D1603242

SCRIABIN
Artist and Mystic

Alexander Scriabin, 1913.

SCRIABIN
Artist and Mystic

By
BORIS DE SCHLOEZER

Translated from the Russian by
NICOLAS SLONIMSKY

With Introductory Essays by
MARINA SCRIABINE

UNIVERSITY OF CALIFORNIA PRESS

Berkeley   Los Angeles

Translated from the Russian A. *Scriabin,* vol. 1:
Personality; Mysterium (Berlin: Grani, 1923).
The astrological study originally appeared in
Capricorne, ed. André Barbault, Collection "Le
Zodiaque," no. 10 (Paris: Editions du Seuil, 1958).
Appendix 1 first published as "Alexandre
Scriabine," by Boris de Schloezer, in *Musique russe,*
ed. Pierre Souvtchinsky, vol. 2 (Paris: Presses
universitaires de France, 1953), 229–48; abridged
and slightly revised by Schloezer in 1957.
Appendix 2 first published as "Scriabine et
l'extase," by Boris de Schloezer, in *Encyclopédie des
musiques sacrées,* ed. Jacques Porte, vol. 3 (Paris:
Editions Labergerie, 1970), 293–98.

University of California Press
Berkeley and Los Angeles, California

**Library of Congress Cataloging-in-Publication
Data**

Schloezer, Boris de, 1881–1969.
   Scriabin : artist and mystic.

   Translation of: A. Skriabin.
   1. Scriabin, Aleksandr Nikolayevich, 1872–1915.
2. Composers—Soviet Union—Biography. I. Scriabine,
Marina. II. Slonimsky, Nicolas, 1894– . III. Title.
ML410.S5988S33 1987 780'.92'4 [B]   86-40109
ISBN 0-520-04384-7 (alk. paper)

Printed in the United States of America

1 2 3 4 5 6 7 8 9

CONTENTS

TRANSLATOR'S FOREWORD

I feel particularly close to both the author and the subject of this book. I met Boris de Schloezer in Kiev, in 1918, as we converged in the capital of the Ukrainian Republic among the multitudes fleeing the famine and cold of Petrograd and Moscow. Schloezer, his widowed sister Tatiana Schloezer-Scriabin (Scriabin died in 1915), and her children Ariadna, Marina, and Julian were guests of the Kiev industrialist Balachowsky, who was a friend and champion of Scriabin. I stayed at the same house, which was the only "skyscraper" in Kiev (it rose six stories and dominated the broad expanse of the Dnieper River). Such a conspicuous building was an obvious target for requisition by various military forces active in the area during the Civil War. (Kiev had changed hands seventeen times in three years.) To protect ourselves against intrusion, we organized a Scriabin Society, and, amazingly enough, the Red Army and some Ukrainian revolutionary groups actually respected our Society as a legitimate shield. At one point an aggressive raiding party of the Soviet military attempted to dislodge us. I remember the intruders as a curiously mixed group led by an officer who carried a tennis racket. During the peculiary internecine struggle, I developed a certain expertise in handling various feuding factions and was particularly adept in confronting the Bolsheviks, with whom I even used the technique of dialectical materialism.

However, my efforts did not avail with the tennis-playing Bolshevik officer, who gave us twenty-four hours to clear out of the "skyscraper." In desperation, I sent off a telegram to Lenin, asking for his intercession as head of the Council of People's Commissars at the Kremlin. "While Moscow is erecting a monument in honor of the great Russian composer Scriabin," my telegram read, "a squad of the Red Army is trying to evict his widow and her children from the apartment they occupy in Kiev. Please intercede for the sake of Russian culture." I knew that Tatiana Schloezer-Scriabin was not legally married to Scriabin because his first wife refused a divorce, but such legalistic niceties would be no obstacle to action for a revolutionary regime. I never found out whether Lenin actually made a ruling on my appeal, but we were left alone, and the tennis-playing officer never bothered us again.

A tragedy darkened our lives when the eleven-year-old Julian Scriabin, who seemed to inherit his father's genius and wrote remarkable piano pieces in the style of Scriabin's last opus numbers (even his physical appearance bore close resemblance to his father's), drowned during an excursion on the Dnieper River. Until this day, nearly seventy years after the event, I shudder at the memory. It was already getting dark when we found him in the island bay, where he had apparently waded and miscalculated the depth of the water; he could not swim. A fisherman in our search party attached his pathetic, slender body to the boat and rowed ashore. His mother was in Moscow and communications were difficult, so Julian was buried in her absence. A Russian Orthodox service was held for the peace of his young soul; his teacher Reinhold Glière, then head of the Kiev Conservatory, made a heartfelt speech, and a school chorus sang the Russian requiem "Let him sleep with the saints." His mother arrived several days later, and Schloezer had to break the news to her; they spoke in French. "Mais non, mais non . . . ," he kept repeating, trying to defer the dreadful news. Some years later Julian's compositions were published in Moscow, and thus he entered the children's paradise of unformed talent.

The inexorable tide of civil war drove Schloezer and myself southward. The next stop in this flight was Yalta, in the Crimean peninsula. It was there that Schloezer began writing his monograph on Scriabin. The White Army, perhaps the most brutal of all Russian warring factions, then mobilized all able-bodied males to defend its last stronghold. Schloezer got caught in a senseless roundup and was sent to the front. A philosopher, writer, and thinker, Schloezer had never handled a gun, but the mindless recruiters were not deterred by his obvious incapacity. He never reached the fighting line, however, because he contracted typhoid fever, a disease that carried thousands of Russians to their death during the Civil War. But he survived.

The next stop was Constantinople, a bustling city occupied by the Allied troops after the defeat of the Ottoman Empire in the First World War. I stayed there for over a year, earning a living by playing piano in restaurants and silent-movie houses, but Schloezer did not tarry long; he took the train to Paris, where he had connections. He became a music critic for the Russian émigré daily, *Les Dernières Nouvelles,* and also contributed articles on music to French magazines.

I renewed my friendship with Schloezer in 1931 when I conducted concerts of American music in Paris. He eagerly attended my orchestral rehearsals and concerts and reviewed them enthusiastically. He said that artistic circles had not been comparably aroused since the exciting days of the Paris avant-garde of the early 1920s. He commended my conducting with friendly caution, remarking that my abilities could be judged only after hearing me conduct the regular classical repertoire. This hope was never realized, however.

Schloezer's book on Scriabin was published by a Russian emigrant press in Berlin in 1923. It was unquestionably the most important account of Scriabin's life, beliefs, and mystical convictions. Scriabin had confided to Schloezer his innermost thoughts; Schloezer's ideas, more pragmatic than those of Scriabin, established a balance between the two. Scriabin had no closer friend than Schloezer; they addressed each other in the intimate form of the second-person singular. A couple of years after Schloezer's death in 1969, Marina Scriabine, the last surviving child of Scriabin and Tatiana (Ariadna perished in the Resistance during the German Occupation), asked me to translate her uncle's book into English. I accepted the task gladly. I had hoped to publish the book on the centennial of Scriabin's birth, which was in 1972 (according to the Old Style, Scriabin was born on Christmas Day 1871, and he felt that the date was symbolic of his mystical Christianity), but typesetting machines grind slowly, and the book now appears well past Scriabin's hundredth birthday, indeed, past Schloezer's own centennial as well.

Schloezer was born in Vitebsk on December 8, 1881 (Old Style). His father was a descendant of the German-born Russian historian von Schloezer, who emigrated from Germany in the eighteenth century. Schloezer's mother was Belgian, and French as well as Russian was spoken in the family. Schloezer's interests from his youth were music and philosophy. He studied sociology at the University of Brussels and received his doctorate in 1901, having written a dissertation on the subject of egoism. Returning to Russia, he became a music critic and contributed articles on aesthetics to various avant-garde periodicals in Moscow and in St. Petersburg. He stayed in St. Petersburg, then renamed Petrograd, for a year after the Revolution. Food became more precious in the hungry year of 1918 than books and musical instruments; he sold his grand piano for the equivalent of fourteen pounds of black bread.

Once established in Paris, he was greatly honored by the intellectual community. The American poet Ezra Pound translated his book on Bach into English. A memorial volume containing articles by ten eminent French writers was published in Paris to mark his centennial. Besides his articles on music and aesthetics, he published a curious short story, "Rapport secret." In this philosophical fantasy immortality is achieved by benevolent aliens. Shortly before his death, he published the novel, *Mon nom est personne,* in which he posited human existence on the necessity of nonbeing. He was intellectually active to his last days, trying to find grounds for the ontological self that he felt should not disappear after death. His greatest affliction was the gradual loss of eyesight; he was compelled to dictate his ideas to his faithful wife or to admiring, young collaborators. When a friend asked him what preoccupied him in the last days of his life, he replied, "J'étudie ma mort." He died on October 7, 1969, at the age of eighty-seven.

Nicolas Slonimsky

INTRODUCTION

This book is the fruit of an encounter or, rather, a collision of two personalities opposed in some respects but possessing in common a certain type of reasoning that allowed them to understand and confront each other—not without some passion—in the spirit of firm friendship and mutual respect.

What brought Boris de Schloezer and Alexander Scriabin together was something that could be called their "dimension," their "format." Both aimed very high; at the summit of their common scale of values were placed art, metaphysics, and the realm of ideals. On this privileged terrain both gave proof of the same passion that animated them in defending their profoundly differing positions. The antagonisms appear especially fruitful as they unfold on these pages. They forced Scriabin to sharpen his ideas, to array them in a better order so as to meet on equal terms the rigorous intellect of an adversary who was as well equipped in the domain of philosophy as in music. During their conversations, Schloezer tells us, "Scriabin rarely expounded his ideas in a finished and fixed form; rather, he improvised his theories, as it were, then and there. These conversations, with their constant exchanges of queries and responses, with their discussions and debates, contributed a great deal to Scriabin's mental discipline, stimulated him, and gave him a sense of direction."

Scriabin's preference for oral exchange explains why he did not write a theoretical tract himself, and why we must rely on the recollections of those who took part in these conversations. A theory improvised in the heat of discussion cannot possess the same rigor of exposition as a text prepared upon mature reflection; formulations differ according to arguments and exchanges between opponents, and the ideas present themselves in forms that vary, if not in essence, then surely in exposition as they develop and deepen.

On account of this peculiarity of oral exchange, many who have written about Scriabin—particularly Leonid Sabaneyev—distorted Scriabin's utterances or misinterpreted them, either because they could not follow attentively the flow of spoken language, or because they mistook a discussion for a contradiction when the debaters approached the same problem, difficult to formulate, from different angles. Boris de Schloezer is in all probability the only person among Scriabin's close associates who was capable of reporting Scriabin's ideas about art in their integrity and unity and of clarifying the concept of the "ultimate act" that was to culminate in an ecstatic union with the supernal Unique Being. Besides having an intimate understanding of Scriabin, Schloezer was his brother-in-law and often stayed with the Scriabins, sharing the daily events of the family. This intimacy enabled him to adequately evaluate the thoughts and the creative processes of the author of *Prométhée*. Schloezer never accentuated the more extreme utterances of Scriabin induced by the heat of a passionate debate; rather, he analyzed Scriabin's spiritual experiences, especially difficult to make explicit, through phases of logical development; he was always careful not to lose hold on the guiding line and get lost in digressions. He clarified obscure points and, thanks to his philosophical skill, was able to arrive at a synthesis and convert into lucid concepts, typical of his own intellect, the ideas, images, and intuitions of the artist, visionary, and mystic that was Scriabin.

Those who are familiar with Boris de Schloezer's writings, who are aware of his influence on musical aesthetics, particularly since the 1947 publication of his *Introduction à J. S. Bach,* know that his greatest concern was precision. He did not harbor preconceived notions and never flaunted his own tastes, although he had plenty of preferences and strong antipathies in music; he based his conclusions only on well-authenticated facts and analyses. Every article, every book he wrote captivated the reader by the logic, unity, and sober clarity of its elegant exposition. But those who know Schloezer only from his writings may imagine that he was a remote intellectual, a man dominated entirely by cold intelligence. This image is far from Schloezer's true character. Not only was he easily carried away by philosophical discussion, but he was also a sensitive, affectionate person vulnerable to life's shocks. These psychological traits made his affinity with Scriabin unaffected and natural.

Toward the end of this life, Schloezer published two works of fiction—a short story, "Rapport secret," and a novel, *Mon nom est personne.* Although Schloezer realized that he lacked professional skill as a fiction writer, these two books demonstrate that he nonetheless possessed a genuine literary gift, particularly effective in developing a fundamental philosophical idea. The characters of his novel, unlike those of Dostoyevsky, were not creatures of the imagination. They were formed from personal experiences and encounters; and yet they possessed a life of their own. His faculty of re-creating a character from real life, his ability to extract vital truth, made it possible for Schloezer to grasp fully the personality of Scriabin, to be fascinated by his very strangeness, and to give us a picture of Scriabin's personality with all the brilliance of a born writer. Schloezer possessed vast intelligence and extensive culture; he was an excellent musician, although he never played an instrument professionally. He was a theorist with a philosophical intellect of the prime order, but he was neither a visionary nor a mystic. He wrote supple, limpid, and lively prose, but even in his fiction he rarely resorted to metaphorical language; he did not feel the need of such language, even though he profoundly admired writers who possessed the gift of picturesque prose. Although he showed proper respect for and interest in mysticism, this type of religious experience was completely alien to him.

Scriabin possessed neither the philosophical erudition nor the dialectical precision of Schloezer, yet Schloezer himself admitted that Scriabin "was a dangerous opponent in debate, always resourceful in repartee, so that anyone contending with him had to be constantly on his guard. It was curious that this musical poet, who moments before could charm us by his art, would immediately afterwards reveal himself as an adroit dialectician capable of clever sparring." But Scriabin was a visionary and mystic. All that he created and lived through, felt or thought, derived from his mystical experiences, essentially incommunicable, which he nonetheless tried to transmit through his musical compositions and poetical writings and expounded in his theories and conversations with those sympathetic to his ideas.

Face-to-face with this original personality, Schloezer listened, observed, and participated in this unique adventure with alert intelligence, understanding, and sensitivity. He could not always agree with Scriabin's views or accept his projections, and he often contested his conclusions; but the spiritual process that he followed in Scriabin was of fundamental importance to him, for it touched upon the meaning and function of art in life and human destiny. Schloezer followed the genesis of Scriabin's philosophy and the parallel outpour of music; hence, the dual plan of Schloezer's book, which was to comprise two sections. The first of these has been completed. It is a passionate and profound study of a unique personality, a singular case examined here not with the circumspect objectivity of a psychologist, but with the clairvoyant penetration of a friend, aided by his own spiritual nobility and philosophical acumen.

A second volume was to be devoted to the composer's musical oeuvre. Owing to a series of untoward circumstances, it was never written. Schloezer emigrated to France in 1920, having lost, like so many other émigrés, all his possessions in the revolutionary upheaval. In Paris he was compelled to meet more immediate demands to make a living. Postponed until a later date, the second volume never materialized. In the meantime Schloezer wrote several articles on Scriabin's music (two of which are included in the present book), not as important perhaps as the second volume might have been, but nonetheless offering some compensation for the abandoned larger work. And yet, if one of the two volumes had to be sacrificed, it is fortunate that it was the second. Scriabin's music is our common heritage. Any competent music scholar ought to be able to study the scores, analyze their technical idiom, and draw certain conclusions. Even if such scholars are few, there may be more in the future. A book on Scriabin's music can thus be written at any given period of time, although it is of course desirable that it be soon. But a life portrait of Scriabin in words—his personality, his theories, his "mythology," as it were—could be given to us in a vivid and picturesque manner only by a writer like Schloezer, with the unique qualifications of musician, philosopher, and friend.

I must now say a few words about the history of the book itself. It was completed in Yalta, Crimea, in 1919, and published in Russian by Grani, a Russian émigré press in Berlin, in 1923. It was Schloezer's first book; before that he wrote mostly for newspapers and magazines. Those who followed Schloezer's career as a writer will be pleased to discover in this volume the familiar stylistic idiosyncrasies he developed in the course of forty-six years between the publication of the book on Scriabin and his death in 1969. In the Scriabin book, Schloezer already applies his method of organizing his materials in a logical sequence, marked by clarity of exposition and lucidity of phraseology. To describe a personality as complex as Scriabin, Schloezer discusses in orderly succession the various aspects of his subject, endeavoring to establish the proper boundaries, at times difficult to define, of his inquiry.

The book is divided into two parts, each comprising three chapters. The first part, on the personality of Scriabin, studies the Thinker, the Artist, and the Mystic. This division may appear somewhat arbitrary. It is quite possible that the author would have made the exposition more flexible in later years, when he learned how to impart to his rigorous architectural plan the elegance typical of his mature style. It is probable also that he would have known how to avoid repeating essential points imposed by the special plan of the text. Thus, ideas about the artist's function concern primarily the Thinker, but they also affect the Artist, whose creative effort they stimulated, and the Mystic, for their deepest origin was Scriabin's spiritual experience. And yet, upon an attentive reading, one finds that there are no literal repetitions, but rather paraphrases with a changed approach from a sharper angle of view. One finds in these recurrences a development, a touch of memory that draws out a trait faintly noted before and enhances its significance. And despite the constraint that the framework of the book imposes on a logical mind, one senses here spontaneity, warmth, and the vivacity of a still-vibrant friendship, qualities that Schloezer's other writings, on abstract subjects less relevant to his personal life, do not possess. Only the pages devoted to the philosopher Léon Chestov, another great friend of Schloezer, reveal a similar underlying emotion.

Reading the titles of the chapters devoted to the personality of Scriabin—the Thinker, the Artist, the Mystic—one may wonder whether the author deliberately omitted the personal element of Scriabin's life. Actually, this personal element was an integral part of Scriabin's inner experience. "Whatever he was doing or saying," Schloezer writes, "an intense inner process of reasoning accompanied his actions, which never ceased and of which he was often unaware himself." At various points Schloezer emphasizes that for Scriabin this mystical inner experience, which he felt with an almost agonizing intensity, was also a source of ineffable delight and the most immediately evident reality, the most absolute certainty, the sole criterion against which all else, including daily occupations, were measured. We therefore owe a debt of gratitude to Boris de Schloezer for preserving in his exploration of Scriabin's personality this perspective, which places in the foreground the fundamental values, relegating all others to lower planes.

The Thinker, the Artist, the Mystic—these three aspects correspond also to Scriabin's three modes of self-expression, which sprang from a common source, his inner experience. Scriabin's grandiose visions of the *Mysterium,* which was to transfigure humanity, and his theoretical speculations that gave these visions a philosophical foundation were not connected with his music in subject matter or development, thematic content or comment, theory or realization. They were parallel actions that enabled Scriabin to communicate the incommunicable. Schloezer writes: "It is entirely possible that there exists a different relationship between the cognitive process and creative activity. Each may be autonomous and independent and yet linked to the other by a vital intuition, which is their common source."

In exploring these three aspects of Scriabin's creative personality, Schloezer does not sacrifice the individuality of Scriabin, but as he relates his encounters with him and their conversations, which invariably revolved around philosophical or aesthetic subjects, he paints for us a vivid portrait of Scriabin the man, with his mannerisms, foibles, frail appearance, characteristic comportment, yearnings, sensitivity, and his reactions to others. We see Scriabin as a human being more vividly than if the author had given us a scrupulously detailed account of his actions or had informed us in minute detail of his daily routine.

The title of the second part of Schloezer's book has an element of surprise. Was it wise to include *Mysterium* in this volume, which discusses the personality and the creative work of Scriabin? Would it not have been more logical to relegate it to the projected second volume, which was to analyze Scriabin's works? And in the second volume, should not this part have been placed at the end, in a chapter devoted to unfinished works—the opera, the *Mysterium,* and the *Acte préalable,* which had never progressed beyond mere sketches? Only a few scenes from the opera had been sketched out, the *Mysterium* always remained a vague project, undergoing numerous alterations; and the *Acte préalable* exists only as a poetic text with unrelated fragments of music, a mass of material in the process of genesis.

In devoting the bulk of his book to these three projected compositions, Boris de Schloezer showed extraordinary insight. As was his custom, he began with the most essential part, the *Mysterium,* and the two other works basic to the musical and philosophical structure of Scriabin's oeuvre. The *Mysterium,* Schloezer wrote, "exists only as a project, but this project, elaborated in detail in some of its parts, constitutes the key to Scriabin's creative personality."

The project of the *Mysterium* circumscribed Scriabin's entire career, musical and philosophical. "This unique project," Schloezer wrote, "had at least begun to be realized. It was not left in the state of a dream, a projection: it was materialized; it was incarnated; it exists objectively, even though in a form completely different from the one that Scriabin envisaged himself." Indeed, all of Scriabin's art is, as it were, "mysterial," to use Schloezer's own expression. He declared: "All of Scriabin's creations are but approximations gradually leading to the *Mysterium*."

In the second part of his book, Schloezer tells us how he came to write his biography of Scriabin, traces its development, and recounts its revision. The original idea was never changed; the nucleus of the book, its organization, even its "mythology" (if we do not attach to this term a pejorative meaning, or equate it with fantasy, fiction, or falsehood) remained essentially unaltered. The central idea of the *Mysterium* is summarized by Schloezer as follows: "It may be described as a dream of the unification of mankind in a common beatitude of ecstasy." This ecstasy was to transfigure, to deify man and the universe. The instrument of this liberating cosmic transfiguration, of this accession to a divine state, was to be art, which alone possesses a unifying demiurgic power.

In his creative life Scriabin varied his spiritual beliefs, his concept of man, God, the mission of the Son of God, the artist's role, and himself. Different stages of this trajectory are traced by Schloezer, who emphasizes the transformation of ideas without ever losing the guiding thread that tied them together.

The writing of this book dates back to 1919. Despite his penetration and insight, Schloezer could not foretell the eventual significance of the *Mysterium,* which seemed but an isolated dream of a feverish imagination, destined to vanish with its originator. He could not imagine that half a century later there would be a fantastic renaissance of Scriabin's mystical ideas, in unexpected forms, aberrant at times, but always recognizable.

In this connection it is pertinent to draw attention to some aspects of Scriabin's philosophy that are quite 'modern' and make Schloezer's book uniquely relevant to our own time. It is Scriabin's 'modernity' that attracts increasing numbers of contemporary music lovers (particularly among nonconformist young people) and imparts special significance to Schloezer's book, appearing in English translation more than one hundred years after the composer's birth. Indeed, as Schloezer points out, Scriabin always lived in the future, the advent of which he so impatiently awaited. Schloezer wrote: "Scriabin took pleasure in playing his works and analyzed their positive and negative features, sometimes criticizing his music with complete candor. But when he dwelled too long on his own past, his spirit seemed to fade. 'This is not what I want,' he would say. But the moment a conversation touched upon his future plans and hopes, he would blossom forth, forget his past disappointments, and become completely absorbed in it, anticipating the joys to come. He often remarked, 'I live only by the hopes of the future.'"

This expectation of a luminous future found its expression in the *Mysterium* and clarified the important role of this work in Scriabin's artistic expression; it also pervades his philosophical theories and fully justifies the space that Schloezer accords to this work that never came to fruition.

Another consideration comes to mind. Scriabin's hope for a future that was to solve all world problems is also characteristic of modern thought, in contradistinction to ancient thought, oriented toward the past, evoking the Golden Age when sorrows and death were unknown. This myth, which fascinated the forerunners of the Renaissance, dominates the philosophy of the nineteenth and twentieth centuries. Laments over a lost Paradise, over the progression of increasingly somber and darksome historical periods that succeeded the Golden Age, yield gradually to a faith in the forward march of humanity toward a brighter future, manifesting itself in a variety of ways. This belief is based on scientific progress, which is to culminate in the domination of nature and control of its elements, while great political systems presage an ideal society with their promise of peace and happiness and a quasireligious, superhuman order resulting from a biological evolution directed by man himself. This inversion of temporal lodestones, swaying between the genesis and the future, leads to incalculable consequences. The prevalent, if somewhat disconcerting, modalities of contemporary art take their inspiration from these anticipations.

If the Golden Age is placed in remote antiquity, then everything that takes us farther away from this brief period of equilibrium and beatitude must necessarily darken its memory, erase its imprint and mask its splendor.

That is the reason we venerate the inherited glories of the past and strive to build monuments that will withstand the erosion of centuries, for the more deeply we are embedded in the past, the greater are the chances for preserving its reflection of paradisiacal light. From this vantage point, all innovation is suspect, and all attempt at abnegation is tantamount to sacrilege. The myths of lost secrets, forgotten wisdom, the powerful continent of Atlantis, and innocent Arcady annihilated by the perversity of man spring from the common lament over the passing of original happiness.

As we project this life in Paradise into the future, no less mythical than the past, our values become inverted. All that we can hope for during a new Golden Age is that it will differ greatly from today's society, that man will be free, powerful, and happy. At that time, instead of cultivating traditional values and keeping vigil over immemorial legacies, all conventions will have been abolished, for only a totally different ideal from ours can capture the reflection of the light to come. All that carries us farther from the past, all that rebels against it, rejects and destroys it, is likely to hasten the advent of the future world. Validation of the new, a search for the original, for something never seen before, and ever bolder experimentation are the logical consequences of this frenzied forward dash to a future Garden of Eden.

There are two distinctly different attitudes, two ways of bringing this experiment to life. The first is to abide in passive expectation with a precise objective in view. We are forced to admit our total ignorance of this future world; we know that it will bring us happiness and freedom, but we cannot even remotely fathom its nature.

This attitude translates into a desire to sweep away the residue of traditions and even abolish all present values, thus opening the path toward the future, without, however, making any effort to bring about the advent of this new world. This course is a sort of desperate gamble, an act of faith in the generating powers of a new chaos.

The second perspective demands obedience to new laws that must correspond to previously drawn plans of reconstruction, yet do not deny the necessity of destroying the present world. There is a certain logic in this destructive scheme, to which Scriabin wholeheartedly subscribed. But the new universe he anticipated was not to be a human society organized according to political plan or based on justice, brotherly love, and happiness. Scriabin dreamed of "a new earth and a new heaven," in the words of the Apocalypse, of a new cosmos, a humanity transfigured, deified and united with the Unique in a common ecstasy. Purely material methods could never carry out this design; wars, revolutions, and social upheavals can only prepare the ground for a final consummation, the unification of the earth. But transfiguration requires a demiurgic act, conceived as a liturgy in which all forms of art are brought together.

One may wonder if ideas of such a distinctly religious nature can have any relevance for our age, one circumscribed by political action and animated by the belief that only politics can resolve the difficulties and contradictions of contemporary society. Variations on these Scriabinesque themes in Schloezer's book possess a special interest for us. The differences of temperament between Scriabin and Schloezer, the composer and the philosopher, shed a novel light on Scriabin's frame of mind, displaying his ideas in modified but essentially authentic modalities as they developed in the course of their conversations. It is interesting to note that the theme of man taking his destiny into his own hands, striving to transcend his condition, and arriving at a state of immortality and deification solely by his conscious effort reappears in Schloezer's novelette, written half a century after Scriabin had confided his grandiose visions to him.

The society pictured by Schloezer in his "Rapport secret," a short story published in *Le Mercure de France* in 1964, differs widely from Scriabin's mystical speculations. Schloezer imagines that the inhabitants of a distant planet, visited by a mission from earth, achieve immortality and divinity through science. These beings, whose origins are human, attain an ultimate union through their yearnings for the future, just as celebrants in the text of Scriabin's *Mysterium* were to do. We can therefore surmise that Schloezer's image of the future was implanted in his mind, however unconsciously, by Scriabin's visionary ideals.

Scriabin's fundamental idea of the great puissance of art is reflected in Schloezer's last publication, the novel *Mon nom est personne*. Here Schloezer describes an imaginary society and then reveals that he himself is a creature of that society. It is a pessimistic and nihilistic notion, a sort of infernal circle signalizing the end of a creative act, an inverted image of Scriabin's liberating liturgy.

In his book *Introduction à J. S. Bach,* Schloezer gives a magisterial exposition of an entity that he calls the "mythical I" of an artist, as opposed to the everyday "I" of an ordinary human being, an individual "someone." This

idea echoes that of "the great I" and "the small I," so elo-
quently evoked by Scriabin in his conversations with
Schloezer. "But which 'I' do we find here?" Schloezer
asked. "Naturally, it is not the 'I' of Alexander Nikolayevich Scriabin perceived in himself, in the consciousness of
the Unique sprung from Scriabin's soul. Of these two 'I's,'
the big and the little, Scriabin speaks very clearly in one
of his notebooks: 'In the dimensions of time and space I
am subject to temporal and spatial laws, but the laws of
time and space are the creatures of my great 'I.'" Certainly
the "mythical I" of Schloezer is the "I" of the creative
artist, not of God the Creator. And yet we witness Schloezer in the process of conjuring up creatures of flesh and
bone in his novel *Mon nom est personne*. There can be no
question of influence, not even subconscious influence de-
riving from Schloezer's memory of his conversations with
Scriabin; we see, rather, a natural continuation of these
discussions, to which Schloezer contributed his personal
ideas. Nothing can better illustrate the coincidences and
divergences of Schloezer's and Scriabin's views in their exchange of ideas that fascinated them both.

We frequently encounter ideas of this nature, even
among people who are completely oblivious to Scriabin's
philosophy. It is surprising to what extent Scriabin anticipated developments of our own time. In his work on the
Mysterium, Scriabin approached the problem of theatrical
presentation. Like modern theater directors, he visualized
a theater without footlights, without a proscenium artificially separating actors and spectators. He intended to have
the entire congregation participate in various degrees in

the dramatic representation. Characteristically, his scheme contained a mystical dimension, which contemporary theater disdains. "For Scriabin, the theater as an edifice, as an entity consisting of a stage and hall separated by footlights," wrote Schloezer, "was but an expression, in terms of space, of the pristine need of man to find a new incarnation, a need that is fulfilled by the masque. Consequently, to Scriabin the entire art of the theater was reduced to a masquerade. He intended to transcend this masque through which humanity seeks to save itself from the spiritual poverty and moral drabness of individual existence." But to attain the efflorescence and plenitude of life, which would lead us to a true—and not merely theatrical—transfiguration, Scriabin insisted that there exists only one path: the path of religious faith culminating in the union of his "I" with the Unique, his fusion with the Unique.

The importance Scriabin attributed to Eros also parallels modern sensibilities. Indeed, Scriabin planned to include among the artistic forms that were to take part in the *Mysterium* the sensations of taste and touch ("caresses"). Schloezer tells us that Scriabin conceived the final ecstasy as a sort of "grandiose sexual act." But here, too, one must not lose sight of the spiritual substance of the *Mysterium,* which taste and touch scarcely epitomized. "It is clear," Schloezer commented, "that [Scriabin] envisioned a consummation of an entirely different dimension. He intended to introduce scents and sensations of touch and taste into the very tissue of the *Mysterium,* interlaced with musical, pictorial, plastic, and poetic elements. Once the unity of all the arts that had been parts of Omni-art was restored, its constituent elements, incapable of autonomous development, would be revivified and resurrected."

This total art, without barriers between its various divisions, approaches contemporary trends, but again on an entirely different plane. In contemporary practice, boundaries between different arts are abolished to fuse art with life. For Scriabin, too, Omni-art was to be resolved on a higher plane of life, but it was not to be dissolved in life. This art was to rise to a superior, exalted, absolute plane; all the imperfect, known arts merely anticipate and remotely approximate it. And while today many seek the sources of a more intense life in spontaneity, in free behavior, by plunging into the subconscious, Scriabin's *Mysterium* was to bring to the level of consciousness, by a creative and voluntary effort, the most obscure senses of the physical body, the darkest depths of the psyche.

Because it was through art that man could hope to attain this unification, Scriabin planned "to include in the *Mysterium* impressions, however diffuse, of inferior sensory organs, which are apt, far more than musical sounds, words, or colors to perturb the psyche. They are also capable, when utilized prudently and cautiously and combined with sounds, gestures, or coloration, of deepening, widening, and reinforcing the tonus of the psyche by increasing and exciting its energies."

Scriabin's irrepressible passion for freedom, a total, absolute, and unlimited freedom, may well find a sympathetic response among contemporary readers. But this freedom was more than simple human freedom. It was not the freedom to act according to one's wishes, which is the choice of the "little I"—a relative freedom, certainly important in everyday life, but much more important as a preliminary to the manifestation of the "great I."

It may appear paradoxical to speak of freedom in light of Scriabin's distrust of spontaneous practices, his dream of a volitional, elaborate art effected by the conscious will of its creator. Let us not forget that the freedom Scriabin sought was an absolute, divine freedom that could only be attained through the ultimate integration of an entire human being, which, in the terrestrial state, is disunited, dismembered, and replete with self-contradictions. This unification could be realized through art, but in order to perfuse the terrestrial man, somber and chaotic, with spiritual light, all the constituent elements of art—sonorous, visual, and otherwise—must be integrated in formal unity. And only after this unification had been attained would inner illumination confer, on a transfigured man, a freedom truly divine, truly universal. "If nothing exists, then everything must be possible," Scriabin often said. And it was from this sensation of sovereign power, which obsessed Scriabin to the point of intoxication, that a conflict arose between the concepts of absolute freedom and truth, which Scriabin believed to be incompatible.

It may well be that in most contemporary trends of art and philosophy, we could find, without forcing a textual identity, the seeds, anticipations, and even occasional explicit declarations similar to those of the visionary musician Scriabin. The search for a new musical language, which led Scriabin to abandon tonality in his last works, the experimental use of a color keyboard in *Prométhée,* and his innumerable innovations in various branches of art—

scenery, lighting, group movements, and so forth—all were paths that logically anticipate the experimentation of contemporary musicians and artists. The reader will find in this book many ideas that have become standard features on our horizon, yet were already discernible between 1910 and 1915 in the fascinating world of Scriabin.

Every time such coincidences come to our attention, we notice that similar elements are reflected in subtly different lights. These encounters invariably take place on disparate planes. When we attempt to pass through the door, which Scriabin left ajar, to a world that appears to be a replica of our own, we must make a choice at the threshold. And those who do not—who, deceived by apparently obvious similarities, venture into Scriabin's world in the belief that it is like our own—risk finding themselves total strangers. They no longer recognize the landscape; the vistas that open before them reveal not the imagined horizons of some ideal human society, living in unity and happiness, but a strangely disquieting world of mystery.

Marina Scriabine
(Translated from the French by Nicolas Slonimsky)

An Astrological Study on
the Natal Chart of Alexander Scriabin

Marina Scriabine

Born on January 6, 1872, at two o'clock in the afternoon (local time) in Moscow, Scriabin had a Sun-Saturn-Mercury conjunction in Capricorn. He is therefore strongly marked by the tenth house. But it is only when we consider the entire aggregate of his tripolar theme that it becomes possible to grasp thoroughly the relationship between Scriabin's creative work, his artistic personality, and the configuration of his natal chart.

Let us begin by distinguishing these three poles of energy and their dominant signs. The ascendant is in Gemini, the sign of mobile, subtle, and swift air. We observe here all the delicate and fragile grace of an adolescent spirit, full of curiosity about the world, free and capricious, and touching the surface of things only to relinquish them at once.

On the other hand, at the cusp of the eighth house, that of death and metamorphosis, we find Capricorn, the

21

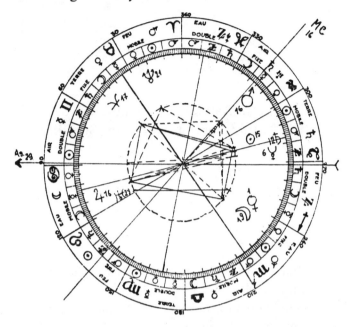

For the delectation of amateur astrologers: Scriabin's natal chart.

somber sign of winter, the sign of the earth, heavy and icebound, symbolizing Saturnian depths (grottoes, underground passages, caverns) and inaccessible peaks, the sign of concentration. In the intellectual domain, this spirit explores and enhances, striving to achieve a totality, a synthesis, a unit. In this universe, the redoubtable conjunction Sun-Saturn, with Jupiter in opposition, accentuates the solitary pride of Capricorn. But mobile Mercury, master of the ascendant, penetrates this mineral universe.

At the third pole is Mars, culminating in midheaven (within a degree), squared with Pluto, the planet of infernal regions, and also squared with the Moon in Scorpio, connoting visionary imagination and initiatory journeys. This violent, explosive combination is rich in energy, particularly in Aquarius, the creative sign.

Let us specify the three aspects: Ascendant (profound entity) in Gemini; eighth house (metamorphosis, death) in Capricorn, with Sun-Saturn-Mercury; and Mars culminating in midheaven (the sector of realizations) in Aquarius. Scriabin's entire oeuvre and philosophy can be summarized as the effort of the imaginative and free spirit of Gemini to liberate itself from the restrictive bonds of Capricornian matter through the power of a creative act (Mars in midheaven).

Two of Scriabin's great symphonic works, the Third Symphony (*Le Poème divin*) and *Prométhée* (*Le Poème du feu*), are the expressions of this inner struggle. This is not program music, but the liberating act of the spirit. This spirit, however, does not disengage itself from matter; rather, it ennobles matter, forming a more intimate union with it. We find here not a disincarnation, inconceivable for a Capricornian, but a more complete and profound incarnation.

The following tempo and mood indications were set down by the composer himself in the score of *Le Poème divin*: (1) Lento, *divin, grandiose;* (2) *Luttes:* Allegro, *mystérieux, tragique* (these two parts belong to the Saturnian world of Capricorn); (3) *Voluptés;* (4) *Jeu divin, avec une joie éclatante* (the spirit of Gemini liberated from the ascendance of darkness).

Other titles and descriptive indications relating to the Capricorn-Saturn aspect are *Poème tragique, Poème sa-*

tanique, Douloureux déchirant, Très lent, Contemplatif, and *Allegro drammatico,* whereas *Fragilité, Poème ailé,* and *Caresse dansée* represent Gemini. The fire of Mars is seen through the more somber light of Pluto (squared with Mars) in *Prométhée (Le Poème du feu), Vers la flamme,* and *Flammes sombres.*

In the structure of Scriabin's music one finds characteristic traits of the two signs locked in struggle; on the one hand, the importance of harmony, of chords (a Capricornian world of aggregations, density, and gravity); on the other hand, the abundance of rapid passages, in subtle rhythms, in palpitating flight, bearing such expression marks as *volando, léger,* and *ailé.*

Let us quote some pertinent passages from Boris de Schloezer's book on Scriabin that corroborate these brief observations. Scriabin's physical aspect—"his frail and delicate appearance, his intense nervousness . . . the frailty and childlike countenance"—is characteristic of Gemini. But there is also the world of Capricorn: "Whatever he was doing or saying, an intense inner process of reasoning accompanied his actions, which never ceased." We are far from the superficial curiosity of Gemini. Here we find a search for perfection without compromise, a very Capricornian image: "a refined, almost pedantic formalist who demanded accuracy . . . perfection of form and precision of execution."

Self-affirmation and pride (conjunction of the sun and Saturn in Capricorn) are also evident. "He was convinced that he was destined to perform an important task in life. . . . Scriabin marked the main subject of *Le Poème divin* with the words *I am.* . . . The nucleus of Scriabin's individuality was encased, as it were, in a strong suit of armor, impenetrable to any sound from the outside."

We now observe how this Capricornian affiliated with Gemini aspired to liberate himself and the universe from the embrace of matter: "The entire evolution of the universe is epitomized by the impact of the spirit on matter, an increasingly close fusion with it, an increasingly deep penetration of it." But this act of liberation signalizes at the same time the death of man and of the present world. For the idea of death dominated Scriabin's creative world as it dominates his natal chart; Saturn, master of the eighth house, is at the same time master of the ninth house (thought) and, with Uranus (at the cusp of the fourth house symbolizing the end of life), master of the tenth house (realization), while present at its own house, the cusp of the eighth house (death). But this death is transfiguration, not annihilation.

If we interpret the natal chart as the symbol of the spiritual duty of mankind, then Scriabin's life and work give us an example of a particularly dramatic response to this challenge.

Translated from the French by
Nicolas Slonimsky

SCRIABIN

Artist and Mystic

by

BORIS DE SCHLOEZER

TO THE MEMORY OF
my sister and friend
TATIANA FEDOROVNA
SCHLOEZER-SCRIABIN
I dedicate this book.
B. Schloezer

PREFACE

There exists a rather extensive literature on Scriabin published in Russia, comprising several books and a number of articles in periodicals. A special issue of the Russian periodical *Musical Contemporary,* dedicated to Scriabin, was published in 1916. It contains a detailed biography prepared by Julius Engel, an excellent article by Viacheslav Karatygin ("Elements of Form in Scriabin's Music"), and an exhaustive commentary by Leonid Sabancyev on the relationship of color and sound in the score of *Prométhée.* This collection is considerable, given how little has been published about other Russian composers, even the most important ones. But it is still not enough to account for Scriabin's actual accomplishment. The wealth and significance of his music can be appreciated by a close study of his works, but to grasp the creative significance of Scriabin's oeuvre in its totality requires a more detailed analysis. Scriabin's expansion of harmonic foundations, his use of a number of new dissonant combinations, and his treatment of such combinations as consonances have not been adequately analyzed. Did Scriabin introduce a truly revolutionary innovation? Did he really transgress the boundaries of our tempered scale, or merely expand its application?

An even wider and deeper problem is Scriabin's contribution to general culture. What place does Scriabin occupy among the builders of the kingdom of artistic beauty? So far, it must be admitted, his personality and his creative accomplishments have been studied totally apart from actuality, outside cultural history. Scholars have duly analyzed the aesthetic importance of his works, they have described in detail personal traits, fundamental tendencies, and leading ideas of his work. But the results of this study are disconnected, so that Scriabin as a phenomenon of general culture remains without definition. The aesthetic influences on Scriabin's music by Chopin, Liszt, and Wagner have been properly discussed, but not in relationship to Scriabin's spiritual world.

Yet the meaning of Scriabin's art can be fully understood only in terms of general culture. His desire to probe the ultimate mystery of unification with the One among the worldly multitudes was an autonomous effort. He found the proper form and images to approach this mystery with the utmost precision, lucidity, and completeness, and he was able to explore it logically. The vision of an ultimate unification has pervaded human history; single individuals and even whole nations have been inspired by this vision. It therefore does not suffice to examine the inner meaning of Scriabin's eschatology; it is imperative to discern its independence and at the same time analyze the relationship of his ideals to those of other mystics. In this light, Scriabin's *Mysterium* must be regarded as one of the greatest human mystical creations, as an individual phenomenon in humanity's mystical life. The same must be said about Scriabin's concept of ecstasy, the rebellious individualism of his early life, and the pantheistic religiosity of his later period. Only after establishing these affinities and differences in their successive appearances can we understand Scriabin's inner world and find a proper place for him among the world's artists.

It is according to this method, which I regard as the only correct approach, that I propose to conduct my discussion of Scriabin's place in culture, and I am fully aware of the tremendous difficulties that are inevitably encountered in this process and must affect the result of my work.

The subject of this book is the art of Scriabin in its totality and its place within his own individuality. The task that I set for myself, which comprises the entirety of Scriabin's personality, falls naturally into three sections. The first section is devoted to a description of Scriabin's personality; the second examines his art within the framework of his most ambitious achievement, the *Mysterium;* and the third analyzes Scriabin's musical compositions.* This division, which treats the results of an artist's work apart from his inner concept, may appear rather artificial, particularly in view of the idiosyncratic subjectivity of Scriabin's art. It is difficult to avoid repetition in such a plan, but the schematization is necessary in order to understand the multifaceted nature of an artist's achievement.

My material for this book has been gathered first of all from the actual works of Scriabin, from my personal impressions and understanding of them. I had access to

* [The present volume comprises the first two sections; the third section was intended for a second volume. See pages 5–6 above.]

Scriabin's diaries, first drafts of his analytic studies, his philosophical and poetic sketches, his verbal observations, and his autobiographical sketches. Finally, I could draw on my personal reminiscences of Scriabin, to whom I was close for many years, and from a feeling of intimacy with him that was, for me, a source of great joy.

Yalta, winter 1919

BIOGRAPHY

Scriabin's father, Nicolai Alexandrovich Scriabin, was born in 1850. In 1871 he married Lubov Alexandrovna Shchetinina, who was born in 1849 and studied with Theodor Leschetizky at the St. Petersburg Conservatory; she was a talented pianist and often gave recitals in St. Petersburg, Moscow, and Russian provincial towns. On December 25, 1871 (Old Style; January 6, 1872, New Style), they became the parents of Alexander Nicolayevich Scriabin. Soon after his birth his mother contracted tuberculosis; she died in 1873 in the southern Tirol.

Scriabin's father served as Russian consul in various countries in the Near East. In 1880 he remarried; his second wife was Olga Fernandez, an Italian citizen who bore him three sons and a daughter. He died in Lausanne in 1914.

From his earliest years Scriabin was taken care of by his paternal grandmother and his maiden aunt, who was a mother to him. As a boy, Scriabin revealed striking musical abilities. He improvised at the piano and tried to play by ear. His aunt was his first piano teacher. In 1882 Scriabin entered the junior military academy in Moscow; his musical talent attracted the attention of his teachers and classmates. He began taking regular piano lessons in 1883 with Georgi Conus, who himself was still a Conservatory pupil; these lessons continued until the spring of 1884.

After a hiatus of a few years, he resumed his piano studies with Nicolai Zverev, a professor at the Moscow Conservatory. Beginning in 1886, he took regular lessons in music theory with Sergei Taneyev. While in his junior year at the military academy he entered the Moscow Conservatory, where he studied piano with Vassily Safonov, continued theory lessons with Taneyev, and took a course in free composition and fugue with Anton Arensky. It was then that he decided to abandon military education and dedicate himself entirely to music. He obtained a finishing diploma in the military academy, however, in 1889. His musical talent developed rapidly during his Conservatory years, but his friends regarded him mainly as a pianist rather than a composer. He graduated from the Moscow Conservatory as a pianist in 1892.

Scriabin's first publisher was Pyotr Jurgenson, who issued several of his piano pieces, among them Valse op. 1, Morceaux op. 2, Mazurkas op. 3, Nocturnes op. 5, and Impromptus à la mazur op. 7. Scriabin had written all these pieces while still a Conservatory student. In 1894 he met Mitrofan Belaieff, his regular publisher for a long time.

In 1895 Scriabin accompanied Belaieff to Europe, where he made his first extensive tour as a pianist: he visited Germany, Holland, Belgium, and Paris, and also spent some time in Switzerland and Italy. After returning to Russia, Scriabin gave several recitals in Moscow and the provinces. In 1897 he married Vera Isakovich, who had just graduated from the Moscow Conservatory. After a brief trip to Paris, they settled in Moscow, where Scriabin was engaged by Safonov, director of the Moscow Conservatory, as a professor of piano. In the spring of 1904 Scriabin went abroad and stayed in Switzerland near Geneva. There he worked on his Third Symphony, which he had begun already in Moscow. In the summer of 1905, upon returning from Paris, he separated from his wife and went to Italy, taking residence near Genoa with his former student Tatiana de Schloezer, who became his constant companion.

In the winter of 1906 the Russian conductor Modest Altschuler, a former student of the Moscow Conservatory who had emigrated to New York, invited Scriabin to take part in one of his concerts of Russian music there. Altschuler conducted Scriabin's First and Third Symphonies and accompanied Scriabin in a performance of his Piano Concerto. Later Scriabin gave piano recitals in Chicago, Boston, and other cities. In the spring of 1907 Scriabin went to Paris. At that time Sergei Diaghilev was presenting his famed Russian concerts, and he included in his programs Scriabin's Second Symphony and Piano Concerto, with Josef Hofmann as soloist. Scriabin and Tatiana spent the summer of 1907 in Switzerland; in the autumn of that year they took residence in Lausanne, where they remained until the following spring. There, in 1908, Scriabin had a visit from Serge Koussevitzky, who at that time established his Editions Russes de Musique and conducted concerts in Moscow and St. Petersburg. Scriabin and Koussevitzky soon became close friends. In the autumn of 1908 Scriabin and Tatiana went to Brussels; early in the winter of 1909 they returned to Russia, where they spent two months in Moscow and St. Petersburg. Scriabin gave numerous recitals in both cities; his programs included his Fifth Piano Sonata op. 53. His Third Symphony and the

Poème de l'extase were also performed in Moscow in that season. Upon returning to Brussels, Scriabin began work on the score of *Prométhée*. In the winter of 1910 he was back in Moscow to complete the score. In 1911 he played concerts in Berlin and Leipzig; in 1912 he made a tour in Holland, where Willem Mengelberg conducted his First Symphony, the Piano Concerto (with Scriabin as soloist), and *Prométhée*. Early in 1914 he went to London, where Henry Wood conducted the *Poème de l'extase* and *Prométhée*. Scriabin also gave piano recitals there. Later that year he stayed in a summer home near Moscow. There he wrote the text of the *Acte préalable,* which he hoped to complete early in 1916. But he did not make much progress on the music; only a few musical sketches were found among his papers after his death.

During the winter of 1915, Scriabin gave three recitals in St. Petersburg; his last public appearance took place on April 15, 1915. Upon returning to Moscow, he became ill. An abcess developed on his upper lip, which led to gangrene, and on the morning of April 27, 1915, he died after days of great suffering. He was buried at the cemetery of the Novodevichi Monastery in Moscow.

LIST OF WORKS

OPUS 1. Valse for piano, f-moll (1885–1886)

OPUS 2. 3 Morceaux for piano (1886)
        No. 1. Etude, cis-moll (Andante)
        No. 2. Prélude, H-dur
        No. 3. Impromptu à la Mazur

OPUS 3. 10 Mazurkas for piano (1888–1889)
        No. 1. h-moll (Tempo giusto)
        No. 2. fis-moll (Allegretto non tanto)
        No. 3. g-moll (Allegretto, semplice)
        No. 4. E-dur (Moderato)
        No. 5. dis-moll (Doloroso, poco rubato)
        No. 6. cis-moll (Scherzando)
        No. 7. e-moll (Con passione)
        No. 8. b-moll (Con moto)
        No. 9. gis-moll
        No. 10. es-moll (Sotto voce)

OPUS 4. "Allegro appassionato" for piano, es-moll
        (1888–1892)

OPUS 5. 2 Nocturnes for piano (1890)
        No. 1. fis-moll (Andante)
        No. 2. A-dur (Allegro)

OPUS 6. First Sonata, f-moll, for piano (1893)
        a. Allegro con fuoco, f-moll
        b. c-moll
        c. Presto, f-moll
        d. Funèbre, f-moll

OPUS 7. 2 Impromptus à la Mazur (1891)
    No. 1. gis-moll
    No. 2. Fis-dur

OPUS 8. 12 Etudes for piano (1894)
    No. 1. C-dur (Vivace)
    No. 2. fis-moll (A capricio, con forza)
    No. 3. h-moll (Tempestoso)
    No. 4. H-dur (Piacevole)
    No. 5. E-dur (4/4, Brioso)
    No. 6. A-dur (3/4, Con grazia)
    No. 7. b-moll (4/4, 12/8, Presto tenebroso, Agitato)
    No. 8. As-dur (3/4, Lento, tempo rubato)
    No. 9. cis-moll (3/4, Alla ballata)
    No. 10. Des-dur (3/8, Allegro)
    No. 11. b-moll (3/4, Andante cantabile)
    No. 12. dis-moll (4/4, Patetico)

OPUS 9. Prelude and Nocturne for Piano, for the left hand alone (1894)
    No. 1. Prélude, cis-moll (3/4, Andante)
    No. 2. Nocturne, Des-dur (6/8, Andante)

OPUS 10. 2 Impromptus for piano (1894)
    No. 1. fis-moll (3/4)
    No. 2. A-dur (3/4)

OPUS 11. 24 Préludes for piano
    No. 1. C-dur (2/2, Vivace), 1895
    No. 2. a-moll (3/4, Allegretto), 1895
    No. 3. C-dur (3/4, Vivo), 1895
    No. 4. e-moll (6/4, Lento), 1888
    No. 5. D-dur (4/2, Andante cantabile), 1896
    No. 6. h-moll (2/4, Allegro), 1889

No. 7.   A-dur (6/8, Allegro assai), 1895
No. 8.   fis-moll (3/4, Allegro agitato), 1895
No. 9.   E-dur (3/4, Andantino), 1894
No. 10.   cis-moll (6/8, Andante), 1894
No. 11.   H-dur (6/8, Allegro assai), 1895
No. 12.   gis-moll (9/8, Andante), 1895
No. 13.   Ges-dur (3/4, Lento), 1895
No. 14.   es-moll (15/8, Presto), 1895
No. 15.   Des-dur (4/4, Lento), 1895
No. 16.   b-moll (5/8, 4/8, Misterioso), 1895
No. 17.   As-dur (3/2, Allegretto), 1895
No. 18.   f-moll (2/4, Allegro agitato), 1895
No. 19.   Es-dur (2/4, Appetuoso), 1895
No. 20.   c-moll (3/4, Appassionato), 1895
No. 21.   B-dur (3/4, Andante), 1895
No. 22.   g-moll (3/4, Lento), 1896
No. 23.   F-dur (3/4, Vivo), 1895
No. 24.   d-moll (6/8, 5/8, Presto), 1895

OPUS 12.   2 Impromptus for piano (1895)
No. 1.   Fis-dur (3/4, Presto)
No. 2.   b-moll (4/4, Andante cantabile)

OPUS 13.   6 Préludes for piano (1895)
No. 1.   C-dur (3/4, Maestoso)
No. 2.   a-moll (6/8, Allegro)
No. 3.   C-dur (3/4, Andante)
No. 4.   e-moll (2/4, Allegro)
No. 5.   D-dur (6/8, Allegro)
No. 6.   h-moll (6/8, Presto)

OPUS 14.   2 Impromptus for piano (1895)
No. 1.   H-dur (3/4, Allegretto)
No. 2.   fis-moll (9/8, Andante cantabile)

OPUS 15.   5 Préludes for piano (1895)
     No. 1.   A-dur (3/4, Andante)
     No. 2.   fis-moll (3/4, Vivo)
     No. 3.   E-dur (6/8, Allegro assai)
     No. 4.   E-dur (3/4, Andantino)
     No. 5.   cis-moll (6/8, Andante)

OPUS 16.   5 Préludes for piano (1895)
     No. 1.   H-dur (3/4, Andante)
     No. 2.   gis-moll (2/4, Allegro)
     No. 3.   C-dur (4/4, Andante cantabile)
     No. 4.   es-moll (3/4, Lento)
     No. 5.   Fis-dur (3/8, Allegretto)

OPUS 17.   7 Préludes for piano (1895)
     No. 1.   d-moll (3/4, Allegretto)
     No. 2.   Es-dur (2/4, Presto)
     No. 3.   D-dur (3/4, Andante rubato)
     No. 4.   b-moll (3/2, Lento)
     No. 5.   f-moll (9/8, Prestissimo)
     No. 6.   B-dur (6/8, Andante doloroso)
     No. 7.   g-moll (9/8, Allegro assai)

OPUS 18.   Allegro de concert for piano, b-moll (4/4,
     Allegro con fuoco) (1896)

OPUS 19.   Second Sonata, gis-moll, sonate-fantaisie for
     piano (1897)
     a. Andante, 3/4, gis-moll; E-dur
     b. Presto, 3/2, gis-moll

OPUS 20.   Concerto fis-moll, for piano, with orchestral
     accompaniment (1897)
     a. Allegro, 3/4, fis-moll
     b. Andante, 4/4, Fis-dur
     c. Allegro moderato, 3/4, fis-moll; Fis-dur

OPUS 21. Polonaise for piano, b-moll (3/4, Allegro
maestoso) (1897)

OPUS 22. 4 Préludes for piano (1897)
No. 1. gis-moll (3/4, Andante)
No. 2. cis-moll (6/8, Andante)
No. 3. H-dur (3/4, Allegretto)
No. 4. h-moll (4/4, Andantino)

OPUS 23. Third Sonata, fis-moll, for piano (1897)
a. Drammatico, 3/4, fis-moll; Fis-dur
b. Allegretto, 4/8, Es-dur
c. Andante, 3/4, H-dur
d. Presto con fuoco, 3/4, fis-moll

OPUS 24. "Rêverie" for orchestra, c-moll (3/4, Andante)
(1898)

OPUS 25. 9 Mazurkas for piano (1899)
No. 1. f-moll (3/4, Allegro)
No. 2. C-dur (3/4, Allegretto)
No. 3. e-moll (3/4, Lento)
No. 4. E-dur (3/4, Vivo)
No. 5. cis-moll (3/4, Agitato)
No. 6. Fis-dur (3/4, Allegretto)
No. 7. fis-moll (3/4, Moderato)
No. 8. H-dur (3/4, Allegretto)
No. 9. es-moll (3/4, Mesto)

OPUS 26. First Symphony, E-dur, for orchestra and
chorus (1900)
a. Lento, 3/4, E-dur
b. Allegro drammatico, 3/4, e-moll
c. Lento, 6/8, H-dur
d. Vivace, 9/8, C-dur

e. Allegro, 3/4, es-moll
f. Andante, 4/4, C-dur

OPUS 27.   2 Préludes for piano (1901)
No. 1.   g-moll (9/8, Patetico)
No. 2.   H-dur (3/4, Andante)

OPUS 28.   Fantaisie for piano, h-moll (3/4, Moderato)
(1901)

OPUS 29.   Second Symphony, c-moll, for orchestra (1902)
a. Andante, 4/4, c-moll
b. Allegro, 6/8, Es-dur
c. Andante, 6/8, H-dur
d. Tempestoso, 12/8
e. Maestoso, 4/4, C-dur

OPUS 30.   Fourth Sonata, Fis-dur, for piano (1903)
a. Andante, 6/8, Fis-dur
b. Prestissimo vollando, 12/8, Fis-dur

OPUS 31.   4 Préludes for piano (1903)
No. 1.   C-dur (3/4, Andante)
No. 2.   fis-moll (2/4, Con stravaganza)
No. 3.   es-moll (2/2, Presto)
No. 4.   C-dur (3/4, Lento)

OPUS 32.   2 Poèmes for piano (1903)
No. 1.   Fis-dur (9/8, Andante cantabile)
No. 2.   D-dur (4/4, Allegro; con eleganza, con
fiduzia)

OPUS 33.   4 Préludes for piano (1900)
No. 1.   E-dur (3/4)
No. 2.   Fis-dur (6/8, Vagamente)
No. 3.   C-dur (3/4)
No. 4.   As-dur (5/4, Ardito, bellicoso)

OPUS 34.   "Poème tragique" for piano, B-dur (12/8, Festivamente, fastoso) (1903)

OPUS 35.   3 Préludes for piano (1903)
    No. 1.   Des-dur (3/4, Allegro)
    No. 2.   B-dur (4/4, Elevato)
    No. 3.   C-dur (3/8, Scherzoso)

OPUS 36.   "Poème satanique" for piano, C-dur (6/8, Allegro) (1903)

OPUS 37.   4 Préludes for piano (1903)
    No. 1.   b-moll (9/8, Mesto)
    No. 2.   Fis-dur (9/8, Maestoso, fiero)
    No. 3.   H-dur (3/4, Andante)
    No. 4.   g-moll (3/4, Irato, impetuoso)

OPUS 38.   Valse for piano, As-dur (3/4, Allegro agevole) (1903)

OPUS 39.   4 Préludes for piano (1903)
    No. 1.   Fis-dur (5/4, Allegro)
    No. 2.   D-dur (2/4, Elevato)
    No. 3.   C-dur (4/2, Languido)
    No. 4.   As-dur (3/4)

OPUS 40.   2 Mazurkas for piano (1903)
    No. 1.   Des-dur (Allegro)
    No. 2.   Fis-dur (3/4, Piacevole)

OPUS 41.   Poème for piano, Des-dur (6/8) (1903)

OPUS 42.   8 Etudes for piano (1903)
    No. 1.   Des-dur (3/4, Presto)
    No. 2.   fis-moll (2/4, MM = 112)
    No. 3.   Fis-dur (6/8, Prestissimo)
    No. 4.   Fis-dur (3/4, Andante)
    No. 5.   cis-moll (12/8, Affanato)

	No. 6.	Des-dur (3/4, Esaltato)
	No. 7.	f-moll (2/4, Agitato)
	No. 8.	Es-dur (4/4, Allegro)

OPUS 43.   Third Symphony, C-dur, "Le Poème divin," for orchestra (1903–1904)
a. 3/2, Lento, divin, grandiose
b. "Luttes," c-moll (3/4, Allegro, Mystérieux, Tragique)
c. Voluptés, Es-dur (3/4, Lento, sublime)
d. "Jeu divin," C-dur (4/4, Allegro, avec une joie éclatante)

OPUS 44.   2 Poèmes for piano (1904)
No. 1.   C-dur (2/4, Lento)
No. 2.   C-dur (3/8, Moderato)

OPUS 45.   3 Morceaux for piano (1904)
No. 1.   Feuillet d'album, Es-dur (3/4, Andante piacevole)
No. 2.   Poème fantastique, C-dur (3/4, Presto)
No. 3.   Prélude, Es-dur (3/4, Andante)

OPUS 46.   Scherzo for piano, C-dur (6/8, Presto) (1905)

OPUS 47.   Quasi-valse for piano, F-dur (3/4) (1905)

OPUS 48.   4 Préludes for piano (1905)
No. 1.   Fis-dur (3/4, Impetuoso, fiero)
No. 2.   C-dur (4/2, Poetico, con delizio)
No. 3.   Des-dur (3/4, Capricciosamente, affanato)
No. 4.   C-dur (3/4, Festivamente)

OPUS 49.   3 Morceaux for piano (1905)
No. 1.   Etude, Es-dur (2/4)
No. 2.   Prélude, F-dur (3/4, Bruscamente)
No. 3.   "Rêverie," C-dur (2/4, Con finezza)

OPUS 50.   Not published

OPUS 51.   4 Morceaux for piano (1906)
   No. 1.   "Fragilité," Es-dur (2/4, Allegretto,
         limpide)
   No. 2.   Prélude, a-moll (6/8, Lugubre)
   No. 3.   Poème ailé, H-dur (3/4)
   No. 4.   Danse languide, G-dur (4/4)

OPUS 52.   3 Morceaux for piano (1907)
   No. 1.   Poème, C-dur (3/8, Lento)
   No. 2.   "Enigme" (3/8, Etrange,
         capricieusement)
   No. 3.   Poème languide, H-dur (9/8, Pas vite)

OPUS 53.   Fifth Sonata for piano (2/4, Allegro impetuoso,
      con stravaganza) (1907)

OPUS 54.   *Le Poème de l'extase* for orchestra (2/4, 6/8,
      Andante languido; Maestoso) (1905–1907)

OPUS 55.   Not published

OPUS 56.   4 Morceaux for piano (1908)
   No. 1.   Prélude, Es-dur (6/8, Violent, très
         accentué)
   No. 2.   "Ironies," C-dur (2/4, Vivo scherzoso)
   No. 3.   "Nuances" (9/8, Fondu, Velouté)
   No. 4.   Etude (2/8, Presto)

OPUS 57.   2 Morceaux for piano (1908)
   No. 1.   "Désir" (12/8)
   No. 2.   "Caresse dansée" (3/8)

OPUS 58.   "Feuillet d'album" for piano (3/4, Con
      delicatezza) (1911)

OPUS 59.   2 Morceaux for piano (1910)
   No. 1.   Poème (6/8, Allegretto)
   No. 2.   Prélude (6/8, Sauvage belliqueux)

OPUS 60. *Prométhée* (*Le Poème du feu*) for orchestra and piano with organ, chorus and clavier à lumières (3/4, Lento, brumeux; 2/4, Dans un vertige) (1909–1910)

OPUS 61. Poème-Nocturne for piano (9/8, Avec une grâce capricieuse) (1911–1912)

OPUS 62. Sixth Sonata for piano (3/4, Modéré) (1911–1912)

OPUS 63. 2 Poèmes for piano (1911–1912)
    No. 1. "Masque" (6/8, Allegretto)
    No. 2. "Etrangeté" (9/8, Gracieux, délicat)

OPUS 64. Seventh Sonata for piano (4/8, Allegro) (1911–1912)

OPUS 65. 3 Etudes for piano (1912)
    No. 1. B-dur (12/16, Allegro fantastico), in ninths
    No. 2. Cis-dur (4/4, Allegretto), in sevenths
    No. 3. C-dur (2/4, Molto vivace), in fifths

OPUS 66. Eighth Sonata for piano, 9/8, Lento (1912–1913)

OPUS 67. 2 Préludes for piano (1912)
    No. 1. 5/8, Andante
    No. 2. 4/8, Presto

OPUS 68. Ninth Sonata for piano (4/8, Moderato, quasi andante) (1912–1913)

OPUS 69. 2 Poèmes for piano (1913)
    No. 1. 3/4, Allegretto
    No. 2. 6/8, Allegretto

OPUS 70. Tenth Sonata for piano (9/16, Moderato) (1913)

OPUS 71. 2 Poèmes for piano (1914)
           No. 1. 6/8, Fantastique
           No. 2. 3/4, En rêvant

OPUS 72. "Vers la flamme," Poème for piano (9/8, Allegro
           moderato) (1914)

OPUS 73. 2 Danses for piano (1914)
           No. 1. "Guirlandes" (3/4, Avec une grâce
                languissante)
           No. 2. "Flammes sombres" (6/8, Avec une
                grâce dolente)

OPUS 74. 5 Préludes for piano (1914)
           No. 1. 3/4, Douloureux déchirant
           No. 2. 4/8, Très lent, contemplatif
           No. 3. 9/8, Allegro drammatico
           No. 4. 3/4, Lent, Vague, indécis
           No. 5. 3/2, Fier, belliqueux

UNPUBLISHED WORKS

1. Romance for French horn in F (1896)
2. Prélude, d-moll, for piano (1881)
3. Prélude, Fis-dur, for piano (1895)
4. Presto—third movement of a Sonata for piano, the
   first movement of which was published under the
   title "Allegro appassionato," es-moll, op. 4 (1887–
   1888)
5. Unfinished ballad, g-moll, for piano
6. Symphonic poem, d-moll, for orchestra (1895)
7. Nocturne, As-dur, for piano (1881–1882)
8. Fugue, e-moll, for five voices (1891)
9. Fantaisie for piano and orchestra (1887–1888)

PART I

PERSONALITY

1

THE THINKER

I saw Scriabin for the first time in the house of my uncle in Moscow, in 1896, when I was only fifteen years old. I was struck by his frail and delicate appearance, his intense nervousness. I was also deeply moved by his piano playing, so unusual, so different from what I was led to expect. He played, if I remember correctly, several preludes from his op. 11. We exchanged but a few words. My impression of this first meeting was so strong that it was not erased for many years. It was still vivid when I met him again in Moscow in the autumn of 1902. Scriabin was then already teaching at the Moscow Conservatory. He was married and was a father, but his outward appearance showed the same tenderness, frailty, and strangely childlike countenance. After a brief talk about mutual acquaintances and other amenities, our conversation assumed a more abstract character and rapidly led to a philosophical debate, impassioned and even embittered. This was the beginning of my long relationship with Scriabin.

At a later meeting, Scriabin and I chuckled recalling how, after a formal introduction and without really knowing each other, we instantly plunged, upon some random pretext, into a debate. I was greatly impressed by the exceptional profundity of his intellect, an impression that intensified the more I saw him.

Unlike most specialists, who regard philosophy merely as a professional occupation separate from everyday life, Scriabin was constantly immersed in philosophical speculation. Whatever he was doing or saying, an intense inner process of reasoning accompanied his actions, which never ceased and of which he was seldom aware himself. But a random remark, a leading question, was sufficient for him to become absorbed in his thoughts, to begin to expound them, persuading, or so it seemed, not so much the listeners as himself.

After a few more years, in 1907, I met Scriabin again in Lausanne. I had arrived there from Russia early in the morning. After spending several sleepless nights in a railroad train, and having barely had time to perform my ablutions properly and to change clothes, I was already drawn by Scriabin into a conversation about theosophy, a doctrine with which he had just become acquainted. This sudden interest did not surprise me at all; it was so typical of Scriabin, who suffered real agony, almost a physical pain, when he found himself unable to cope with a thorny problem. He would not admit that there was anything that he could not immediately grasp, and he abhorred superficiality and approximation in his thinking.

This metaphysical passion, if one may so describe it, possessed him to the very end of his life. A few hours before he died he continued to discuss problems for which his spirit eternally sought solutions.

But what was the purpose of this intense speculation? What did he seek to achieve in this self-abandonment to metaphysical passions? An understanding of life? The truth of reality? And can one speak of the truth in a precise, scientific, and philosophical way?

Undoubtedly the thirst for inner knowledge was strong in Scriabin, but this was not the impulse that set his thoughts in motion when he was preoccupied with the solution of some of the most difficult problems that faced him. To Scriabin, spiritual action always exercised priority over theoretical thought. He was a man of action first and of ratiocination second. He was convinced that he was destined to perform an important task in life, and he interpreted events in the outside world in such a way as to make his own actions appear not only entirely natural, but even inevitable. He took an interest in the reality of life only insofar as it concerned the present, and both were for him only actions designed to build the temple of the future. At our early meeting he seemed to be absorbed in purely theoretical speculations that were quite unrelated to reality. But it was only an appearance. Actually all his tenets and corollaries were pragmatic in their nature, for they gave him the needed support for the psychological, logical, and moral inevitability of certain events in the future. They were reasons for action and a commentary on his own hopes and aspirations, as well as a rational justification of his creative artistic work.

This is not to say that Scriabin's philosophy was secondary to his artistic activity and that it performed merely an ancillary or auxiliary function—that would be to underestimate the importance of his beliefs. But the coincidence of his desiderata and aspirations with the results he obtained is explainable by the existence of a special relationship between his philosophy and his artistic aims, a relationship different from that of subordination.

I had frequent occasion to observe Scriabin during his conversations with others, particularly with those who were inclined to agree with his ideas, such as the poet Viacheslav Ivanov. And I invariably noticed that when his interlocutor paused, as if satisfied by theoretical conclusions, Scriabin would go further beyond theoretical positions, categorically deducing the desirability, necessity, and inevitability of certain actions and events, the arrival of which he was anxious to expedite.

In his thinking, Scriabin did not proceed from existing premises but from that future to which he aspired, a vision of which was constantly before him and whose advent he passionately awaited. This future he interpreted as a reality to be materialized here on earth. When he strove to depict our world in rational terms, when he tried to grasp its meaning, he was guided by an ardent desire to master the material needed for the consummation of these visions perceptible through the ultimate transparency of reality.

I recall that at the very inception of our friendship, in 1902 and 1903, I pointed out to Scriabin the utopian, fantastic character of his speculations and prognoses, arguing from historic considerations. He admitted that his familiarity with history and science was scant, but he insisted that historical data were important to him only for a greater understanding of his objectives. In this sense one might say that his desire to acquire knowledge was not unselfish. Factual information as such held no attraction for him, and he was completely uninterested in assembling and cataloguing scientific data, a scholarly pursuit that has now become so popular.

Scriabin's regard for the world as it appears to us at the present time was conditioned by his vision of the future, of a world that ought to be, of a world that will assume a new form inconceivable to our senses. He sought his personal truth not as an external, separate, and alien entity; he saw it by intuition. To him the birth of that new world signalized the completion of the entire cosmic cycle. And yet in this poet, in this prophet, there lived a refined, almost pedantic formalist who demanded accuracy in all that concerned his creative work. Perfection of form and precision of execution were his characteristic traits. He was aware of contradictions, disharmonies, and inconsistencies in life, and he strove to reconcile them, to find their resolution, not only on a psychological and intuitive plane, but also in rational thought.

In this tendency to formulate and schematize, in this peculiar rationalism, was Scriabin's salvation. I am convinced that if his intellect had not been so strong, he would have perished, driven to madness by the impetuosity of his own creative forces. His rationalism was a mask that concealed his irrational self, a mask that unconsciously but wisely held in check his creative spirit, essentially limitless and transcendental. "To create is to limit oneself," Scriabin liked to say. Hence the formulas and schemes designed to limit, to confine, to reveal in a word the flame burning within him, threatening to consume him. In meditation, in speculation, Scriabin seemed to find a welcome repose, a saving grace, a retreat to a stable, definite, albeit confining world, a harbor where he could find a temporary refuge from his visions, from the tempestuous tensions of his inner self.

Characteristically, this tendency grew stronger over time, as his spiritual life deepened, widened, and was enriched by new ideas. The farther he retreated from human logic, from rational categories and rubrics, the more perfect and pure grew his own self-contemplation, the more vivid his visions, indescribable in human words. Then, as if fearful of losing himself and perishing in the unknown, he relied more firmly on formulas and schemes of our plane. Each formula, each scheme was for him a support needed to bring about his dreams and visions here on earth.

Scriabin's metaphysical constructions were not only logical, but also graphical; he drew them out, using ruler and compass, with great diligence and accuracy. He endeavored to represent in lines and geometric figures the interrelations he intuitively perceived between the world and the individual, between God and reality, in art, religion, and science. Among his drawings, there were also diagrams of the Supernal Temple to be built when Time comes to an end. He designed these drawings with a particular tenderness that at times bordered on the naive. He would constantly refer to them during our conversations. "Here, look at my diagram," he would say. "Everything here is so clear, logical, and vivid. It is impossible to mis-construe these drawings." That an idea could be fitted so easily into a graceful, schematic design he regarded as ir-refutable proof of its basic truth. Some of these drawings are still extant, but without a text and devoid of Scriabin's vivid and personal comments, they now stand mute.

The most extraordinary aspect of Scriabin's cognitive striv-ings was his perseverance toward maximum clarity and logic. He constantly questioned his conclusions, no matter how well they suited his desires and his hopes. He sub-mitted these conclusions to harsh criticism and carefully checked on the process of his own thinking. To some who did not know him well, it appeared, particularly in the last years of his life, that he had become something of a doc-trinaire, that his faith was absolute and his dogmas were immutable. One could indeed gain this impression from the tone of his argumentation, his self-confidence, even his occasional intolerance. Such was my own impression at our first meeting. Actually, there was nothing intransigent or adamant about him. True, there was in him an unlimited and fanatical faith, but its subject was not ideology, not philosophy, not those rational constructions that he erected with such care but was willing to destroy without pity once he had realized their fallacy. This faith, which excluded all compromise, was generated by the irrational impulse which possessed him and which he tried to ra-

tionalize, an impulse that demanded its realization in himself. He never doubted the absolute truth and importance
of the inner voice that he heard in his soul. When it was
questioned, he responded as a fanatic, refusing to grant
any concessions and categorically dismissing all arguments
by referring to his own inner experience as an *ultima ratio.*
Scriabin readily accepted criticism of his work; he even
conceded doubts regarding his own intellectual constructions and debated freely on the subject. The validity of his
vision, on the other hand, his peculiar sense of being, the
reality of the world within him, were not to be challenged.
I remember well a conversation I had with him about his
projected opera. To my candid doubts concerning some
fragments from his libretto and its character, he reacted
by agreeing with what I had to say. But when I raised the
question of the fundamental idea of the opera, which was
the union of all humankind into one indivisible entity,
when I observed that such a union is not only impossible
but is not even desirable, he disagreed with me violently.
Our discussion grew more and more impassioned, leading
almost to a quarrel. Scriabin was perfectly willing to concede deficiencies in this or that work, but he never yielded
to the argument that our world within its terrestrial limitations excludes the idea of oneness and that therefore
such oneness is unattainable. This was to him a question
of life or death, for he lived only by this dream. As a result,
only those who accepted, at least theoretically, the possibility of the ultimate achievement of absolute unity on
earth, or at the very least responded by silence when this
question was posed, could enter into an intimate relationship with him.

Scriabin's intellectualism was also revealed in his passion for debate. He loved the very process of discussion, and he was carried away by argument as much as he could be by music. A dangerous opponent in debate, he was always resourceful in repartee, and anyone contending with him had to be constantly on guard. It was strange at times to observe how this poet who had moments before charmed us by his art could immediately afterward reveal himself as an adroit dialectician capable of clever sparring. In his debates there was nothing vague, nothing elusive — the qualities so richly reflected in his musical compositions. On the contrary, everything in his discourse was clear, lucid, and transparent. He never tolerated any terminological ambiguity in himself or in others and always tried to achieve perfect definition and precision in the concepts with which he operated. A fine conversationalist, he was always delighted when he succeeded in catching his opponent unawares. I can almost see before me his mocking face and a curiously childlike smile on his lips. Scriabin was extremely honest, and when a debate ended and passions subsided, he was the first to point out flaws in his arguments. When a subject under discussion moved him deeply, when it touched on the fundamental principles, then he abandoned all thought of debate or contention and was no longer preoccupied with victory over his opponent; then the discussion became a common search, a friendly exploration.

I must observe parenthetically that Scriabin's subtle fastidiousness and dialectical skill led sometimes to casuistry verging on the ridiculous. When he analyzed the music of someone else, he showed even a certain pettiness.

He was himself aware of this foible, and the only reason that I mention it at all is to point out that this trait was intimately connected with his desire to achieve precision and accuracy. He was repelled by anything that was disordered or inconsistent within itself, any sign of sloppiness in thinking, feeling, and acting.

And yet this precise and sharp intellect fought rationalism as a personal enemy. "As a rationalist you cannot understand what I have to say"—how often he tossed such phrases at me in the heat of discussion. Indeed, rationalism, a doctrine of integral, total apperception of the world in the categories of pure reason, of the falsity and irreality of all that cannot be expressed in categorical concepts, was entirely unacceptable to him. As for his own formulas and schematic constructions, he regarded them merely as auxiliary tools, and very imperfect ones at that; he knew that the more adequate expression of his prophetic visions was his own musical oeuvre, and not at all the theories in which he always found an insoluble residue. He always had more faith in psychology than in logic. "Logically, it may be an impossibility," he would say, "but in this instance, one must take a psychological view; logical contradictions abound in spiritual life, and I have more confidence in what I feel intuitively than in any ratiocination."

During our long friendship, Scriabin's ideology underwent considerable changes and his philosophical attitude frequently altered. Summing up my impressions of our discussions and debates now, when he is no longer with us, I see clearly that these changes occurred on the periphery of his intellect, in the rational formulas and images that arose in his consciousness. And although these formulas were constantly evolving, they expressed the same unchanging thoughts, the same central idea. But he perceived this idea from different angles, which depended on the general development of his intellectual and volitional self. A great distance separates the concepts of phenomenological empiricism and naturalism from religious mysticism. But the distance between amoral individualism and universal oneness is immense. Yet Scriabin found this path and traversed it, never deviating from the course once undertaken. He intended to achieve human and cosmic oneness; his ideology was essentially a theory of oneness and the means by which it could be achieved. During our early meetings, his perception of this oneness was simple, perhaps too simple—almost mechanical. He used to say, "Almost all human disagreements stem from a lack of mutual understanding, from misinterpretation of words that have different meanings for different persons. If we all could agree on the meaning of the most elementary concepts that are most frequently used, then the first step toward the unification of mankind would have been made." A few years later he would not have said that, for he would have understood that such an external unification of mankind would be futile and illusory. When he was writing *Le Poème de l'extase,* he already realized that oneness could be attained only by the deepening and sharpening of contradictions, and not by their negation or forcible unification.

However, this change in his attitude concerned the means but not the ultimate end.

In his search for new forms of expression, in his attempts to rationalize his intuitive perceptions and to impart to them the character of a universal imperative, Scriabin proceeded with complete independence from others.

Critics have pointed out that Scriabin's music was influenced by Chopin, Liszt, and Wagner. The presence of these influences is undeniable. Much more autonomous, however, was the development of Scriabin's philosophical thought. This assertion may at first seem unusual and even paradoxical, for Scriabin was not a professional philosopher. And yet when I was once asked under whose influence Scriabin's ideology was generated, I was at a loss to reply. Such influences could be discernible only on the periphery of his thinking, in his manner of expression perhaps, but not in the substance of his ideology. He occasionally made use of conventional formulas and propositions, but he filled them with his own peculiar meaning, which was sometimes at odds with the semantic value of the original concept. When he encountered a person whose mental attitude was opposed to his, he resisted any possible influence, no matter how intellectually strong his opponent was. A typical example was his relationship with Prince Sergei Troubetzkoy and with the famous socialist

Georgi Plekhanov. At our early meeting in 1902 Scriabin spoke to me about Troubetzkoy with great admiration and affection. He was impressed by Troubetzkoy's intelligence and erudition. But it was obvious that his attitude toward the ideas and aspirations of Troubetzkoy and his circle was independent and even hostile. He felt equally out of sympathy with the religious mysticism of Vladimir Soloviev and spoke of it with a certain condescension and even derision. Religiosity was to him at that time a symptom of weakness of will, and he equated mysticism with superstition. The determining factor of Scriabin's ideology at that time was solipsism and metaphysical nihilism. "Nothing exists," he used to say, "the only thing that is, is what I create." In his usage, "I" represented an empirical person. He strove to achieve oneness, a confluence of All in All; he aspired to be the center of this confluence and regarded this consummation as an absolute, unconditional, and free act. At that time he was a member of the Moscow Philosophical Society, into which he was introduced by Prince Troubetzkoy. He attended the meetings regularly, but he rejected the spiritual and idealistic disciplines of Troubetzkoy and Leo Lopatin that dominated the society, regarding them as obstacles on his own path.

Had Scriabin met Troubetzkoy two or three years earlier, they might have formed a much more intimate relationship. They might have found a common language, understood, and perhaps influenced each other. For as time went on, Scriabin's spiritual life acquired a new depth and gradually assumed a religious character as a result of the growing awareness of his mission—a conviction that he was predestined to perform a certain appointed task entrusted to him from a source independent of his own volition.

In 1905 Scriabin met Georgi Plekhanov. Their relationship followed a course similar to the association with Troubetzkoy. Despite the fact that they formed a close acquaintance—almost a friendship—despite the respect and admiration that Scriabin had for Plekhanov, the latter remained spiritually alien to him. Scriabin was antagonistic to Plekhanov's materialistic philosophy, which he regarded as a peculiarly crude and rudimentary form of realism and substantialism. His ideas were repugnant to him, for they constricted, in his opinion, the free flight of his creative imagination. Yet it was under Plekhanov's influence that Scriabin became acquainted with Marxism—he even read the first chapters of *Das Kapital.* The dialectic strength of Karl Marx and the structural symmetry and orderly exposition of his theories greatly impressed him. From then on he never doubted the economic (but only economic) strength of Marxism and never questioned the dialectical inevitability of the collapse of capitalist society. But economic and political upheavals, however spectacular, had for Scriabin only a secondary importance, for he posited the supremacy of spiritual life, in opposition to Plekhanov's basic thesis that consciousness is determined by environment. Scriabin's attitude toward historical materialism was sharply negative; on the other hand, he injected into socialist doctrines some religious and mystical elements, which were, of course, quite unacceptable to Plekhanov.

Scriabin first became acquainted with theosophy in Paris in 1906, when a friend told him that his vision of

Mysterium, of the union of humanity with divinity and the return of the world to oneness, had much in common with theosophy. Here we can definitely speak of an influence, for when I saw Scriabin a few months later in Switzerland he was deeply engaged in reading works by Mme. Blavatsky, Annie Besant, C. W. Leadbeater, and other theosophists. His conversation was full of theosophical allusions to Manvantara, Pralaya, Seven Planes, Seven Races, and the like; he used these terms volubly as if they were familiar to all and as if they reflected incontrovertible truths. With the intransigence of a neophyte, he dismissed my doubts about theosophical postulates. "Read it," he would say, "I refuse to discuss the subject until you have read, even if superficially, the first volume of *The Secret Doctrine* of Mme. Blavatsky." I followed Scriabin's advice, but when I began to read theosophic literature I became aware that Scriabin used theosophical terms quite loosely. He adapted them to his own ideas, aspirations, and yearnings and employed theosophical postulates as formulas to describe his own experiences. When his infatuation with theosophy subsided somewhat, he said to me, "You may not accept the doctrine of Seven Planes as the ultimate truth, but to me it serves as a convenient framework for classifying natural phenomena and for creating order out of the chaos of factual data." The doctrine of Seven Races attracted Scriabin with its psychological ramifications, even when he no longer tried to interpret it in a literal sense. Each race, according to this interpretation, reflects a certain phase in the evolution of man's spiritual life, so that the history of the races becomes a history of the human psyche, which acquires senses and desires vested in the flesh and then

gradually denudes itself, abandoning its belongings and returning to the simplicity of the primordial oneness. Having
accepted this postulate, Scriabin reorganized in his own
terms the entire history of humanity, of which the cycle
of his own psychic life was a particular case. This gave him
a key to the understanding of world history. In the winter
of 1907–1908, he formalized the content and the subject
of his *Mysterium,* which he understood as a history of the
races of man and of individual consciousness or, more accurately, as an evolutionary psychology of the human
races. This phase of Scriabin's spiritual development owed
most to theosophy, which supplied him with the necessary
formulas and schemes, particularly in the notion of Seven
Races, which incarnated in space and time the gradual
descent of the psyche into matter. Even when he began to
retreat from theosophy he still felt greatly beholden to
Mme. Blavatsky's *Secret Doctrine* in his own development;
indeed, he felt tremendous admiration for Mme. Blavatsky
to the end of his life. He was particularly fascinated by her
courage in essaying a grandiose synthesis and by the
breadth and depth of her concepts, which he likened to
the grandeur of Wagner's music dramas. On the other
hand, his closer acquaintance with later theosophists tempered his early enthusiasm and in the end drove him away
from theosophy altogether. In Switzerland and Belgium he
subscribed to the theosophical publication *Le Lotus bleu,*
and in Russia he received the *Journal of Theosophy.* But he
rarely read either of these publications; the pages of the
Russian one remained uncut for a very long time. He said
that Mme. Blavatsky was the only great theosophist and
that her followers contributed little to her doctrine. He

was shocked by the lack of appreciation of the fine arts among Russian and foreign theosophists and by their unwillingness to give music its rightful place in their writings. Musical tastes in the theosophic circles of Moscow and St. Petersburg filled him with horror. "Can you imagine," he used to say, and his voice betrayed real anguish, "they adore Massenet!" He was greatly incensed against some English women theosophists who tried to interpret his music in theosophical terms and exploit it as theosophic propaganda. The artist in him rebelled against such misinterpretation. "They do not understand, they do not understand, they do not love art," he used to complain.

Music remained for Scriabin the primary concern, his destined calling, and in theosophy he found an interpretation of the cosmos that provided the foundation, the justification, and even, so he believed, the anticipation of the future. The theosophic vision of the world served as an incentive for his own work. "I will not discuss with you the truth of theosophy," he declared to me in Moscow, "but I know that Mme. Blavatsky's ideas helped me in my work and gave me power to accomplish my task."

Was Scriabin really influenced by Indian philosophy? His acquaintance with it came mainly through various theosophic tracts, among them *Religions de l'Inde,* by Auguste Barth; *The Light of Asia,* by Sir Edwin Arnold; *The Life of Buddha,* by Asvaghosa (in the translation of Konstantin Balmont); and several travel guides to India. This type of material was, of course, insufficient for a real understanding of the subject. As for European philosophy, Scriabin became familiar with it relatively late in life. In one of his notebooks we find the following entry: "At the age of twenty, first reading of Schopenhauer." At our early meetings I had an impression that Scriabin's philosophical knowledge was quite extensive. Later on, however, I realized that it was rather scant and that his knowledge of history and the exact sciences was also superficial. When we became close friends he often chuckled, remembering how he had fooled me by flaunting his alleged erudition. This lack of education often depressed him, although he was able to conceal it cleverly from those who did not pay close attention to what he said. "I lack general knowledge," he would declare, "but for my work such knowledge is needed not in order to become a specialist, but to be able to orient myself in all branches of science and not run the risk of discovering America for the second time."

Scriabin frequently expressed regrets that he never attended university classes but was instead enrolled in a military school. On the other hand, he found a certain consolation in this lack of formal education: "I do not have to spend time trying to overcome the troubles which beset men of science and interfere with their work." He made an attempt, however, to remedy this deficiency. Thanks to his love of conversation on abstract subjects, he acquired considerable skill in philosophical debate. He was not an assiduous reader; moreover, he lacked the ability to see clearly another person's viewpoint, but he could listen with interest to the exposition of some system or discipline, interjecting well-placed remarks. Reading gave him no opportunity to engage in direct debate, and this kept him away from books. As a result, almost all information he possessed on science and philosophy was derived from conversation on these topics.

His philosophical library was not large. In 1902–1903 in Moscow it included Friedrich Paulsen's *Introduction to Philosophy;* a volume of Plato's *Dialogues,* among them the *Symposium* in the translation of Vladimir Soloviev; *The Doctrine of Logos* by Troubetzkoy, of which he read only the initial few chapters; Alfred Fouillée's *History of Philosophy;* Goethe's *Faust;* and Nietzsche's *Also sprach Zarathustra.* Several other books were added later, among them the *History of Modern Philosophy* by Friedrich Ueberweg; *Logic* by Christoph Sigwart, of which he read only a few pages; two or three bulletins of philosophical congresses; the first volume of Kuno Fischer's *Immanuel Kant;* Wilhelm Windelband's *History of Philosophy;* and several books on theosophy.

Scriabin could admire only such writings as were in harmony with his own mode of thinking. He read Mme. Blavatsky's *The Secret Doctrine* (in a French translation) many times, marking in pencil the most significant passages. But he could not follow the reasoning of authors who were ideologically antagonistic to him; he simply put their books aside after reading a few pages. "I have very little time," he explained, "and I cannot afford to divide my attention."

Scriabin had a similar attitude toward the phenomena of everyday life, toward persons and actual events. He was unable to render an objective judgment; he was interested in facts, events, persons, or objects only if they were relevant to his ideas and aspirations.

As the years went by, this characteristic attitude became more pronounced. Scriabin seemed to lose the capacity for contemplating the world's reality and was entirely absorbed by the desire to exploit this reality for his purposes. Whomever he met, whatever subject he tackled, his sole criteria were whether they would hasten or impede his progress and be allies or enemies. As his will grew firmer and his visions seemed closer to realization, he almost lost the faculty of normal perception and became completely enthralled by these phantoms. Nothing existed for him except insofar as it affected his plans, positively or negatively. This is the reason why he seemed incapable of admiring art for art's sake.

Concluding my remarks about Scriabin as a thinker, I should like to shed some light on his mode of ratiocination. It was that of intuition and analogy. Analogical constructions guided his intuition in a definite direction. I should say that Scriabin in this respect is akin to Goethe, and this is perhaps the only point of contact between these two men who are in other respects so different from each other. Logic served Scriabin only as a tool to demonstrate and to expound his ideas, and he made use of logical constructions only as premises for already confirmed conclusions. Scriabin displayed a certain skill in deductive reasoning, having acquired it through arduous practice. Although he had a highly developed analytic sense, he could never master the scientific aspect of logic. While analyzing himself and his own process of thinking, he applied a psychological approach, discovering that his own reasoning progressed by juxtapositions and analogies and that only with the aid of these analogies could he arrive at helpful deductions. These deductions he then endeavored to justify by syllogism or some other device of formal logic.

It may appear that the analogies that he sought between phenomena were arbitrary. They evoked natural objections. But observing how he manipulated the points of similarity and dissimilarity, one had to grant a certain validity to this rather primitive method, which he steadfastly defended against all criticism. Of course his insufficiently disciplined and sometimes deluded intellect led to grave errors, but these cannot invalidate such intuitive perceptions, which stimulate one's cognitive faculties. By the juxtaposition of analogies Scriabin systematized amorphous material in his thinking, introduced order, distinguished the ingredients from each other, and, by so doing, intensified the power of his concentration.

2

THE ARTIST

There are two categories of artists. To the first category belong those whose creative work is not conditioned by consciousness, who are sagacious without being aware of their wisdom. They give birth to their creations in joy or in sorrow, but the true value of these creations remains unclear and inaccessible even to themselves, their creators. Having projected their ideas in musical tones, colors, or verbal images, they can no longer describe in terms of formal logic what they themselves had discovered. Inherently obscure and mysterious, they lack the desire to clarify the subject through their reasoning powers and to communicate to themselves and others the true meaning of their own work. The words in Plato's dialogue *Ion,* spoken by Socrates, are applicable to such artists: "Just as the corybantic celebrants dance in a state of frenzy, so do poets compose their beautiful lyric poems. Falling under the power of music and meter, they are stricken with Bacchic madness, just as the Bacchic maidens draw milk and honey from the rivers, when they are possessed by frenzy."

There are other artists who make an earnest effort to understand themselves, their creative work, and the world in which they live. They try to attain clarity, lucidity, and comprehensibility. They aspire to reveal themselves in rational terms, to articulate the elements that reflect their ideas. Having created something, they attempt to reconstruct intellectually the inexpressible and to rationalize the transcendental. They intend to illuminate the apperception of their desire by appropriate ideology. Leonardo da Vinci, Michelangelo, Beethoven, Goethe, and Wagner were among the creative spirits who strove to achieve such wisdom. Scriabin, too, belongs in this category, for in him this desire for cognition was combined with a passion for formal perfection and systematization. Those who were close to Scriabin were often struck by the grandeur of his creative designs, over which he himself seemed to lack control, and by the earnestness and intensity of his intellect. His creative and theoretical tools operated with equal acuteness. We witness in Scriabin a very strange phenomenon in which the artist fails to be satisfied solely by his artistic achievement and is constantly striving to justify it morally, religiously, and scientifically, to explain to others the meaning of his productions, to reveal their significance not only from an aesthetic but also from a metaphysical standpoint.

Ideological theories proposed by artists are customarily treated either as curious whims or annoying eccentricities. Such is, generally speaking, the attitude of specialists, but it is also a sentiment of the multitudes who do not tolerate a departure from traditions and firmly established norms. Scriabin's ideology, too, was subjected to this criticism.

Such an attitude stems from an erroneous view concerning the connection between the ideological and aesthetic products of an artist. It is commonly thought that one of these must be subordinated to the other. Here we face a dilemma: either the artist strives to expound a certain system of philosophy in order to preach a doctrine of his own or else he attempts to express himself in personal terms. In the first instance, creative effort is vitiated by cerebration and tendentiousness, and the art itself is subordinated to an external purpose. In the second instance, philosophy becomes subservient to art and is compelled to follow obediently the free flight of the artist's imagination. We deal in the first case with an unsuccessful artist who is also a propagandist, and in the second with an unsuccessful thinker. That is why many intellectual artists are suspected of deliberate contrivance to justify their way in art. The ideology of Wagner and even that of Goethe, whose artistic genius cannot be questioned, is therefore deprived a priori of its philosophical and scientific validity, just because both were creators within the realm of beauty. A philosophizing artist must perforce be either a poor philosopher or a poor artist, as we realize that either his art is subordinated to reasoning or, conversely, his ideology is in the service of his art.

It is, however, entirely possible that there exists a different relationship between the cognitive process and creative activity. Each may be autonomous and independent and yet linked to the other by a vital intuition, which is their common source.

If we assume that creative effort, whether philosophical or artistic, thrives on intuition, then the former transforms that intuition into an object of abstract knowledge, while the latter exhibits that creative effort to our cognition in concrete images. Then it becomes clear that both endeavors may develop in a thinking artist in parallels and possess equal validity. Graphically this can be represented as follows: if we assign the symbol A to a work of art and the symbol B to a philosophical system that corresponds to the artist's ideology, then the common but erroneous relationship between the two can be represented by the following diagram:

A 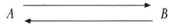 B

In this diagram a work of art is the formative factor that determines the artist's ideology; conversely, ideology becomes the determining factor of a work of art.

The following diagram gives a more adequate representation of the relationship between these two factors:

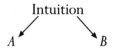
Intuition
A B

Here a work of art is not directly dependent on ideology, and ideology is not a direct reflection of, or a transcription into, a conceptual language of the artist's aesthetic code.

The first corollary to this proposition is that no aesthetically valid work of art can realize in concrete images any theory or discipline, whether philosophical, religious, or moral, but presents only a reflection of concrete, vital existence. The second corollary, positive in its nature, states that an artist's ideology possesses an objective, cognitive, and not merely subjective psychological validity. Indeed, genuine works of art demonstrate that the artist came down from Mount Sinai, so to speak, in full possession of the gift of prophecy, and that his thinking reflects his visions with complete clarity, but does so in a different form, on a different plane. Valid works of a poet, a musician, or a painter cannot be described with ideal completeness in the form of systematic categories. Some artists, however, strive to present their visions in both concrete and abstract aspects, addressing themselves simultaneously to realistic observation and discursive thinking. Both the artist and the thinker within a single person create autonomously and yet derive their inspiration from the common source of intuition. Most artists never formulate their own ideology, not even a fragmentary one, and create their works without excessive cogitation. Carried away by beautiful but, for the reasoning intellect, mute creations, we must fix their content within the terms of reason. The only possible avenue to this comprehension is the aesthetic apperception of the work in its vital oneness, in which the artist's intuition causes an autonomous emergence of abstract formulas that disclose the contents of that intuition.

It follows from these premises that we must regard the ideology of great thinking artists as essential to their art. The common and superficial attitude to the contrary notwithstanding, we must trust a priori the utterances of these messengers from another world, at the same time taking care to separate the original from the traditional in their messages, the essential from the incidental, remembering that much that seems either naive or paradoxical appears so on account of the artist's insufficient mastery of discursive reasoning, which results from inadequate philosophical training.

These general considerations impose themselves upon all to whom Scriabin opened the gates of his inner world. The parallelism between Scriabin's words and works, between his doctrine and his music, is clearly apparent. Anyone listening carefully to what he has to say in his music and in his ideological utterances must realize with utmost clarity that these are two facets of the same subject and that the supposition that one is a transcription of the other is absurd. When Scriabin wrote music, he never derived his ideas from imagined theories, whether philosophical or otherwise, or even from purely aesthetic musical considerations, for he never regarded his art as a means of expressing his thoughts, as a propaganda tool intended to charm the listeners by an appeal to their senses. His artistry was never the result of artificially contrived reasoning. On the other hand, his theories and his system of thought were never translations of his art into a language of concepts. Scriabin's thoughts did not follow his artistic creations like shadows, nor did they precede them as guiding beacons. It is difficult to determine the origin of his thought or to trace its translation into art; both must be regarded as spontaneous, primary, equally autonomous, and commonly dependent on the focal light, which he perceived intuitively. I do not propose to enter into an analysis and evaluation of his ideology and his art of words. The question is not whether he reasoned correctly from a certain standpoint or whether the poet in him was equal to the musician. To understand the nature of Scriabin's personality, which can be so easily misconstrued in all his multifarious activities—as a musician, poet, philosopher, and even as a prophet—we must realize that they all represent different aspects of the same essence. If, however, as it appears certain, the artist in Scriabin dominated the philosopher, and the musician guided the poet, the problem is not to decide which of these activities was of a primary or a secondary nature, but to emphasize that his creative powers had a certain qualitative individuality, that he had greater mastery over musical sounds than over verbal concepts or vivid writing. In him the auditory images were predominant. He was not able to create a structurally solid and self-consistent philosophical system. His text for *Le Poème de l'extase* has much less aesthetic validity than his music to this text, but his poetry has the same immediacy as his music. His treatment of this text is as indicative of his method as his later use of the poem for the *Acte préalable.*

Scriabin began to compose the music for *Le Poème de l'extase* in 1905; the text, originally titled "Poème orgiaque," was begun even earlier, the first sketches dating from 1904. When he started its composition he did not try to draw a precise and strict correspondence between the music and the text. The poetry did not annotate the music; conversely, the words were not translated into musical terms. In 1907, while in Lausanne, I was writing an article on *Le Poème de l'extase* for the *Russian Musical Gazette* in anticipation of its performance in St. Petersburg. When working with Scriabin, I tried to correlate the text with the music; I realized that the music in its free flow accurately followed the progress of the poem. I recall how gratified and even astounded Scriabin was when I pointed out this parallelism to him. But it was not an artificial or intentional parallelism; rather it was a natural result of the oneness of Scriabin's intuitive perception of the total image of the work, which appeared to him in its two aspects. Only when the score was completed and sent to the publishers did Scriabin mark down the principal motives of the work: Motive of Self-Assertion, Motive of Horror, Motive of Will, Ominous Rhythm, and so forth. It follows that there was no preliminary design in Scriabin's mind conditioned or determined by extramusical considerations.

Scriabin was a musician, and only a musician, when he wrote his symphonies and sonatas; he was a poet, and only a poet, when he wrote the text for *Le Poème de l'extase* and the *Acte préalable.* He was a religious thinker in his conversations, and in his diaries he expounded his doctrine of art in action. But the products of this musician, this poet, this thinker coincided in their essence, for they all stemmed from a common source.

Scriabin marked the main subject of *Le Poème divin* with the words *I Am* and designated it as the theme of Self-Assertion. This motto was printed in the program notes with his approval. As a result, the rumor spread that Scriabin composed music according to a formula, seeking combinations of sound that would express previously formulated ideas, thoughts, and theories. But chronology belies this supposition. Scriabin began working on *Le Poème divin* in the autumn of 1902. Several sections of the work were already completed in the spring of 1903, and the theme of the introduction was one of the earliest. Scriabin played it on the piano for me and asked, "Do you not feel that this theme has such power, majesty, and conviction that it may be called a declaration of self-assertion?" I replied, "Yes, it sounds as if it proclaims *I am!*" He was delighted with this phrase, and it remained attached to the main motive of the work.

In the Andante of *Le Poème divin,* there is a motive for the trombone marked *élan sublime.* Scriabin had a difficult time with this passage and left several blank measures to be filled out after completing most of the movement. He intended to connect the sections preceding and following the trombone motive with material of a sensuous and even erotic nature. He needed a contrast to interrupt this flowing and caressing current. Finally he found what he wanted: a fanfare-like call in the trombone, which satisfied him aesthetically and musically. He described this fanfare as the protest of the spirit against the sensuality that had invaded the music.

Only a few disconnected musical fragments of the *Acte préalable* were found among Scriabin's manuscripts after his death, but its text was completed, although its second part remained unedited. The evolution of this work was characteristic of Scriabin's creative habits. He appears here as thinker, poet, and musician, revealing the unity of his entire personality and its direct dependence on a primary source. The text of the *Acte* was completed in the late autumn of 1914, but the major part of musical sketches relate to a later period; some of them were written barely a few days before Scriabin died. He did not use the text of the *Acte préalable* as a libretto in the manner of Wagner but began to write music afresh, as if the text had never existed, following only a general outline inspired by the vision of his ideal of oneness. From this image, by dint of perseverance, step by step, Scriabin derived its formative elements—first the words, then the music. If death had not cut short his work, he might have added to the score visual images, perhaps gestures and motions. The text of the poem was preceded by an exposition of its ideological content. It was not, however, the philosophical concept, formulated in definite terms, that determined the progress of the *Acte préalable*. Scriabin did not recapitulate in this text the train of his thought; it was not a poetical rendition of some previously formulated ideology. Scriabin detested philosophical and didactic poetry and often asked, with some anxiety, "Does this seem too intellectualized?" And he said, "I am not expounding theories, I express ideas." Ideas were to him concrete events. If in the text of the *Acte préalable* there still remained traces of theorizing, he intended to edit the text so as to eliminate such intellectualization. Death put an end to his plans.

Scriabin's synthesis of the arts was based on the idea of an intimate intermingling of all artistic disciplines. He called this process "counterpoint," as opposed to Wagner's parallelism of music and drama. Scriabin's method was the result of his musical philosophy. He reduced the Wagnerian synthesis to a system of intricate multilayered constructions flowing from poetic expression. Such "counterpointing" of the arts in an intimate interpenetration represents a denial of the separateness of different arts and the assertion of their essential oneness in an all-embracing Omni-art. To Scriabin this Omni-art, or synthetic art, was not a vestige of the past. He did not evoke remote antiquity in his art, nor did he defer it to a distant future. It was to him a living presence, the content of his own psychological experience.

Scriabin possessed a special sense of color in musical sounds. In his desire to invest musical images with verbal ideas, he dreamed of symphonies of odors and tastes; he intended to introduce tactile sensations into the score of *Mysterium,* so as to transform the entire human body into a sounding instrument. In this respect Scriabin extended, systematized, and projected onto the outside world his own inner experience. Whatever one may think of the keyboard of colored lights in the score of *Prométhée* or of the aesthetic validity of color in music, it is certain that to Scriabin himself the music of *Prométhée* radiated light and scintillated colors. As he played its opening bars on the piano for me, he remarked that violet light should permeate the concert hall at this point, and it became clear that the "Prometheus chord" represented to his mind both a sound and a tone, a sound-color, not a sound accompanied by violet or any other light. But this grandiose conception, portending a synthesis of all the arts, can be understood only by taking into consideration the idiosyncratic traits of Scriabin's personality.

Scriabin first realized that universal art was a function of his own artistic personality during the composition of his Fifth Piano Sonata, which immediately followed *Le Poème de l'extase*. When he played this sonata for me in Lausanne in the winter of 1908, he remarked that the music existed outside him in images that could not be expressed verbally. He was not creating this music out of nothing, he declared, but rather he had removed a veil that obscured it, and thus made it visible. His task was to render this inner image into sounds, without distortion; he liked to call this image a "sounding body" possessing a color of its own. He observed it in his inner self and at the same time separate from him or, rather, above him. He sensed it with his entire self, not only through the medium of sense organs. In trying to describe this extraordinary state, he had, despite his skill in self-analysis, a great difficulty of expression. That is why he sometimes used different terms in referring to the same psychological state.

Motives and successions of chords were associated in Scriabin's consciousness with outside forces guiding his composition. When Scriabin worked on his thematic material, gradually building the sonorous edifice of the Fifth Piano Sonata, he sensed with different degrees of clarity the basic image that seemed to exist outside the framework of time. "I am but the translator," he once blurted out, speaking about his Fifth Piano Sonata. During the process of its composition he felt as though he were projecting a three-dimensional body on a flat surface, stretching and flattening in time and space a prophetic vision that he experienced as an instant revelation, simplifying and at the same time impoverishing it. The integral vision that he perceived with his entire being, in which all the human senses participated, he reduced to a system of sounds, thus utilizing only one sensory medium. He also said that in the apperception of this primary vision he did not feel that he was merely a passive recipient, but was at all times creatively active.

In the light of Scriabin's propensity for schematization and rationalization, we may conclude that he unconsciously emphasized a certain element of his inner experience in order to impart to it a more subtle and yet more definite form. But the difference here is only in details. In the process of work, Scriabin always progressed from the general to the particular, from oneness to individual moments. These moments did not exist autonomously beyond the general vision; Scriabin postulated them as parts of the whole. From this whole he deduced its constituent parts, and his creative process became therefore a revealing analysis of the object envisioned by him in an act of synthetic contemplation—an analysis which was followed by a synthesis of the whole. When Scriabin composed, his work never went in a single direction, from inception to conclusion. Rather, previously fixed elements served as the coordinates that defined the system of sound, through which he drew corresponding lines. His work progressed simultaneously in all directions, developing from different points of departure according to a plan worked out in the most minute details. This plan, which determined the general form of a musical composition and its structure, whether it be a sonata, a symphony, or a tone poem, was sketched by Scriabin in advance, when the thematic material was only beginning to shape itself. He followed this plan with unswerving logic, never deviating from it. Sometimes, carried away by his imagination, he was tempted to break away from the scheme, but upon reflection he invariably returned to it, even if he had to sacrifice some of his abundant materials. Indeed, when his creative strength failed him, Scriabin would interrupt his work and seek to regain the idealized image. He called it, in theosophic parlance, "to place oneself on the plane of oneness." I have already referred to this transference onto another plane in connection with *Le Poème divin*. It was not until three or four years later that Scriabin himself became aware of such transferences.

Scriabin was not alone among creative artists in this respect. No one could accuse Mozart of theorizing, needless self-consciousness, or excessive self-analysis. Describing the process of his creative work, Mozart declared, to quote Oulibyscheff: "My ideas are growing and I constantly broaden and clarify them; my work is almost ready in my mind, no matter how long it is, so that at a later time I can embrace it in my soul with a single glance, like a beautiful picture of a fine human being. I hear it in my imagination not in successive stages, but as it should appear in its entirety. What joy! The invention and development of an idea proceed as in a deep and beautiful dream."

Before undertaking the writing of a tragedy, Racine said, "Ma pièce est faite." Delacroix, as his biographers assert, "saw his picture before he painted it, visualizing its outline, color and lighting. All that externally reflects the main idea of the work appeared to him at once, so that the beginning of his work, as well as its completion, formed a harmonious whole."

Here we find an exact analogy with Scriabin's creative process of composition, which proceeded from an intuition of the entire work. The act of synthesis, harmonious unity, constitutes the first phase; the act of analysis, the separation of the idealized image intuitively observed, forms the second phase; and reconstruction, during which a new and integral image is created and harmony is transferred to another plane, is the third phase.

But here we are faced with a new problem: If to Scriabin the ultimate reality was Omni-art, of which music is only a component part, why did he cultivate exclusively instrumental music and never write a single work of synthetic art—an opera or a music drama, or at least a song in which music is blended with words? This question is tentatively answered by Viacheslav Karatygin in his book on Scriabin. He sees the reason for this aversion to declamation or vocalization in the voice being "an instrument . . . too concrete, too naturalistic and realistic." He further finds a contributing cause in Scriabin's idealistic individualism, because he feared the "intrusion into the sphere of idealism of an alien element reflecting nature and reality." But I would prefer a different and a more natural explanation of this paradoxical phenomenon.

Scriabin could not set a ready-made text to music, because he could not and would not subordinate the process of musical thought to an unrelated entity. Any adjustment to words was to him a violation of the essence of music; every time he heard an art song, he listened to it with mixed irony and disdain. Sometimes he was asked by people who did not know him well why he never wrote for voice. He usually evaded the question; it was unthinkable to him that his music could be united with words in a relationship in which the former would be subordinated to the latter. But if it was impossible for him to set words by someone else to music, why did he not himself, like Wagner, write both the poetry and the music? The reason for this self-denial (which he reconsidered only in the last years of his life, in the *Acte préalable*), I believe, was the inadequacy of his verbal self-expression. He became aware of this inadequacy by the failure of his only attempt to set words to music which was in the finale of his First Symphony.

It was characteristic of Scriabin that, although he

fully appreciated the validity and significance of his musical achievement, for which he never sought approbation, he always solicited the opinion of others about his literary ventures. Until he began work on the *Acte préalable* in 1914, he was extremely diffident about his ability to write. He used to say, "I have no misgivings about my music. Here I appear fully armed; I am a complete master of the art. But in literature I feel like an amateur. I have no formal mastery of literary expression such as I possess in music." When he played fragments from the *Acte préalable* for friends whose opinion he valued, he never sought their approval, but merely desired to share his experience with them. In composing a literary text, however, he desperately needed encouragement from professional poets and writers, such as Viacheslav Ivanov or Jurus Baltrushaitis.

Scriabin's ventures into poetry were many; the earliest of them date back to the years 1901–1902, in sketches for a contemplated opera. But its progress was uncertain; Scriabin constantly changed the libretto. Although he labored over it some two years, his lack of literary skill was the cause of its failure. Unlike his musical ideas, his verbal images were encumbered by artificial constructions and amounted to little more than imperfect poetic sketches. When in 1904 he tackled a literary form once more in the program for *Le Poème de l'extase,* he published it separately as a poetic commentary to a purely musical work. Although poetry and music were to him dual aspects of a single artistic creation, he knew that the aesthetic value of his poetry was greatly inferior to that of his music. His literary self-expression was of a cerebral type, for he was incapable of painting in words the vision that was so clearly revealed to him in music.

The perfection that marks every work of Scriabin is also characteristic of the entire evolution of his creative life. Here I do not need to indulge in generalities but can speak from personal knowledge of his artistic personality. When Scriabin wrote his Fifth Piano Sonata and *Prométhée* (subtitled *Le Poème du feu*), he transcended the dimension of time. His entire oeuvre, from the early sonatas to the last, from *Le Poème divin* to *Prométhée,* can be construed as a single work of grandiose dimensions, of which his sonatas, tone poems, symphonies, and preludes were but transitory phenomena. This is not merely a figure of speech or a picturesque metaphor, but a statement of fact clearly evident to anyone who has closely followed the path of Scriabin's creative individuality and watched the progress of his work. One may say that the totality of Scriabin's oeuvre is the sum of individual attempts to realize in concrete form something that had never before been rendered in the categories of time and space. Each of his major works was to him a definitive and conclusive act. Each successive work was to him an act of perfection; each was unexcelled. But as soon as a sonata or a symphony was finished, he immediately noticed its inadequacies. He then embarked on a new work in which he hoped to achieve a closer approximation of his ideal, an ultimate consummation. His whole life was spent in an attempt to create a unique work that would make all additional creative efforts superfluous. But while striving to achieve this dream, he gave us a series of beautiful compositions. Yet no matter how high their quality, to him they signalized a failure by their very number. He believed that he had reached perfection in *Le Poème de L'extase* and that the living dream of his life had finally found its realization. But once the work was completed, he saw in it but a shadow of an ideal image.

Scriabin always loved with a special tenderness each piece he was working on at a particular moment and to which he gave all his energies. At the same time he would experience disillusionment with the immediately preceding work. Scriabin, who had a reputation, even among his friends, for being in love with himself and his music, who treated other composers with condescension and thinly veiled contempt, in reality was beset by doubts about the validity of his own works as soon as they were completed. He acutely felt the inadequacy of his music in contrast with the lofty vision that he had tried to realize in the world here on earth. He seemed to possess unbounded faith in himself as one divinely anointed; he was seemingly enamored of himself, but actually he worshiped his ultimate vision. He strove to achieve the perfection of what he longed to express, and what he had already accomplished never gave him the needed satisfaction. Each work served only as a stepping-stone to a new creative effort.

Scriabin took pleasure in playing his works and analyzed their positive and negative features, sometimes criticizing his music with complete candor. But when he dwelled too long on his own past, his spirit seemed to fade. "This is not what I want," he would say. But the moment a conversation touched upon his future plans and hopes, he would blossom forth, forget his past disappointments, and become completely absorbed in it, anticipating the joys to come. He often remarked, "I live only by the hopes of the future."

During Scriabin's last years of life this longing for things to come reached a particularly acute stage. Disheartened by the seeming failure of his endeavor to express the inexpressible by musical means alone, he became impatient. He hurried in his work as if he were constantly pursued, as if he had a premonition that he had little time to live. "No more words, I must get to work, I must proceed faster, I have lost too much time already," he would say.

It is understandable that, with such an attitude toward his own work, he was critical of compositions by others. His notorious lack of interest in their music was regarded as a symptom of egotism and overweening pride. The truth is that he lost all capacity for enjoying a work of art as such, irrespective of its authorship. He was equally incapable of studying doctrines that were out of harmony with his own aspirations, even when he was willing to admit their theoretical value. A work of art demands a pure, objective judgment that Scriabin could never render, particularly in the last five or six years of his life. Often he was simply bored by music, although out of politeness he concealed this boredom. Among his own works he especially liked the Lento and Andante of his First Symphony and the first movement and Andante of his Second Symphony, for in them he seemed to foresee the later works in which he expressed similar moods with greater perfection. They brought before him the hope of ultimate consummation.

Scriabin had definite musical antipathies. Among them was even Beethoven. (It is known that Chopin, too, had little appreciation of Beethoven.) Scriabin recognized Beethoven's tremendous historical significance, of course, but he felt no artistic affinity with him. His attitude toward Tchaikovsky's music was almost pathological. He suffered agonies when he had to listen to Tchaikovsky's piano pieces. The only composer who was capable of moving Scriabin deeply, and even causing him to forget his own musical problems, was Wagner. His admiration for Wagner can be explained by the philosophical grandeur of Wagner's music dramas. And yet Scriabin was not familiar with the entire *Ring* cycle. He heard *Siegfried* for the first time in Moscow in 1902; he attended a performance of *Götterdämmerung* years later; he never went to a complete stage production of *Das Rheingold;* he never heard *Tristan und Isolde* or *Parsifal*. He never read any of Wagner's major theoretical publications or the writings of Wagnerian exponents Houston Stewart Chamberlain or Henri Lichtenberger. He gained information about Wagner's personality chiefly from popular magazine articles. And yet he succeeded amazingly well in penetrating the essence of Wagner's musical philosophy.

Scriabin's attitude toward other arts was equally personal. He took great interest in literature, painting, and architecture, but only insofar as they related to his own preoccupations. He ignored subjects that were not immediately useful for his work. The only exception was poetry, particularly works that gave him an intimate aesthetic satisfaction, such as Konstantin Balmont's and Viacheslav Ivanov's. As for the so-called belles lettres, I never saw Scriabin read a novel, a short story, or any other book. Occasionally he would look at a volume of Chekhov or a magazine article, but even that not very often. For his intellectual nourishment, he preferred a living exchange of ideas. Although he was fond of painting he let years pass without attending an art show. Contemporary paintings, with their emphasis on purely pictorial representation without any spiritual overtones, left him indifferent.

Scriabin's philosophy of art is reflected in his definition of his own works as stages on the road to the ultimate consummation of his dreams, visions, and theories; each composition was to him but a closer approximation of this final goal by increasingly bold efforts toward its attainment. He conceived all art as being in a state of flux; in his estimation no single work of art could be regarded as self-sufficient. He made no exception for his own compositions, which were to him only links of a chain, moments of a continuous progress in time. True, he reserved a special niche for himself, but only because he felt that he was destined to complete the cycle of evolution and connect the links of the chain. Hence his rejection of purely aesthetic pleasures that derived from the appreciation of a certain work of art and its enjoyment per se—such artistic gourmandism was to him a symptom of spiritual poverty and psychological decadence. A work of art, he never tired of repeating, must carry the observer beyond its own appointed limitations; it must stimulate action and creative effort and animate further developments. To Scriabin, art was a means of transforming phenomenological reality, of liberating it and making it transcend its limits; it was also the reflection of the revolutionary essence of his own being.

Indeed, Scriabin was a revolutionary in his innermost self. He was not satisfied with the creation of new artistic forms within the premises and limitations of the material world; he was not satisfied with transcending these limitations even at a greatly accelerated pace within a given period of time. His objective was an instantaneous, catastrophic abolition of reality and a spiritual translation to a higher plane of consciousness. Scriabin believed in the disparate nature of the historical process, a view typical of his revolutionary state of mind; he sensed gaping chasms in the fabric of reality that had to be spanned by leaps and bounds. He harbored apocalyptic expectations of a new earth, a new heaven, awaiting the palpitating fulfillment of the promise of that angel who vowed to the "eternally living" that "time will cease to be."

Hegel said that quantity, growing indefinitely, transcends into quality. Scriabin frequently quoted this dictum during our discussions on philosophical subjects to vindicate his theory of "catastrophism." It was for him not only a theoretical postulate, but a manifestation of inner experience. He felt in his own being how this tremendous tension continued to increase until it suddenly brought forth a new state qualitatively different from the preceding. Projecting his inner experience outwardly, he speculated that the entire history of the world also obeyed this evolutionary process of gradual accumulation and growth, that, upon reaching a degree of saturation, must terminate in a world catastrophe, leading in turn to a new evolution, a new increase in tension, and a new crisis. Scriabin associated this philosophy of life with the specific structure of his major works, which to him represented a series of gradual expansions systematically and logically evolving in the direction of a final ecstasy. Indeed, all Scriabin's works, beginning with the Third Piano Sonata and ending with the Tenth Piano Sonata, are built according to a uniform succession of states—languor, longing, impetuous striving, dance, ecstasy, and transfiguration. This outline is basically simple; it is built on a series of upswings, with each successive wave rising higher and higher toward a final effort, liberation, and ecstasy.

To whom was Scriabin closer, Apollo or Dionysus? By definition, all art must be Apollonian, for it requires regulation, rhythm, measure, and self-limitation, leading to a spiritual transfiguration. In this sense, Scriabin was a votary of Apollo Musagetes, the leader of the muses. Indeed, Scriabin was one of the most devout Apollonian builders of the temple of sounds; yet music is a Dionysian art. He possessed an extraordinary capacity for the formulation of his spiritual experience and a willingness to limit himself, to perform a psychological sacrifice, which is the *conditio sine qua non* of artistic creativity. He knew how to confine himself within fixed limits, to sweep away without pity all that was superfluous, even if artistically valid, for the sake of the symmetry and lucidity of sonorous edifices. Particularly significant in this respect are his last major works, whose fiery nature is contained within the boundaries of a rigid formal structure. In this respect his works are classical in the Hegelian sense of the word; the two elements that are analytically discernible in every work of art—form and content—maintain in Scriabin's music an almost perfect equilibrium, with formal configurations comprising the totality of the content, and with content in turn totally absorbed by form. Hence the extraordinary autonomy of his works, which, like all masterpieces, lead their own independent lives and even counterpose themselves to him, their creator, as separate phenomena. It is thanks to this perfection of form that Scriabin's works possess a transpersonal, superindividual quality.

If we abandon for a moment the discussion of Scriabin's works as a perfect product of his artistry and address ourselves to the reality of his individual self, we shall arrive at different conclusions regarding Scriabin's classical views on art. The most typical representative of such a classical view is, it seems to me, Flaubert. For him a work of art, as revealed in his correspondence, possesses an absolute value and significance per se. The objective of an artist, according to Flaubert, is not the pure joy of invention, but the completion of a perfect work, which by its very existence vindicates and justifies the artist's effort. The creator himself is only the worker, the master, and the builder. He is inferior to his own creations. Life is only raw material for art. Scriabin's attitude toward these attributes of the creator was quite different from Flaubert's; it was anticlassical, romantic. Fully absorbed in the turbulent element of life, he strove not merely to create beauty, but to sense the living process of creation. He saw his goal not in the achievement of aesthetically valid products, but in the attainment of an intensified mode of existence. He wanted *to be*. He yearned for a realistic transfiguration, not merely its shadowy simulacrum. Scriabin valued life above art; in art, he saw the means of enrichment, of enhancement, of subtilization of life, culminating in the acquisition of mystical power. To him it was the man himself, the artist, who occupied the center, not the crystallized products of his creation. He once told me that the crisis that Gogol suffered in the last years of his life, which led him to destroy the second part of his novel *Dead Souls,* is of greater import, not only for Gogol himself but for all humanity, than the fate of the novel itself. Gogol was bound to sacrifice his creation for the sake of enhancing and intensifying his spiritual life. Scriabin interpreted along similar lines the lives of Dante, Leonardo da Vinci (whom he prized greatly), Byron, and Goethe. They attracted him as human beings first and as creators of artistic values second. They were closer to him than their greatest creations. This attitude explains his negation of absolute aesthetic values and eternal masterpieces, or rather masterpieces existing beyond time. Works of art, even the greatest among them, are creations of time and, as such, subject to corruption. Their lifetime may be reckoned by centuries, but in the end they are bound to grow old and die; they are not above life, not beyond life, but within the stream of life. This viewpoint is, of course, diametrically opposed to the classical theory of art. For Flaubert, for instance, the true work of art is beyond the dimension of time. Human tastes change; a work of genius may be temporarily forgotten, but such oblivion does not affect its intrinsic value, which is never diminished.

Scriabin erected truly classical edifices of sound fashioned in a perfectly finished form, consistent within themselves, and independent in the classical sense. Yet he regarded these edifices as transitory monuments, not as objects possessing an autonomous existence. "Art is only an intoxicating drink, a miraculous wine," he once re-marked. This intentionally paradoxical statement epito-mizes his view of artistic values. He enters the temple of Apollo only to carry out in reality the images that he be-held there. He summarized his philosophy in this motto: "From our present life to another life through art."

While composing, Scriabin never regarded a given work as a means to an end, but as a creative reality. He was his own severest critic, a conscientious technician of art, a master builder, a formalist, even a pedant. This dual-ity of creative philosophy was typical of Scriabin; it per-meated his entire being and assumed many different forms. Although Scriabin was a mystic who rejected rationalism, in his mode of thinking he maintained a logical sequence, always seeking justification for his spiritual experience. This free and rebellious spirit was willing to observe con-ventional social customs and mundane fashions in his manner of dress, his conversation, and his general behavior; he even flaunted his conventional pose as a challenge. Similarly, in his artistic expression, Scriabin the romantic composer rigorously followed the conventions of formal classicism.

Scriabin realized very early in life that his art was completely integrated with his philosophy; he always knew what he wanted and visualized his objective with utmost clarity. This awareness, this careful planning was to him fundamental; he had little regard for men of genius who were not conscious of their intentions in art, who created masterpieces by intuition alone. It is for this reason that his appreciation of Haydn, Mozart, or Raphael, who were natural geniuses, was qualified, while he greatly admired Leonardo da Vinci and Wagner as conscious originators of new forms of art. But when he read in Julius Kapp's biography of Wagner that external events sometimes influenced his philosophy of art, he was disillusioned. "I always thought that Wagner knew exactly what he wanted to accomplish," he commented ruefully.

This consciousness of his ideal combined with something that may be called a demonic possession. There were moments when his mind seemed to wander, and yet at these very moments new visions appeared most clearly before his eyes. I watched him in such states of creative ecstasy. He seemed intoxicated by the potent wine poured into his soul from beyond; he seemed to be possessed by a mysterious force. At such moments the real Alexander Nikolayevich Scriabin, whom we knew so well from daily contact, seemed to dissolve in the rays of the one who rose in him and took possession of his spirit. One felt strangely affected and disturbed by his transfigured visage and at the same time irresistibly attracted by it. All categories seemed to merge in him, and the structure of his personality itself seemed to vanish. Such was Scriabin's state during the composition of *Le Poème divin,* the Fifth Piano Sonata, *Prométhée,* and the *Acte préalable.* We saw this transfigured Scriabin when he played his works at home for a close circle of friends.

"The Spirit came down upon us," Russian religious sectarians used to say to describe the peculiar state of mind of worshipers who became conscious of being possessed. I recall this state of possession at the last concert Scriabin played in Petrograd in 1915, two weeks before he died. An inexpressible otherworldly look flashed in his eyes as he played his Third Piano Sonata, among other works. When I accompanied him home after the concert, late at night, I told him about my impression. He said that indeed he felt completely oblivious of playing before an audience; he was not even fully aware of what he was playing, not even conscious of being the performer. "I rarely experience such a feeling on the concert stage," he added. His self-possession on the podium was usually total; he could even follow his own interpretation as if supervising himself from outside, so as to prevent himself from being carried away.

During our last meetings, in the winter of 1914–1915, Scriabin often played for me sections from his unfinished *Acte préalable,* revealing his visions of the future. Sometimes I felt that he was then already removed from earthly life, that his eternal self had already passed over to another plane. And I instinctively wondered what retained him here on earth. How could he continue to dwell on our plane of existence if he had apparently severed all connection with it? But his psychic structure was such that immediately after, when he still seemed to be irradiated by the sunrays of a world different from ours, he could return and proceed to analyze, to justify, to formulate, and to describe his prophetic visions for us.

Even at moments of the highest spiritual transports, Scriabin never resorted to musical improvisation, never attempted to pour out his feelings by improvising at the keyboard. He would either plunge into work on a new composition or play over some of his old pieces. During the course of our long friendship, I heard him improvise only once or twice. If, yielding to requests, he sat down at the piano to play, he might try out a few improvised chords or passages but then would start playing one of his published compositions. And it was only for intimate friends that he ever volunteered to play fragments of works not yet completed.

This reluctance to improvise is explained not only by Scriabin's insistence on chiseled and strictly organized forms, but also by his peculiar idealism; all realistic portrayal of human sentiments in art, even in a most subtle way, was unacceptable to him. He steered away not only from realistic art, but from any psychological allusion in music. Art to him was synonymous with spiritual transfiguration. His idealism referred not to the content of an artistic work, but to the manner of its realization. That is why he felt compelled to reject Mussorgsky's realistic art, despite the evident sincerity and immediacy of Mussorgsky's musical images, the qualities most admired in the creator of *Boris Godunov.* To Scriabin the word *artlessness* always had a pejorative ring, because he was convinced that art must perforce be artful in order to overcome and overwhelm the realism of life.

One of the most remarkable traits of Scriabin's artistic personality was his sense of absolute freedom in creative work. I was always impressed by this autonomous quality of his labors, his total unconcern for external events, conditions, or influences. I do not recall any other artist who has ever attained such freedom and autonomy in his work. The nucleus of Scriabin's individuality was encased, as it were, in a strong suit of armor, impenetrable to any sound from outside. He led his life, he created, he experienced desires behind this protective shield in complete tranquility and solitude. This isolation is not to be confused with indifference or a lack of humanity. Scriabin reacted with lively interest to external events, and he showed sincere and intimate concern for others. He formed warm friendships easily, but he could as easily terminate them; and he could freely yield to influences. But in all these relationships only one side of his individuality seemed to be in action; his innermost self remained free. This inner self was protected against invasion. There were periods of extreme difficulty in Scriabin's personal life, both materially and morally, but it is quite impossible to find any reflection of these experiences in his musical compositions, with the exception, perhaps, of the funeral march in the First Piano Sonata, which Scriabin wrote during a time of great turmoil caused by a seemingly incurable hand ailment.

Scriabin wrote *Le Poème de l'extase* in the most trying financial circumstances; at times he did not even have enough money to buy postage stamps for his correspondence. The death of his daughter by his first marriage, who was his favorite child, nearly crushed him; he cried all day long, but he never interrupted his work. His luminous Fourth Piano Sonata was written at the time of a great crisis, when he was faced with a crucial decision that was to change his entire life.

When the war broke out in 1914, Scriabin was at work on the text of the *Acte préalable*. He was greatly disturbed by the war, although he failed to realize its critical significance in world history. I recall with what impatience he awaited the daily newspapers, for which we had to walk to the station some six kilometers away. But after he had read the dispatches and we exchanged views, he would go to the balcony upstairs to continue his work, often under a scorching sun, forgetting all else until the next morning, when once more he set aside an hour or two to discuss the war, as if he were studying a lesson or performing a necessary daily task. I repeat, this ability to abstract himself from the world of reality was not a symptom of indifference. He took an interest in everything that was going on in life; he tried to embrace all branches of human knowledge. Only when he felt that the outside world would somehow encroach on his inner life did he seek seclusion. So vast, so profound, so rich was his inner world, so powerful were the forces bursting into realization, that nothing could obscure even temporarily the vision that loomed so vividly before him.

One of the most characteristic qualities of Scriabin's personality was his confidence in people, his readiness to disclose his plans and aspirations and even to confide in them the working processes of his life. He was always ready to lavish his inner riches on others, as if suffocating from an overabundance of ideas; he experienced a real joy in sharing his treasures. But although many were called, few were chosen. It was not the result of fastidiousness; it sufficed for someone to show interest in religion, philosophy, or art to make Scriabin reveal his most intimate hopes and intentions. He often regretted his eagerness and vowed to be more circumspect in his relationships, but he seldom succeeded in carrying out this resolution. His desire to communicate his inner experiences, to share the vital nourishment he received from his spiritual resources, was too strong to be contained.

Personally, Scriabin was not an optimist. He always viewed life in a somewhat somber light; he was ever suspicious of others. He expected everyone to share his longings, the aspirations and visions that sustained his own spirit, and he imagined that all he had to do was to stimulate these ideals in others in order to make them join his cause. He believed that he spoke the language of all mankind. He was overjoyed when he glimpsed a spark of sympathy in others. But he was bitterly disillusioned when his friendship was not fully reciprocated. He was oversensitive; he was easily disheartened by a lack of understanding. He was not intolerant and was quite willing to engage in discussion with his most determined critics, but the moment he encountered a callous indifference, he would retreat into himself for a very long time.

3

THE MYSTIC

In the preceding chapters I have attempted to recreate the image of Scriabin the thinker and the artist mainly from my own remembrance of him. I followed the path from the periphery to the center, until it brought me to the inner core of Scriabin's personality, to his most intimate essence, to that deeply hidden subsoil that nurtured his philosophy and artistry. Here, in its primordial state, is found the source of his creative self. In the darkness of this subsoil were submerged the closely intertwining roots of his philosophy and his art. Everything he believed in, everything that he aspired to, everything that he created, was determined by his intuitive experience. Scriabin was a mystic, and the mystic in him governed his philosophy and his artistic convictions. The uniqueness of his philosophical and artistic individuality is reduced in the last analysis to the uniqueness of his mystical experience. Therefore, in order to understand Scriabin, one must descend into these depths and try to dispel the darkness that reigned there. This can be accomplished only by another artist intuitively capable of embracing Scriabin's individuality in its vital oneness. An analytic method of approach would fail here completely, for it is impossible to express in rational terms an entity that is irrational by nature. We have no other pathway to Scriabin; we must either abandon all attempt to penetrate his personality and thus confine ourselves only to art, or discuss the mysteries of his innermost individuality in terms of logical concepts, attempting to gain access to the inaccessible and rationalize the irrational.

In order to comprehend Scriabin as a mystic, we must first define this term that has been used in many different ways. We must distinguish mystique from mysticism. The former designates the totality of mystical experience; the latter represents the body of more or less systematically assembled doctrines and disciplines in which mystique finds expression. The former relates to intuitive apperception, the latter to the system of ideas and concepts in which the personal mystique finds congenial expression. Mysticism is unthinkable without a mystique, for there can be no mystical doctrine without the personal experience that enters a mystique. Conversely, such a mystique cannot be entirely free of mysticism. Every mystical experience finds expression in a more or less organized system embodied by a mystical doctrine that is the flower and the fruit of the mystique, even if it is not fully blossomed or ripe.

Strictly speaking, every time a mystic tries to recount his experience, he partakes of mysticism. The mystical experience of Plotinus cannot be doubted; for the

mystical system he created is a grandiose projection of this
mystical experience. St. Francis of Assisi and St. Seraphim
of Sarov never constructed original, self-contained mystical disciplines, but communicated their mystical experiences in religious terms sanctioned by the Church. But
they often injected their personal experience, which became a part of their theoretical mystical doctrine. Mysticism is a specific discipline that interprets the world in
specific terms, a transcription in images and concepts of a
personal mystical experience.

Mystical experience can be analyzed from two
standpoints: from the object itself and from the relationship entered by an observer. A mystic experiences something that is ordinarily inaccessible to consciousness, and
he experiences that something in a totally different way,
outside of ordinary modes of perception. What is the object of mystical contemplation? Obviously it cannot be
something that possesses a qualitative peculiarity; it cannot
be a known *this* as differentiated from a known *that*, but
rather an entity in which *this* and *that* are merged and
unified. The object of mystical experience is a totality, a
single, indefinite, unqualified entity. This lack of qualitative
definition and this vagueness are not the results of spiritual
poverty and emptiness, but on the contrary derive from
the overabundance and plenitude of existence. Being *all* in
its oneness, this entity is not a mere abstraction for the
mystic, as it is to an ordinary consciousness, but represents
a complete, living reality, in which the mystic distinguishes
individual components. But how is this reality revealed to
him? He experiences it not as something alien or external,
not by discursive reasoning or analytic dissection, but in-

tuitively by direct cognition, embracing it in its totality. In this experience there is no relationship between subject and object, no orientation toward a transcendental object, for this object is immanent in the consciousness of the mystic. A mystic perceives this object in himself, and it reveals itself to him as his own essence, or as some infinitely powerful force with which he is totally identified. He dwells in it; it embraces and permeates him. Thus in mystical experience an individual observes the immanence of the Infinite; hence the self-identification of a mystic in his ultimate depth with the Absolute, his self-assertion through it, or else, on the contrary, the recognition of his utter inferiority face-to-face with It. Naturally there are numerous gradations, nuances, and forms, sometimes contradicting each other and ranging from daring theomachy to humble recognition of the utter sinfulness in any claim for separateness or selfness.

Forms of mystical experience are many and multifarious, and mystical doctrines are numerous, but no matter how a mystic experiences his sensations and yearnings, their foundation remains a unique and direct perception of the Infinite.

Since Scriabin expressed his mystical experience in images and concepts, we must analyze not only his individual mystique, but also his mystical code. We must answer two basic questions: What was Scriabin's mystical experience?

What was the nature of his mystical doctrine? We must first examine Scriabin's personal experience, for his mysticism informed his creative work and crystallized his action which must be examined from a psychological standpoint in order to view its vital flow.

Mystical experiences are polymorphous and often elusive in their manifestations, but it is possible to organize them in certain categories, to classify them according to certain traits, always bearing in mind that such classification is purely schematic and serves merely an auxiliary function. Its foundation is the object of mystical experience itself, the *what* of the mystique, that infinitude intuitively perceived by the mystic, in which he participates as a communicant. It is perceived by some mystics as a presence closed in upon itself, consummated, and dwelling in a state of absolute perfection. It is immobile, bottomless, and without boundaries, an ocean that absorbs all differences, so that any change, any motion, becomes an illusion, a deception, and a transgression. The only realities are It, Nothing, and All. Other mystics see Omnipresence as a burning fire; to them the Unique is not repose, but movement, impetus, and ever-renewed creation. They behold not a perfect and immobile Verity, but the stream of Life Eternal, in which they are immersed and with which they merge.

Undoubtedly this scheme is rudimentary and crude; pure types are extremely rare. Still, it is possible to include in the first category the mysticism of the Hindus and perhaps the doctrine of Meister Eckhart, and in the second the doctrine of Heraclitus in all its transformations, and, to a certain degree, that of Plotinus and Jakob Böhme. If we draw our categories according to the relationship between the mystic and the Unique, it is possible to posit two types of mystical experience, passive and active, feminine and masculine. Meister Eckhart is an outstanding representative of the first category, insofar as we can judge by his orations and sermons. His ecstatic transports were marked by the utmost passivity; in these states his own individuality and his will were extinguished, and his soul, now free to receive the revelation, was completely permeated by the Deity—hence, Eckhart's doctrine of self-abnegation as the supreme virtue. The mystique of Eckhart's disciple Suso was of a similar nature, but it was compounded by love, specifically love for a woman. Closely resembling Suso's mystique is that of St. Angela of Foligno. On the other hand, the mystique of Jakob Böhme is active and virile, a mystique of willpower. It is encountered much more rarely than the passive type, which represents the median form of mystical experience. In the mystique of Mme. Guyon this passivity reaches an extreme state imperiling the very existence of the individual.

It is possible to construe another criterion for the classification of mystical experiences that is determined by the individuality of the mystic himself and not by his particular image of the Unique. In this classification, too, we find the familiar alternation of active and passive types. There are contemplative mystics and there are active mystics. Strictly speaking, contemplation is the basis of all mystical experience, which manifests only through contemplation. Some mystics dwell in complete inactivity during the sometimes protracted periods between moments of ecstatic revelation, awaiting new ecstasies and longing for them; others are in a state of constant activity. The character of their visions is such that they experience an imperative need to act in order to make their visions come true, either by their own effort or by appeal to a higher, divine authority, thus becoming obedient servants of the Deity. In the experience of most mystics, periods of contemplation and inaction alternate with periods of heightened activity. Such was the case with St. Francis of Assisi, St. Seraphim of Sarov, St. Sergius of Radonezh, and particularly St. Teresa of Avila. The last period of her life was marked by energetic, practical activities that she perceived as divine action realized through her.

Scriabin's mystical experience can be reduced to the second of these two basic types of mysticism. He experienced the Infinite as a dynamic existence, a living flame; he actively strove to reach the elevated mystical plane by willing it. His mystique was of a masculine and volitional, rather than a feminine or receptive, character; it was marked by a strongly pronounced pragmatism that rendered his contemplations dynamic, their power being derived from his visions. His mystical experience urged him to action. Reality was to him an act in which he was a participant. If the mystique of Suso is that of love, and the mystiques of St. Francis, St. Teresa, and St. Angela those of love permeated with suffering, then the mystique of Scriabin was that of creative action.

÷

In his childhood and early youth, Scriabin was very religious. He underwent a crisis of religious consciousness
when he was in the twentieth year of his life. It passed, as
Scriabin himself told me, without complications; in this
lack of a sense of crisis he was probably helped by his
feeling of pride and self-assurance. In one of Scriabin's
notebooks, dated about 1906, there are to be found some
remarkable autobiographical revelations. Here is a frag-
ment:

> Early childhood: Love of fairy tales, vivid imagination,
> religious moods. Entry into the military school at the
> age of ten. Unbounded faith in teachers and in the
> priest. Naive belief in the Old Testament. Prayers . . .
> A very serious participation in the mystery of the Eu-
> charist . . . At sixteen, a remarkable absence of self-
> analysis . . . At twenty, an ominous hand ailment, a
> most decisive event of my life. Fate puts an obstacle,
> incurable according to the doctors, to the attainment
> of an ardently desired goal—brilliance, fame. The first
> serious failure in life. The first earnest attempt at phi-
> losophy; the beginning of self-analysis. Reluctance to
> admit that my ailment is incurable, and yet an obses-
> sion with somber moods. First reflections on the value
> of life, religion, God. Continued strong faith—in God
> the Father rather than Christ. Ardent, long prayers,
> constant church attendance . . . Reproaches addressed
> to fate and to God. Composition of the First Piano
> Sonata with a funeral march.

These random observations are typical of Scriabin's
early doubts. He jotted them down for himself only, never
imagining that anyone else would read them. He was al-

ways secretive about his notebooks; he did not show them even to his closest friends and kept them under lock and key in his desk drawer. When by accident or through absentmindedness he forgot to put away any of them, he betrayed apprehension, fearing that someone might read them. These notes are therefore undoubtedly sincere and truthful. Scriabin's casual reference to his strong faith in God the Father, rather than Christ, appears all the more revealing in regard to his mystical life, which was totally absorbed by the creative aspect of the Deity. It was God the Father, the omnipotent creator of heaven and earth, to whom he pledged his allegiance, to whom he felt closest. He adhered to the teachings of the Russian Orthodox Church, but he worshiped the first person of the Trinity, the Creator, rather than the Redeemer. Even when he became interested in theosophy and accepted the doctrine of Logos, God the Son remained alien to his soul. Theoretically he accepted Christ, but he lived by the Lord of Hosts. This rejection is all the more strange because Christian mysticism surrounds mainly God the Son, with the mystery of redemption placed in the center. At the foundation of the experience of all mystics, whether in the West or in the East, lies a consciousness of one's sinfulness, a sense of guilt that oppresses the soul. This sense of guilt, however, was completely alien to Scriabin. The problem of Redemption occupied him little; consequently, he never experienced a need for Christ, whom he accepted only in his creative aspect as the Word, the Logos that was in the Beginning. It was only much later, two years before his death, that Scriabin began to feel nearer to the Redeemer and accept the notion of the guilt of individual existence.

Testimony to this change is found in the text of the *Acte préalable,* where Scriabin for the first time addressed himself to the problem of morality. Scriabin's philosophy of life before his religious crisis, which came upon him unexpectedly in his twenty-first year, was determined by his consciousness of having a vital link with the Creator, of a personal participation in the divine creative act and immersion in world action, in the contemplation of the world in its motive and creative aspects. The intensification of this religious crisis was in all probability caused by his first acquaintance with philosophy, which destroyed the youthful wholesomeness of his beliefs. It was not philosophical speculation alone, however, that determined the direction and character of his spiritual life but the increasing awareness of his own creative power, of his seemingly unbounded strength, accompanied by a growing clarity of judgment. The crisis passed rapidly, without complications, culminating in a theomachy of self-assertion. Some vestiges of this struggle are found in the fragments of his unfinished opera libretto. Here are some excerpts:

I.   Beatitude. Ideal, Truth. The goal outside me. Faith in God, which fills me with longing for high ideals and a hope of their attainment through divine power.

II.   Disillusion in the possibility of this attainment; reproaches to God.

III.   Search for the ideal in my own self. Protest. Freedom.

IV.   Scientific justification of freedom.

V.   Religion.

These notes represent a scheme by which Scriabin hoped to retrace the path of his development. The following passage on a separate piece of paper is of a more personal nature; it apparently refers to the period immediately following his religious crisis, about 1894, when Scriabin was composing the *Etudes* op. 8:

> Whoever it was who mocked me, who cast me into a dark dungeon, who raised me aloft only to hurl me down, who gave me gifts only to take them back, who lavished caresses on me only to torment me, I forgive you, I do not reproach you. I am still alive, I still love life, and I love humanity. . . . I will go forth to announce to everyone my victory over you and over myself. I will go forth to warn them not to place their hopes in you, not to expect anything from life, except what they can create for themselves. I thank you for all the trials and tribulations to which you subjected me, for you gave me the knowledge of my endless power, my unbounded strength, my invincibility. You endowed me with creative power. I will go forth to carry to all humanity the message of strength and power, tell them that they should not despair, that nothing is lost.

The elevated rhetorical style of this declaration does not necessarily impugn Scriabin's sincerity, for he wrote it exclusively for himself, and a certain flamboyance was characteristic of his natural writing style. Such a state of rebellion could not, however, continue, for negative attitudes were inherently repugnant to Scriabin. He asserted himself through himself, rather than by opposing himself to others. His path was from the God outside and above him to the

God within. But such a transposition, in transferring the center into himself, could lead only (in view of Scriabin's consciousness of his own powers and his enormous inner tension) to self-deification. Theomachy was the prelude to Scriabin's attribution of creative force, the symbol of which was God, to himself. The crisis was over; Scriabin remained alone, but he never again relied on an extraneous power, never deified this power. He asserted himself as the source of power. These Byronic moods found their reflection in the libretto he sketched for the opera that he never completed. In his music this mood of rebellion, this challenge to higher powers, manifested itself later in the *Poème* op. 32, no. 2, which Scriabin himself described as Byronic and the *Poème tragique* op. 34.

When I first met Scriabin, he produced in me the impression of an extremely egocentric person; his own self seemed to possess for him an absolute validity. Nothing existed outside his individual will, which governed everything according to its own laws. Scriabin seemed a typical product of Nietzscheanism. Only when I came to know him better did I realize that his egocentrism concealed something quite different from Nietzsche's precepts. In the depth of his soul Scriabin did not project himself to another plane of existence; to him there was no other plane. Examination of his writings shows that his individualistic, Nietzschean moods neither lasted long nor made deep inroads into his consciousness. Solipsistic individualism was to him only the means to an end, not the goal in itself.

My characterization of Scriabin's state of mind radically contradicts the widely accepted notion of Scriabin as an extreme individualist, an opinion that is systematically fostered by Scriabin's critic Viacheslav Karatygin. He finds departures from individualism only in the last works. Leonid Sabaneyev, Scriabin's biographer, voices a similar opinion. In the light of my many discussions with Scriabin, I must categorically reject this view. Scriabin's philosophy of life was much more complex and original.

Scriabin wrote in one of his notebooks:

> Individuality exists only in relation to other individualities; it represents a coloration, an epiphany of the Spirit in the framework of time and space. The will to live is one and the same in all humanity; variations represent but a passing phenomenon. . . . Longing creates the instrument of its own fulfillment. The highest synthesis is revealed in man and human society; its goal is the preservation of life and the furtherance of individual progress. But there is a higher synthesis that is of a divine nature, and which at the supreme moment of existence is bound to engulf the entire universe and impart to it a harmonious flowering, that is, ecstasy, returning it to the primordial state of repose that is nonbeing. Such a synthesis can be consummated only by human consciousness, elevated to a superior consciousness of the world, freeing the spirit from the chains of the past and carrying all living souls away in its divine creative flight. This will be the last ecstasy, but it is already close at hand.

There were moments in Scriabin's life when he wanted to take possession of the world as something foreign, something that had to be conquered. In his mystical experiences he beheld the cosmos as an attribute of himself, and he envisioned himself in the center of the flame that symbolized the universe. This was not a profession of solipsism; for solipsism entails languishment, vacuity, and deficiency, rooted in an egotistic proclamation of self-sufficiency. For Scriabin the assertion of his uniqueness and his divinity was not the revelation of egocentrism, but the categorical imperative of his personal will. He did not maintain that the external world was illusory. The existence of others was as real or unreal as his own. The only difference between the two realities was that he identified himself with the creative act that gave life to him and to others. In his soul he anticipated the moment of becoming conscious of this act. And he felt that in his own individuality this active force became cognizant of itself.

All these figures of speech are, of course, metaphorical. Words are powerless here. One can only suggest what Scriabin himself tried to clarify verbally—the awakening of his consciousness, felt with such intensity, so rich in content, so complex, and at the same time so simple. The formulas he designed failed to satisfy him; he constantly amended and supplemented his definitions. His inability to find a verbal equivalent for the extraordinary intensity of his spiritual life caused special difficulty. The category of substantiality eluded him; he contemplated all things *sub specie actus*. For him only action possessed reality; of the substratum of the act, of its nature, he knew little.

Having never read Henri Bergson, Scriabin asserted the primacy of motion and denied the existence of the subject of the motion. I remember with what satisfaction he told me, upon reading Windelband's *History of New Philosophy,* that Fichte also interpreted the world as a system of pure processes and recognized only acts, not substances, as valid entities.

The following excerpts from Scriabin's notebooks date from 1903–1905, the time at which he composed *Le Poème divin* and *Le Poème de l'extase.*

The universe represents the unconscious process of my creative work. The sensory world is a part of it, illuminated by my attention. I am nothing, I have a will to live. Through the force of my desire I create myself and my feeling for life. Life. Creative élan. All is in us, and in us only. O you, the depths of the past born in the rays of my memory. O you, the summits of the future created by my dream: you do not exist; you constantly dance and change, just as my desire, free and unique, dances and changes. I am free. I have a will to live. I yearn for the new and the unknown. I want to create, create consciously. I want to ascend the summit. I want to enthrall the world by my creative work, by its wondrous beauty. I want to be the brightest imaginable light, the largest sun. I want to illumine the universe by my light. I want to engulf everything and absorb everything in my individuality. I want to give delight to the world. I want to take the world as one takes a woman. I need the world. I am what my senses feel. And I create the world by these senses. I create the infinite past, the growth of my consciousness, the desire to be myself. I create the infinite future, the repose in me, the sorrow and joy in me. I am nothing. I am only what I create. The destiny of the universe is clear. I have a will to live. I love life. I am God. I am nothing. I want to be all. I have generated my antithesis—time, space, and plurality. This antithesis is myself; for I am only what I engender. I want to be God. I want to return to myself. The world seeks God. I seek myself. The world is a yearning for God. I am a yearning for myself. I am the world. I am the search for God, for I am only what I seek. The history of human consciousness begins with my search and with my return.

The phrase "I am nothing" occurs on almost every page. It was also a constant refrain during our conversations. Having destroyed everything in the Spirit, Scriabin equated the Spirit with nothing. I recall his joy when this idea suddenly dawned on him. "Nothing exists!" he exclaimed. "I do not exist! But if nothing exists in reality, then everything exists if I ordain it to exist by an act of creation." This refrain, "I am nothing," expressed Scriabin's antisubstantialism, his postulate of the pliable nature of existence—obedient to the commands of the creator—and his feeling of boundless freedom. "If nothing exists," he used to say, "then all is possible."

All these utterances betray a curiously egocentric state of mind. The world is the product of my imagination, Scriabin seems to declare; I am divine; and nothing exists outside of me. The real meaning of these pronouncements must be sought in connection with Scriabin's idea of the reality of others. Scriabin poses this question unambiguously and tries to prove that the negation of others' reality entails the negation of his own reality. I quote verbatim the concluding section of Scriabin's declaration, which confirms what I had to say about his philosophy of life.

Individual consciousnesses differ only in their contents, but the bearers of these contents are identical. They are beyond space and time. We are faced here not with a multiplicity of conscious states, but with a universal consciousness that experiences a multitude of states of consciousness vertically (in time) and horizontally (in space). We should not be surprised by a world in which the same consciousness reveals itself in different individuals. Much more mysterious is that the universal consciousness contains the consciousness of Ivan in one place and of Peter in some other place. . . . Therefore the concept of individual consciousness is relative. There exists only one universal consciousness, in which an individual finds himself, according to the content that this consciousness experiences at a certain moment of time at a certain point in space. As a creative entity, an individual consciousness is nothing but potentially everything; but individualities exist only in the categories of space and time. . . . By individually sensing something, I create not an imaginary but a true multiplicity of centers reflecting the interplay of a unique creative entity, which is equally conscious of all the separate individualities it contains. At the present moment, at a given point in space, I am an individual conscious of myself, but I am also an act defined by my relationship to the external world. But in the absolute, I am God; I am a consciousness simultaneously experiencing all other consciousnesses. I am you. I am all. I have unconsciously created the world as many times as there are living creatures. Now I have elevated myself to the level of conscious creation.

Scriabin continued:

> The true center of the universe is the all-embracing
> consciousness. Our past, which had not yet reached
> the level of consciousness, and our future are parts of
> this consciousness. The past and the future emanate
> from it, as does the infinity of space. They exist only
> as attributes of creation. The universe is identical with
> God's will and is created by God. God is an all-
> embracing consciousness, a free creative impulse. In-
> sofar as I am conscious of the world as my creation,
> everything must be the product of my free will, and
> nothing can exist outside me. I am an absolute being.
> All the rest are phenomena born in the rays of my
> consciousness.

But who is this "I"? It cannot be Alexander Nikolayevich
Scriabin, located at a certain point in space and time and
embodying a certain individual consciousness, but rather
the universal "I" that Alexander Nikolayevich Scriabin beheld in himself, that the consciousness of the Unique had
burst into flame in him. Of these two "I's" Scriabin wrote
explicitly in one of his journals:

> In time and in space I obey the laws of time and space,
> but these laws are formulated by my greater "I." It
> seems to me that the only reason events do not follow
> my wishes is that I am concentrated on my little "I,"
> which must be subordinated to the laws of time and
> space created by my greater "I."

We must remember that these words are not the
fruits of Scriabin's reasoning; they do not represent the
logical process of his thoughts, but rather constitute an

attempt to formulate and explain in rational terms, not so much to others as to himself, the psychological phenomena he experienced. These experiences are unparalleled; for in them Scriabin not only postulated his identity with the world outside and consciousness of being rooted in God, but proclaimed himself an active cause of the entire cosmic process, devoid of all material support and of all purpose save self-joy and self-delight. Scriabin sensed the world as theater; in conversation he often described life as a cosmic play. Scriabin wrote:

> If the world is my unique and absolutely free act, then what is truth? I do not find it within me; it causes me untold agonies. I search for truth all the time. I long for it. . . . If I do not sense the truth in myself and can posit only what I create, then there can be no truth. . . . The world has always thirsted for freedom and yet always feared it, it needed the truth as its support. What a fatuous pursuit! Truth and freedom are mutually exclusive. Let us not be afraid of this bottomless void! But if there is no truth, what is the purpose of life? Can it be that all our sorrows, all our joys, all the great and lofty values in life, are but phantasmagoria and illusion? But there is a consolation. All this exists only because we want it to exist; all existence is created by the power of our desire. The consciousness of our strength and freedom prevents the world from vanishing into nothingness. If I want to fly, I can fly in any direction I want. Nothing but void surrounds us.

Scriabin did not negate truth by reasoning, but rather by his innate opposition to anything as stable and abiding as a truth that sets insurmountable obstacles to absolute freedom.

In Scriabin's consciousness, so unified, so simple, and yet so difficult to analyze, one trait is dominant—his joy in life. He wrote: "My joy is so great that myriad universes could be submerged in it without disturbing its surface." He exclaimed: "If I impart to the world but a single grain of my joy, its jubilation will never cease."

All who were close to Scriabin sensed a palpitating, intoxicating joy in him. Whatever preoccupied him, whether he was perturbed, indignant, or suffering physical or moral agony, there was joy in the depths of his soul. His whole life was spent in the light of this inner sun that illumined his spiritual life. He did not know the tranquil repose of a man of wisdom who by an effort of his will places himself above life's turmoil; nor the beatific quietude of a mystic absorbed in contemplation of his object of worship. What Scriabin perceived were ripples and currents, palpitations and trepidations, the undulant joy of cosmic creative force, in which he was immersed and with which he merged. At times this sensation took possession of him forcefully, tearing down all obstacles on its way and flooding his consciousness, so that he was as though intoxicated, but there was always something light and winged in him at such moments. He could then indulge in a schoolboy's pranks and practical jokes. When I surprised him once in such a mood, I was momentarily shocked, for I could not believe that a grown-up person could behave so like a child. I even suspected him of deliberate clowning and posturing. But later I realized that it was just at such moments that he was totally sincere and natural. It has been said that Scriabin was an elf rather than a titan. There is some truth in this description, if the word *elf* connotes joyful wingedness and a lambent dancing step. But this description is entirely false if the contrast between elf and titan refers to the miniature quality of his music, its tenderness and subtlety. For his winged spirit was strong, vast, and deep. Titanism was alien to Scriabin's nature because it implies struggle and rebellion, self-aggrandizement through the humiliation of others—traits that were repugnant to him. He did not cultivate tragedy in his works, and titanism is tragic by definition. Scriabin had his share of tragedy in his own life, pain and suffering, despair and despondency, but he was not conscious of the tragedy of all humanity. He always felt completely free and independent in the oneness of life. He knew that there was disharmony in the world—he recognized its existence and even postulated its necessity—but his constructions were purely theoretical. That is why he was so eager to reconcile contradictions in a synthesis that he could obtain without too great an effort and in a relatively short time.

Such a reconciliation was for him not caprice, but inner necessity. The opposite is usually true in the lives of artists who strive to free themselves from life's contradictions and to attain psychological harmony by building an artificial paradise, reconciling the abiding antinomies, and glossing over the disharmonies of life. Scriabin dwelt in a paradise of his own devising; he achieved spiritual harmony and had to make a special effort to emerge into the outside world, realize the existence of contradictions, and form an idea of life's tragedy. This venture to the outside disrupted the vital equilibrium of his inner self. It was often a calculated game, a play of the spirit that was revealed with a particularly striking force in his last creations, Le Poème de l'extase and Prométhée.

Scriabin passed through titanism and its concomitant theomachy when he detached himself from the God beyond and above him; only then could he begin to perceive his own inner illumination. Like many other mystics, he went forth in search of oneness, which eluded him. He suffered agonies that forced him to create consoling images, but they proved stillborn and false. At a later stage of his creative career, during the period when he saw the light ahead more clearly, images of struggle and suffering lingered. It is, of course, impossible to set up boundary lines between periods in Scriabin's artistic career. But, consider that in the autumn of 1902, at the inception of my friendship with Scriabin, he was already illumined by the vibrant light of life's joys, which burst forth in flame through his entire being. Recalling that the first sketches of his unrealized opera date from 1900 to 1901, we can properly mark the end of this period of rebellion with the Second Symphony. Composed in 1902, this piece signalized the beginning of the ecstatic period that continued to the end of his life.

Ecstasy of spirit—this phrase best describes Scriabin's peculiar state of mind. He placed himself, so to speak, outside his own being; he broke down the restraining bonds of time and space and beheld the cosmos directly in its perennial motion, its dance.

One of the most striking traits of Scriabin's mystical experience is its eroticism. In this, too, Scriabin departs from the mystical traditions. Indeed, only the mystique of the passive, receptive type is perfused by erotic sexuality. Such is the mystique of St. Teresa, St. Angela of Foligno, Mme. Guyon, Suso, and St. Ignatius Loyola. They ardently worshiped all that was revealed to them in their visions. They were erotically enamored of their images, but their love was of a feminine type. Mystics who worship God and nature display a feminine attitude toward the object of their adoration; they are receptive and yielding, not active or conquering. Such attitudes often assume pathological forms. The history of mysticism records but few instances of masculine love. Mystical experience of the volitional type is usually devoid of erotic or sexual elements; this absence of sensuality finds its counterpart also in the doctrines of ascetic mystics. Jakob Böhme cultivated a doctrine free of feminine connotations. Volitional, active relationship to the object of mystical experience is not touched by devotional love. The feeling of polarity here is not sensual; it is asexual. Scriabin is a unique exception to these categories; for he was a mystic lover with a masculine relationship to God. His philosophy of life was sensual, strongly imbued with sexuality.

During his individualistic period, Scriabin posited himself in relation to the world outside as actively masculine, as an antithesis to the passivity of the world, which dwelled in a state of "awaiting" and "languishing," as Scriabin expressed it in *Le Poème de l'extase.* "I want to take the world as one takes a woman," Scriabin said. In his visions of conquering the world through the enchantment of his art, he put these words in his hero's mouth: "I came here not to teach, but to caress."

At a later stage of his development, when Scriabin tore down the wall between himself and the universe, when the world became a part of him and he became submerged in it, when the cosmos became a supernal creative stream, he identified himself with the active element of this stream. Its symbol became to him the Eternal Masculine of the *Acte préalable,* while the world, "playing in the rays of a creative dream," as Scriabin described it in *Le Poème de l'extase,* continued to be the Eternal Feminine. The polarity of "myself" and "not myself" is here reduced to a sexual polarity.

Scriabin relished the free interplay of his senses, colored by a subtle but profound eroticism. Always fastidiously polite and solicitous, he nonetheless could, at times, in a friendly conversation among men, indulge in frank comments touched with cynicism. On occasion he displayed a boyish coquetry, but his sensuality was never coarse; it was marked by the same winged quality that characterized his longings, feelings, and creative impulses. Despite its strength and intensity, his sensuality was free of carnal materialism; it was indeed infused with a spiritual quality. In this flaming soul, which seemed to consume itself so rapidly, all earthly senses were transfigured, or, to use the terminology of theosophy, dematerialized.

Scriabin the sensualist, perpetually in love with life and its joys, had nothing but contempt for the flesh as the embodiment of the material element; he felt toward it a sort of revulsion of which only the great ascetics of the past had been capable. In Christian doctrine, it was mainly the dogma of the resurrection of the flesh that he inwardly found incomprehensible, even self-contradictory. To him the flesh was something inferior and coarse, something that had to be overcome and eventually discarded. This conviction grew stronger with time. I recall our conversations on this subject at his summer home in 1914. I was particularly struck by the energy and passion with which he spoke of the ultimate divestment of fleshly garments, of dematerialization, of a return to a state of pure spirituality. I understood then that his theoretical rejection of the material universe and his metaphysical activism were predicated on the perishability of all matter and on the deceptive character of its solidity.

Scriabin was enamored of color and form. He took delight in the multitudinous offerings of life, which were to him the revelation of a living fantasy. He was fascinated by the very process of the birth, the blossoming, and the withering of life. This curious antimaterialism also explains Scriabin's strange insensitivity to nature. It is indeed remarkable that although he proclaimed his oneness with the cosmos, of which nature is a part, nature itself had no charm for him. To be sure, he appreciated the beauties of nature as an artist, and he had a fine understanding of the variety of life forms around him, but the mystic in him could never enjoy nature's autonomous existence. Mountains, forests and rivers, the ocean, land animals and birds of the air had little attraction for Scriabin; they signified nothing more than beautiful combinations of colors and forms, intricate symbols and signs whose mysterious meaning he was to divine. He perceived in the beauties of nature certain psychic processes, cosmic volitions and sensations, and he could be fully absorbed in these phenomena; to him events of the outside world were but the temporal and spatial signs of psychic states. Once when we took a walk together in Switzerland, Scriabin suddenly declared that to him the Alps symbolized only certain mountainous states in his own psyche, marking an increase of energy, a sharp intensification of action, and its subsequent dissipation. These terms were not just metaphors; they reflected his innermost psychological states. He wrote in one of his notebooks:

O you, rocks of my wrath! O you, tender lines of my caresses! O you, gentle flowers of my dreams, you, stars, lightning flashes of my eyes, you, the sun of my delight, you, interpreters of my fleeting sensations in space! Thus I speak, immersed in time, severed from space.

Scriabin's antinaturalistic mystique can be described as anthropocentric, for he saw man, and nothing but man, in the universe. All material objects, all events were to him simply functions and creations of man, and he saw the entire history of the cosmos in its human perspective. But the man in his cosmology was not a man of flesh and bone, but a spiritual man, totally denuded of fleshly vestments. The cosmos appeared to him as a complex of spiritual or perhaps psychic acts whose consciousness he bore.

Did Scriabin really love humanity? His soul was aflame with human love. I spoke earlier of his constant eagerness to share with others the joys that were overflowing in his soul; this desire was unquestionably one of the principal incentives to creative work. He introduced others into his luminous world and let them partake of its blessedness. He wrote: "O my world, fill yourself to the brim with my freedom and my joy!"

Scriabin's entire being seemed to exult when he shared his experience with others. Not for him were the satisfactions of the recluse or the solitary happiness of the egotist. Yet it must be admitted that Scriabin did not lavish his spiritual gifts on individual humans. His interest was not directed toward a particular person, but to the ideal of Man with a capital *M*. A particular Ivan or Peter was to him but the raw material of universal consciousness. He did not address himself to the souls of specific people, but to the Spirit of Man in its unique manifestations, of which all Ivans and Peters are but individual phenomena.

The ecstasy of Scriabin, averse as he was to struggle or tragedy, his absolute spirituality, his otherworldliness often seemed to be the marks of coldness and aloofness. The flaming world of Scriabin's mystique, too joyful and luminous for common comprehension, seemed to lack human warmth; ordinary people were dazzled by the blinding rays of Scriabin's sun and so could not enter his world.

÷

The mystique of the will is related to some form of magic. A man pure of soul abhors magic as a diabolical temptation and a sin. To approach God and to submerge himself in the divine essence, man must deny himself, sacrifice his free will, "gnaw himself to the bone," in the horrifying phrase of St. Gregory of Nyssa. Any expression of personal will on the path toward divinity is an impediment in the quest of beatitude. But an imperious willpower dominates mystics of the volitional type who actively strive to achieve divinity. The effort of will that a mystic makes in order to be permeated with divine essence is an act of coercion toward the Deity. A ritual of magic conjurations, which denies miracles yet invests the magician with power over the infinite, grows luxuriantly in mystical practice. In an article on mystical doctrines published in *Logos* (1912–13), Georg Melis contrasts a religious magus and a mystic of the contemplative type: "The religious magus strives to bind God; a mystic wants to be bound by God; the former wants to coerce God; the latter wants to be coerced by God; the former wants to be God; the latter wants to come to God; the former strives to be God; the latter wants to be in God."

Such imagery is typical of religious writing, but its terms are rarely adequate. All mystics are to a certain degree either magi or contemplators, but "these contradictions are frequently reconciled in a single individual," to quote Melis again.

Scriabin was undoubtedly a magus, but his magical consciousness underwent considerable change as he gradually vanquished his individualism. His mystique between 1900 and 1902 reveals traits of magical consciousness, but it did not include the state of beatitude, for Scriabin felt that what he had accomplished was not through divine illumination, a benevolent dispensation of the Deity, but through his own effort of will. Some years later, further sensing his life's destiny and his doom, he became conscious of his divine anointment. He talked volubly of his mission, of the exalted but arduous task that he could not relinquish. At the same time he identified himself ever deeper, ever more intimately with the world community; he no longer strove to take possession of the world for his own purposes, and he could no longer aspire to the conquest of God, who never existed beyond his own consciousness. Thus both forms of magic—naturalistic magic, whose object is nature, and religious magic, which aspires toward God—were completely transfigured in Scriabin's world outlook. Scriabin belonged to the category of masculine, active mysticism, and his brand of magic became a species of theurgy, which was not directed outward, to external objects, but inward; the Theurgist personified by Scriabin concentrated his activity on his inner self, that unique, divine state of being which, when pierced by consciousness, would be transfigured and returned to the state of oneness. This magic act was bound to lose its coercive character, for the object of its enchantments was the Theurgist himself, and its purpose was to awaken to new life the elements dormant in him. Magic was reduced to caresses and began to assume an erotic character.

The magic of Scriabin's creative mystique was intimately connected with his ardent curiosity about the darker aspects of life, which he perceived around him and the reality of which, not only psychologically, but also metaphysically, he proclaimed. He liked to invoke dark visions and abandon himself to a perilous game; he longed to bring to light "all the vital embryos," as he phrased it in the text he wrote for *Le Poème de l'extase,* no matter how monstrous or repellent they were.

From this somber region Scriabin received inspiration for his works. It is undeniable that his complex and vast intellect sought contact, at least in some part of his being, with satanism. This diabolical element, whether we regard it metaphorically or mystically, tempted him upon occasion; he liked to gaze into it, courting the danger of being engulfed in it. In this respect, Scriabin had an affinity with Wagner, Liszt, Byron, Baudelaire, and perhaps also Leonardo da Vinci. Hence his profound divergence from Beethoven and Mozart, who were, as men and as artists, totally removed from any kind of diabolism insofar as it could be considered human at all.

These somber, disruptive forces could never take full possession of Scriabin. He conquered them, subdued them, just as Wagner, Liszt, Byron, and Baudelaire did before him, for they all were creators in the kingdom of the beautiful, artists of genius. The stages on Scriabin's path to liberation, the landmarks of his victories, were *Le Poème satanique* and the Ninth Piano Sonata. Goethe had Mephistopheles in him, but once having created Mephistopheles, he freed himself from him and completed his conquest of the demon. Similarly, Scriabin vindicated his independence

from diabolical elements by bringing them into the light
of day, subjecting them to the laws of proportion, and
guiding them into the realm of the beautiful. I therefore
cannot assign this diabolical element the important place
in the spiritual life of Scriabin that Leonid Sabaneyev does.
"In diabolism," Sabaneyev wrote, "I find the solution to
many puzzles in Scriabin's life and in his spiritual tragedy. . . . Undoubtedly, the entire spiritual and creative
physiognomy of Scriabin's consciousness was conditioned
by Satanism. . . . Considering the entire aggregate of Scriabin's spiritual elements, as reflected in his philosophy and
his art, we are astounded and shocked to behold the visage
of Satan, born of the confluence of all constituent parts of
Scriabin's nature." We see that Sabaneyev definitely views
Scriabin in the light of artistic satanism.

To describe Scriabin as an artist-satanist seems to
me as preposterous and absurd as the expression "wooden
iron." It is easy to form erroneous judgments regarding
Scriabin's personality, but one thing is beyond doubt: Scriabin was a great artist, a creator of genius, whereas diabolism is completely sterile, lacking creative power. It can
deceive and parody; masques and grimaces are the means
of expression in satanism, for it bears the stigma of im-
potence. This is freely acknowledged by psychologists (or
rather psychopathologists since the various forms of de-
monism and satanism are abnormal phenomena) and by
adepts of religious mysticism, who regard diabolism as the
possession of the soul by dark forces.

The judgment of Sabaneyev and similar verdicts of
those who like to expatiate on the subject of morbid genius, immoral art, corrupt beauty, and so forth, appear to

result from misapprehension of the true meaning of the creative effort in art. According to Sabaneyev and others, Scriabin's Ninth Piano Sonata, *Le Poème satanique,* "Etrangeté" (op. 63, no. 2), and other works of a similar nature betray explicit symptoms of satanism emerging from the world of darkness and taking possession of the artist. Exactly the reverse is true; these works are proofs of the artistic strength, basic purity, and clarity of Scriabin's spirit through which all phenomena were spiritually transfigured and sanctified. If Scriabin had not written his Ninth Piano Sonata or *Le Poème satanique,* those who knew him intimately, who listened attentively to what he had to say and observed his expression, might have imagined that Scriabin courted unknown dangers, that dark, destructive forces were about to overpower him, for his ambitions and designs were too bold, too presumptuous, his faith in victory too great and his ignorance of reality too profound. His moral stance, which gave paramount consideration to power and vital intensity, might also have been a source of concern.

In discussing Scriabin as a magus, one cannot ignore his infatuation with occult sciences. So-called exact disciplines, such as physics and chemistry, failed to interest him, although new discoveries in the field of radiology fascinated him. It was the mystical physics of occultism that entranced him as soon as he began to read books on theosophy and other occult sciences by Mme. Blavatsky and Leadbeater. But here again Scriabin revealed his typical trait, which I would call pragmatism. Occult manifestations and their impact interested him not for their subject matter, but only insofar as they could give him power over outside phenomena. He saw in them a vehicle of influence, a weapon of unparalleled strength. He sought knowledge as a means to power, but his inadequate scientific training, his lack of intellectual discipline and critical methodology, impeded his progress. When his intuition was silent, he surrendered easily to passing influences, be they Mme. Blavatsky, Leadbeater, or Annie Besant. Scriabin, who was always proud of his liberty and his independence, was perfectly willing to follow unquestioningly these theosophic mentors. He trusted them; he acknowledged their authority and took on faith their most fantastic claims. I emphasize that this was the case only when his intuition was silent which, unfortunately, happened just as he entered the mysterious world of the occult.

What was Scriabin's method of mystical cognition? By this method I do not mean a system of rules and regulations employed consciously or unconsciously by a mystic in the belief that he can thus perceive certain truths; rather, I mean the path Scriabin followed toward the Unique, even if he was not aware of direction.

Mystical cognition is intuitive; it connotes spontaneous perception. I am not touching on the problem of the value of such intuitive cognition, but merely stating the fact that it exists. We are offered here a choice of two paths. Some mystics unconsciously select one to the exclusion of the other; but there are those who are familiar with both paths, and they sometimes succeed in uniting them. The first path may be defined as subjective, psychological, or microcosmic, and the second as objective, naturalistic, and macrocosmic.

Some mystics achieve cognition by introspection. Absorbed in themselves, they judge everything through the medium of their own psyches. Their "I" is the path that leads them to cognition of God and the world. This path is a true mirror of life, whose reflective surface they study intently, lovingly seeking and finding in it the reflection of the Unique. Such was the mystical consciousness of Meister Eckhart, Suso, and almost all ecclesiastical mystics, both Greek Orthodox and Catholic. Hindu mystics followed the same path. Other mystics, however, seem to have averted their gaze from themselves and directed their attention toward the outside world. They knew how to observe nature; they understood, loved, and penetrated it. Their path lay in nature, and through it they arrived at the vision of the Unique. Among these mystics of nature are Jakob Böhme, St. Martin, and St. Yves d'Alveydre; they are occult visionaries for whom nature is a reality and not merely a phantom or symbol.

The first path leads to the absorption in nature of a personal "I"; the second leads to the Unique, in which "I" and nature merge. Of course, the methods employed by mystics, whether consciously or unconsciously, determine to a certain extent the character of their personal mystical experience and entire doctrine of mysticism. Mysticism reaches its greatest development, its highest organization and most detailed systematization, among mystics of the objective, naturalistic type. Occult sciences, beginning with cosmogony and ending with esoteric theories of physics and zoology, flourish luxuriantly among contemplative mystics. But Scriabin belonged to a different type. He conceived of nature as a stream of spiritual or psychic processes, a system of acts. He created the image of nature according to his own likeness. The subject of his intuition was always himself, the individuality in which he discovered God; his cognition of the world was therefore formed in terms of a living, creative individuality. He was cognizant only of himself and observed the world only through himself; this led him to a philosophy of panpsychism combined with antisubstantialism and actualism. Constantly striving toward some undefined objective, seeking an indefinite goal, he inevitably plunged deeper and deeper into himself, discovering new riches, sensing his inexhaustible nature, his own infinite dimension. He recognized only one measure—man, that is, the microcosm. He was himself no more than a microcosm, a cosmos in miniature, a reflection of the universe; but he also viewed himself as a macrocosm. The little and the large worlds were identical in him, and he contained this unique cosmos in his own self.

During his work on the text of the *Acte préalable,* Scriabin translated his theogony, cosmogony, and anthropogenesis into poetic images, but while doing so he actually only relied on self-cognition and introspective exploration. His intuition was vast and profound, but its object was always inherent in himself; he seemed unable to emerge from his inner world, although he widened and deepened his consciousness to the point of infinity. Whatever he touched, whatever he studied, was immediately psychologized, acquiring the characteristics of a spiritual state of being. He was incapable of grasping a state of being governed by logic or any reality not permeated with human qualities. Hence his typical religious anthropomorphism, which made him view God in human terms and man in divine.

Needless to say, Scriabin was not an ordinary psychologist preoccupied with introspection and self-analysis. He had experienced moments of clairvoyance and ecstasy, but these states of mind seemed to take place in his own psyche, which to him was at the same time a cosmic sphere. A comparison with the remarkable Russian mystic Anna Schmidt, whose manuscripts have recently come to light, is revealing. Anna Schmidt knew mystical experience through the contemplation of the macrocosm. Her insight was not directed toward herself, but toward the vast expanse of the world at large, of which she was only a particle when immersed in herself. This self-immersion led to a yearning to exteriorize herself. The object of her visions and revelations was the macrocosm, which she contemplated intuitively and without the personal microcosm as medium.

Anna Schmidt believed in the reality of mystical experience, which she analyzed in great detail and illumined by the ontological doctrine of divinity and of the spirit world. In contradistinction to this view, Scriabin treated divinity entirely from a psychological point of view; combined with his rejection of materialism and substantialism, this attitude bore the ominous stigmata of metaphysical nihilism, which he could not escape.

The mysticism of mystics belonging to the subjective category is usually imperfectly developed and without systematic classification. Scriabin was spared this dreamy vagueness and nebulous imprecision, common to subjective mystics, by his sense of formal perfection, his intellectual astuteness, pragmatism, and insatiable dedication to philosophical activity. Hence his predilection for scientific-sounding formulas and his infatuation with the occult, in which he hoped to find support for his theories. The subjective quality of Scriabin's mysticism is reflected in the striking idiosyncrasies of his musical compositions. Deeply subjective, emotional, and saturated with personal feelings, his music succeeds at the same time in transcending the individual to assume a rigorously objective meaning.

Apocalyptic expectations, fanatical belief in the world's imminent end, are characteristic of many mystics, but few have matched the intensity and penetration of Scriabin's eschatological vigil, particularly during the last years of his life. His conviction that the end of the world was near, that cosmic history was approaching its consummation, was so intense and his manner of discussing it so matter-of-fact and sober that one felt somewhat uncomfortable talking to him about it. It was eerie to hear him, a man of the twentieth century, dressed in ordinary clothes and behaving in normal fashion, speak unaffectedly about subjects usually treated as religious abstractions. Those who did not know him well might have thought that he was playing a role for some unfathomable reason, that he was dissembling or indulging in poetical rhetoric with some strange, arcane implications. And yet Scriabin was never more sincere, more direct, or more true to himself than when he was volubly proclaiming the imminence and inevitability of a world catastrophe and the consequent transfiguration of man.

Such apocalyptic pronouncements, rather puzzling in our own time, may have been common in the tenth century or among early Christians. There was a profound difference, however, between the mentality of Scriabin and these millennial mystics. The early Christians and Catholic Europe of the tenth century awaited the end of the world and the Second Coming of the Redeemer as an inevitable event, whereas Scriabin believed that it was his destiny to assume the awesome burden of bringing about this consummation. Were he to fail, someone else would have to take over the task, in which case the world would obtain a remission. He envisioned himself as an active participant in the concluding act of the world drama; his yearning for the final fulfillment, he was convinced, would precipitate that event. In contradistinction to the mystics of the tenth century, Scriabin was an active participant; he was not merely the object of divine action or a passive celebrant, but a working agent. Did he entertain any misgivings or doubts on that account? He was convinced that the day of Universal Ecstasy was bound to come, and he was equally convinced of his own momentous role. But he also had moments of doubt in his own powers. He never admitted such doubts directly, but hesitations and fears persisted, and toward the end of his life they became more intense as he realized the slowness of his progress and the swiftness with which the years passed by. One could detect such doubts indirectly when, for instance, he sought moral support from others. I recall Scriabin asking me several times:

> Does not the fact that this mystery was revealed to me prove conclusively that I, and no one else, have the power to bring about this fulfillment? It is unthinkable that another person would be able to follow my design, to understand my central purpose! I was the first to behold the ultimate vision, and I must be the one to reveal it!

The idea of the *Acte préalable* must have originated in these doubts and fears. Scriabin seized eagerly upon it and plunged into his work with total dedication, for he harbored a secret fear that he would not be vouchsafed enough time and strength to achieve the creation of the *Mysterium*. He decided, therefore, to sketch out at least its approximation, a faint reflection of the grand design. One of Scriabin's intimates observed, very much to the point, that in Scriabin's innermost consciousness, undertaking the *Acte préalable* signalized abandoning the project of the *Mysterium*.

Scriabin had absolute faith in the unlimited power of man's free will. He was convinced that man possesses total power over himself, his body, and certain elements of his soul. He struggled to achieve this power over himself and attained remarkable results in this endeavor. The most striking demonstration of his power was his victory over a seemingly intractable condition of his right hand, which he suffered when he was twenty. From his autobiographical journal, quoted in a previous chapter, one can see how deeply this ailment affected Scriabin and to what despair he was driven by the verdict of his doctors. He continued his medical treatment, but he was helped much more by practicing a species of autosuggestion, for his ailment was mainly of a nervous nature. The cure came as a result of his belief that it was crucial for him to overcome his condition and return to work. His organism was frail and delicate, but he developed a tremendous power of resistance through psychological means. He had never tried to undergo physical training, and he was constantly susceptible to imaginary ailments. Gradually his health improved, despite the psychological tension that threatened his physical well-being. In the 1890s Scriabin suffered from acute neurasthenia. Even his piano playing and his music seemed to be marked by a morbid neuroticism. "A sickly talent"—this cliché described Scriabin accurately at that time. When I first met him, the thought crossed my mind that Scriabin was not destined to live long, that his bodily frame was too weak to withstand the tensions of his inner forces. But he succeeded in overcoming this imbalance; he recreated his body not through physical therapy, but through persistent work on his own constitution, by a curious concentration of his spiritual powers. To the end of his life, he remained

extremely nervous, excessively irritable, and easily provoked. Yet he managed to preserve a certain inner harmony
and stability, even at moments of the greatest spiritual exaltation, when he seemed to transcend his physical being
and was, almost literally, beside himself. But at such moments his inventive powers achieved great ingenuity, he
was illumined to the depth of his soul, and his spirit acquired a monolithic firmness and stability.

If madness is chaos, then superior organization and
harmoniousness are polar to madness. Scriabin often came
near catastrophe, reaching the borderline between sunlit
ecstasy and outer darkness and despair. But despite this
impetuous influx of mysterious psychic energy into his
sphere of consciousness, Scriabin was able, by sheer power
of will, to gain control of himself and preserve the unity
of his psyche. States of ecstasy, crystallized in musical
sound in such works as his Seventh Piano Sonata and *Prométhée,* combined a superpersonal detachment with an exceptional strength of organization and spiritual integrity.
Ecstasy transcends the normal limits of an individual human being through infinite expansion; at the same time
the conflicting elements contained in these works moved
toward their center, organizing themselves around it in
obedience to the creator's will. The question arises: Was it
Scriabin's own will that was in command? It must be emphasized that to Scriabin the state of ecstasy was not chaos,
disarray, confusion, and formlessness; on the contrary, it
was a structure of perfection in a harmonious form, compared to which the unstable system of so-called normal
consciousness appears chaotic. The following quotation
from Scriabin's notes illustrates the point:

> Ecstasy is the highest exaltation of action; ecstasy is a summit. . . . Intellectually, ecstasy is the highest synthesis; emotionally, it is the greatest happiness.

Empirical consciousness vanishes at the brief moments of ecstasy; what Scriabin experienced he never related to the person named Alexander Nikolayevich Scriabin. The consciousness of his selfness disappeared completely, giving way to a new superpersonal oneness. Reflecting on it, Scriabin was inclined to explain it by the theory of his two "I's"—the small, empirical "I" representing human consciousness of one particular unit of Omni-consciousness, and the large "I" representing divine consciousness of this Omni-consciousness. In the state of ecstasy, the little "I" identifies itself with the large "I." This was Scriabin's symbolic interpretation of his relationship with the superior power of divinity.

Scriabin's nature was exceptionally volitional, but his will had a superpersonal character, particularly during the last years of his life, so that its energy proceeded not from Scriabin but, so to speak, through him. It is in this sense that one can describe Scriabin as possessed. The process of gradual consolidation, expansion, and enhancement of his individuality, the process of organizing his entire physical and spiritual powers, which his intimates constantly witnessed, suggested a gradual penetration of his soul by some superior state of being. I use this description to emphasize that far from being "possessed," that is, subdued, Scriabin experienced a remarkable efflorescence of all his faculties, as abundantly demonstrated by his music. Scriabin's ecstasy was the fountainhead of his inspiration, whose products were distinguished by a formal perfection of design. Thus Scriabin's mystique was artistically fruitful, and it may well be said, "by their fruits ye shall know them." This judgment allows no exception. It is therefore incorrect to compare Scriabin's state of creative ecstasy with the ecstatic delirium among some Russian religious sects, the flagellants, for example, just as it is unthinkable to equate the visions of St. Teresa with the hallucinations of a hysterical woman. These sets of phenomena are of a totally different order, and the difference here is not of degree, but of essence.

In this connection I should like to mention a seemingly trivial but actually very significant fact. In his early years, before the composition of the last five piano sonatas and *Prométhée,* Scriabin sometimes claimed that intoxication may be beneficial to creative activity, and that one gains a temporary freedom in wine. Scriabin liked to drink wine in congenial company, but he showed a remarkable tolerance for intoxicants, particularly in view of his delicate health. I never saw him intoxicated, no matter how much he drank; at most, drinking made him more loquacious and voluble. But later he changed his attitude toward alcohol completely. He came to see in it a symptom of spiritual decadence; the need for artificial stimulants became for him an index of inferiority, immaturity, and lack of mystical insight. Although he occasionally drank wine, particularly after his concert appearances, he never abused this practice. "I have no need of wine," he used to say.

The concept of the Deity, with which Scriabin wrestled so painfully in his youth and thought he had exorcised, apparently came to possess him again. Many Christian mystics of the active type have been possessed in this sense. Among them were St. Teresa and her mentor, John of the Cross. St. Teresa described the mystical possession as a "spiritual wedding." In his remarkable treatise *Etudes d'histoire et de psychologie du mysticisme,* Delacroix gives the following description of such a spiritual marriage, imparting to it a rather strong rhetorical coloration:

> In the state of possession we witness a radical transformation of the soul and of life itself, imbued by a continuous, permanent, and conscious element of divinity. The soul partakes of the divine spirit not only during a brief moment of intuition, but through the entire life of the individual; thus, intuition assumes a lifelike form. The soul, illumined by God, experiences its divinity in its actions; the individual feels that all spiritual states are born in the Deity, that his entire life and mode of thinking spring from a divine source. . . . An individual then is identical with divine action. . . . Hence the consciousness of a superior control that is exercised throughout one's life, a sensation of automatism and of freedom combined, created by the conversion of individual consciousness into divine guidance. Here the soul is in a state of continuous possession by divinity, a species of theopathy analogous to demonopathy. The Deity is perceived by the inner soul of man, becoming flesh of the flesh and the consciousness of consciousness, an integral part of the will. It is an operation that finds its natural expression in action. . . . True spiritual life demands utilization of the divine force that penetrates the body and

brings about the conquest of the outside world and of human souls. . . . Contemplation and action exist in the soul, which is at once divine and human. It is only in this theopathic state that one's life assumes the meaning of a divine act, so that vital activities actually express the divine element and exhaust it by an infinite, creative action.

÷

The reality of the phenomenon of possession cannot be refuted, but it can be interpreted in various ways, depending on the standpoint, scientific or religious, taken by the commentator. It is possible to explain it exclusively in psychological terms, as Delacroix does, making use of the theory of subconscious spiritual energy (a theory which really explains nothing). Possession can also be explained in terms of mysticism, as in the case of St. Teresa, who was a strict Catholic, or Scriabin himself, whose faith in his mission on earth and of his sacrificial role stemmed from his own mystical experience.

This missionary awareness, a sense of predestination and the expectation of a unique achievement, gradually displaced Scriabin's vision of a freely selected goal toward which he moved in a spirit of play and could abandon at any moment, obeying a passing whim. We witness in Scriabin the absorption of the individual consciousness by the consciousness of an appointed action. Scriabin always said that the vision of cosmic ecstasy captivated him by its grandeur, by its fantastic challenge. But in the last years of his life he relinquished the personal element and concentrated on the objective itself; he felt that his empirical "I" was subordinated to a superior imperative and that his role as an individual was to do his utmost to bring about an ecstatic consummation.

As this realization grew, the personal element in Scriabin's creative activity gradually receded. His early dreams had concerned the attainment of personal power over humanity; he had craved glory and fame, and he had hoped to exalt himself by his accomplishments. But later he became less absorbed in his own person and transferred his allegiance to the work itself. Shortly before his death, when I jocularly remarked to him that he was apparently enjoying the atmosphere of admiration and adulation by which he was surrounded and that it flattered his vanity, he answered me with an unexpected earnestness, even solemnity: "I swear to you that if there were someone greater than I am, capable of creating a greater joy on earth than I can, I would immediately withdraw and hand my task over to him. But, of course, I would then cease to live." This was not mere rhetoric on his part; he meant every word of it.

Scriabin always believed in the greatness of his power. In early life he took immense pride and delight in the consciousness of his superior abilities. Later on, however, he changed his attitude and spoke of his mission as ordained by a higher being. And when, toward the end of his life, he tasted glory, triumphs, and universal recognition, his *amour propre,* vanity, and pride gradually faded away. Then he could truly say: "Not unto us, Lord, not unto us, but unto thy name give glory." Scriabin's "I" became a path to divinity.

Having recognized his own "I" as the medium of divine communion, Scriabin perceived the dual nature of man: constricting and constricted, determining and determined, delimiting and delimited, sacrificer and sacrificed. The empirical individuality is a sacrificial offering, Scriabin believed. But who offers it? The answer is the individual consciousness, insofar as it is not detached in its aspect of a delimiting, determining entity reposing in the bosom of the Unique. Scriabin regarded himself as such a sacrificial offering, doomed by his own will, which he identified with the will of the Unique, and yearning to consume the world in the fires of ecstasy. He posited his individual consciousness as a means to an end, subject to his own power, which was also the power of God. Through his inner experience, from theomachy and self-deification, Scriabin arrived at the recognition of his own nature, and human nature in general, as the self-sacrificial act of the Deity.

PART II

THE MYSTERY

4

THE OPERA

Scriabin's music, seemingly so complex, appears upon examination extraordinarily transparent and lucid. It is complex in the number and variety of its constituent elements, in its yearnings, emotions, and ideas. But at the same time it is remarkably simple when grasped in its entirety; then it appears classically sculptured and harmoniously proportioned. The multifarious ingredients of Scriabin's music are intimately interconnected, with each part related to the image of the whole. This whole does not represent a simple sum of addenda, an arrangement of different parts; it exists over and above such individual parts. That is why only the integral image is real and concrete, whereas its constituent parts become visible only upon analysis or dissection.

The entire mass of Scriabin's creative works represents the revelation and incarnation, in terms of our own world, of some form of clairvoyance, of a spiritual act that is not a function of the intellect, a state of contemplation, or a sensory impression, but a superior entity transcending the mind, the emotions, and the senses while subsuming them.

In all his endeavors, whether he tried to create new artistic forms or strove to define his mission in rational concepts, Scriabin concentrated on the formulation in clear and graphic terms of his still vague visions. In this respect Scriabin was a striking exception among artists and thinkers. No other artist has ever achieved such completeness, systematic organization, and simplicity in his philosophy of life. Only among religious seers, saints, visionaries, and great mystics of the past can we find such oneness of thought, sentiment, desire, and mood, all seemingly springing from the same source pierced by a unifying beam of light. This idiosyncrasy presents the greatest difficulty for an analysis of Scriabin's work and, paradoxically, makes it relatively simple. Indeed, it suffices to establish the principle of oneness that animated Scriabin's creative endeavor in order to divine the vital forces behind his expressive methods. His creative path is thus illuminated with the utmost clarity of detail, revealing the secret interconnection among his compositions, their meaning, and their import. We must grasp Scriabin's creative message in its integrity, or else we will fail to understand it altogether. It is revelated in an instant, but only a special key can unlock its mystery. How can we find this key? How can we penetrate the enigma of Scriabin? It is clear from the preceding paragraphs that a mere summation and collation of Scriabin's works in their chronological succession, an analysis, a dissection, will never solve the problem. To arrange

Scriabin's works in their true perspective, we must have some generic idea not only of Scriabin's creative evolution, but also of his sources of inspiration. We must ascertain what concepts were incarnated in the procession of sonatas, tone poems, and symphonies. Even if we attempt a psychological analysis of Scriabin's works in order to discover their constituent elements, we must still have a definite idea of Scriabin's entire oeuvre, for only in its totality can we divine the inner nature of these elements. A technical analysis of Scriabin's music, therefore, cannot provide us with the necessary key to unlock his secret; it cannot enlighten us on the meaning of his creative design, its objectives, and its vital resources. The solution of Scriabin's mystery seems possible only by way of artistic intuition, an aesthetic contemplation of his musical works. Thus we have to proceed in reverse, from the particular to the abstract—a course made possible by Scriabin's self-revelation in the *Mysterium*. This work never materialized, but its design, elaborated in detail in some of its parts, provides the key to Scriabin's creative intent. However, we must not trust Scriabin implicitly and accept on faith his declarations concerning his work and his aims, for in the last analysis, the music itself must determine the value of his ideas. We must render our judgment impartially by proper study and without prejudice, disregarding Scriabin's own pronouncements, however authoritative.

From a psychological standpoint, the *Mysterium* is central to Scriabin's creative biography. His thought centered on realizing the *Mysterium;* all other works were incidental to it, successive stages of a gradual crystallization, signposts of the artist's progress toward his goal.

But even if we disregard the psychological aspect of Scriabin's moods, longings, and expectations and consider his creative work in its entirety, we must recognize that this grand design was not a fantastic dream, but a project that achieved an objective existence, although in a form quite different from that originally planned.

It is therefore imperative to begin examining Scriabin's creative catalogue with the *Mysterium,* rather than placing it at the end, even though this work (if it can be called a work in a sense of a completed project) was never put on paper, was never even begun, and never existed except conceptually (the material originally designated for the *Mysterium* was eventually incorporated in the score of the *Acte préalable*). We are, therefore, compelled to rely on reports of what Scriabin told his friends about its nature and on its faint reflection in the *Acte préalable*. Thus we find ourselves forced to pronounce judgment on a work that is a design without content, because the evaluation, not only aesthetic but philosophical, of Scriabin's entire career depends on the status of the *Mysterium.*

The fundamental idea behind the *Mysterium* underwent numerous changes, progressed in different directions, and assumed different forms during the successive stages of Scriabin's inner evolution. We can distinguish four such stages.

In the early period of Scriabin's life the *Mysterium*

did not exist even as a concept. At that time Scriabin did not seek to realize his ideas in any particular artistic form. And yet his art was already suffused with the thought of the *Mysterium;* it was inherently "mysterial," so to speak, and consequently vital and active.

In its general scheme, the central design of the *Mysterium* may be described as a dream of the unification of mankind in a single instant of ecstatic revelation. This dream pervaded Scriabin's entire artistic and philosophical evolution; it permeated and determined his activity through the years. The difference between this early period, covering the last decade of the nineteenth century, and subsequent periods was that, although he came to believe that the main purpose of his life was the realization of this dream, he did not initially limit this objective to a single work, such as the *Mysterium,* but attached equal significance to all his compositions. In Scriabin's judgment at that time, all his works served but a single purpose, all were directed toward the same goal, all preparing humanity for a final transfiguration through their impact. In theory this notion postulated the saving and liberating power of art, not merely as an aesthetic phenomenon, but also as a social and metaphysical factor. Scriabin was willing to abandon the cult of aesthetic values and began to view art as an active force capable of bringing about a substantial change in the nature of man. In this sense one can recognize the "mysterial" substance of Scriabin's art even in the earliest years of his creative evolution.

Scriabin's First Symphony—particularly its musically unsuccessful finale, a hymn to art—reveals the longings and aspirations of the young composer in a strikingly forceful manner. This hymn, which is weak from a poetic standpoint, represents a preliminary sketch of the *Mysterium;* it is in fact the only instance in Scriabin's entire body of work where he applies a grandiose, transcendental style. In it Scriabin expressed for the first time, in a definite and fully intentional design, his idea of the unifying, illuminating, and transfiguring power of art, which became the dominant concept of his philosophy of life. He affirmed the religious role of all art, but it was a religion without God. Man is lonely; there is no superior divine power watching over him, so he must achieve his joy solely through his art. This concept spells a fundamental difference between Scriabin's glorification of art in his First Symphony and Beethoven's apotheosis of joy in the Ninth Symphony. But did Scriabin really glorify art in his hymn? He told me once, "This is not a paean to art, but to the artist, that is, to myself." Scriabin was at that time so deeply engrossed in himself, in his own personality, that he also identified himself with his art.

As early as 1901 the idea of the *Mysterium* began to take a definite shape in Scriabin's mind. He thought of composing an opera. This was the second stage. In the summer of 1903 Scriabin wrote me, "If you only knew how eager I am to write an opera!" But, obeying the command of some inner voice, he made a decisive choice to extend his action beyond the boundary of art. The idea of the *Mysterium* was born. In full awareness of his intentions, he embarked on the composition of a work to be called *Act of the Last Fulfillment.* He hoped to complete it in a short time, but the project assumed increasingly grandiose dimensions; it seemed to recede from him farther the closer he approached it, hoping to place it within definite limits. This was the third stage.

During this period of impatient expectation and constant procrastination, Scriabin decided to write an *Acte préalable,* which was to serve as the threshold to the *Mysterium,* as its preliminary act, a species of initiation. It was a compromise between the grand design of the *Mysterium* and practical realities, achieved by dint of considerable abridgment and simplification.

The main subject of my early conversations with Scriabin, in the autumn of 1902, was his opera. I had the impression that he had been working on it for two or three years and that something prevented its completion, even though the libretto and some of the music were partly finished. He spoke to me frequently and almost passionately about it and read to me parts of the libretto. But he was already involved in other projects. The overpowering vision of the *Mysterium* apparently interfered with the completion of the opera, for there were premonitions in the libretto of elements that were designated for the *Mysterium.* Before he left Russia in the spring of 1904, Scriabin still intended to continue his work on the opera and even set a definite date for its completion in the following year, so that he could embark seriously on the *Mysterium.* But it became clear to me that there would be no opera at all, because the alluring phantom of the *Mysterium* patently displaced it in Scriabin's

mind. My premonitions were justified; after the completion of *Le Poème divin,* Scriabin began work on *Le Poème de
l'extase,* while at the same time continuing to elaborate his
plans for the *Mysterium.* He even ceased mentioning the
opera in his conversations. Its musical material was eventually incorporated into various minor pieces; as for the
libretto, it is preserved only in fragments. Some scattered
verses from it I later recognized in the text Scriabin wrote
for *Le Poème de l'extase.* When I saw Scriabin again in 1907,
in Lausanne, he spoke of the opera as an abandoned project, a preliminary sketch of some value but, on the whole,
immature and not self-sufficient. And yet he felt a certain
tenderness toward fragments from this music; it was the
feeling of a father for his firstborn; besides, he saw in it
the germinal motives of the *Mysterium,* and that alone re-
dounded to its value.

Scriabin read some of the libretto to me; it consisted of set pieces, some lyric monologues, and various
disparate sketches. There were gaps in the text, which
Scriabin filled by verbal comments. I recall how impressed
I was by the directness of purpose and the naive sincerity
of the plot, by the engaging, although somewhat stilted,
style of Scriabin's prose, by its élan, power, and very personal thoughts and moods. But the rhetorical manner, the
cerebral abstraction of the images, the deadening sche-
maticism of the dramatis personae, and the absence of action and dramatic tension, despite abundant melodramatic
disasters—all contributed to an air of confusion.

The best part of the libretto is contained in the
lyric episodes; unfortunately, they are few in number. The

main portion of the text is a versified tract reflecting Scriabin's philosophical, sociological, and artistic notions. Some verses have a pleasing quality, thanks to their verbal sonority, but the prosody is monotonous and dull. Scriabin's unfinished opera seemed to be in the form more of a cantata or oratorio than a music drama.

The hero of the opera, never named, is described as a philosopher, a musician, and a poet. It becomes immediately clear that the hero is Scriabin himself and that the drama on the stage reflects an idealized image of Scriabin's own life and works.

Addressing the cast of characters, the hero apostrophizes:

> When will you, O King, reveal
> The power of your will?
> When will you, O slave, decide
> To break the chains of shame?
> In this life of misery
> Who can have any hope?
> Oh, Paradise is but an empty dream!

The hero then vows to free the people from slavery and distress:

> If only I could give you
> A grain of my blessed self,
> If only a ray of the caressing light
> That inhabits my soul
> Could for a moment illumine
> The sorrowful lives of people
> Devoid of happiness, without a future!

Loved by the King's daughter, he exclaims:

> The victorious beginning of my bold adventure
> Became known to her at last.

She abandons her family and the court of her royal father to follow the hero who preaches the blessedness of a new life. But he is seized by his foes, who represent the dark forces that keep men in spiritual slavery; he is cast into prison. From Scriabin's readings, I recall the scene of the hero's interrogation (that was not preserved in the extant manuscripts). To the questions, "Who are you? What message are you bringing to our people? Where would you lead them? What do you hope to accomplish?" the hero replies with a single word: "Freedom!" This word epitomizes his entire state of being, his readiness to rise even against himself in the name of freedom.

The hero sets himself against the world; he wants to conquer it and force it to serve his purposes:

> By my audacious fight
> I shall possess the world!

The hero is rescued from prison by the people who rebel against the forces of darkness and salute him. In the last act, Scriabin planned to present the apotheosis of the hero, the victory of his mission, and his death on the summit of blessedness, hailed by men to whom he brought salvation.

÷

The inception of Scriabin's opera relates to the years 1900–1901, when his solipsism reached its peak, when the idea that dominated his soul was a Nietzschean will to power, a yearning for an absolute unfettered freedom, a desire to challenge and conquer the world, an assertion of his personal "I." But even in this early period, Scriabin's individualistic concentration did not eliminate conflicting tendencies. Other sentiments and yearnings animated him—a loving tenderness for the world that he dreamed of conquering, an ardent desire to be at one with it, and a hope to unite all mankind in a common bond of blessedness. This spiritual state of mind, which eventually displaced his solipsism, found its reflection, however indistinct, in the finale of the First Symphony and was gradually developed and reinforced in later works. Hence the complexity of the psychological fabric of the opera and its intrinsic duality.

The motive of a single individual challenging the world, the image of a suffering and unrecognized hero, tormented and persecuted by wretched adversaries, is sharply emphasized in the opera. I recall individual scenes built entirely on this antithesis of the hero and the multitudes, crowds that the author mocked and despised, for whom he felt nothing but utter contempt, making no distinction of class or station between the nobility and the plebs. Characteristic of this attitude are the scenes of the ball at the court and the popular rebellion, first directed against the hero and later rallying for his cause and freeing him. The dominant idea of the opera is the superiority of an individual who is spiritually stronger than the nameless masses; its corollary is that the hero has the right to subject the people to his own will. It is not difficult to recognize here the spirit of Nietzsche as revealed in *Also sprach Zara-thustra,* Scriabin's favorite work by Nietzsche. At that time Scriabin regarded Nietzsche as one of the greatest of all thinkers; later, however, when he read Nietzsche's attacks on Wagner, he moderated his enthusiasm. One also finds here echoes of Byronic moods. Yet both Byron and Nietzsche had a compensating element in their writings; purely individualistic moods were interlaced with conflict-ing motives. Scriabin envisioned the hero of his opera as a Superman, but this Superman called mankind to freedom. Moved by his loving concern for the people, he hoped to fire them with the sun of joy and fuse with them in their joyfulness. For this end he was willing to undergo any sac-rifice, any suffering. In this construct, people were not raw material from which the hero could fashion a new world at his command, but his spiritual brothers, called to achieve a universal ecstasy through the power of art:

> By my enchantments of celestial harmony
> I will waft to men caressing dreams,
> By my power of magical love
> I shall make them blossom in the spring!

The hero sought power only for this end. He wanted to possess the world in order to invest it with the joy that overwhelmed him in his solitude. "Take all, I need no recognition!" he exclaimed.

According to Scriabin, the hero's will towered above all else; it was not regulated by anyone or anything. The unification of all men in the spirit of joy was the goal he set for himself. But behind this solipsistic anarchism there was an endless love for humanity. The hero, that is, Scriabin himself, could have no other goal, for it was an imperative demand of his abundant creative spirit.

The ethical element is completely absent in Scriabin's opera. He did not even pose the problem of good and evil. Perhaps this problem simply did not exist for him at the time, although he was confronted with it in the *Acte préalable*. But in his early years he subscribed to the popular Nietzschean notion that good and evil were purely biological categories; in this respect Scriabin was, like Nietzsche, a pragmatist. He did not pursue a moral or religious purpose in his dream of unifying all mankind. The hero of the opera did not regard conciliation or unity as moral ideals; they were superseded by the ideals of blessedness and joy, for only in the unification of mankind, in the universal fusion into a single body and a single spirit, could life reach the ultimate efflorescence. This image of physical and spiritual flowering retained its central position in Scriabin's philosophy for a long time.

Apart from the rejection of conventional morality, Scriabin adopted in his opera an attitude of open and belligerent atheism; later he modified it as he delved more earnestly into the nature of individual existence. His atheistic consciousness may be summarized as follows: There is no God; religion is a sweet deception; there is no other creator than man himself, or rather a Superman, a hero. To a superhuman hero, human multitudes are of no account; at best they are younger brothers whose duty is to respond obediently to the hero's call, to abandon themselves unconditionally to his power and his enchantments.

÷

The hero takes the initiative. The attainment of the ultimate ecstasy is his appointed task. He is the only actor. He
is the sole creator. These dogmas of the hero mark the
profound difference between Scriabin's concepts at the
time of his writing the opera and his later mature realization that although the hero must initiate, encourage, and
stimulate action, the task of salvation and transfiguration
belongs to the people. They must be summoned to action,
to creative work as participants, not as passive workers in
the hero's behalf. In the opera this attitude of the hero
toward the masses, who symbolize respectively the active
and the passive principles, had an erotic character. The
king's daughter, who is the first to respond to the hero's
call, represents the Eternal Feminine; she symbolizes the
masses awaiting the Superman's call and obediently, lovingly accepting his command. The erotic love that springs
forth between the hero and the king's daughter symbolizes
the Superman's love for the world and its responsive, feminine yielding to him. The consummation of this love is a
prototype of the final ecstasy. This symbolic act of love was
later fully expressed in the text of *Le Poème de l'extase* and
in some episodes of the *Mysterium*.

As I have pointed out previously, Scriabin conceived the unification of humanity in a somewhat mechanical manner. He believed that the establishment of political
and social unity was a necessary prelude to realizing a spiritual unification of mankind. Hence his dream of an all-
embracing world kingdom built on socialist foundations

and unified by a single autocratic, spiritual, and political sovereign hero; around him, in a strict hierarchic order, are disposed his collaborators, representatives of the spiritual aristocracy. The hero of Scriabin's opera personifies a social reformer, a socialistic propagandist, and, at the same time, an adherent to a peculiar order of theocracy that worships no God but is headed by a high priest. This vision may have been suggested to Scriabin by Dostoyevsky's Grand Inquisitor. Unfortunately the corresponding scenes are not found among Scriabin's papers. They may have been jotted down on scattered pages and eventually lost.

The idea of the ultimate transfiguration of mankind in death, which dominates the design of the *Mysterium,* is but indistinctly outlined in the opera. Its finale was to conclude with the hero's death after fulfilling his task to sow the seeds of his doctrine among men, uniting them into a physical and spiritual entity and attaining the supreme state of beatitude. Scriabin never completed this finale, but he freely outlined its content to his intimates. The hero finds his death during a great festival, which crowns the attainment of universal unification with the production of a grandiose musical drama created by the hero. He dies in a state of ecstasy, joined in death by the king's daughter and surrounded by jubilant multitudes united in exultation. Thus the hero, who has called upon humanity to achieve a universal ecstasy, which in the physical world would result in the death of all mankind, dies alone. His transfiguration becomes a personal, subjective act. He lives through the blessedness of dissolution, but in the categories of time and space the only external reality is the fact of his death. Men and nature continue to follow their regular course of life, ignoring his dead body. Time no longer exists for the hero and space enfolds him like a scroll, but his end does not bring about the end of the world and its transfiguration. The fulfillment in ecstasy, from which there is no return, is for only the hero and the king's daughter, who symbolizes the world of humanity awaiting the end in languid expectancy. The people around them are mere spectators. Scriabin's individualistic conviction, whereby he accords the state of being only to himself, as an individual particle torn away from the cosmos, and counterposes himself as his own antithesis, is expressed here with ultimate clarity.

By identifying himself with the hero of his opera, Scriabin seriously suggested that he, too, must die with the hero at the climactic moment of the opera, should it ever be produced. This expectation of death applied only to him, to Scriabin, and not to the world at large. Possessed by extreme egocentrism and subjectivism, Scriabin regarded the death of all humanity and the end of the world as of secondary importance to the death and transfiguration of the hero. In the depths of his soul, he apparently believed that with his own death the world, too, would fall and vanish.

÷

Enamored of art, convinced that it possesses an over-
whelming and unique power, Scriabin had not yet endowed
it with that mystical aura that was present during his work
on the *Mysterium*. His opera is permeated with the same
sentiment toward art as the choral finale of the First Symphony; namely, that art is a powerful means of psychological pressure, the strongest stimulus to unify the multitudes in a single experience. But at the time he had not
yet dreamed of art as a phenomenon of cosmic dimensions,
capable of transfixing all nature. The myths of Orpheus
and Amphion had not yet acquired a peculiarly personal
meaning for Scriabin. His opera was still encompassed
within the boundaries of a work of art. It was a reproduction, an image, a representation, a musical drama, the performance of which was to shatter and transfigure the souls
of men and lead them to ecstasy. But in the center stood
the image of the creator himself; the opera served as a
vehicle for his own joy, his own intoxication and transfiguration, his own ecstasy, which was a reality only for
himself, while remaining but a symbol to the rest of
humanity.

Scriabin's opera represents his only attempt to create a
dramatic work, discounting the melodramas he tried to
write in his adolescence. In it Scriabin posited with complete clarity his creative premises as subjective and psychological. He never went beyond the boundaries of his

specific design; he did not attempt to make his characters live, as did Shakespeare, Goethe, Tolstoy, and Flaubert. In Scriabin's opera there is only one person who thinks and acts—Scriabin himself. The hero, the king's daughter, their followers, their adversaries, and the people are but divers aspects of his own personality. The opera is thus a dramatized poem describing Scriabin's inner life; it is reduced to a continuous monologue. But Scriabin failed to delve deeply enough into his own self. He was unaware of the inexhaustible riches and limitless potentialities of his creative spirit. He had not learned to divine the macrocosm through his inner microcosm; he had been unable to ascend to a higher state of being. This is the reason for the meagerness of his characterizations and essential sameness of the dramatis personae of his opera in spite of the external differences of their functions in the plot.

Undoubtedly Scriabin was inspired during the composition of his opera by characters in Wagner's music dramas; he even dreamed of surpassing the master of Bayreuth. He thought that in rejecting history in favor of legend and myth, Wagner and his successors were eventually bound to abandon any historical or legendary references and create an abstract philosophical drama. In this way Scriabin believed it would be possible to attain perfect purity and clarity of artistic images and invest them with universal characteristics free of mundane particularities. But Siegfried lives because Wagner created in him a true image capable of reincarnation, whereas the hero of Scriabin's opera, lacking the requisite legendary and historical prototypes, remains, despite his active masculinity, a stillborn creation. Having failed to attain his objectives in his opera, Scriabin nevertheless continued to pursue his subjective course; any other was closed for him. Where it led him, what he accomplished by it, will be made clear in the discussion of the *Acte préalable*.

The influence of Wagner is evident also in the musical sketches of Scriabin's opera, in which he had intended to build a wide-ranging system of leitmotivs. It is unfortunately impossible to judge the music of Scriabin's opera, which exists only in the form of disparate themes and motives. For some of the dramatic moments Scriabin had already found fitting musical phrases illustrating the action, but he made use of these unorganized materials in other compositions, while indefinitely postponing the completion of the opera. The utilization of these rich materials continued through the years. Thus a phrase that Scriabin jotted down in 1903 as a leitmotiv of the opera found its way into his Sixth Piano Sonata, written in 1911. I recall his playing the scene of the court ball in the opera at its climactic point, when the princess abandons her father and joins the hero. In it Scriabin intended to parody some operas that were to him monsters of banality and spiritual decadence, particularly those of Tchaikovsky, whose music he violently disliked. Some of these parodies, in which commonplace melodies were set in luxuriant harmonies, were quite ingenious, but apparently Scriabin did not write any of them down.

Had Scriabin completed his opera in 1903, we would have had a brilliant, though stylistically eclectic, work—ambiguous in design, containing interesting musical and poetic episodes but lacking any independent significance—at best, a premonition of a future work of real importance.

5

MYSTERIUM

Toward the end of 1902, at the time when Scriabin was engaged in the composition of his opera, a new idea took possession of his mind. He thought of creating a work of truly grandiose dimensions, a *Mysterium*. It was to encompass the vision of an apocalyptic ecstasy and the end of the world. Scriabin firmly believed that the production of this work would actually lead to cosmic collapse and universal death. Obviously this design is a transference to another plane of art, utterly without precedent.

The *Mysterium* was to be the ultimate fulfillment of Scriabin's creative path. But he wanted to prepare the world for it by a preliminary work—a tragedy whose hero brings joy into the world and inflames it with ecstasy. After the production of the tragedy, the *Mysterium* would reveal the ultimate prophesy. Beset by doubts and indecision, Scriabin changed his creative plans many times. But by the

middle of 1904, he became completely absorbed in his
"mysterial" visions.

Preliminary sketches were made during his stay in
Switzerland; afterward he hoped to travel to India, which
exercised tremendous attraction for him. It was there he
hoped to build a great temple for the production of the
Mysterium. He showed little concern about the material side
of the project; he was somehow sure that once he revealed
his plans, offers of financial assistance would follow in
abundance. These illusions were quickly dispelled. Besides,
Scriabin himself was uncertain about the precise nature of
the *Mysterium*. In 1902 he hoped to complete the work in
four or five years; in 1907 he said he needed five or ten
years more. Then he decided to write a preliminary work,
an *Acte préalable,* to prepare both humanity and himself for
the revelation in the *Mysterium*. From the inception of
Scriabin's "mysterial" period, in 1902, to the time of his
death in April 1915, the outline of the *Mysterium* remained
without significant change. Its grand design acquired
greater precision, and its planned realization became more
brilliant and colorful. But all this was already embodied,
as a flower in a seed, in the original idea of the *Mysterium*.
Scriabin added little to it and deleted nothing from it. He
only examined it more closely with an ever-increasing degree of absorption. Unquestionably, he was influenced by
theosophy, but only insofar as the theosophical doctrine
helped him to clarify his own ideas and facilitate the realization of what he regarded as the most important work
in his life.

In analyzing the *Mysterium,* we must consider its

form as it became fixed in Scriabin's conversations with friends during the last three or four years of his life, when he was at the peak of his creative powers. The *Mysterium* assumed its most developed and perfect form in 1913, when he began work on the *Acte préalable;* he transferred the material originally destined for the *Mysterium* to the *Acte préalable,* which was to serve as its close approximation, a simulacrum of the major work. By temporizing, Scriabin regained complete freedom in regard to the *Mysterium;* he was no longer anxious to complete this grandiose project within a stipulated period of time. He was not worried about its patently utopian quality, and he cared little about what others might think of it. In the process, the design of the *Mysterium* was enlarged, purified, and freed of all temporal and spatial restrictions. Scriabin still dreamed of a voyage to India in his quest for occult knowledge; he even made detailed plans for such a journey in the winter of 1914, but the war put an end to them. That the *Mysterium* would someday be completed he never doubted. In the meantime he plunged into work on the *Acte préalable.* During the last period of his life, the image of the *Mysterium* gradually assumed an unreal, phantomlike appearance, even though its outlines were precisely drawn. The *Acte préalable* became a practical version of the *Mysterium,* reduced to terrestrial dimensions and subject to rational planning.

As the *Mysterium* receded into the misty distance of remote temporal and spatial categories untainted by earthly impurities, dwelling entirely on the idealistic plane and absolved of reality, it became a peculiarly powerful vehicle for the ancient dream of a universal reunion of humanity with divinity, whose agent Scriabin believed himself to be.

The title *Mysterium,* which Scriabin selected for his crowning work, came to him at a time when he was not yet a confirmed mystic, when he could speak with irony about proponents of mystical philosophy like Vladimir Soloviev and professed atheism and phenomenalism. His knowledge of ancient mystery plays was practically nil, and he did not augment it until much later. He took no interest in the theater of ancient Greece and still less in medieval mystery plays, so the title *Mysterium* bore no relation to its historical antecedents. He attempted to establish such a connection at a later stage of his creative work, when he was searching for analogies between antiquity and his own aspirations. He joyfully noted down the imagined similarities and gradually became convinced that his work embodied ancient traditions, that by dint of intuitive power he had succeeded in discovering something which eluded even professional historians, and that his discoveries enabled him to transmit the magic message presaged by the participants in ancient mysteries. When Scriabin first conceived the idea of the *Mysterium* in 1902, he was not concerned with historical precedents; he regarded himself as a solitary figure standing outside history, a mystical exception. He relished his exclusivity and solitude and made no attempt to establish

a connection with the past, to find predecessors or precursors. In his imagination the concept of the *Mysterium*
had totally different connotations; it signified to him the
magical nature of an act he intended to perform. This active quality, of which Scriabin was deeply conscious, still
retained its mystery, so that although the *Mysterium* was to
be a magical action, the magus who designed it was unable
to penetrate its mystery. But it was just this mysterious
quality that Scriabin intended to exploit. In Scriabin's
understanding the word *Mysterium* evoked the insuperable
barrier between all works of art and his unique artistic
design.

Scriabin's opera was intended to be a theatrical production
and nothing more. It was to portray a spectacle of ecstasy,
of individual death and spiritual transfiguration. On the
other hand, the *Mysterium* was to be the actual realization
and consummation of this ecstasy, the collapse and transfiguration of the entire cosmos, including all humanity. It
was to be a fulfillment rather than a representation, a universal downfall rather than an individual death. These were
the two principal points of the *Mysterium* on which Scriabin
erected his majestic design. All that was subsequently built
upon this foundation served his determined intent to bring
about the joyful communion of all mankind.

Psychologically these two elements were connected in Scriabin's mind so intimately that they became

inseparable. Because he strove to avoid a mere representation of ecstasy and realize the actual event, he was compelled to aspire to a cosmic, rather than an individual, state of ecstasy. Conversely, a dream of cosmic transfiguration necessitated an actual, rather than a representational, fulfillment.

Striving toward this ultimate ecstasy, after which humanity was to awaken in heaven, so to speak, Scriabin had initially intended to depict the death scene on the stage, as if harboring a secret hope that it would bring about his own death through identification with his hero and transfigure his innermost state of being. But in his continuous speculation on this subject, Scriabin became convinced of the essential identity of his individuality with other individualities. In the depths of his soul, he had a direct knowledge of himself as Alexander Nikolayevich Scriabin, while the individualities of a Peter or an Ivan were but points in the stream of universal activity; for "individual consciousnesses differ from one another only in their content, but as bearers of these contents they are identical." But how could these projections be reconciled with Scriabin's expectation of his exclusive transfiguration, which, in spite of its subjective certainty to him, would have left us, in the framework of time and space, with nothing but a dead body? If Scriabin were really an extreme individualist, as many believed, then he would have found a very simple solution to his problem: Everything is my own creation; time and space are but categories of my activity; other consciousnesses are nothing but creatures of my imagination. It follows, therefore, that the only significant ecstasy is my own, and it must find expression in the collapse of the entire physical world and the abolition of time and space. Until then, Scriabin would speculate, while he was still an individual, he had to discriminate between objective and subjective states of being, a distinction that would disappear at the moment of universal ecstasy. It was on this foundation that Scriabin began to build his opera. But when he conquered his solipsism, he abandoned the opera and began work on the *Mysterium*.

Nursing his desire for ecstasy, Scriabin recognized his essential identity with the rest of humanity and the entire universe in its creative aspect. To him, the dream of universal union was a precognition of mysterious, obscure, and inchoate cravings of all nature for eventual transfiguration. But at the same time he was forced to acknowledge that the realization of his personal ecstasy amid an indifferent world was impossible and self-contradictory. The specific number of people experiencing the sensation of ecstasy was, of course, immaterial. What does it matter if two million people or a thousand million people experience the state of ecstasy, when a single soul remains excluded from universal light? Such a partial consummation cannot be imagined; either all mankind and nature undergo transfiguration, or none do. Scriabin understood very well that the transfiguration of a single individual, or, to use his own terminology, of one of the centers of a universal consciousness, had no validity, for universal consummation must perforce be total. In other words, cosmic ecstasy is not the sum of single ecstasies, but individual ecstasies are manifestations of the cosmic ecstasy. An individual ecstasy is necessarily partial and therefore temporal; it constitutes, so to speak, a temporary suspension of time, a momentary break in the linking chain of multiple states of being. Only universal ecstasy can grant absolute freedom, all the little "I's" transfigured in a single moment in the Unique.

As the concept of a cosmic ecstasy developed in Scriabin's mind, he was bound to realize the inner contradiction of his design for the opera and the falsity in the notion of a theatrical representation of doomsday. As long as Scriabin associated the creative act exclusively with his operatic hero (with whom he secretly hoped to identify himself at the crucial moment), it was possible for him to accept the division inherent in every dramatic play into two groups—actors who represent, perform, and reproduce human feelings on the one hand and those who perceive and contemplate their production on the other. The very concept of an individual and subjective ecstasy not involving the universe in its entirety implies this separation between an acting individual and a great, passively receptive mass of people, that is, actor and spectator. But the idea of a cosmic ecstasy must by necessity exclude the roles of actor and spectator; for it can be realized only as a collective act drawing everyone into its circle without opposing anyone to anyone else. Such a collective act ceases to be a representation or reproduction of an event, but becomes its actual fulfillment. True, such an act may fail. But it also may succeed and must therefore be attempted.

It may appear, at first glance, that there should be no essential difference between a collective act, that is, a cosmic exploit as envisioned by Scriabin, and a staged representation perceived from the outside; for a theatrical element is inherent in any action, no matter how earnestly or sincerely performed. Spectators are not necessarily passive and may actually be absorbed in the dramatic events on stage no less fully than the actors themselves. They thus become participants in theatrical performance. Judged from this standpoint, Scriabin's *Mysterium* appears as a dramatic production whose peculiarity consists in the fact that its participants perform it for their own advantage, thus becoming at the same time actors and spectators of their own production.

Theatrical representations in which spectators are equated with actors are, of course, entirely within the realm of possibility. Some modern theater directors have already experimented with such productions. Indeed, Scriabin's *Mysterium* might well have been reduced to a performance by both actors and spectators. But it should be emphasized that Scriabin's fundamental design had nothing in common with a mundane theatrical reform. For Scriabin the separation between the audience and the stage, between spectator and actor, of which the footlights are a visual symbol, reflected but the external aspect of theatrical performance, an expression on the dramatic plane of everyday experiences. The art of the theater, according to Scriabin, originated in a duality, which he intended to abolish. Here we touch upon one of the basic points of Scriabin's creative philosophy, heretofore ignored in the analysis of his achievements.

Scriabin always felt a deep aversion to the theatrical art as such, to the nature of a dramatic representation in general, rather than to some particular genre. Through the years, this aversion increased to the point of complete intolerance. Everything associated with the theater, the acting profession itself and even the sets, provoked in him a strange and almost incomprehensible hostility. He rarely went to the theater even as a young man, and toward the end of his life he almost ceased to attend any theatrical performances. And yet on those rare occasions when he did go to the theater, he was often carried away by the action on the stage; he was, for instance, profoundly moved by the dramatization of *The Brothers Karamazov* at the Moscow Art Theater, but immediately afterward he tried to fight off his favorable impression. He was himself at a loss to explain this strange idiosyncrasy, except as an instinctive opposition to any type of theatrical action. Only when he became conscious of the mystical connotations of his ideas of life and its theatrical counterpart did he begin to understand the human yearning for acting, which constitutes the vital core of the theater.

Scriabin acknowledged the existence of the theatrical instinct in man no less categorically than the most extreme proponents of the modern "theater for oneself." For Scriabin, as for theatrical reformers, the theater as an edifice, as an entity consisting of stage and hall separated by footlights, was but an expression, in terms of space, of the pristine need of man to find a new incarnation, a need that is fulfilled by the masque. Consequently, to Scriabin the entire art of the theater was reduced to a masquerade. He intended to transcend this masquerade through which humanity seeks to save itself from the spiritual poverty and moral drabness of individual existence.

Humanity is not granted a full, rich, and free state of being. Spiritually we languish in a cramped space, within prison walls, in a servitude imposed on us by some alien power. Hence the yearning for reincarnation—a desire to escape from ourselves and forget our state of being; to save ourselves from our own selfness and transfer ourselves to another plane of existence; to live several successive lives; to enter Peter; then Ivan, and dissolve in them; to drink from all chalices; to reflect ourselves in many mirrors; to overcome the inborn isolation of individual existence by a multiplicity of reincarnations. Yet these are not the proper ways to achieve true enlightenment. It is not vouchsafed to man to transpose himself to another man; we are obliged to be content with an illusion, a simulacrum, of another personality. We perform an act. In a theatrical representation, in a play, an individual can hope to find momentary liberation from his chains, because a masque provides the appearance of a multiform, multivalued, inexhaustibly polymorphous life. In this respect theater is but a surrogate of life. The function of theater is to offer us solace, to provide distraction, to delude us, poor prisoners of life, and intoxicate us with stimulants in order to create an artificial, illusory paradise on earth. Like most mystics, Scriabin postulated the exclusive reality of a different path of life, at the end of which man will enter a universal state of being that leads to a true reincarnation, making it possible for him to discover someone else in himself and himself in someone else. This is a religious path, a way of uniting the small "I" with the Unique. Rejecting the masque and every type of representation and theatrical image, an individual can outlive his selfness in the bosom of Omni-consciousness and obtain absolute freedom and an overabundant richness of existence. For a mystic like Scriabin, the theater (taken in its broadest sense) is basically antireligious and thus sinful. It substitutes a masque of multiple reincarnations for the dwelling in God and thus supports the illusion of life. Scriabin maintained that Christianity was justified in its negative attitude and outright hostility toward the theater and masquerade of all kinds.

In man's passion for the theater, this parody of life, Scriabin saw a symptom of the deepest spiritual degradation, a warning of the advent of the darkest night of history that would be succeeded by a new dawn in which man would become conscious of his divine nature.

The cult of the theater that prevailed in Moscow during Scriabin's last years of life repelled him and made him feel that the downfall of modern society was imminent. Paris on the eve of the outbreak of war in 1914 was equally repugnant to Scriabin for its noisy, luxurious, nervous, and decadent theatrical life. "Our entire society is being converted into a theatrical production," he used to say. "It tries to achieve a semblance of life in its deliberate artificiality. Our own lives begin to acquire a theatrical character because of inner division and outward dispersion. We become stage actors performing for ourselves, possessed by a passion for self-analysis." Scriabin regarded the lack of sincerity as a typical trait of modern man, an actor and spectator at once, who puts on makeup for his own gratification.

Scriabin's appeal to sincerity and simplicity may seem odd in a person who never ceased to analyze himself, constantly probed his own psyche, and urged humanity to join him in a playful game that was to be brought to life and destroyed at the artist's whim. While emphasizing the importance of self-analysis, Scriabin nonetheless saw in it but an intermediary phase, a transition; he deemed it necessary that the world pass through a period of ambivalence in order to achieve a higher state of being. He believed that harmonious integrity of the soul is not necessarily an unconscious state, and that it is entirely possible to attain a perfect unity between action and cognition. The spirit of play he promulgated had nothing in common with representational acting on the stage. The symbol of the theater is the masque, whereby "A" assumes the appearance of "B" while remaining "A." No matter how artistically this switch of personae is effected, acting still remains a masque. "A" does not actually become "B," but merely assumes his appearance, although this impersonation may so fascinate "A" that he temporarily loses consciousness of his real identity and imagines himself to be the one whose makeup he wears. Such a switch of identities often occurs in children's games. But Scriabin's idea of life as a play posited life as its own aim, enacted with absolute freedom. The principal trait of such a play is total sincerity. When Scriabin declared that to him ecstasy was but a play, he did not imply that he was playing a game of ecstasy, mimicking it or wearing its mask, but that his yearning for ecstasy possessed an independent value in actual existence, not as a means or a transition, but as an essential entity.

The role of the *Mysterium* was to overthrow theater,

to destroy theatricality, externally and internally. In his thirst for absolute freedom and eternal life, his yearning to tear down the bonds of his own personality, man could resort to the masque for solace, but in the *Mysterium* he was to place himself in the bosom of the Unique and by so doing become universal.

To a man divided within himself, wrestling with himself, deprived of immediacy and pristine innocence by an intensified self-consciousness, the *Mysterium* promised to restore the integrity of self-unity. For man had once possessed innocence, sincerity, and integrity, but he became blind. As soon as he developed consciousness of himself, he lost his inner unity. The task of the *Mysterium* was to recreate this unity in the light of consciousness, so that man could acquire wisdom and knowledge of himself and yet preserve his innocence. He would then be clarified to himself, while retaining his sincerity and integrity.

In his search for lost innocence Scriabin found precursors in remote antiquity. He hoped that the *Mysterium* would revive the forgotten achievements of the ancient mystagogues. But in the ancient mysteries, particularly the Eleusinian, to which Scriabin often reverted in his conversations, there already existed an element of play, of representation; they already carried the taint of decadence. They had lost their religious and liturgical character and were rapidly approaching the theatrical genre. This trend did not, however, completely deprive the Greek theater of the character of a mystery play. It is present in the works of Aeschylus, whose *Prometheus* Scriabin greatly prized. An absolute hegemony of theatricality succeeded the classical Greek period. Not until the emergence of medieval mystery plays was there a return to the religious origins of the theater. But in our time the masque became the predominant theatrical form. With it the art of the theater reached its lowest point.

Before embarking on an analysis of the *Mysterium* from the standpoint of form and content, before defining its meaning and purpose, we must trace the general schematic outline of Scriabin's ideology, the fundamental principle of which is contained in his doctrine of the *Mysterium*.

Throughout his philosophically conscious period of life Scriabin was an actualist. Only action was ontologically valid in his view; substance, whether material or spiritual, lacked the attribute of being. If the individual psyche was an active agent of creation, so was the universe itself. The world, and man in it, constituted a stream of active phenomena. This curious dynamism which derived from Scriabin's acute awareness of his own creative powers, stood in opposition to theosophy. As a highly complex and somewhat eclectic doctrine, theosophy also contains motives of action. Yet the basic text of theosophy, *The Secret Doctrine* of Mme. Blavatsky, preaches substantialism. Following his customary procedure of attributing his own ideas to his favorite authors, Scriabin sought to discover in Mme. Blavatsky's writings an emphasis on actualism and the negation of substantialism. When I tried to refute this contention with direct quotations from Mme. Blavatsky's text, Scriabin parried my arguments with the clever assertion that Mme. Blavatsky used the terminology of substantialism only as a concession to the traditional mode of reasoning, that each action can be traced to some definite agency that in turn describes all action as an attribute of substance.

What is the ultimate goal of this stream of actions? What is the purpose of cosmic acts? What is the meaning of the universe and individual existence? There is no aim and no meaning in the universe, Scriabin averred. There is no predestined path for the stream of world action. I recall Scriabin's delight when he came upon Mme. Blavatsky's declaration that "the universe is the sport of Brahma," his triumphant expression as he read this sentence to me as proof of the intuitive genius of the founder of the theosophical doctrine!

The tenet that the state of being has no purpose, but carries meaning and significance in itself, as its own reason and vindication, was basic to Scriabin's philosophy. As time went by, this set of beliefs underwent certain modifications, partly under the influence of theosophy and, more important, because of his growing understanding of his own vital task. Acknowledging the existence of a "sporting" element in life and accepting the world as a product of divine play, as a self-validated act, he conceded that individual lives are meaningful. The purpose of their existence resides outside them; they are assigned to perform certain missions, the fulfillment of which would justify their existence.

Continuing along similar lines of reasoning, Scriabin asserted that individual nations and certain historic periods are also assigned definite missions and that the course of human life presupposes a predictable terminal point, the end of mankind on earth. Carrying this idea to its logical conclusion, Scriabin reasoned that the universe as a whole must also possess a certain purpose, expressed in the spirit of play, whereby the universe becomes its own goal.

In his opera, as we have seen, Scriabin viewed the world as a realm of caprice and free fantasy. He postulated that each individual must create his own aim and follow his natural inclinations. The hero alone introduces into these variegated and discordant phenomena some sort of order and regularity, subordinating all separate efforts and yearnings to a single common purpose, and thus imparting a certain meaning to history. But what particular meaning? Any meaning that the hero may wish to impose. But while Scriabin-as-hero intended to lead the world to unity and ecstasy, he did not exclude an alternative solution that could reveal a totally different design.

This chain of thought and feeling is reflected in *Le Poème de l'extase,* which is, however, interlinked with new ideas. The state of ecstasy no longer represents Scriabin's exclusive personal aspiration, with humanity forced by the magic of his art to embrace his ideal and share his yearnings. This goal is no longer imposed from without, no longer transcendental to humanity, but immanent in it. Scriabin's role thus becomes important only because he was the first to formulate this grand design, and had therefore been chosen to bring it into being. This schema was the foundation of Scriabin's philosophy of history and cosmogony; theosophical doctrines added concrete terminology and factual material, but the premises of Scriabin's thinking were formulated long before his acquaintance with Mme. Blavatsky's books.

In postulating a pure actuality of existence, free of subjective references, possessing no definite goal, and autonomous in its nature, Scriabin asserted a unity of being that absorbed all possible multiplicities of all possible individuals. Scriabin remained faithful to this credo throughout his life, but this doctrine, like that of the inherent validity of existence, underwent considerable modification during its development.

Scriabin's opera combined elements of monism with individualistic pluralism in a somewhat curious manner. He was an atheist when he was working on the opera and conceded creative powers only to man, refusing to admit any superior imperative or moral norm. A state of being had no substance in his belief; it was empty, although created spontaneously and blossoming forth in all possible colors and images. The problem of reality was no longer of any consequence to Scriabin. The unity of beings was not an inner unity to him, or a unity of substance traditionally contrasted with the phenomena of external multiple events. Nor was it a unity of origin; Scriabin yearned for the ideal future, which he eagerly awaited and whose advent he strove to expedite. He had no interest in the mystery of cosmic beginnings. The past was to him an immediate presence in the multiplicity of individuals to be united in a monistic entity.

What was the state of the world in the beginning? Scriabin wrote:

It is useless to ask how the world began. The nature
of time allows me to deduce from each given moment
an infinite past and an infinite future. . . . What I desire, I desire here and now, but I need to posit the
entire history of humanity to make this moment a
reality. I create the past, and I create the future, by my
whim, by my fugitive desire. Everything is but my desire and my dream. Everything is my creation.

He wrote elsewhere:

I need you, O dark depths of the past. For my infinite
exaltation I need an infinite development, an infinite
growth of the past. To achieve a state of bliss I need a
world that would languish in pain. I had to pass
through an infinitude of centuries in order to awaken
to my present state. I had to undergo brutality and
savagery in order to achieve the refinement of today. I
need strife in the past.

It follows that Scriabin deduced the past from the
present. The past was determined by the present and specifically by his own desires. The past of the world up to
that moment was what it was, and nothing else, because
of Scriabin's yearning for oneness. The world was built
according to the laws of time and space, ineluctably following Scriabin's expectations as it culminated in a cosmic
ecstasy. Scriabin conceived his dream first and adapted history to it afterward; he wrote down the sum and then
inscribed its addends.

It was at this time that Scriabin attempted to outline a scheme of cosmogony, once more following a tripar-

tite dialectical formula: chaos and void; definite state of being; chaos. This formula cannot be verified as to its correctness or falseness. It does not pretend to express a given reality. Scriabin was interested only in creating a certain dialectical symmetry and eliminating inner contradictions.

Prior to 1903, Scriabin posited the unity of existence as the aim of a creative effort, as an ideal he freely chose and, in his view, could realize. As he expressed it, the state of being is both nothing and potentially everything. Unification is the consummation of the vital process willed by the hero. With the passing of years, this expectation shifted from the transcendental category to the immanent presence; he began to think of himself as a missionary called upon to bring about the ultimate unity. But if unity, so ardently desired by the world, was immanent, then it must have been already inherent in it, concealed in it, or lost in some remote antiquity. During this period of philosophical transition, Scriabin wrote the text to *Le Poème de l'extase,* which was preceded by relevant entries in his diary. His thoughts and feelings as reflected in these writings are ambiguous. What is the spirit to whose self-illumination this text is devoted? Is it an individual spirit deified by the consciousness of its absolute freedom? Is it a cosmic spirit that attains self-knowledge through its own creatures or in one of its acts? When I posed this question to Scriabin, he was apparently at a loss for a definite answer, hesitating between two conflicting interpretations. Scriabin's text to *Le Poème de l'extase* and the diary entries, however, generally refer to a unified spirit, to a deity in the farthest recesses of the individual soul, the creation of God by man, but not of man by God. What attributes did Scriabin attach to God at that time? God is absolutely free, having achieved the identification of his "I" with his "non-I":

> By identifying "I" with "non-I," I annex "non-I." From this point on, the consciousnesses of all men are dissolved in my individual consciousness. I become for them the fulfillment of all their yearnings; the world becomes a unified action, an ecstasy. All men become identical with my individuality and my activity, so that they can perceive only my action and can experience only my consciousness. All men must have faith in me as in God and recognize my identity with themselves in order to obtain their peace and their death in God. I desire the flowering of mankind, and mankind must have a reciprocal desire. Everything in the world is the result of mankind's creative activity, because everything is my creation. Mankind, that is, I, is the Deity. Strife and death will be vanquished, and universal joy without measure will spring forth in a triumphant torrent of life.

In these declarations, as in *Le Poème de l'extase* itself, we find the ideal of inner unity; for all must coalesce with all, achieving oneness, because all is one by its very nature: "Therefore, everything, the entire visible world, is a creative act, which is my creative act, the only one, the result of my untrammeled volition."

How are we to interpret these utterances—"my creative act," "my untrammeled volition," and so forth? We already know the nature of "I" whose creation is the world itself—it is the superpersonal "I" that an individual must discover in himself. In harmony with these declarations, Scriabin wrote:

> From the standpoint of creative power, the world must be explained as it is, namely, as the projection of my will. Let us examine the nature of the creative effort. The world is pluralistic. Why? The answer is this: If there existed but a single entity, then nothing would exist. The act of creation is an act of discrimination. To create something is to delimit something by something else. It is possible to create only a multiplicity. Space and time are categories of creation; sensations are its content.

The following declaration is even more explicit:

> I desire to create. By this desire I produce a multiplicity, comprising a multiplicity in a multiplicity, and a singularity in a multiplicity: "non-I" and "I." "Non-I" is necessary so that "I" can create within "I." "I" and "non-I" are aspects of action. This does not mean that these aspects take precedence over action itself; for action, like everything in the world, is a unique, free creativity.

Gradually this early individualistic and atheistic formula—whereby the world achieves oneness through the heroic Superman, who ordains his own oneness by free will and builds the history of the world and mankind around himself—evolved into the final postulate: the world is unique in its origin, unique in its nature, but it recognizes its uniqueness only when it ends.

Here Scriabin once again constructed a tripartite scheme of life, cosmos, and man, but now he filled it with a different meaning. In his earlier speculations, he consciously recreated the past from his will to achieve final oneness; now, however, he regarded his desire as the result of centuries of creativity, the efflorescence of nature seeking its lost, pristine innocence.

These schemes were outlined by Scriabin long before his acquaintance with theosophy. He had not yet heard of either the doctrine of Mme. Blavatsky or Indian lore that she related so profusely. It is doubtful whether he could have benefited from such treatises as *Les Religions de l'Inde,* by Auguste Barth, or *The Light of Asia,* by Sir Edwin Arnold. But after reading *The Secret Doctrine* of Mme. Blavatsky, he had little to change in his cosmological formulas, besides introducing terms such as Manvantara, Pralaya, and so on.

In one respect, however, Scriabin yielded to theosophy. According to his early tenets, the cosmic process had but a single cycle to run; having proceeded from nothingness, that is, from total equality and blessedness, it was to return forever to this nothingness, this blessedness. But theosophy postulates a multiplicity of cosmic cycles in time and space. The "sporting" of Brahma knows no end; a Manvantara follows a Manvantara, a Pralaya follows a Pralaya in the infinity of time. Having accepted this doctrine, Scriabin had to abandon his idea of a final and absolute ecstasy, the uniqueness of his mission, and the act with which he was to crown the life of the universe. He was compelled to be content with a "private ecstasy," as he expressed it, after which, following a Pralaya, there would come another Manvantara culminating in yet another ecstasy, ad infinitum. However, in his conversations he often reverted to his initial faith in the exclusivity, uniqueness, and irreproducibility of cosmic ecstasy without the recurrent cycle, so that Brahma would eventually have eternal repose. In several other respects, Scriabin also remained true to his original beliefs, refusing to abandon old positions that were irreconcilable with the theosophic doctrine. As usual, he tried to smooth down this contradiction by liberally interpreting theosophic texts to suit his purpose.

Probably under the influence of Schopenhauer's *Die Welt als Wille und Vorstellung,* the first philosophical book that Scriabin ever read, he admitted of no state of being except subjective consciousness. "Esse est percipi," Berkeley said, and Scriabin liked to repeat this aphorism. He wrote in his journal:

> Actuality is a sphere of our sensations, of our emotions and of our consciousness. . . . This is the only proposition which may be regarded as infallible. In other words, actuality is perceived by us immediately only in the sphere of our sensations and our psychic states. . . . The saying that we perceive everything through the prism of our consciousness is false, for nothing exists and nothing can exist outside subjective consciousness.

Scriabin returned to this idea constantly in his conversations and writings. Human history is the evolution of consciousness. But whose consciousness? In Scriabin's solipsistic phase, it was his own consciousness that, gradually developing, created the present and, by the same token, posited the past and the future. Later he ascribed this creative attribute to Omni-consciousness, divine consciousness, and finally to God, who achieves self-cognition in his sons. To Scriabin, consciousness was never a spiritual substance; he defined it as an active principle, an action and nothing else. Consciousness per se was a nullity; universal consciousness was oneness, a cohesion of coexistent processes, a system of relationships. Each member of this system, each state of being, negates all other consciousnesses and at the same time affirms them through their mutual relationship. Outside these states, outside a system, consciousness is impossible. All phenomena take place within consciousness, although it is not a separate entity independent of these phenomena. When they are removed from consciousness, nothing is left except their formal connections, which are abstract. But this abstract scheme has the attribute of reality in the life of phenomena; it is exhaustively represented at every moment by a given phenomenon. This latter negates all other phenomena and by so doing posits them. Scriabin defined consciousness as a state of being that possesses reality only in relation to other states of being, not in itself. A state of being can be absolute only in its oneness, but it does not acquire the attribute of being unless (or until) it experiences a moment of ecstasy in which the whole world recognizes its oneness, that is, at its moment of self-cognition, of Omniconsciousness.

Self-cognition is a creative process that reveals itself only in its creations. Each moment generates a subsequent moment; the act of creation is the totality of these moments. Similarly, an individual consciousness, which is a nullity in itself, cannot be conceived outside coexistent processes. Scriabin equated creativity with consciousness. The state of consciousness is an act of creation and vice versa:

> To create is to discriminate. All states of consciousness are connected by this act of discrimination. . . . To experience a certain state of consciousness is to separate it from other states of consciousness, only in relation to which it can exist.

In the final analysis Scriabin reduced the creative act to a process of attentive perception, which selects certain entities and summons them to life by affirming one element and negating another. An individuality builds its life by the concentration of attention. This process is analogous to the condensation of stellar material born from primordial, inchoate nebulas. A further condensation leads to the formation of stars and fixes them in the firmament.

Scriabin frequently reverted to the notions of consciousness and creativity, in different guises, stressing a negation of the old and a yearning for a new and different state of being. But he had to admit that these fundamental concepts were indefinable, that they could only be suggested or alluded to, and only illuminated obliquely, by way of comparisons and analogies. Scriabin wrote:

> It is impossible to describe a creative act by words alone. All that exists is my creation. But it exists only in its creatures, with which it is identical. . . . Abstract

concepts, such as existence, essence, etc., fail by far to express the meaning of world reality.

The obvious subjectivity of these announcements gives a clue to Scriabin's method and reveals the sources of his theories. This method was self-analysis and introspection, and the source was his own psyche. Scriabin was well aware of his subjectivity but regarded it as the only possible and correct procedure. "Man can explain the universe by studying himself alone," he used to say. He wrote in one of his journals: "To analyze actuality one must study the nature of my active consciousness and of my free creativity."

Scriabin sought to justify his theories by arguing that the evolution of the universe is coextensive with the evolution of consciousness, and that there can be no state of being other than consciousness. He established these propositions introspectively, but he did not select his methods a priori. Rather, he chose them because he found the macrocosm in the microcosm and realized that the truth could be revealed only in subjective psychological terms. Particularly interesting in this respect are his writings, mostly of a lyrical nature, in which the cosmic and subjective elements are so closely intermingled as to become inseparable. This merging of elements was not rhetoric, but a sincere and immediate expression of his innermost thoughts. The text of *Le Poème de l'extase* is deeply imbued with these sentiments.

Anyone who received Scriabin's confidences regarding his subjective experiences, anyone who read his psychological writings, must have realized that for him there was no separation of the two spheres of being. They both were unified in the psychic world. The following fragments relating to the character of Omni-consciousness are germane:

> When I have no desire, I am nothing; but when I experience a desire, I become the substance of my own yearning. This individual longing gives rise to all other yearnings, because it can exist only in relation to my other desires. . . . Different states of consciousness co-exist. My consciousness can exist only in relation to other consciousnesses, not only with actually existing consciousnesses, but with all potential consciousnesses that are present in each psyche as a possibility, as an unconscious process taking place beyond the horizon of consciousness. In this sense, each person contains the entire universe as a process lying outside his consciousness.

Here Scriabin probes individual psychology. However, all that he has to say about the psyche is a variant of his propositions relating to the cosmic consciousness. Scriabin's conditions for psychic experience must be interpreted on the individual and cosmic planes simultaneously:

1. Separateness from all others.
2. Connection with all others.
3. Individualism (multiplicity).
4. Divinity (oneness).

Only under these conditions can an individual consciousness assert itself, for one can be conscious only of something that is sui generis, something that is different

from other entities and at the same time connected with
them because of this difference. These entities are thus
both mutually exclusive to and identical with it. These
conditions retain their validity also in regard to cosmic
consciousness, for they must satisfy the prerequisites of all
parts of cosmic consciousness, that is, all states of being.
   Scriabin's cosmogonic and anthropogenetic formulas, which he elaborated by analysis of his creative
products, are similar in nature. He introduced new details
into these analyses, but the fundamental scheme remained
unaltered. He described these dialectical constructions as
"rhythmic figures." He wrote this outline:

> Period preceding the awakening of consciousness. Pe-
> riod of conscious life. Period of postconsciousness,
> which coalesces with the period before the awakening
> of consciousness. . . . The following is the first rhyth-
> mic figure: unconscious state; consciousness (sensation
> of life); unconscious state.

   This scheme later assumed the following extended
formulation:

0.   Nothingness—Beatitude.
1.   I desire (before Chaos).
2.   I begin to discriminate vaguely.
3.   I discern. I begin to distribute elements (time and
     space) and foresee the future of the universe.
4.   I ascend to the summit and experience oneness.
0.   Beatitude—Nothingness.

   The original state of being lies outside time, because time must evolve from it. Scriabin variously defined

this pristine state as chaos, nothingness, inchoateness, blessedness, unconsciousness, oneness, and God. Later, after he made his acquaintance with theosophy, he called it Pralaya. He equated all these terms, while emphasizing that this equation was to be understood as an approximation, an inadequate description of the state of being before the world began (if the expression *state of being* can be used at all with reference to a time before time began). He compared this period with sleep, unperturbed repose, when all is silent for a brief moment after strenuous activity. During the last years of his life, Scriabin resorted to this terminology less frequently. He preferred to speak of oneness, God, "I." How did he define these concepts? In his philosophy oneness could exist only in multiplicity, as the unity of an aggregate, the law of a system. Scriabin similarly equated "I" with only his individual experience, yearnings, and creativity. Consciousness, on the other hand, was to him the accumulation of coexistent states of mind, with God existing only in his creatures. To queries on these subjects, Scriabin replied as follows: One must distinguish the oneness correlated to multiplicity from the absolute oneness, which includes both oneness and multiplicity in mutual coordination. From the unrevealed God one must distinguish the God revealed in divinely created beings as correlated to God during the process of creation. One must distinguish the absolute "I" from the correlated "I" and "You" included in the absolute "I." The state of being in a Pralaya is a unity of oneness and multiplicity—that is, a God in whom the creator and his creatures are inseparably present, a large "I" that in a Manvantara will divide into "I" and "You."

One naturally thinks of Nicholas of Cusa and his doctrine of the absolute as a union of contradictions, and of his modern disciples, particularly the Russian philosopher Simeon Frank. But what little Scriabin knew about Nicholas of Cusa must have come from reading Fouillée's *Histoire de la philosophie*. As for Simeon Frank, his most important work, *The Object of Knowledge,* was not published until after Scriabin's death. Scriabin's view of the absolute as distinguished from unity correlated to multiplicity evolved quite independently of these sources, exclusively from subjective motivation.

Entering this field of speculation, Scriabin had to renounce his original assertion that a state of being can exist only in a consciousness; he also abandoned his phenomenalism, though reluctant to admit it even to himself, and he desperately tried to reconcile irreconcilables. Ostensibly he still adhered to the principle "Esse est percipi" long after having forsaken both phenomenalism and relativism. He did not enter this new path under the compulsion of logical arguments. It was not as a result of his introspective probings that he finally had to concede the possibility of a state of being outside consciousness, that is, of an absolute being; rather his thinking was conditioned by his steadily growing apperception of divinity within himself, increasing faith in God, a loving, filial attitude toward the Deity, and consciousness of a mission entrusted to him by some superior power. Such sentiments were completely at odds with Scriabin's early philosophy, in which all states of being were reduced to their relationship to other states of being. The divergence continued for a number of years, until Scriabin, intolerant of disharmony, finally realized that it was impossible to formulate a vast religiophilosophical system on the foundation of phenom-enalism and relativism. It was then that he began to add building stones to this foundation. These new elements, however, did not alter the essential character and general spirit of Scriabin's concept of states of being, the objective of which remained the achievement of blissful ecstasy in the ultimate union of all in all. In this state of pre-temporal, absolute oneness immanent in itself, the palpi-tating will to life and a dream of creative activity arose in Scriabin's soul:

> I do not know yet what I ought to create or how to create it, but my desire to create is in itself an act of creation. A creative impulse disrupts divine harmony and gives rise to matter on which the divine thought is to be imprinted.

Scriabin's cosmogony embodied a gradually inten-sified differentiation in cosmic evolution. Absolute oneness disintegrates, giving birth to multiplicity, and together they form a correlative oneness—a reflection in multiplic-ity of the original absolute oneness. The Deity sacrificially disappears in its own creatures, but its image is preserved in them as the formal principle of this multiplicity. Scriabin here introduced into his system a new element—Deity as an absolute, autonomous state of being revealing itself in the cosmos. Yet he continued to insist that in the process of evolution and gradual differentiation there can be no other state of being than mutually related multiplicities, the product of the final disintegration of the Deity. In

Manvantara the Deity continues to exist only in its creatures and cannot rise above the process of cosmic evolution; at the same time it cannot become its substratum or substance. The life of the cosmos is a creative act, which in turn consists of a series of new creative acts. Each reflects in its structure the original act of creation and recapitulates the act and its rhythm in a steadily growing process of differentiation that refracts and divides the creative impulse.

We have established that creation is an act of differentiating and delimiting constituent elements. Creation necessarily posits multiplicity. "One can create only a multiplicity," Scriabin declared. "If something were unique, it would be a nullity."

Each successive act of creation increases multiplicity. The first creative act in time, or rather the first act that gave rise to time and was repeated in all subsequent acts, represents the self-differentiation of the Unique—the self-contemplation precipitating its disintegration and the rise of the duality of spirit and matter, "I" and "You," Eternal Masculine and Eternal Feminine. Members of each of these basic pairs, progenitors of all others, are correlated; thus a single act of creation summons to the state of being the categories of both "I" and "non-I," spirit and matter, the active and passive principles. Scriabin wrote: " 'Non-I' complements 'I' to equal zero." The same equation can be applied to spirit and matter, to the masculine and feminine principles; when paired and added together, they equal zero, which is absolute oneness according to Scriabin's terminology. Although mutually exclusive, they set in motion, when combined, the evolution of the universe and of man

in it. Duality is pristine multiplicity. Three pairs of its
premises reflect the triune nature of the original duality;
they illuminate a typical creative act from three points of
view, thus positing the entire evolution of the state of
being, the overcoming of resistance, as self-enlightenment,
as love.

What is matter? It is the limit set by the spirit determined
to conquer it, surpass it, and impress itself on it, thus momentarily restoring the equilibrium between them, de-
scending, in the process, to a lower grade. The balance is
then disturbed by a new impulse, until the entire resource
of power is exhausted in the activity of Manvantara. Scriabin declared: "The world is given birth by resistance ordained by me. Life is the overcoming of this resistance."

From Scriabin's point of view, the process of evolution is the history of the impregnation of matter with
spirit, which is also the immersion of spirit in matter, leading to constantly increasing interpenetration. Scriabin,
however, did not grant priority or superiority to spirit;
spirit sets matter as its own limit, as a resistance to itself,
exhausting itself in the process. This self-exhaustion is its
purpose and allows spirit and matter to be correlated on
equal terms. Matter does not exist outside the spirit. Conversely, the spirit cannot exist without matter capable of
receiving it. Both spirit and matter are intimately rooted
in the Unique, as common products of its fission and rev-

elation. At first this dichotomy of spirit and matter appears indistinct, but it becomes more and more pronounced in the process of evolution, reaching, at a certain moment, a maximum of tension. This moment of the greatest antagonism between spirit and matter as fundamental principles is at the same time the moment of their most intimate fusion in the concrete phenomena of life.

The act of self-limitation is also an act of self-enlightenment, that is, of consciousness of oneself. Just as the Unique, sacrificially limiting itself, is differentiated into spirit and matter, so a creative act, in the process of self-cognition, is divided into "I" and "non-I." Further creative acts are further disintegrations of this "non-I," each of which posits an "I." Scriabin wrote:

> To create is to separate, to desire something new, something different. In order to create, it is necessary to postulate a source, a multiplicity, a "non-I," and also an entity that is being separated, an individuality, an "I." Let us suppose that "non-I" is, at a certain moment, an element designated by a. The next act of creation would consist in the differentiation in that a of x and y or else in the negation of a and in the generation of b as an opposite of a.

From this standpoint the evolution of the world is the history of the Unique's self-cognition. The nascent palpitation of life, the yearning for creativity within the Unique, is a thirst for cognition.

The act of self-limitation and self-cognition is at the same time an act of love, an erotic act. The primary polarity of spirit and matter is the polarity of the masculine, impregnating principle and the feminine, receiving principle. This erotic aspect of the cosmic evolution dominated Scriabin in his last years of life, and his understanding of the nature of eroticism underwent considerable changes then. It was highly sensual during his work on *Le Poème de l'extase;* the sexual aspect was foremost in his creative imagination. Scriabin's words, "I want to take the world as one takes a woman," were not mere poetic metaphor. This sensuality, despite its refinement, sophistication, and even spirituality, was totally devoid of any moral element and completely alien to spiritual love, in which physical fusion is only a means to an end, a pathway to love. In his imagination, the cosmic finale assumed the dimensions of a grandiose sexual act. Trying to explain the nature of ecstasy to himself and others, Scriabin invariably resorted to erotic analogies and similes. Even the design of the temple in which the *Mysterium* was to be enacted was an intricate network of sexual symbols. The erotic aspect of Scriabin's philosophy was the only subject that he was reluctant to discuss, despite his candor in conversations with friends, fearing, not without reason, that his ideas would be distorted, demeaned, and debased. But the sexual element was never absent from Scriabin's creative speculations. He saw in the sexual act the physical prototype of ecstasy. His eroticism was imbued with sexuality without absorbing external elements; it seemed to probe deeper into itself, so that sexual gratification gradually assumed the character of altruistic love. A creator, Scriabin reasoned, does not limit himself to sensual delights in the act of creation; he also loves his creatures. He not only enjoys taking possession of another life, as one picks a flower, but, overflowing with abundance, he enjoys giving life to his creations, impregnating them with the joy of being. This sentiment is reciprocal; it invites a feeling of love on the part of one's creations for the one who bestowed the gift of life upon them. Considered from this point of view, the history of the world is the history of God's love for his creatures and of their responsive, joyful love for their creator. The self-sacrifice of the Unique is a creative act and also an act of love; it posits the beginning of time and sets in motion the process of the world's evolution through continued self-sacrifice—an uninterrupted creation of the new at the price of the death of the old, which at the same time evokes a reciprocal yearning of the created for its creator, a loving gratitude for him and a longing to return to his bosom. God is love, Scriabin proclaimed. This sounds like a Christian profession of faith, but for Scriabin this love contained an erotic and sensual element incompatible with Christianity. In his cosmogony the creator remained, at all stages of the evolutionary process, the Eternal Masculine and his creatures the Eternal Feminine.

A gradual increase of multiplicity, the world's retreat from the Unique, and the materialization of the spirit in concrete phenomena—all make up the scheme of world evolution. But evolution implies the potentiality of a reverse process. A centripetal movement is ineluctably followed by a centrifugal movement; the world must eventually undergo the process of involution, resulting in demateriization, depersonification, and a concomitant decrease in polarity. For Scriabin, who always looked forward, who was engrossed in visions of the future, cosmic history was the history of the end of the world. This end was both the goal and the motive force of his thought. He wrote:

> The first stage of cognition is the first step on my road back. My voyage of search and return marks the beginning of the history of human consciousness, of cognition, of its creativity and of mine.

The drama of world evolution fascinated Scriabin because it was bound to end soon, and because its first act contained its epilogue *in spe*. Scriabin's interpretation of involution as the opposite of evolution was affected by his study of theosophy. The very notion of return was a rather late accession to Scriabin's philosophical vocabulary; for if there were no common origin, no Father, there could be no return to Father. Before his acquaintance with theosophy, he never used the term *involution* and was familiar only with the popular notion of evolution. In his constructs evolution lasted for ages, but ceased in a moment. Soon, however, Scriabin began to see more clearly the difficulties lying ahead in the realization of the *Mysterium* and decided to shorten the preliminary period. "We have already entered the process of inner unification of all mankind," he said. "We have already gone over the summit; we have already passed the moment of the highest tension, signalizing the first vision of ecstasy, and we now find ourselves in the period of concentration and fusion which must be culminated in death."

When Scriabin made his first acquaintance with theosophy, and specifically with the doctrine of involution, he was prepared to accept it. He even extended the doctrine of involution to cover a process that retraces the evolutionary stages in reverse order, possessing an attribute analogous to gradual unfolding. The universe, he contended, describes in its evolution a parabolic or hyperbolic curve similar to the orbits of comets in their course toward the sun. They move from the darkness of the void toward warmth and light, to the sun of life, and back into eternity. But here Scriabin met with insuperable difficulties. According to theosophical doctrine, we are now situated near the middle of the path, on the mounting branch of the curve. Ours is the fifth race; it is to be followed by the sixth and the seventh, which is the last. The end is still distant, so we can only dream of a return. Obviously Scriabin could not accept this position; he was determined to precipitate the return. He was willing to wait a few years, but not thousands upon thousands of centuries, as prescribed by Manvantara. On the other hand, he was reluctant to reject the attractive theosophic concept of cycles and races, congenial with his philosophy in many other respects. He recognized that the descent of the spirit into matter must perforce result in dematerialization as a protracted, historic, and objective process, which cannot be compressed into an instantaneous psychological outburst.

Unable to resolve this difficulty, he was forced to obviate it, as he had with the problem of the multiplicity of Manvantaras and the recurrent ecstasies inherent in them. Ostensibly he accepted the theosophic doctrine, which promised ecstasy only for our time; thus the *Mysterium* would conclude not an entire Manvantara, but only the cycle of the fifth race. There could be no return of a multiplicity of states of being to the bosom of the Unique, no universal death, but only the death and enlightenment of our race and of the new race of children of the Unique. In the depths of his soul, however, Scriabin continued to believe that he would somehow expedite this process, that he would preside at the conclusion of the entire Manvantara, and that the sixth and the seventh races could be speeded up and culminate with the production of the *Mysterium*. Scriabin therefore developed a theory postulating the possibility and even the inevitability of a tremendous acceleration of the involutionary process in its last stages. Involution would traverse the same path as evolution, but at an infinitely faster pace—not because it would consume less time, but because time itself would contract. The evolutionary process of differentiation distends time, whereas involution pulls time together, folds it in, and causes it to vanish completely at the moment of ecstasy. It is, therefore, possible to live a million years in one second; whole periods of history can occur instantaneously, like a flash of lightning, setting off a cosmic whirlwind in a wild dance. All this was, of course, nothing but a fantasy; Scriabin's theories would probably have assumed a more organized form had he lived longer. In his last years he was obsessed by the thought of precipitating world processes in the only domain in which they are operative, that is, in the consciousness of man.

÷

To what extent was this intricate and vast concept Scriabin's own, and to what extent was it derived from other sources? As we know, his main influence was theosophy and some Oriental, especially Indian, doctrines. We must therefore determine which part of Scriabin's scheme came from theosophy, particularly the writings of Mme. Blavatsky, which are intimately related to Hindu cosmogony. The fundamental theosophical doctrine concerns the Manvantaras and Pralayas and postulates the plurality of world periods, each corresponding to a single breath of Brahma, followed by his repose in sleep and succeeded by a new breath. Scriabin began to use the name *Brahma* in place of *the Unique* only after he became acquainted with theosophy. But he independently developed the doctrine of the Unique as an absolute state of being that is identical in our consciousness with nonbeing and comprises, in a latent state, the correlated concepts of unity and multiplicity. The concept of the disappearance of the Unique in its own creatures during their creative periods was also original.

A related theosophical doctrine posits the Seven Planes of being, the Seven Races, the septuple nature of the individual soul, and, ultimately, metempsychosis. Scriabin accepted the latter doctrine, which plays an important role in Oriental religions and philosophical systems, without reservation. But he never attempted to develop it fully, perhaps because he was indifferent to the ethical problems inherent in the doctrine of reincarnation.

He only became interested in the ethical implications a few years before his death. Through theosophy Scriabin absorbed the occult doctrines, which greatly extended the boundaries of his world in time and space; occultism also enabled him to discover the infinite perspectives reckoned in millions of years before historical time.

Above and beyond the world circumscribed by our senses Scriabin postulated another world, much more complex, vast, and rich; this world became for Scriabin as real and immediate as the visible world is to us. Did Scriabin actually perceive other planes of existence by direct experience or intuition? He spoke at times of his visions on the mental plane of the astral region, but his references were desultory and confused. The astral world was not his domain.

Scriabin found vindication for his own mission in the lives of consecrated votaries, missionaries of superior powers sent to earth to reveal the secret truth in its various aspects for the benefit of humanity. He regarded himself as a member of this select fraternity of messengers of the Unique and as a custodian and restorer of ancient wisdom. During the last years of his life he even thought of assuming a formal title in that fraternity, known in mystical lore as the "White Lodge," in whose existence he earnestly believed and which, he was sure, secretly awaited his coming.

Scriabin mainly made use of these disparate elements to elaborate, systematize, and organize according to an already fixed design his eschatological doctrine. It concerned the end of the world as a communal act bound to bring about the fusion of spirit with matter and their extinction in the bosom of the Unique. This act was to be an act of man—the *Mysterium*.

What was the purpose of the *Mysterium?* It was to experience ecstasy in human consciousness and death in time and space. Ecstasy and death were for Scriabin the two aspects, internal and external, of Manvantara, the return of mankind and nature to God, followed by the absorption of time and space in the Deity.

Man possesses a natural yearning for the abolition of all boundaries confining him to relativistic, individual existence. This yearning is the determining attribute of man and of all living creatures. As soon as an individual consciousness realizes that it is limited, imperfect, and isolated, it ardently desires to transcend the boundaries of a conditional, relativistic state of being and violate the restricting laws of a segregated existence, that it may attain absolute freedom and become integrated with All. This freedom can be interpreted in various ways. It may be regarded as a return to God, to primordial chaos, or as deification of the individual, the reassertion of one's "I" as a unique value, the only reality that absorbs all other states of being. These yearnings and their accompanying visions are but the expression and interpretation of our eternal and tormenting thirst for a full, unbounded life, a sign of our liberation from the shackles of a limited state of being. The moments of liberation, necessarily transitory and fleeting in terrestrial existence, the moments when our chains are broken and our souls set free, constitute, in the broadest sense of the word, an ecstasy. The tortuous quest for this ecstasy is conditioned by the acute sense of our limitations, imperfection, and inadequacy.

The character of ecstatic consciousness differs according to how we regard this liberation, how we intend to achieve it, and to what causes we ascribe it. Its character depends also on the intensity of our yearning for a reunion with God, a life in God, absorption and dissolution in an impersonal and formless state of being, immersion into nothingness, into death. Ecstasy has different connotations for a bacchanalian, for Plotinus, for St. Teresa, and for a contemplative Hindu. Its aspects are diversified in individual religious convictions and beliefs. But its essence, a unique blessedness of liberation, a triumphant assertion of boundless freedom, perfection, and inexhaustible plenitude of being, remains unchanged.

We do not sufficiently appreciate the magnitude of the effort needed to maintain our individualities in a well-ordered and equilibrated state. Because this psychological tension, this strenuous effort to preserve self-control, is never absent from our minds, it forms a constant background to our spiritual lives. We become aware of it only at moments when it is sharply increased or in those rare instances when we succeed in freeing ourselves from it completely. The psyche is much too complex, much too unstable a system to maintain equilibrium without a constant effort. Our senses, thoughts, desires, and ideas are engaged in a constant inner struggle. We constitute a synthesis, albeit an imperfect one, which is constantly disrupted and instantly restored. Only a vigilant self-control saves our psyches from total disruption. Sensations, emotions, and desires strive to invade the entire disequilibrated sphere of our individuality, to seize full command in order to accomplish their particular aims. It is imperative, therefore, to preserve a mutual interdependence in the hierarchy of our psychic elements; for if it fails, the individual is threatened by madness and, ultimately, physical death. It is essential to subordinate our individualities to certain norms, to arrange compromises in this curious inner struggle, so that order can be established in our psyches. Whether this ordering is the result of many centuries of external pressures, which conditioned our consciousnesses from generation to generation, or whether it is dictated by inner impulses does not concern us here. For Scriabin himself there could be no questioning the origin of this ordering; to him it was axiomatic that man is ordered exclusively by forces operating within himself. But we must accept the fact that the psyche has been organized in an orderly manner, that its activity is now controlled by certain obligatory norms. And yet these redeeming norms, which necessarily correct our imperfections and inadequacies, torture the psyche, for they restrict the extent of its action, which essentially and potentially is boundless.

What is the nature of orgiastic ecstasy? It is the destruction of all barriers, boundaries, and norms. The path of Dionysus leads to liberation through ecstasy. And yet we can live only by prescribed norms; even the soul is a norm, albeit an imperfect one. The gift of Dionysus, orgiastic ecstasy, thus leads to the destruction of the psyche, liberty in chaos. The soul is darkened and torn asunder by the Dionysiac excitation of all the senses, by the intensification of conflicting drives. Seized by a whirlwind dance, the psyche is hurled into chaos; its unity is destroyed, its boundaries demolished, and its norms abolished. But this chaos also brings great joy, a joy of liberation from the dark prison of our beings, a joy of salvation and freedom from the agonies of disjointed existence. There are no more limitations, whether internal or external; there are no longer any boundaries, any obstacles. All becomes possible. This Dionysian ecstasy, this blessedness of disintegration, represents the rebellion of the psyche's irrational forces against consciousness, the victory of amorphous chaos over the organizing, defining, and analyzing individual will. The darkening of the consciousness is a prerequisite for this ecstasy, which signalizes a return to primordial unity, formlessness, and heterogeneity. Intoxication with wine offers us but a degraded simulacrum of ecstasy.

Christian mystics reject the return to primeval chaos but speak of a loving reunion with the Deity. The mystical lore of ecstasy is diversified and enriched by colorful nuances. Some pantheistically inclined mystics describe ecstasy in terms differing little from those of the Dionysian ritual. Their mysticism and the cult of Dionysus, seemingly so different from each other, possess striking similarities. Both speak of the disintegration of the individual. For the followers of Dionysus, it is brought about by a sudden shock and a tremendous intensification of the vital tonus, sometimes aided by artificial means; for mystics the same result is attained by a simple life and mortification of the flesh, sometimes entailing physiological measures, such as fasting. But their goal is the same: dissolution in the fires of chaos or a return to the bosom of the omniperfect Father. Some mystics rebel against the idea of the individual soul's total destruction and teach eternal life in Christ, in which ecstasy becomes a delirious enlightenment of the soul, its communion with God, its return to the Unique, and its dwelling in God forever. Absolute freedom and a state of blessedness are then achieved through the inner identification of one's personal will with divinity. The Christian interpretation of ecstasy is diametrically opposed to the Dionysian. The former's protagonist is St. Paul, unless we interpret his teachings from a pantheistic point of view. Scriabin's doctrine of ecstasy combines elements of both Christian and mystic teachings, forming a rather curious synthesis whereby the state of blessedness is included in dissolution and personal will is identified with the divine command. Ecstasy, which is the crucial point of Scriabin's eschatology, inspired almost all his major works—*Le Poème divin, Le Poème de l'extase, Prométhée,* and the *Acte préalable*—expressive of that final moment of blessed liberation inherent in the Dionysian cults. But there is a cardinal difference between the freedom demanded by Scriabin and the orgiastic freedom. The Dionysian concept is purely negative; the element of salvation in it coincides with that of disintegration. Scriabin's ecstasy, however, is a positive phenomenon somewhat akin to the mystique of St. Paul; the freedom it bestows entails no element of destruction in the rebirth of the soul. The soul disappears in ecstasy, but is resurrected, while the fiery baptism of ecstasy mortifies the flesh and transfigures it in a spiritual enlightenment. The negation here is of a creative nature. But Scriabin does not halt at this point; he draws further conclusions from the negation of all individuality, its final disappearance in the bosom of the Unique, and its fusion with it. Scriabin's concept is pantheistic; in his philosophy, the human psyche lacks the attribute of eternal life. But whereas the Dionysian path leads its votaries to an immediate enlightenment through the death of individuality, Scriabin attains the same goal by a circuitous route, by efflorescence, the enlightenment of the individual psyche, and its confirmation in God as the necessary prelude to a death in God.

This concept, which may appear strange at first glance, was conditioned by Scriabin's direct intuition of the deepest essence of the individual state of being. Even during his most individualistic period, Scriabin posited the liberation of individuality in the abolition of all norms, demolition of all boundaries, overcoming of all limitations, and destruction of all obstacles. Ecstasy was for him an act of individual self-assertion; it comes to pass in a realm where individuality reigns supreme. Rather than accept liberation through dissolution in chaos or fusion with the Deity, Scriabin proclaimed the deification of individuality, which legislates for itself, limits itself by sportive play, and builds and destroys its own norms, obeying only the momentary whims that dictate its sovereign laws. But even in this simplified form, predicated on the desire to impart a cosmic character to his "I" and endow it with the attribute of absolute being, one can already find a valuable idea that caused Scriabin to regard individuality as an autonomous, self-limiting, self-defining entity. Still later Scriabin was moved to broaden this concept and impart to it a religious character.

Driven by Eros, we rush toward ecstasy; our psyches thirst for liberation from restricting norms. These norms are the chains they seek to break; hence the rebellion against all bonds and obstacles, which are imposed on our psyches from without. They are conscious of their own heteronomy, cognizant of their own form being determined by an alien power, whose purpose they cannot understand but whose action they experience by direct contact. If such bonds are obstacles, if laws are chains, then existence is not autonomous, but is willed by a force from without. This is the existence of a slave; the only possible escape from it is self-annihilation, for the norms that restrict an individuality cannot be destroyed without causing the psyche itself to disintegrate.

Orgiastic cults are fundamentally pessimistic, predicated on the propositions that humanity is doomed to suffering and horror and that a curse hangs over the individual state of being, whose essence is a forcible restriction, the elimination of which destroys individual consciousness. The moment of blessedness is therefore also a moment of dissolution. This pessimistic philosophy, nurtured by an acute consciousness of the sinfulness of individual existence, was entirely alien to Scriabin. Life was to him a state of continuous joy. But how can there be joy if human individuality is heteronomous? On the other hand, the concept of an entirely autonomous creative individuality willfully setting up obstacles to itself, shackling itself in order to be forced to tear off its chains, substitutes anarchy for liberty and destroys all forms, all definition of individuality, which then crumbles into dust.

To Scriabin, however, the essence of the individual state of being consisted not in the limitations imposed on the psyche from without, but in self-limitation, in which liberty is equated to autonomy. He therefore sought liberation not in the destruction of all norms and abolition of all limits, but in the overcoming of their alien, forcible character and in a joyful acquiescence to these limitations set by a freely posited will—not necessarily one's personal will, but one inherent in the sacrificial character of separate existence. The psyche experiences its freedom in ecstasy as a precognition of its autonomy, without destroying its defining forms, but affirming them as its own creation, even though this creation is not willed autonomously. The latter point marks a recession from Scriabin's extreme individualism and solipsism. In the light of these ideas, ecstasy appears as the restoration of the true meaning of individual existence, a renascence of an individuality that has gained cognition of the freedom hidden behind a consciously willed norm.

If the individual state of being is autonomous, if it is not restrained by alien forces but is limited by an act of will, if imperfection, imprecision, and isolation connote self-abdication, then individual existence must be an act of self-immolation and individuality itself the result of a freely offered sacrifice. But how can an individual account for a natural limitation as an act of will? Only by the intuitive perception of the Unique, whose law is autonomous, by identification of oneself with the Unique; that is, by ecstasy. It is in ecstasy that an individual gains insight into its divine nature and perceives himself in the aspect of divinity, that is, in the aspect of freedom.

From the standpoint of ordinary consciousness, which predicates its "I" by opposing it to "non-I" and recognizes the state of being only by the existence of its external boundaries, even divinely illuminated ecstasy would signalize the death of an individual, since it would expose the illusory nature of forcible limitations. But if we admit that the individual state of being is an act of self-abdication on the part of divinity, then it becomes clear that by performing an act of will, the individual obeys the will of the Father, that the final ecstasy signalizes not the death of the individual, not the destruction of the individual state of being, but its enlightenment. This enlightenment leads to the generation of a new race of freely submissive children of the Unique, consciously dwelling in its bosom, fused with it and separated from it, voluntarily subdividing themselves to carry out the mission of the Unique, which becomes both the gift and the giver.

Here we seem to perceive Christian submission, "Thy will be done." But this devotional sentiment is intermingled with conflicting feelings. Scriabin did not take it from Christianity; it arose when he realized that he had a mission to perform on earth. His conception of the world and of man was far removed from Christian dogma; it actually was nearer to the Hindu understanding of the outside world. "Life in God" was for Scriabin but a transitional formula, a penultimate rather than ultimate stage of cosmic history. He believed that man is consubstantial with God, that man was created out of God's substance, and that God's substance was dissolved in its descent into the material body. The birth of the world and the birth of man were processes taking place within God, as acts of divine resignation and the consequent death of the Deity. For a Christian such a construct is blasphemous, for Christianity proclaims divine creation out of the void. But it comes very close to Hindu cosmogony, in which we are given a choice between God and man and his world. The Unique exists only in the Pralaya; it disappears in the Manvantara, in which only God's children survive. History begins with the death of God and the birth of man and concludes with the death of man and the resurrection of the Unique, whose sacrificial body undergoes restoration in the Pralaya, an act hidden from our perception. The apotheosis of cosmic history consists in the total absorption of the individuality in the Unique. If in the beginning there was self-limitation of man and self-multiplication of the Unique, then at the end there must be the reacquisition of oneness or, in other words, resurrection. It is, therefore, possible to assert that, after the enlightenment of the individual psyche in ecstasy, all children of the Unique must be reunited in it and thus lose their selfness. Clearly, there can be no temporal succession of events in the state of ecstasy. There can be no sequence of cause and effect; their relationship cannot lie in the temporal category. We can speak here only of a logical sequence. An act of ecstasy is autonomous; in it the psyche recognizes the Unique and becomes consubstantial with it. Ecstasy thus constitutes a free and voluntary transubstantiation. But it is impossible to accomplish, Scriabin maintained, as long as the human psyche is shackled by alien norms; it can come to pass only when the individual self acquires the consciousness of its divinity and sacrificial nature. Only in a state of ecstasy can the children of God find one another, return to the bosom of the Father, and regain peace.

This act of free and conscious return to the bosom of the Father was, in Scriabin's view, an expression of filial devotion and parental revelation, involving a reciprocal sacrifice. As the Deity disintegrates into multiplicity and endows that multiplicity with life, thus dooming itself to death in its hypostasis of the Unique, so mankind, having recognized God's image, yearns to reach God, thirsts for God's resurrection, and, by so doing, dooms itself to death in its hypostasis of multiplicity.

We must distinguish this mutual love of God and man from the mutual attraction between spirit and matter, between the Eternal Masculine and the Eternal Feminine. The entire history of the world is epitomized by this mutual attraction and interpenetration. Both the world and man are products of this love, partaking of both principles. Nature is the union of these principles as well; for without their mutual interpenetration and ensuing conflict there can be no concrete existence. The Unique possesses no inborn polarity. Conflicts arise only at the time of its sacrificial disintegration. At first this inner polarity is weak and uncertain; then it grows and develops, reaching its highest tension at the point of the closest encounter, its most intimate fusion of the two basic principles, in the emergence of man. With the dematerialization of the spirit, this tension subsides, decreasing proportionately to the increase of distances between the two poles. At the end of the process of involution, the conflict becomes less pronounced and, at the moment of ecstasy, vanishes completely.

In man's love for God, in his yearning for a reunion with his spiritual brothers, and in his expectation of the resurrection of the Father, there is nothing specifically feminine or masculine. Man's nature is "actipassive," "femimasculine." Man appears, therefore, in the image of God, as its simulacrum; his reflection mirrors God's oneness, which, however, is cleft. The oneness of man is a tense combination of two polar principles, which are fused in absolute oneness only in God. In this sense man is the entity both closest to and most distant from God.

Man's love of God, like God's love of man (in this scheme man is a substitute for the universe), is completely devoid of all sexuality. This is not a love of two opposite entities yearning for a union; on the contrary, their union sharpens their polarity. This is not a yearning to replenish oneself, which inevitably entails an element of slavish submission. This is a love freely given, enhancing itself and generating reciprocal love. But its nonsexual character does not exclude eroticism; it is not less erotic than a passionate mutual attraction between the active masculine and passive feminine principles.

At this point Scriabin seems to be completely free from the obsessive notion of sexual polarity, with its sensual and egocentric need of replenishment. He approaches the Christian ideal of altruistic love, which is devoid of egotistic connotations. But even when he had already passed through what could be called his Hindu period, Scriabin was still far from the spirit of Christianity. His filial love for the Father retained an element he called "caress," infused with sensuality, which found its expression in the concept of the *Mysterium*.

The state of ecstasy appears to us as an instant, a point, a flash of lightning, immediately followed by a darkness hurling us back into the realm of necessity and subjecting us again to the torments inflicted from without. The actual duration of a state of ecstasy is immaterial. Whether it lasts only a second or thousands of years, it must inevitably be followed by a return to the ordinary condition of life. But Scriabin denied the necessity, or even the possibility, of such a return, arguing that the state of ecstasy is the goal and end of the entire historical and cosmic process, which is bound to bring about a total metamorphosis of the world and of man in it. The universe must either remain unchanged or be transformed forever, without a return to its erstwhile slavish condition, because time itself will be swallowed at that last moment, carrying down with it space and multiplicity, which are its attributes. The following notation in one of Scriabin's journals, dated about 1906, before he became infatuated with theosophy, is indicative of his train of thought:

> Absolute being, as opposed to absolute nonbeing, is being in All, and as such it is realized at a moment that must illumine the past; it will recreate the past at the moment of fulfillment of divine creativity, at the moment of ecstasy. Time and space and all that they contain will be consumed at that supreme moment of great efflorescence and divine synthesis. . . . The state of absolute being is an all-embracing divine creation, which marks, in terms of time and space, the ultimate boundary, the final moment that radiates eternity. Cosmic history is the awakening of consciousness, its gradual illumination, its continuous evolution. All moments of time and all points of space will acquire their truthful definition, their true meaning, at the moment of universal fulfillment. We can assess the value of a work of art only when it has been completed; similarly we can define the categories of time and space only when they have been consummated. A moment of ecstasy will cease to be a moment in time, for it will compress time into itself. This moment represents a state of absolute being.

In accordance with these idealistic speculations, Scriabin regarded the ultimate cataclysm, bound to supervene at the moment of ecstasy, as the expression, on the physical plane, of a spiritual upheaval. Ecstasy leads to the cessation of time and space, the transfiguration of flesh in the universal conflagration is its direct consequence. Later Scriabin saw the end of the spatial-temporal world and the advent of the universal cataclysm, culminating in ecstasy, as the natural conclusion of the cosmic process. Man's recognition that his sacrificial nature partakes of divinity, his dissolution in the Unique, and the consequent extinction of all multiplicity, of time and space, which are submerged in the Unique, result from the dematerialization of the spirit, the diminution of polarity and the return into Nothingness, which is All. But this consummation, which according to the theosophic doctrine takes many millions of years and passes through a long series of intermediate stages, was to Scriabin an imminent event. Rushing in like an avalanche, it would take place within his lifetime. Scriabin was not content with the vision of an individual ecstasy. Individuals can be leaders, inspirers and instigators, centers of excitation, but not even the greatest geniuses can achieve ecstasy in isolation. On the other hand, the multitudes are, in Scriabin's words, "protuberances of the consciousness of a genius, his mirrorlike reflections." A genius "contains all possible gradations of the senses of separate individuals and consequently engulfs the consciousness of all his fellow men."

Earlier in his philosophical development, Scriabin believed that the world had no grand design, that ecstasy was his own prerogative, that the decision to confer the blessed gift of ecstasy on humankind and decree the end of world history were matters of his personal choice. Gradually, however, he came to regard ecstasy as a perfectly natural phenomenon, which obeyed the laws of a cyclic Manvantara, determined by the preceding history of the cosmos. The advent of the Manvantara could either be precipitated or delayed by man, but it had to take place sooner or later, when humanity was fired with a yearning for fulfillment. Such a view of the final cataclysm is very much in the spirit of theosophy and Hinduism. But Scriabin gave it a new interpretation, restoring to man his sovereign power; in his scheme, the end of the world cycle is ordained by man, who becomes both priest and sacrificial offering at that supreme moment. Man is free to sacrifice himself, for when man exists, nothing else exists; only man can transform multiplicity into oneness. Through his own death, man resurrects God. This liturgical act lies at the foundation of Scriabin's *Mysterium*.

By what means did Scriabin expect to achieve this end? The answer is: through art. Scriabin's *Mysterium* must therefore be an artistic event. Ordinarily, art is supposed to have definite connotations and perform a specific function. But the *Mysterium* transcends the limits of ordinary art and becomes a religious as well as an artistic act. Scriabin refused to separate art from religion; in his view religion is immanent to art, which itself becomes a religious phenomenon. Scriabin's case is unique in that he, an artist of genius, was determined to transcend his art, to cease to be an artist, to become a prophet, a votary, a predicant. Yet such appellations would have been unacceptable to Scriabin, for he refused to admit that his design reached beyond art, that he violated the frontiers of art and thus ceased to be an artist. On the contrary, he argued that the commonly accepted view of art was too narrow, its true meaning lost, and its significance obscured. It was his destiny to restore art to its original role; consequently he was much more an artist than any other, because to him art was the religion of which he was the sacristan.

Far from claiming to be the originator of this concept, Scriabin insisted that he was merely reviving a lost tradition. A reference to a "religio-artistic work" was to him a tautology. Art is either religious or nonexistent, he argued, for its subject, beauty, is an imprint of spirit upon matter, which is a definitely religious concept.

The religious nature of art was to Scriabin the source of its active power. Art is either active or Orphic. An artist is an Orpheus unconscious of his strength, unaware of his power over men and nature, both animate and inanimate, over the vast world of spirits, superior and inferior, dark and luminous. The myth of Orpheus was Scriabin's favorite legend; to him it represented the vestigial remembrance of a historic man who once wielded great power, the true nature and significance of which has been lost. But man's incomprehension of the magical power of Orpheus's art could not destroy this magic; its memory may be alive only in fairytales, but its power is real and continues to influence the life of the world. An artist is therefore an unconscious magus. Scriabin believed that he was the first to rescue this magic from the long night of oblivion and restore its power. But he welcomed reminders that others before him knew of this power, and he was eager to find Orphic traditions in the history of man. He was elated when Viacheslav Ivanov told him that Novalis, in his novel *Heinrich von Ofterdingen,* portrays a hero who achieves the enlightenment of the physical world through the magical power of his art. He was also greatly impressed by the findings of the French music historian Jules Combarieu, who sought the origin of music in ancient magical incantations; this supporting view of a scholar who never entertained any mystical notions was for Scriabin a significant confirmation of his own beliefs. Whatever the value of these speculations, Scriabin was the first creative artist to develop the magical principle of art into a systematic doctrine and use it as an aesthetic foundation for his own compositions. It was to him not a speculative hypothesis, a superstructure on his artistic activity—its appendix, as it were—but an integral part of his work, an earnest endeavor to rationalize his intuitive previsions. Indeed, he regarded himself as an Orpheus, wielding power through his art over both the psychic and physical worlds. It was thanks to this self-identification with Orpheus that Scriabin was able to form the idea of the *Mysterium.* The power of an artist, Scriabin was convinced, would be all the more effective in the hands of one who consciously strove toward an all-important spiritual goal. Art is Orphic in its vital principle; not only music, but painting, sculpture, architecture, poetry, and dance possess the Orphic power of enchantment. But how is it manifested? How can a sonata, a picture, a poem be realistically effective? To answer these questions, I must engage in some observations of a polemical nature.

The only detailed account of Scriabin's doctrine of the magical power of art is found in Leonid Sabaneyev's book on Scriabin (Moscow, 1916). But his account is in my opinion misleading, and my own memory of Scriabin's views contradicts Sabaneyev on every point. Unfortunately, Scriabin left nothing in writing concerning his ideas on the subject. He barely touched on it in his diaries. In the last years of his life, Scriabin was fully absorbed in his work on the text of the *Acte préalable* and rarely committed his thoughts to paper. The reminiscences of his intimates are therefore the only source of available information. But our conversations were free exchanges of opinion. Far from postulating his ideas in an explicit form, Scriabin let his mind wander. Dialogue and debate stimulated his thinking and to some extent directed its course. Scriabin never concluded his sentences with a period, so to speak. A theory expressed in definitive terms on one day could be followed by a question mark on the next, debated anew, and assume an unexpected or novel formulation, gradually deepening and broadening in response to searching questions.

Scriabin's theory of the magical power of art may well have existed as Sabaneyev recounts it. Scriabin often indulged in speculations along such lines, but he certainly would have modified his conclusions as soon as he realized their logical flaws. In the light of Scriabin's constant revisions of his theories, these flaws would have eventually become evident to him. According to Sabaneyev, Scriabin's theory of the Orphic character of art is as follows:

> Art is a sorcerer, possessing a magical power over the human mind, acting by means of a mysterious, incantatory, rhythmic force manifested in it and transmitted directly from the substance of the creator's will. This rhythmic force enhances immeasurably the magical power of art. Just as regular beats, however weak, can set in motion a huge bell; just as the periodic vibrations of a sounding body are capable of destroying solid objects by a steadily increasing amplitude, so psychic vibrations, set in motion by an interplay of sounds, lights, and other sensory impressions, can be reinforced so enormously as to precipitate a veritable psychic storm. The power of art is immense in this respect. The impact of art on the psyche may be of a purely aesthetic nature, but it may be powerful enough to induce a catharsis, inner illumination, and purification; in its most extreme manifestations it will generate a state of artistic ecstasy. Just as there are two types of magic, white and black, so the magic power of art may be psychically benign or malignant. If it results in an inner illumination, the effect of such an art becomes theurgic. Once we accept the principle of effective action on the psychic plane, each performance of a work of art becomes an act of magic, a sacrament. Both the creator of a work of art and its performer become magicians, or votaries, who stir psychological storms and cast spells upon the souls of men. Such a theurgic art, leading toward a catharsis and an ecstasy, may become either a liturgical act or an act of Satanism, according to the direction taken by its effective action.

Thus, according to Sabaneyev, the magic power of art is limited to the psychic world and has no effect upon the realm of matter. But then it becomes incomprehensible by what means Scriabin expected to influence the material world. Can it be that he attributed to art only a psychological power, to the exclusion of all cosmic effect? But if so, why was he fascinated by the myth of Orpheus, who enchanted trees and stones by his playing? It is quite true, as Sabaneyev reminds us, that rhythmic vibrations can destroy solid objects by dint of continuous increase in amplitude. But the analogy does not hold true for art. Does art produce an impression by the sheer intensity of sounds employed by the composer? Or does music affect material objects by psychic means alone? And if so, then by what particular means? In Sabaneyev's account, Scriabin's theory applies only to music. Nothing is said about other arts. Are they deprived of power? And if so, what remains of Scriabin's dream of a synthesis of all arts? These problems require a thorough analysis.

The fundamental flaw of Sabaneyev's report is that it fails to examine the aesthetic ingredients of a work of art, apparently relegating the concept of the beautiful to a subsidiary position, neutral in its magical essence and thus ineffectual. But this attitude radically contradicts Scriabin's basic philosophical premises. He might have voiced such ideas upon occasion, but he would never have made use of them with reference to the *Mysterium*. It is incongruous to contrapose the aesthetic effect of art to its catharsis, which produces the sense of "illumination and purification," because an aesthetic sensation implies, by definition, a process of illumination and purification. The magic power of art cannot be alternately benign and malignant; a corollary would posit the existence of an art aesthetically valuable but noxious, unhealthy, and immoral—a contingency inconceivable to Scriabin. Sabaneyev himself quotes a verse from the choral finale of Scriabin's First Symphony: "O wondrous image of divinity, O pure art of harmony!" An image of divinity cannot exercise a negative influence on the world. There is no room for the forces of darkness where divinity presides. This should be clear to anyone who knows what an exceptionally exalted place Scriabin assigned to art in both his life and his philosophy, how dedicated he was to art and how firmly he believed in its saving grace. It is therefore impossible to imagine that Scriabin could describe any art as an act of satanism, for in Scriabin's belief a work of art is inherently incapable of serving the forces of darkness. An artist cannot be a malevolent magus as long as he acts as an artist, embodying a divine image. If we are to accept Sabaneyev's interpretation of Orphism, then we must believe that to Scriabin, great artist as he was, art possesses no specificity and is totally absorbed by magic. If so, then there would be no difference between a sonata and a magical incantation; Scriabin's Ninth Piano Sonata would be an aesthetic equivalent of some repulsive and abhorrent conjuration by means of which a satanist cult summons its master. The Ninth Piano Sonata is a great work of art infused with beauty, and yet, according to Sabaneyev's account of Scriabin's doctrine, its aesthetic value has no bearing on the nature and direction of its magic power, which must be negative despite the inherent beauty of the work itself. But if so, then why did Scriabin only respond to those magic incantations and sacraments that possess an aesthetic value, that contain an element of beauty? Can it be that they were simply more pleasing to him? This supposition leads to absurdities and contradictions. Sabaneyev could, of course, have cited Scriabin's own words and diverted our criticism to him. But the point is that Scriabin could never have expressed himself in the terms imputed to him by Sabaneyev. I am willing to concede that Scriabin might have uttered such ideas spontaneously, but upon consideration, he was bound to reject them and evolve a different theory, one that analyzed and clarified his inner experience and was organically connected with his personal views, designs, and aspirations. I shall attempt to expound Scriabin's theory as it crystallized in the light of my own discussions with him.

Any influence exercised by a work of art must be of a material nature. A work of art, specifically a musical work, produces an impact on matter, altering it in a certain way. This impact is physical, but in Scriabin's idealization it extended to all states of being, including the astral and mental. Although the nature of this impact has not been thoroughly evaluated and its manifestations may not be immediately evident, they are present in the artist's creative design. One must always bear in mind that the material element of artistic impact is combined with other impressions. A system of sounds in any musical composition affects the entire world of matter and alters it in various ways. Strictly speaking, any object, even if it is totally devoid of aesthetic value, exerts some influence on its milieu. The very emergence of such an object disrupts, to a certain extent, the equilibrium existing before its appearance and must therefore create a new interrelationship among other objects. And since even the most minute part of the world system is intimately connected with all other parts, it may be said that the building of the pyramids in Egypt or the sailing of a boat from Europe to America alters the entire equilibrium of the universe. From this standpoint there is no difference, in principle, between Scriabin's Third Symphony and some grandiose engineering project, such as the construction of the Panama Canal. Naturally one thinks of the physical identity of air waves in music and explosions. Destructive results of explosive air waves are in evidence all around us, but it is at least conceivable that their energy can be directed, organized, and systematized for constructive projects as well. We must not conclude that constructive use would require an amplification of vibrations and the employment of sounds of maximum intensity. The same result can be achieved not only by a quantitative increase in the power of sound waves, but by a greater intricacy of sound combinations. One can conjure up a vision of the reconstitution of dead flesh and reorganization of matter effected by an especially complicated system of sound waves. There is no doubt that if we could make visible all vibrations of the air mass produced in the vicinity of a sound source—as a result, say, of a performance of Scriabin's *Prométhée*—we would find that all objects, including our own bodies, vibrate in such complex rhythms as to induce the disintegration and transformation of matter. This physical impact does not depend on the will of a creative artist. He may not even be aware that it is possible; and yet the sounding body created by his work does alter, to a certain extent, the surrounding medium. According to Scriabin, this sounding body influences not only the physical environment, but also the astral and mental planes of being, thus acting invisibly upon invisible objects, producing perturbations of matter in all its states. But, Scriabin insists, similar perturbations are produced not only by works of art but by the intrusion of any object into the world.

There are, however, substantial variations in the nature and direction of these effects. A work of art, as an aesthetically valuable object, has a reforming and positive character; it is constructive, unifying, and formative. A medium subjected to its action becomes organized; a certain harmonious order is established in it. The strength, depth, and duration of this effect can vary, but its direction remains constant. An artist possesses a powerful tool; its application can only be beneficent, sometimes contrary to the intentions of the creator himself. The beauty of an object of art becomes, so to speak, a guarantee of its positive influence on the material world in all its aspects.

What has been said about music is also applicable to dance, poetry, painting, and architecture. But it is only through the art of dance (taking this term in its broadest sense) that the human body becomes a completely unified, harmonious entity. In everyday life our bodies, affected by external circumstances and internal necessities and desires, are deprived of unity, which is fully attainable only in plas-

tic, aesthetically pleasing motions. Dance affects first of all
the body of the dancer himself, and not only his physical
body, which is directly visible and perceivable, but also his
invisible bodies—astral and mental—and through them
alters the material medium, imbuing it with a harmonizing
motion. It further affects the bodies of the spectators, who
inwardly follow his rhythmical movements. Dance, therefore, may be described as the highest type of organization of living matter. Latent in its rhythm are grandiose
and heretofore unexplored potentialities, which Scriabin
hoped to bring to life in his *Mysterium.* Of course, not
all forms of dance possess this organizing and exalting virtue. There are dances—particularly those of primitive
tribes—that produce a deleterious effect on living matter,
disrupting whatever degree of unity and harmony already
achieved and injecting the spirit of disorder and turmoil
into the human body. Their destructive effect is analogous
to that exerted on organized matter by air waves that are
mutually out of phase. Such primitive dances are devoid
of aesthetic value, which is the prime requirement for a
positive influence on matter, and consequently must be
placed outside the artistic category.

In static forms even inert matter can attain great
beauty, as, for instance, in a perfect architectural structure.
A living body receives this organization in motion, in action regulated by rhythm, that is, in dance. Its harmony is
dynamic. But inert matter reflects only static harmony, a
harmony of position like that created by architects. In music and dance the impact of art is not limited to the sounding medium or to a human body in rhythmic motion; similarly, a master builder, by distributing masses of stone in

predetermined proportions, subordinates to the laws of harmony not only the stone itself but also the boundless material universe around it, altering it in the direction of greater organization. Thus every work of art becomes a powerful source of motive forces whose organizing action invades all states of being.

Apart from its impact on matter, art acts powerfully on the mental world. The notion of art's power over matter may appear odd, even absurd; but no one will deny that musicians, poets, and painters exercise a peculiar power over the souls of men. All artists, and particularly musicians, have known moments when an intimate sympathy arises between listeners or spectators and themselves. The artist's commands, sentiments, and thoughts are instantly communicated to those in attendance, inviting their response in the spirit of yielding obedience. This power is stronger and more enduring than that exerted by material forces. Art enthralls and bewitches; an artist compels the perceiver's psyche to fall into agreement with his own rhythmic pulse and becomes the center of far-reaching forces, which establish a psychic order congenial to their creator. Each psychic unit drawn into the creator's sphere of influence becomes, in turn, the center of new radiations interacting with the creator, urging him on, and increasing or diminishing his activity as if by interference of phases. If a performance of *Prométhée* can pierce the bodies of the listeners with specific vibrations, invisibly introducing perturbations into both animate and inanimate matter, drawing it into a regulated, rhythmic motion, then this performance generates in the concert hall a collective soul, which embraces in an orderly action all individual psyches, including that of the generator himself. There may be other interpretations and explanations of this phenomenon. For Scriabin, at any rate, the collective soul was as real as the individual psyche; it was not an arithmetical sum resulting from additions and combinations of individual souls, but an integral and organic entity.

Here we witness a phenomenon frequently and plainly observable, and Scriabin seemingly discovered nothing new. The new element lies in the extent of this psychic impact and in its specific nature. For it must be remembered that Scriabin believed in the actual existence of spiritual beings other than man, dwelling on both the superior and inferior planes. Art must then influence these beings as well, indirectly, through the senses, and directly, through intuition. Beings dwelling on the astral plane, for instance, ought to be as sensitive to music, as responsive to its charms and enchantments, as man himself. In this view, psychic organisms created by art and containing myriads of diversified beings, visible and invisible, of whatever consistency and degree of consciousness, become inwardly united and infinitely complex. In its relation to the creative artist, the psychic medium becomes a resonator of enormous power, greatly amplifying the original pulse.

This phenomenon reflects the quantitative aspect of art's impact upon human souls. Much more important is the qualitative aspect; we find that art serves not only as a powerful resonator, but also transforms and reconstructs the psychic medium, which acquires under the influence of art a specific and, despite its diversity, homogeneous character. In my previous discussion of the impact of art upon matter I pointed out that, according to Scriabin, this impact is invariably beneficial, that it brings order into matter and contributes to its unification and fusion with the spirit, elevating it to a superior plane of formal organization. A similar phenomenon takes place in the psychic medium. The impact produced upon it by art can be described by a single word—*efflorescence,* which connotes a harmonious enhancement, expansion, and diversification of the psyche. This efflorescence of the psyche constitutes a total revelation, a realization of all its hidden potentialities. Contemplating a work of art—a painting, symphony, poem, or statue—man effloresces, assumes a deeper, fuller, more intense, and more harmonious mode of life; art organizes his soul and imparts to it a unity that human souls ordinarily lack. An aesthetic sensation, in Scriabin's understanding, is characterized by so great an intensification, so vast an expansion and enhancement of spirituality, that its synthesis achieves a greater cohesion, its unification becomes more complete, its form more perfect. The artist then becomes a benign magus, whose wand makes everything bloom around him. We picture him occupying the center of a whole system of concentric spherical waves spreading in all directions like light waves. All material bodies, all consciousnesses in the sphere of action of these waves are unified in a superior entity; their ingredients preserve their specific characteristics and individuality, but they effloresce and transfigure themselves in the revelation of oneness.

The corollary of these premises is that true art can never produce a depressing or debilitating influence on the soul; even melancholy, sad, and mournful works of art invariably introduce into the psyche an element of reconciliation, unity, and harmony, as if purifying it. This is the catharsis of Aristotle, which saves the soul from an ominously lurking, menacing chaos.

Herein lies the radical difference between a peculiar spiritual exhilaration induced by works of art, even those of the most passionate and tempestuous nature, and the excitement resulting from emotional stress, irritations, and the various natural and artificial stimulants that disturb the psyche and disrupt its unity. In contradistinction to the Bacchic delirium that engulfs human consciousness in its whirlwind, the impact of art enhances the vital tonus, quickens the pulse, and sharpens and invigorates the senses, thoughts, and desires to the point of saturation, while still retaining its formative power. Its effect is elevating, organizing, and unifying. A collective soul, formed through this process and marked by harmonious organization, is distinct from the psychic phenomena that manifest themselves in crowds, at public meetings, and under the influence of excitement, passions, and emotions. An eloquent political speaker can become the center of a whole system of powerful psychic vibrations and thus create a certain unity in the surrounding psychic medium. But personal distinctions are lost in a homogeneous crowd. Individuals are carried away in a psychic torrent without asserting themselves, without attaining a superior organization and form, which only art can bestow. Art thereby differs from all types of magic and public manifestations. What are the prerequisites for art's specific and positive impact upon both the material and psychic worlds? Art is the realization of beauty, which is the "wondrous image of the Deity." Art impresses oneness upon matter. An artistic work of music, poetry, or painting is a reflection of the Deity in matter. We hear in these pronouncements an echo of the ancient doctrine of beauty, going back to Plotinus and still farther to Plato. But by postulating the active power of art, Scriabin introduces an entirely new element into these historical antecedents.

Art, according to Scriabin, is a sacrament that exercises a positive influence on the souls and bodies of men. No aesthetically valid work of art can ever be likened to a Black Mass, even one that reveals obvious demoniac or satanic traits, as Liszt's "Mephisto Waltz." In the alembic of art, a Black Mass is inevitably converted into a White Mass. Such a transformation is also a prerequisite of catharsis, which is a positive phenomenon, no matter what the subject of the work that induces it, whether it presents morbid images inciting horror or erotic scenes exciting lust. If catharsis does not take place, the fault lies either with the spectators and listeners who fail to appreciate an artistic interpretation of reality or with the artist himself, if he lacks the intuitive power or technical ability to transfigure reality, or if he is too deeply absorbed in phenomenal reality, which inhibits his capacity to transfigure certain aspects of life, particularly those of an erotic nature. In light of these considerations, the mystical connotations of a work like Scriabin's Ninth Piano Sonata become clear. Its music transfigures man by introducing harmony, order, and form into the deepest recesses of his soul; it exorcises the dark and evil forces—which to Scriabin possessed an objective existence—and compels them to assume an image of divinity, thus divesting them of malevolent power and elevating them to a superior state of being.

In Scriabin's theosophic cosmogony, the Unique tears itself asunder and disintegrates into the correlative formal aspects of unity and multiplicity, but preserves its primordial oneness in artistic beauty, which embodies the remembrance of God and anticipates the Deity's return to concrete reality. We grant the attribute of beauty to objects preserving this memory of unity. The impact of art upon nature, objects, and living beings intensifies their positive qualities and endows them with divinity. But the task of an artist consists not in creating beautiful objects that refract in inert matter the image of the Deity, but in enabling these objects to impress themselves upon the cosmos and humanity. The necessity of art is the result of man's inability to act upon the world directly, Godlike, to enhance its organization. He is therefore forced to adopt an oblique course of action, to concentrate his efforts on a specific point in space and time, which subsequently becomes an active center, a transmitting station, and an energy accumulator serving the ultimate goal of creative art.

Each concrete phenomenon is the result of either the materialization of the spirit or of the spiritualization of matter. The closer, the more intimately spirit and matter are fused in a phenomenon, the more intense is their polarity. At this point we reach the last frontier; we have climbed over the highest peak. From here the road inevitably leads back to absolute oneness through the dematerialization of the spirit and despiritualization of matter; the polarity and specificity of spirit and matter diminish until their eventual reunion. The artist's role in this process is that of a divine deputy in the Manvantara. Artistic creativity continues the work of cosmic creativity.

In an evolutionary process, characterized by the descent, differentiation, multiplication, disintegration, and intensification of antinomies, the creative artist, whose aim is unity, acts as a conservative, restraining, and regulating agent. In a world that tends toward atomization and a maximal heterogeneity, he preserves the image of the Unique, a memory of absolute oneness, and, by impressing this image upon matter, sustains the interconnection of individual objects.

A diametrically opposite task faces the creative artist in the process of involution, ascent, and integration, which tends toward absolute oneness. But in this role, too, he remains a regulating agent. Whereas in the process of differentiation he endeavors to maintain the principle of concrete unity, in the reverse process of integration he contributes an element of multiplicity and specificity. However, the efflorescence of the psyche evoked by contemplating a work of art is not a manifestation of formless heterogeneity, but a harmonious enhancement, expansion, and diversification leading to a state of formal perfection. In this view, the sense of the beautiful provides the key to the redemption of the world. In the evolutionary process, it precludes disintegration into an infinite number of mutually incompatible elements; in the involutionary process, it prevents incoherent distribution in a chaotic homogeneity. But does not this descent into nothingness, that is, into the Unique, constitute the goal of the cosmic process? Yes, but this reunion must be freely chosen; it must pass through consciousness and can only be realized through art.

÷

Two fundamental ideas animate the artistic design of Scriabin's *Mysterium:* a synthesis of all arts and the inclusion in
the sphere of art of elements outside the field of aesthetics.
As I have pointed out before, the theory of the intrinsic
and genetic unity of all the arts arose from Scriabin's own
intuitive experience. To him sounds had no separate existence from colors, images, or concepts. This unity was
basic to his doctrine of Omni-art, which gradually differentiated into categories of music, dance, painting, and
plastic arts. Here Scriabin was influenced by Wagner; but
he never sought to reestablish the unity of all arts as prac-
ticed in antiquity, for this primordial unity only reflected
the relatively weak development of the individual branches
of Omni-art. The luxuriant growth and efflorescence of
these elements was predicated on their differentiation,
whereby sounds, colors, and motion evolved gradually and
independently into separate arts. At the dawn of history,
humanity knew only an inchoate Omni-art, in which diverse elements formed a confused tissue of visual, auditory,
and motoric sensations. According to Scriabin, the memory of this ancient period of Omni-art survived in the
Greek theater, in which the arts of music, poetry, and
dance were so closely interrelated that none could be separated from the others without losing its individual validity.
This parallelism, a summation of separate arts emerging
from their primordial, undifferentiated, incoherent unity,
represented the first attempt to create a synthetic art, one

calculated to revive the remembered unity and, at the same time, develop each art independently. But the process of differentiation within each art became so rapid that the remembrance of primordial unity was eventually lost.

The most consistent attempt to reinstate the original unity of the arts, denied by theorists but affirmed in one form or another by creative artists, was Wagner's operatic reform. But despite Scriabin's acknowledgment of Wagner's genius, he rejected Wagner's method of uniting arts by parallel development. This was not the path to the unity demanded by our artistic instinct, Scriabin maintained. We must never retrace the past.

What is the force that guides an artist in his desire to unify independent arts, separated from one another by apparently insuperable barriers? He is guided not only by the remembrance of their primeval union, but by a growing sense of their essential unity—the realization that a work of art must represent a certain entity, in which a chosen aspect is outlined in sharp contours, whether musical or pictorial, and is revealed at the expense of all other arts, although they are potentially inherent in it. The problem of the creative artist consists in realizing the potentialities of all arts, while reserving the right to give preference to a single one. He must pursue the analytic path before undertaking a synthesis. According to this method, which appears to be the only correct one, we will never arrive at a simple parallelism, a mere summation of arts, a purely mechanical and extrinsic unification—the inescapable result of the efforts of Wagner's followers, who probe the historical unity of all arts and strive to restore it by reassembling its dismembered ingredients. Wagner preached the dogma of artistic synthesis, but he failed to realize that such a synthesis must be preceded by an intuitive analysis of the pre-existing entity. Still, the Wagnerian principle of artistic parallelism provides a working formula for the realization of artistic synthesis. Scriabin expanded this formula and generalized its application, regarding the Wagnerian principle as a particular case. According to Scriabin, Omni-art is a species of counterpoint of individual arts. True, Scriabin was fascinated by Wagner's concept of synthetic art, but he avoided this term, for it seemed to imply a unification of heterogeneous elements by mechanical summation or juxtaposition. During the last years of his life, Scriabin emphasized the ideal of a compound art of auditory, visual, and motoric elements. In this formulation, Omni-art embraces all possible combinations of heterogeneous ingredients. Scriabin saw the main advantage of this formula as its flexibility and general applicability, protecting the artist from the perils of formalism that Wagner was unable to escape.

The counterpoint of individual arts consists in their free association. But the exact nature of this association cannot be determined in advance; it emerges spontaneously during the process of artistic invention. A creative artist cannot accept restrictions imposed by a predetermined theory; he must be completely free. The simplest formula is, of course, a parallel construction such as Wagner proposed, in which words and actions are accompanied by music, and a unified content evolves on two parallel lines, like two streams flowing next to each other but never crossing. Instances of such literal parallelism are very rare; usually the tissue of an artistic work presents a much more intricate design. A verbal sequence may be interrupted by a musical interlude; a poem may be concluded with a gesture, a visual scene with a chord. A symphony, representing a single art, that of music, can be described as integrally homophonic, for its system of sounds, no matter how diversified, constitutes only one component of Omni-art. With this symphonic element Wagner combines, in his music dramas, the element represented by the poetic text. Here we find an embryo of a complex polyphony of arts, which in Scriabin's design was to be fulfilled in the *Mysterium,* having already evolved in the *Acte préalable.* The narrow formula of parallelism derives from the thesis of an intrinsic heterogeneity of separate arts, whereas the free formula of polyphonic combinations rests on the realization of an intrinsic homogeneity of all elements of Omni-art. In the latter verbal expression is, in a sense, also a color, an action, a movement, and a chord.

The polyphonic design, in which the many branches of art function as contrapuntal voices, represented by poetry, music, painting, sculpture, and choreography, naturally makes the problem of creative work immensely complicated. Scriabin fully understood the magnitude of the task he undertook in the *Mysterium,* which was to embody such a counterpoint of the arts. He explained to us that it would defeat his purpose to first write the text and then the music, then outline the mise-en-scène, plan the choreography, design the scenery, and so on, section by section. All these ingredients had to be coordinated simultaneously, with each component art reflecting the corresponding aspects of the entire composition. In other words, the *Mysterium* had to be written like an orchestral score, in which the composer distributes instrumental parts, guided by his aesthetic sense and technical knowledge. In the *Mysterium* several individual arts were to be treated as contrapuntal voices are in a polyphonic work. Scriabin began to experiment with a counterpoint of the arts, at first somewhat diffidently, in the *Acte préalable*. But in this work he had to deal mainly with two component parts—words and music—while other ingredients were temporarily left in abeyance.

The contrapuntal tissue of the *Mysterium* grew enormously complex with the inclusion in the score of the so-called inferior organic senses—tactile, gustatory, and olfactory. From the standpoint of traditional aesthetics, his grand design was doomed to failure, because sensations of touch, taste, and smell differ fundamentally from auditory and visual sensations. They cannot be organized, graded, arranged, or otherwise systematized, and any attempt to do so produces an inchoate mass of incoherent impressions. The specific properties of the tactile, gustatory, and olfactory senses preclude their integration into systems analogous to those derived from the senses of sight and sound. But to Scriabin these properties were not intrinsically incompatible with the idea of a primordial unified Omni-art that includes all the senses. The fact that the systematization of organic senses, besides those of sight and sound, is not viable points only to the accident of their failure to give rise to individual arts in the process of evolution. Scriabin felt that this exclusion was not inevitable, for in a creative process all senses take part. Through an intuitive understanding, he lent support to the psychological theory that deduces all the senses from a primordial, undifferentiated vital sense, which was neither visual, tactile, nor auditory, and had subdivided into specific senses in the process of evolution.

To the ancients, art expressed a sense of the beautiful through formal organization of spiritual and material elements. This primordial art comprised all senses, thus contributing to the efflorescence of the psyche. Senses capable of artistic development gave birth to separate branches of art, while others, not possessing this capability, remained sterile. As a result, the remembrance of the original union of arts vanished among men, remaining only in the imaginations of those who could identify and analyze the objects of their intuitive contemplation. That is why the idea of incorporating the senses of touch, taste, and smell into an artistic work was strange to most artists, who regarded it as a paradox and an absurdity.

Of course Scriabin never seriously intended to create a work of art based on olfactory or tactile sensations. Yet one must admit that Scriabin himself contributed to the propagation of such myths by talking volubly about symphonies of perfumes and caresses, which the *Mysterium* was to include. It is clear that he envisioned a consummation of an entirely different dimension. He intended to introduce scents and sensations of touch and taste into the very tissue of the *Mysterium,* interlaced with musical, pictorial, plastic, and poetic elements. Once the unity of all the arts that had been parts of Omni-art was restored, its constituent elements, incapable of autonomous development, would be revivified and resurrected.

To summarize: a spoken word is a harmony, gesture, and color; it is also a scent, taste, and caress. The inclusion of all the senses into the polyphony of the *Mysterium* was intended to enrich it enormously; its fabric would be differentiated into sound, color, movement, odors, and tactile actions. This does not mean, of course, that all these elements would occur simultaneously. But just as in a fugue, where some voices are silent at certain times, so the continuity of odors and tastes could be disrupted, restored, and broken again at will.

It was to scents that Scriabin attached especial importance, for it is well known that olfactory sensations form numerous intense, complex, and suggestive psychological associations. No less important to him were the sensations of touch or, as he preferred to call them, with obvious erotic implications, caresses. The sensations of taste, however, were to be included in the *Mysterium* mainly for the sake of completeness, formal perfection, and logical consistency.

In the design of the *Mysterium,* Scriabin clearly indicated that art is merely a medium, a tool necessary for the ascent to a higher state of being; in other words, he subordinated art to life. The specific properties of the inferior organic senses, their unsuitability for classification, deprive them of aesthetic value in the judgment of those to whom aesthetically valuable entities must invariably be self-sufficient and totally independent, justifying and vindicating themselves by virtue of their own existence and thereby ruling out any extraneous intrusions. But Scriabin measured the value of an art by its ability to serve as a medium for the elevation to a new, more perfect plane of being. That is why he was impelled to include in the *Mysterium* impressions, however diffuse, of inferior sensory organs, which are apt to perturb the psyche far more than musical sounds, words, or colors. They are also capable, when utilized prudently and cautiously and combined with sounds, gestures, or coloration, of deepening, widening, and reinforcing the tonus of the psyche by increasing and exciting its energies.

In the fulfillment of the *Mysterium* as a truly universal act, the use of a single language, even the most commonly spoken in the world, such as English or French, seemed quite inadequate to Scriabin. A language expresses the specific spirit of the nation that created it, and carries with it a number of historical connotations, thereby lacking the universal quality that Scriabin so eagerly sought. Also, contemporary languages, in the course of their evolution, had become abstractions and lost the etymological precision of ancient languages.

In remote antiquity human speech was suffused with concrete images; it was pictorial and dynamic. The verbal element was still part of the primordial synthesis and possessed a high emotional tonus. Speech, inseparable from motion and music, deeply affected and invigorated the souls of men. Modern languages, however, have degenerated into a system of signals and abstract symbols; they have lost all connection with real objects and become interchangeable with any other medium of communication, a condition undoubtedly convenient for the language of science, which is abstract, unambiguous, and precise. Hence the recent experimentation with artificial languages, which possess, in comparison with living tongues, the advantages of logic and simplicity. Scriabin urged a return to the natural sources of speech, to song and music, in order to retrieve the living word as a direct link to the essence of material objects.

At one time Scriabin became interested in Sanskrit, which, according to popular opinion, was the primordial Aryan language. He even purchased a Sanskrit grammar and began to study it, but soon gave it up when he realized that it would take too much time. Besides, he decided that Sanskrit, in spite of its antiquity, was already too highly developed and therefore could not provide a clue to the origin of speech. Shortly before his death he declared: "I may have to create my own language for my works and to immerse myself in the spirit of music and dance. Modern speech is too inflexible, too firmly fixed; it is imperative to restore to the spoken word its original lightness, to make it more fluid, more pliant, to reinforce its songful quality. Sanskrit may be an intermediate stage, but we must delve more deeply for the roots of speech."

÷

Scriabin's *Mysterium* was to be a unified work of Omni-art consisting of visual, auditory, tactile, motoric, olfactory, and gustatory ingredients. Its tissue is analytically divisible into separate but intimately connected parts, among them musical, poetic, and plastic, constituting a grandiose system of sonorous edifices, colors, forms, motions, and physical contacts. But none of these components possesses self-sufficient validity; none can be performed or even evaluated separately from the others.

Like all works of art, the *Mysterium* creates a beautiful form in time and space; it imprints upon matter the essence of unity, which is the image of the Deity. Ideally, the *Mysterium* was to embody the most perfect organization of matter, which is constantly disintegrating and reassembling, perpetually disturbed by mutually interfering currents; from this incoherent mass the *Mysterium* was to emerge as a harmonious system, an island in the middle of the ocean. This system, however, was not an aim in itself; its significance is measured by its capacity to influence the surrounding mediums, psychic and material, on all planes of being, to move in the positive direction, contributing to their efflorescence and impressing upon them the image of the Unique. The difference between traditional works of art and the *Mysterium* lies only in the extent and power of their impact. According to Hegel's formula, which Scriabin liked to quote, quantity here becomes quality. Prior to the origination of the *Mysterium,* the impact of a work of art could sustain but a transitory efflorescence, which could not protect the psyche from chaos. The sense of unity imparted by these artistic phenomena to the psychic and material worlds was necessarily unstable, since it failed to embrace the universe in its totality. The moments of ecstasy experienced by listeners and spectators in a concert hall or a museum, witnessing masterpieces of genius, invariably give way to fatigue and exhaustion upon return to reality in the framework of time and space. But after the production of the *Mysterium,* its participants, in Scriabin's phrase, were to "awaken in heaven" as free sons of the Unique. The *Mysterium* thus becomes the focal point of universal efflorescence and imprints the cosmos with the attribute of oneness. The aim of the *Mysterium* was to make the world beautiful, endow it with aesthetic value, and transfigure it for all eternity. The creator of the *Mysterium* was not assigned to a given point in the spatial and temporal world but was to communicate, directly or indirectly, with the entire sphere of being.

Despite the grandeur of this design, its realization, in the light of Scriabin's aesthetic system, appeared entirely possible. The principal problem was the manner of production. Here, each performer becomes the focus of forces that affect all the other performers, so that the cumulative energy of the resulting impact is directly proportional to the number of participants. Precise mathematical calculation is, of course, impossible, but it may be said that as the number of participants increases in the arithmetical progression, the energy of the entire system increases in the geometric progression. The creator, exerting his influence on the listeners (supposing the action is musical in nature), is reciprocally influenced by them, so that the collective soul born in the process, whether in a concert hall or the theater, represents the aggregate of all participating individual psyches raised to the nth power.

By what criterion can the impact of a work of art upon the public be measured? It can be measured by the degree of perfection with which artistic beauty is realized or, in other words, by its aesthetic value. It follows that the magical, incantatory power of Scriabin's *Mysterium* over all nature, both animate and inanimate, must infinitely exceed the influence exercised by, say, Wagner's *Parsifal*. But the *Mysterium* would not demonstrate greater aesthetic value merely because it arrays a greater number of participants or lasts longer, but because of the greater perfection of its inner organization, higher artistic cohesion, and faithful transmission of the image of the Deity. True, in Scriabin's aesthetics the qualitative and quantitative aspects were never reconciled, but as the years went by, the qualitative aspect assumed the dominating position. I recall that Scriabin spoke of the entire population of the world participating in the *Mysterium*. Later he realized the impossibility of such a fantastic idea, yet his penchant for grandiose designs was too strong for compromise. He was reluctant to consider a production of the *Mysterium* for a small circle of consecrated devotees; his vision of universality demanded mass participation.

The impression made by the *Mysterium* was to be

infinitely stronger than that of even the most formidable productions of traditional art. This expectation was predicated on the high aesthetic value of the work itself (constituting its qualitative aspect) and its magnitude in terms of time and space, taking into consideration the number of participants and the complexity, multiplicity, and diversity of its components (constituting its quantitative aspect).

Scriabin envisaged the subject of the *Mysterium* as world history from the cosmogenic and anthropogenic standpoint, the evolution of the human race regarded not as a series of external events, but a gradual materialization of the Spirit, its immersion in matter.

But such a history of the universe must be at the same time a history of the individual psyche. Psychology here becomes cosmology, and vice versa. The *Mysterium* unfolds before us the evolution of the cosmos, mankind, and the individual; all three traverse the trajectory from incoherent homogeneity to specific multiplicity, returning to pristine unity. This history was to be enacted in the *Mysterium*. In accordance with the number of human races in Mme. Blavatsky's doctrine, the *Mysterium* was divided into seven parts. The performance of each part was to occupy a whole day, and the entire *Mysterium* was to last a period of seven days or multiples thereof. The production itself was to be preceded by a series of "preliminary acts" corresponding to the ancient purification rites. These acts were to include the physical, moral, aesthetic, religious, and philosophical training of the participants and also incorporate the landscaping of the area and the building of a temple.

Scriabin had a fairly definite idea for the geographical location of the *Mysterium*. It was to be in India, either in the mountainous north, popularly believed to be the cradle of humanity, or in the southern, tropical part of the peninsula. Later he no longer specified a definite geographical location, for his grand design had outgrown terrestrial boundaries. He was content with a general indication: "in tropical surroundings." His project of a temple underwent a similar process of dematerialization. During the period between 1903 and 1906 Scriabin had a definite vision of the temple, which was to be a gigantic circular edifice topped by a high cupola. He even left some drawings of its architectural design, which consisted of a hemisphere surrounded by water, so that its reflection would create the visual impression of a complete sphere. Around the temple he planned to build terraced gardens. In private conversation Scriabin let his imagination run freely; he envisioned a group of buildings placed in the middle of a forest, and forming an intricate sexual symbol. The landscaping itself was to be part of the score of the *Mysterium,* and the workers and builders were to become themselves participants in the production. Eventually Scriabin abandoned concrete indications of the external aspect of the project, although he continued to speak of a temple or a number of temples occupying a large area.

One of Scriabin's most ambitious projects was the artistic fashioning of nature itself, with its daily changes of light and dark, noises of the forest, singing of the birds, and planetary motion above. He rejected artificial staging. The sky at night, the fragrance of the woods, were to be integral parts of the symphony of colors, shapes, and odors in the score of the *Mysterium*.

Scriabin's design included constantly varying architectural forms (inertia and immobility of even the most beautiful buildings oppressed him). In order to realize this "architectural dance," as Scriabin phrased it, he envisioned luminous mirages of buildings produced by special projectors. He also imagined fragrant curtains of haze, with pillars of incense rising to the sky, and transparent surfaces made visible by beams of light directed toward them at an angle. Above all, he wanted everything to move, to overcome gravity, so that not a single stone would disrupt by its inertness the universal joy making the whole world dance. Carried away by his imaginings, he once blurted out: "It may be necessary, at the last moment, to destroy the temple itself, to demolish its walls in order to emerge into open air, under the skies."

It was the task of the participants in the *Mysterium* to identify themselves with special states of being corresponding to the seven human races of the theosophic doctrine. Some were to assume the inner aspects of the Lemurians (the third race in Mme. Blavatsky's scheme) or Atlants (the fourth race). The fifth day of the *Mysterium* corresponded to the time of our own race. On that day, a symphony of sounds, colors, motions, forms, and caresses was to be raised to the highest possible degree of spontaneity, the finest perfection of design, leading to an ultimate fusion in a disembodied, phantomlike mirage.

With the aid of sorceries and enchantments of Omni-art, the *Mysterium* was to take humanity back to its

primordial state. But this was not to be a mere recapitulation of the past; it was to be an illumination, a transfiguration, so that the participants would identify themselves
with their remote ancestors, infusing their past with
beauty and investing it with a sense of oneness, greater
organization, and perfection. In this manner, the past was
to join the higher states of being through its reorganization
in the *Mysterium,* and the power of art would reach the
remotest periods of antiquity, with each successive stage
permeated by the spirit of divinity. As for the stages of
ascendance, they were projected into the future. By the
magical agency of art, humanity could pass through the
stages of the sixth and the seventh races in the shortest
possible time and be reincarnated successively, while the
corresponding psychic and material states of being would
be illumined by beauty. The initial days of the cycle were
to project the idealized and transfigured images of extinct
races; the last two races were to be revealed on the sixth
and seventh days in forms infused with oneness. The human spirit, the human body, and all nature would recapitulate their cosmic cycles in their alternations of descent
and ascent. These cycles would culminate in the apotheosis
of the kingdom of the beautiful, inaugurated by the mighty
impact of the art of sounds, colors, forms, plastic motion,
caresses, and perfumes. This was to be a crowning theophany of seven days, realizing a complete transfiguration
of the world.

The question arises: Does not this resurrection of the past and insight into the future possess the character of the theatrical representation Scriabin so vehemently deprecated? The answer must be in the negative. In the *Mysterium*, there is no room for actors or passively receptive listeners and spectators; its participants—from the protagonists to every artist in the symphony of odors and lights—all, without exception, were to perform not only their appointed tasks, as subjects of the action, but also to react to performances by the rest of the cast, as objects of their own action. Singers, musicians, and dancers, in mutual interaction, were to reach a higher state of being and receive, at the same time, the sensations induced in them by symphonies of aromas and caresses. The participants in the *Mysterium* were not to be actors, but rather votaries in the sacrament of theophany, a liturgical act in which their flesh and souls would undergo the miracle of transubstantiation. This communion could no more be called a theatrical production than could a religious service during which devout celebrants identify themselves with priests performing a bloodless sacrifice and the choir in their prayers.

In the sacrament envisaged by Scriabin, the gift of transfiguration was not only for the immediate participants, but for all who were aware of the event, even if they did not actually attend it. Scriabin realized that even in his grandiose design there could be no question of compulsory attendance, for the sphere of action of the *Mysterium*, though it would take place at a certain point in time and space, would actually embrace the entire universe, and millions of people would spiritually participate, even if physically they happened to be far away. Scriabin compared mankind with the human body, the organs of which perform specific functions while participating in the life of the entire body. Enlarging on this simile, Scriabin told me, during one of our last conversations, that his temple was to be a grandiose altar, the focal point of the act, a sacrificial place. The true temple was to be the earth itself. In vast Gothic cathedrals, worshipers assemble in multitudes, crowding the doorways and the lateral naves; they listen to the voice of the priest and the singing of the choir from a distance and watch the flickering candles from afar. Yet, in their prayers, they are true celebrants of the divine service. Thus all mankind was to participate in the *Mysterium,* which would then become a truly communal act, not only by virtue of the great number of performers, but by its quality and spirit of communion.

What role did Scriabin assign to himself in the *Mysterium?* It is difficult to give a definite answer to this question, in view of Scriabin's own ambiguities in his pronouncements on the subject. He was inclined as the years went by to diminish rather than enhance his part in the event. During his solipsistic period, at the time of the composition of his opera, he placed himself in the center of the *Mysterium,* regarding it as a primarily personal act. But as early as 1907 his views underwent significant modification. He spoke about the importance of attracting large masses of people to witness the *Mysterium,* and he emphasized that the masses should join the action spontaneously, obeying the clarion call of love. He was content with the role of guiding spirit. "The storm is already stirring," he used to say; "the movement will grow rapidly." As the rumors of his project spread, he complained that he could not find sympathetic allies. "I need support," he lamented; "I cannot do all my work alone. It is imperative that people realize the universal importance of the *Mysterium*. Its success is vital to all humanity, not just for my personal gratification." If, during his early period, he was apt to regard humanity as the raw material on which he would bestow the gift of blessedness, he later declared that the salvation of mankind and its transfiguration must be a universal concern, that if he should fail to awaken in men the loving memory of the Father and the longing for a reunion in him, then the fulfillment of the *Mysterium* would be indefinitely delayed.

Scriabin often envisioned himself standing at the altar of a universal temple as high priest performing the holy eucharist, or presiding at the last ritual as teacher, educator, and supreme leader of celebrants in the *Mysterium,* aided in his work by devout votaries. Toward the end of his life, however, Scriabin no longer dwelt on his own role; what was uniquely important to him was the act itself, and he was willing to be dissolved in it.

According to Scriabin's early design, the *Mysterium* was to culminate in the spectacle of cosmic conflagration, which would precipitate an apocalyptic doomsday. The element of theatrical representation would not disappear until

later. Eventually Scriabin abandoned all plans to compose
the finale of the *Mysterium,* for in his expectations this finale
was to mark the end of the world and the resurrection of
God. Obviously it was impossible for him to describe this
end, but it would reunite mankind in the Unique, and its
enactment was to be entrusted to a new, transfigured man,
a celebrant in the sacrament. The finale of the *Mysterium*
was therefore to be determined during its actual performance. The Seventh Day (days, of course, symbolized periods of human history) was to be the last, during which
man and nature would come nearest to the Unique, elevated by the magic of all-powerful Omni-art. They would
actually be transfigured: exaltation, as immeasurable and
deep as the ocean, would reach its greatest imaginable intensity; the spirit and matter, liberated from their chains,
would approach nothingness, and the polarity of the masculine and feminine principles would fall to the vanishing
point. The cosmos would be hurled into the sunlit abyss
of ecstasy. At that instant the universal consciousness
would burst into comprehension of the Unique. Mankind
would experience filial freedom and become aware of its
divine essence, its sacrificial nature. But the advent of the
Father cannot come to pass as long as man, free and conscious, still partakes of the nature of multiplicity. Art has
performed its mission; the creation of beauty is accomplished, the world is impregnated with the image of the
Deity. The Seventh Day is ended; the *Mysterium* has
brought mankind, and the whole universe with it, to the
threshold of death. The ineffable arrives in the loving surrender of man to God; a blessed immersion into God takes
place, a fusion with God, now resurrected and lovingly

receiving his sons unto himself. The Manvantara will have been consummated.

÷

Scriabin's design, awesome in its grandeur, surpassed all precedent and bordered on sacrilege in its audacity; it inspired admiration, but also evoked wonderment and doubt. It was a majestic, strange, perhaps mad design, impossible to carry out but somehow immediately understandable, capable of firing the hearts of men with love, intoxicating them. The *Mysterium* may be the most unattainable of all dreams, but it is also the proudest affirmation of man's powers—a challenge made not for self-aggrandizement, but in the spirit of humility, as a sacrificial and plenary surrender, a hymn to life that glorifies death.

Clearly, the philosophy underlying Scriabin's *Mysterium* is not apt to find supporters among the adepts of contemporary religious and philosophical doctrines. At best they would regard it as a fanciful mirage devoid of substance, a lofty but dangerously misleading scheme. Indeed, Scriabin's notions are incompatible with current doctrines, even though his opponents may sympathize with him and perhaps secretly admire him. Materialists, positivists, Kantians, occultists, theosophists, orthodox Christians—all have reason to take a hostile attitude toward Scriabin's pronouncements, as indeed they did. But what was the result of their rebuke? It isolated Scriabin's position still further, leading to a still more intense individualization in his philosophy and blocking all avenues of approach to its inner meaning. From the standpoint of science, Scriabin's *Mysterium* is folly; for an orthodox Christian it is blasphemy; for the followers of Kant it is naively dogmatic. As for occultists and theosophists, they recognized in Scriabin's grand designs the fruit of a richly endowed, powerful but undisciplined spirit lost in the corridor of mirages. The superficially critical attitude of Scriabin's opponents only confirms the acknowledged fact that he was neither a theosophist nor a positivist, neither a neo-Kantian nor an orthodox Christian.

Formal criticism of Scriabin's position, regardless of the opponent's personal convictions, is useless. The only purposeful method of inquiry is impartial analysis of the sources of Scriabin's philosophy and its relationship to other doctrines. This is the objective of the present study.

The simplest way of dealing with the *Mysterium* is to dismiss it altogether as a curious and whimsical apparition and devote oneself to the study of Scriabin's art, to enjoy his musical compositions and ascribe his philosophical speculations to personal aberration. But we recall that a similar attitude was taken toward the unorthodox religious philosophy of Tolstoy, whose critics preferred to dissect the personality of a genius, expressing admiration for the novelist while shamefacedly veiling the moralist. But Scriabin was an even more complex personality than Tolstoy, and it would be quite impossible to perform a similar operation on him, for his entire art is "mysterial." All his works were to him but preliminary approaches to the *Mysterium,* a succession of approximations. It would be incongruous to examine his music and his philosophy separately.

By comparing Scriabin's *Mysterium* with other creations of genius, I do not mean to imply that he was in any way influenced by others. Even if influences existed, they could not have affected his fundamental design. But there might have been points of contact with other philosophical doctrines, parallelisms of thought that often lead to an incidental similarity between two alien doctrines. It is as though these doctrines were originally connected on a different plane, grew out from the same root and on the same stem, but developed independently and lost all trace of their common origin. Such an intimate parallelism, in the absence of all ascertainable links and interactions, has a profound significance, since it demonstrates that a given religious, philosophical, or artistic phenomenon is not accidental, the outcome of a random confluence of external factors, nor peculiar to an individual; rather it is part of a current of human thought, immanent in a definitely recognizable spiritual trend.

Upon analysis the *Mysterium* reveals two fundamental aspects: first, a faith in the boundless creative power of man as an anointed continuator of divine labor; and second, the belief in the imminence and inevitability of cosmic ecstasy accomplished through art.

Faith in the magical power of man had been voiced a generation earlier by an obscure Russian philosopher of genius named Fyodorov. Scriabin never knew of Fyodorov's existence, and yet their ideas bear a close resemblance. Taking as his point of departure a strictly orthodox Christian position, Fyodorov promulgated the doctrine of man's Godlike nature and postulated man's responsibility for redemption and transfiguration. He also proclaimed man's unconscious power over nature. The aim of man, according to Fyodorov, is the resurrection of ancestors, generation after generation, a total victory over death, and eternal life on an earth transfigured by man's own power. Fyodorov's goal differs from Scriabin's, but the means by which the Russian philosopher hoped to attain it were similar. Fyodorov was deeply convinced that art had a magic origin, and, like Scriabin, he endeavored to vindicate his conviction by scientific arguments. For both Fyodorov and Scriabin art was an activating medium, a mystical technique; both regarded art as a practical tool. In fact, Fyodorov's mystical doctrine is permeated with this practical sense, perhaps even to a greater extent than Scriabin's. The religious and philosophical substance of Fyodorov's book, *Philosophy of Common Action,* constitutes a species of superior technology. Fyodorov equated science with art, and it is through science that he sought the means to the transfiguration of the world and man. Hence the extraordinary and sometimes bewildering mixture, both in Scriabin's and Fyodorov's speculations, of infinitely grandiose and fantastic elements with abundant minutiae, in ostensibly logical and scientific-sounding formulations. In boldness and grandeur of design, Fyodorov matches Scriabin's vision of the apocalyptic consummation of man's destiny. But Fyodorov derived his mystique from blood kinship, a notion quite alien to Scriabin. In Fyodorov's desire to vanquish death, which he regarded as the greatest evil, there is a deep, warm, childlike attachment to the world, to man, to all living creatures. He hoped to achieve redemption by freeing the flesh from corruption, that is, from evil. Scriabin's yearnings were born of life on earth; his thinking was pragmatic and transcendental at the same time, because he was forever seeking the unknown, the new. There is another important difference between the two philosophers: Fyodorov expected the redemption of the world to be accomplished by future generations; he was humble in the face of reality and never hoped to witness the transfiguration of mankind. Scriabin, on the other hand, expected to participate in this apocalyptic act. Had Scriabin known Fyodorov, he might have been repelled by Fyodorov's necromancy, his mystique of the flesh, worship of the past, and devotion to his earthly forefathers. And yet for those who are acquainted with the teachings of both Fyodorov and Scriabin, their inner kinship is clear.

About a year after Scriabin's death, the Russian philosopher Nikolai Berdyayev published his book *The Meaning of Creativity,* subtitled *An Essay on the Vindication of Man.* The appearance of this book was symptomatic of the times; its guiding thought was the deification of man as a participant in the act of divine creation. God is in need of man, Berdyayev wrote; man is indispensable in the work of God. Here we encounter the idea of a Godlike man as creator. Berdyayev's book crystallizes his thoughts evolved many years earlier. Although Scriabin and Berdyayev were personally acquainted, they knew little of each other's ideas, and there could not have been any reciprocal influence between them. But both the philosopher and the musician arrived at the same ideas of man's redemption through art and of man as creator, whose divinity derived not from grace but ontological spirituality. But Berdyayev opposed the doctrine of God's immanence in all its forms, especially Hinduism. He postulated the transcendency of God over man, a notion that impressed Scriabin as monstrous and absurd. But Berdyayev's sparring against Hinduism did not obscure his deep sense of God's immanency. He cited the words of St. Angela of Foligno in one of her visions: "I beheld the Trinity and saw myself on the cross in it." This awesome testimony could well be an epigraph to Berdyayev's book, and the same mystical vision corresponds to Scriabin's belief in Godlike men. Such blasphemy would probably have horrified Fyodorov, even though the words of St. Angela reflect some of his own ideas. The anthropological aspect of Fyodorov, Berdyayev, and Scriabin is here reduced to theology; but Scriabin is more direct, outspoken, and candid in his doctrine of man's sacrificial creation of God, whereas Fyodorov and Berdyayev, assigning God's labor to man, leave unfilled the chasm that separates man from God.

All beliefs in the divine nature of man, whatever their current form, whether mystically religious or biologically positivistic, can be traced to Dostoyevsky and Nietzsche. Dostoyevsky was familiar with Fyodorov's writings and, in one of his letters, comments enthusiastically on the Russian philosopher's ideas being close to his own. Scriabin likewise felt a kinship with Dostoyevsky; he was particularly fond of the suicidal mystic Kirillov in *The Possessed.*

The influence that Nietzsche, particularly in his final phase (represented by *The Antichrist*) exercised upon Berdyayev was very strong. Their ideas coincided: man's redemption could be achieved only through art. For Scriabin, too, the quintessence of man was creativity, which, as in Nietzsche, absorbs all other attributes. Scriabin's attitude toward Nietzsche was complex. He felt an inner kinship with Nietzsche, but the connection was oblique, as if their philosophies grew from the same root but effloresced on different branches. Whereas Berdyayev absorbed the deepest essence of Nietzsche's thought directly, Scriabin absorbed only his solipsism, amorality, and the biological aspect of the Superman doctrine, completely ignoring the mystical quality in Nietzsche. This is not surprising, for Scriabin became acquainted with Nietzsche's writings at the time when he himself regarded mysticism as a symptom of decadence. As Scriabin's philosophical acumen grew, he gradually corrected his false image of Nietzsche. In fact, Scriabin, unbeknownst to himself, approached Nietzsche on another plane. Nietzsche's idea of man as the sole creator of values developed, in Scriabin's philosophy, into man's becoming the demiurge of a new earth and heaven. But Nietzsche's Superman who impresses himself upon the masses, his legislator who toys with human destinies, disappears completely in Scriabin's construction. This image made a brief appearance in Scriabin's opera, but soon vanished when Scriabin abandoned his preoccupation with individuality and became concerned with universal destiny.

The origins of Scriabin's doctrine of an activating art cannot be found in Nietzsche, even though this doctrine may have its roots in Nietzschean mysticism. Berdyayev raises the possibility of this derivation in his book *The Meaning of Creativity,* in which his faith in man's messianic mission leads to the recognition, albeit circumspect, of the incantatory power of art. Similar ideas are found in German romanticism, especially the works of Novalis, but by then Scriabin was well on his way to Orphism. For him, as for Novalis, Orphism was more than a poetic fairy tale, a remembrance of an ancient power over nature, and a fascinating subject for literary discussion. Novalis never consciously sought vestiges of Orphism in remote antiquity but directed his interest toward a future, Orphic apotheosis. Therein lies the essential difference between Novalis and Scriabin, for whom the magical power of art was a proven phenomenon inherent in the idea of the beautiful. There is also another difference. Scriabin tried to find a logical formulation for his contention that art directly affects the material world, a notion absent in Novalis. Their ultimate aims differed as well: what was for Novalis the transfiguration of nature and man was for Scriabin but the means for communication with the Unique, a yearning to immerse oneself in the Unique. These differences, however, do not obscure the spiritual kinship between the poet and the musician or, in a broader sense, between Scriabin's philosophy and German romanticism, which also was the breeding ground for Nietzsche. Since there can be no question of any direct influence, the similarities between Nietzsche and Scriabin are all the more remarkable.

It is important to point out that the historically varying manifestations of the romantic state of mind are all activated by the same motive force. It is in this eternal romanticism that we find the origins of the messianic destiny of man, basic to Scriabin's *Mysterium,* which leads to supreme efflorescence in the gift of ecstasy.

An infallible criterion in judging the romantic or classical character of a given work of art is found in an objective or subjective attitude toward general culture. A classical artist judges the aggregate of all entities, material and spiritual, that a given nation accumulates during a particular epoch as an objective system, significant in itself. For a classicist, all products of the creative effort are formally crystallized; they possess an autonomous existence, generate their own standard of values, and live and evolve all by themselves. Once separated from their creator, they become a part of the objective world of reality and obey its laws, so that their originator begins to feel like a stranger among them and regards them as natural objects. The world of culture, for a classical intellect, becomes as autonomous as nature itself. As a result, the classicist posits life as a means for the realization, materialization, and objectivization of values, which invest life with a specific significance and meaning. He strives to organize life, to combat its elusive fluidity, capricious inconstancy, and pervading dynamism by systematizing its individual elements. He tries to escape immediate experience; in his creative effort he attempts to break through to the Absolute, which he posits as an immobile entity, quiescent in itself. Dedicated to the creation of independent, imperishable objects, the classicist's apperception of life is transcendental. His ideal, which is unattainable, is a hermetically closed, perfect, self-sufficient system of realized values that has no room for man, the creator of this system. Classical culture is fundamentally materialistic and static; therein lies the ever-present danger of its degeneration into fetishism and formalism.

For the classical mind the world of culture, though manufactured by man, possesses an objective reality equivalent to the world of nature's. For a romantic mind, however, products of human creativity are not valuable in themselves; the romantic regards culture, formed by the crystallization of collective creativity, subjectively and judges it only insofar as it contributes to the meaning of life itself and makes it more intense, complex, rewarding, and diversified. Entirely immersed in the stream of life, the romantic refuses to recognize cultural values outside life's domain. He restores culture, represented by a system of crystallized products, to its source, to life, to the vital creativity of a concrete individual; he endows it again with fluidity, mutability, and mobility.

The course of classicism is from life to culture; it subordinates life to culture as a means to an end. Romanticism also takes its point of departure in life, but it returns to life through culture, which enriches life. Romantic creativity is directed, in the final analysis, toward life; it is immanent to life. Its ideal, perhaps unattainable, is absolute freedom of creativity, in which the creator toys with his products and delights in them. Romantic culture is dynamic and revolutionary; it is independent from the world of objects. But this independence carries with it the danger of degeneration into inchoate sterility.

Inasmuch as pure types do not occur in the world of reality, there cannot exist an unallayed romantic culture. At their most extreme, both romanticism and classicism would destroy themselves. Throughout history the preponderance of either tendency has fluctuated considerably.

I have already mentioned that Scriabin was a typical romantic in his attitude toward art. But we are concerned here not with Scriabin as an individual, but with Scriabin as a creator. Indeed, Scriabin's creativity, as revealed in the *Mysterium,* is profoundly romantic. Never before had the romantic spirit reached such exaltation; the *Mysterium* marks the logical and psychological acme of romantic culture. It is impossible to conceive the existence of a work transcending the *Mysterium,* for it embraces the total spectrum of Omni-art.

Half in jest, half seriously, Scriabin used to call himself a true Hindu, in the sense that his spiritual fatherland was India. Of course, any localization of the creative spirit is inherently faulty, but Scriabin was undoubtedly right in stressing his inner kinship with the Orient, and particularly with India. Ancient Hindu culture, before it had accepted the total cult of Brahma and become static, was definitely romantic; there are some vestigial elements of romanticism in India even in our own day. Hindu culture also had its classical traits, which predominated for a certain period of time, but the romantic strain asserted itself in the end, as it did in other cultures of the Orient, with the possible exception of China and Japan. This romanticism accounts for the fundamental difference between the classicism of Greco-Roman culture and that of ancient India. Western antiquity, as expressed so vividly in the myth of the Golden Age, also had its romantic elements. But the classical design unquestionably dominated Grecian, Hellenistic, and Roman cultures, which emphasized the objectivity of the values they created. For the sake of schematic classification, it may be said that Western antiquity is the spiritual fatherland of classicism and India the spiritual motherland of romanticism. Indeed, in Europe the rise of interest for Eastern poetry, philosophy and religion, and especially for the arts of India, coincided with the efflorescence of German romanticism.

Scriabin's philosophical and religious affinity with the immanent systems of India was not the result of his reading theosophic literature, whether Mme. Blavatsky's *Secret Doctrine, Religions de l'Inde* by Auguste Barth, or *The Light of Asia* by Sir Edwin Arnold. Rather, it indicates certain common beliefs; for the affirmation of God's immanence to life and the subject of knowledge to the act of cognition are typical romantic ideas. The God of romanticism is, in a sense, a romantic artist; his creatures have no objective reality or value and cannot be contraposed to the Deity as autonomous beings. For the classical mind, however, God transcends to life, and the act of cognition does not include the object of knowledge. The God of classical philosophy is a classical artist, who creates self-sufficient images possessing autonomous values.

The immanent quality of romantic thinking is commonly associated with the psychological and metaphysical doctrines of voluntarism and dynamism, characteristic of Scriabin's personal philosophy as well as Hindu teachings. The integral intellectualism of ancient philosophy is equally remarkable. As for romantic religious consciousness, it always gravitated toward pantheism, which is, of course, closely related to Hindu religious systems. Scriabin, too, was in a sense an adept of pantheism. To conclude, Scriabin's romanticism, as revealed in the design of the *Mysterium,* was cardinal to his philosophy. And this provides a ready answer to the natural question: What is Scriabin's rightful place in contemporary culture?

Scriabin expressed himself quite explicitly in regard to Western culture, to which he was definitely antagonistic. He believed that his art would play a revolutionary, indeed destructive, role in Western culture. There is some truth in this evaluation, but Scriabin made the common error of identifying contemporary cultural forms with culture in general and thus appeared to be in the false position of an opponent to all culture. But if we consider Scriabin's fundamental beliefs, we must realize that he fought only what Hegel described as "bad infinity." He opposed the classical elements of contemporary culture while vigorously promoting the contrasting ideals of romanticism. It could not be otherwise, because an artist, *nolens volens,* must be a protector of cultural attainments.

Scriabin's art is intrinsically incompatible with the Western European mode of life, both emotionally and intellectually. In order to accept and even to approach Scriabin's ideas, Western culture would have to undergo a total spiritual reform. Even Scriabin himself never fully realized how far removed his spiritual world was from that of Western Europe. The philosophical design of the *Mysterium* was organically alien to European culture, and it was not by accident that the idea for this work originated in Russia in the creative mind of a Russian.

This mutual antagonism stems from the classical trend of Western European culture as expressed in its cult of materialism. Western European culture naturally contains romantic elements, but its coloration is predominantly classical. Its system of values comprises a conglomeration of manufactured objects that tend to assume an autonomous existence, forming a rigid world often hostile to man's emotional life. Products of man's creative labor are separated from their makers and embark on an independent development outside the sphere of human action; moreover, these objects exert a reciprocal influence on their creators, stimulating further production of ready-made forms that correspond to the already accomplished crystallization. It therefore requires great perseverance on the part of the creator to modify his product in order to reverse the trend toward objectivization. Thus the creator encounters resistance not so much from the inertia of his working materials or from the psychological obstacles to the inventive process, but from manufactured objects themselves. Their continuous differentiation and systematization complicate the creator's task by depriving him of free choice, imposing on him an inflexible course of action, a categorical imperative directing him on a predetermined path. Whatever field of cultural endeavor we examine, we find an oppression of man by his manufactured products, which come to life and begin to proliferate in total disregard of his intentions. They, in turn, give rise to new autonomous formations, sometimes quite startling and monstrous to their manufacturer. We encounter an analogous situation in economics, law, religion, and art. Georg Simmel pointed out this curious development in one of his articles, but he regarded it as a natural phenomenon.

We are confronted here with the abnormal development of "machinism," which constitutes the most extreme and ugliest form of human servitude. Classicism demands the subordination of the inventor to material objects, a submission of the creator to his own products. Taking humanism as its point of departure, Western European culture reduces man, or in a broader sense the vital principle itself, to the level of a laborer subservient to the dictates of manufactured cultural entities. In the last analysis, such a culture lacks humanity; its ideal is a refined, hermetically sealed aggregate of values, in which there is no room for man, not even as a worker, because this perfected system is capable of independent, spontaneous evolution. Despite the presence of some romantic relics in contemporary culture, it has already, as we have said before, been corrupted by the prevailing plague of all classical cultures—a fetishism of deified objects.

A reaction against such extreme "machinism" was inevitable. Political revolutions occurred in rapid succession, but they were powerless to alter the direction and nature of cultural evolution or even retard its decline. The most powerful clarion calls to oppose cultural automatism were sounded by Nietzsche and, for religious reasons, by Tolstoy. But they, and many others who combatted the materialism of contemporary culture, found themselves opposing culture in general. They and their disciples engaged in polemics against all cultural establishments, particularly the church and the government as representatives of traditional, objective reality. This attack was conducted mainly in the name of the rights of man, under the banners of political and ethical freedom and individualism. Nietzsche, Tolstoy, and also Ruskin opposed contemporary civilization as an obstacle to creative freedom, which, they felt, could be regained only by destroying all stereotypes of culture.

Scriabin's position was quite different. He never rejected civilization, never called for its destruction. He urged man to forge ahead not by evading culture, but by transcending it, by vanquishing it and utilizing its values for achievements exceeding its boundaries. Nietzsche and Tolstoy preached the destruction of the mighty edifice of European culture, whereas Scriabin hoped to endow it with dynamic power, to restore to civilization its former plasticity, its lost mobility, and resurrect in man's consciousness the intuitive knowledge of his creative power. Scriabin's protest was therefore neither anarchistic nor individualistic; he never rebelled against established institutions, against the church or government, as Tolstoy did; he simply denied these institutions all independent significance. He regarded them as mere appurtenances, which to a true romanticist served as an intermediate stage on the road to a superior state of being. His *Mysterium* was to be an act transcending individual effort, a communal act built on strict hierarchic organization, both political and religious. This supreme achievement was then to be consumed in the fire of creation, raised to the greatest imaginable power.

Scriabin aspired to death. He eagerly awaited the end of creativity itself. It appears, therefore, that he turned against that same romantic culture he so brilliantly represented. But this contradiction is in appearance only. Romanticism and classicism differ radically in their sense of the future. To a romanticist immersed in the stream of life, this sense of the future is an aim in itself; to a classicist it is a signpost indicating the direction to a transcendent objective. For the classicist, the present is always a transition, a stepping-stone to the future, in which all objectives are to be attained. The future is the field of objectives, the classicist contends, and they alone possess reality and value. Hence the highest achievement of the future, in the classical view, is measured by its relationship to the ephemeral present. In classical cultures, in which workers and masters labor together, the future is conceived as an accumulation of cultural values, a development and reinforcement of the system whose ultimate aim is perfection in isolation. But such an absolute ideal is manifestly unattainable, for the road leading to it must be infinite. This notion is the crux of the idea of infinite progress, a never-ending process of realizing ideal values. It is a classical idea par excellence; the concept of an end as a fulfillment is absent in classical philosophy. It is also absent in our civilization, which has classical foundations. History is of indefinite duration, and no single moment signalizes an end. Specific civilizations, in this view, may be mortal; they decline after they have discharged their functions and have solved their particular problems. But a total fulfillment of these ideals, embodying the solution of cosmic problems, is unthinkable in the classical mode of reasoning; only an infinite approach to that solution is conceivable. The end of human history, according to the classical scheme, will be the consequence of external events—a change in the natural environment, for instance. A similarly external event must also cause the death of the cosmos. But death as a fulfillment, as the only moment in which all beings find their meaning and vindication, in which the world ends internally, is to a classicist complete nonsense. The classical mind can comprehend only a relative fulfillment; for total fulfillment and perfection are attributes only of a finite universe, whereas infinity is unbounded and therefore indefinite.

It has often been pointed out that the idea of infinity is alien to classicism. This is not quite true. Classicism does not accept the world of transfinite numbers, that of Georg Cantor's calculus, which postulates infinity as an entity. It offers instead an indefinite infinity, an imperfect infinity, a potential infinity, or, in Hegel's term, "bad infinity." Discomfited by its lack of precision, the classical mind prefers to reject infinity altogether in favor of a finite entity. Hence its prudent self-limitation, its reticence, its quest for formal perfection, and its cult of form for form's sake, whereby imperfect entities acquire a certain definition and completion. The classical mind uncompromisingly adheres to relativism; it is unable to imagine the fulfillment of the cosmic process and the attainment of absolutes except as an infinite approach to a limit or to a transcendental state of being, because it has retreated from the tide of life and obscured the immediate apprehension of the creative act.

The idea of infinite progress is often illustrated by the myth of the Golden Age. Historically these two concepts have much in common; yet they are fundamentally incompatible. The concept of the Golden Age became popular in the era of Emperor Augustus and came down to us through a famous poem by Virgil. It is essentially a romantic idea, portraying the fulfillment of a historical process. Infinite progress cannot lead to a Golden Age, no matter how long this progress continues or what heights it attains, because it is unable to transcend the limitations of relative values and thus complete the series of finite events. For the Golden Age is a departure from a historic series, a transfer to another plane. The legend of a lost Paradise expresses in symbolic form the psychological axiom that Paradise can be found again only upon a return to the tide of life. That is why the Golden Age represents not a self-sufficient, immutable myth, but a joyous, playful action, an exultant state of wise childhood.

Romantic consciousness, intoxicated by the vision of infinite blessedness, builds an imaginary paradise as an idealized form of life on earth. This vision alternately assumed chiliastic and eschatological aspects, particularly pronounced in the history of Christianity, which, despite its domination by classical modes of thinking, always revealed romantic moods; for romanticism is the living soul of religion. Chiliastic and eschatological aspirations are often regarded as incompatible, but both invoke mankind's desire to escape relativism and recover self-sufficiency in

life. The only distinction between them is that chiliasm
stresses the element of joy and grants it a certain duration
within the framework of terrestrial sensory forms, whereas
the eschatological doctrine treats of events pertaining to
the end of our spatial and temporal world and seeks to
justify life, thereby investing the cosmic process with
meaning.

As a romantic, Scriabin was naturally fascinated by
the legend of the Golden Age. The vision of a blessed kingdom was the motive force of Scriabin's opera and provided
the chiliastic inspiration for *Le Poème de l'extase*. It is evoked
in the *Mysterium* as the constant counterpart to the dominating motive of death. But inevitably this exalted state of
being draws to an end; cosmic ecstasy is reduced to a single
instant and is absorbed in it when man becomes conscious
of his regained freedom. This is the limiting moment toward which the cosmos rushes in its headlong flight, finding its fulfillment in death.

Thus the blessed life and the fulfilling death, both
expressing the human longing for the absolute, are united
in Scriabin's *Mysterium* in a single image of loving death, of
sweet annihilation.

6

ACTE PRÉALABLE

Scriabin conceived the idea of writing the *Acte préalable* as a preliminary to the *Mysterium* in about 1913. Beginning in the winter of 1914, he prepared materials, both musical and poetical, for the *Acte préalable,* making ample use of sketches originally designated for the *Mysterium* itself. He undertook systematic work on the *Acte préalable* in the spring of 1914, and by the autumn of that year the text was almost finished. Scriabin read it to his friends, the poets Viacheslav Ivanov, Juris Baltrushaitis, and Konstantin Balmont, for whose literary judgment he had great respect. He had hoped to complete the first drafts of the musical score in the spring of 1915, but his busy concert season left him little time to concentrate on composition. When he died in April 1915, all that could be found among his manuscripts were the text for the *Acte préalable* and numerous disjointed fragments of music consisting mainly of scattered thematic motives and outlines of harmonic progressions.

In discussing the *Acte préalable,* we are perforce limited to the text. Although it was virtually completed, Scriabin left it not fully edited. There are lacunae; individual verses and sometimes whole stanzas appear in variant forms. And we must remember that the text was not to be recited, but performed simultaneously with music, dance, and pantomime.

As the title indicates, the *Acte préalable* was to be an introductory act, preliminary to the composition of the *Mysterium.* Scriabin altered the original plan under the stress of his creative turmoil, engendered, perhaps, by his lack of self-confidence. He felt that he had to test his powers at once before embarking on the grandiose project of the *Mysterium.* He could no longer go on composing sonatas and tone poems. The image of the *Mysterium* loomed large in his imagination, but in the meantime the *Acte préalable* absorbed more and more of the material originally designated for the major work. Scriabin felt that he had to accomplish something tangible, here and now, and so the *Acte préalable* became an abridged version of the *Mysterium.* In it Scriabin returned to the obsessive image of cosmic death in a state of ecstasy, along the lines of his operatic libretto but elevated to a much higher plane. Scriabin fully realized the contradictions inherent in this creative imperative. The *Acte préalable* was to prepare mankind for the acceptance of his message to demonstrate the goal to which he had summoned them, to recall before them the entire history of the world from its birth to its immersion in the bosom of the Unique. This element constitutes the fundamental difference between the *Acte préalable* and Scriabin's opera, which was to portray an individual ecstasy. Another important difference lies in the philosophic aspect. The *Acte préalable* was not meant to be an ordinary theatrical performance by actors for spectators; it was to be played out by the participants for themselves.

There was no longer a line of demarcation between actors and audience; for all to some extent contributed to the action. Still, the theatrical aspect was not completely eliminated from the *Acte préalable*. Despite the abolition of footlights and proscenium separating the stage from the hall, the personae, the masks, were still to be exorcised.

There were moments during the composition of the *Acte préalable* when Scriabin decided to enlarge it to preternatural dimensions; at times he barely resisted the temptation to transform it into a full-fledged *Mysterium*. But the necessity of completing the score made him yield to the demands of reality. At first he still dreamed of a temple for the performance of the *Acte préalable;* he made drawings of an edifice in the form of a rotunda with a dome, its floor consisting of concentric terraces rising toward an altar at the center, visible from all parts of the arena. Participants were to be placed on terraced concentric steps. But again he compromised; he was willing to stage the *Acte préalable* in a suitable concert hall or theater. Abandoning all hope for a production in India, he considered London, a city he especially liked. But his greatest preoccupation was with the performers. The *Acte préalable* made high technical demands on its participants, yet he expected them to be completely free of all theatricalism, of all self-consciousness, which even the greatest artists are often unable to escape. They had to be more than just good actors or good singers; they had to be adepts in Scriabin's ideas, or at least sympathetic to them, equipped intellectually and artistically for their tasks. Scriabin even thought of establishing a special training school for future participants offering instruction in artistic, intellectual, and religious subjects. "My actors," Scriabin used to say, "will have to forget their theatrical habits and learn something entirely new!"

The production of the *Acte préalable* was to be a hermetic and esoteric event. There would be no audience; only adepts were to be admitted. A strict hierarchy was to be established among them. High, near the altar, would be placed the principal artists, directing the act and performing important roles. A lower tier would be assigned to choristers, participants in religious processions, and dancers. There would be no set pieces. Separate scenes, in the theatrical sense, would be reduced to a minimum and expressed mainly by symbolic pantomime. In this respect the

Acte préalable is closer to a cantata or oratorio than to a music drama of the Wagnerian type. There would be no presentation of dramatic events, no realistic sets to complement the action; the narrative would be conveyed symbolically by gestures and dancing movements, with the content communicated in various lyrical forms. The lyric passages are the most significant in Scriabin's text for the *Acte préalable;* they are most beautiful poetically, most expressive philosophically, and most moving emotionally. In this text Scriabin reveals to us, for the last time and with the utmost penetration, the predominantly lyrical character of his genius and the peculiarly subjective insight of his prophetic visions. This subjective lyricism achieves great profundity and great power, so that it transcends the individual self-revelation and enters the domain of cosmic pantheism. The poem is a lyric song, but Scriabin sings not about himself but about the universe; his individual self here acquires cosmic stature. And yet Scriabin could grasp the universal conception only by transforming it into his own. He does not always succeed in this transmutation; the lyricist in him often becomes an epic narrator who describes and paraphrases the events. These epical moments are the weakest parts in the *Acte préalable,* for here Scriabin the poet loses the power of spontaneous imagery. He becomes a rationalist and a theorist; his natural expressiveness loses its brilliance, strength, and originality. The difference between the lyrical exultation of some episodes and the ponderous cerebration of others is so striking that one gets the impression that the poem was written by two different people, an extraordinary poet possessing a gift of prophetic vision and a didactic theoretician paraphrasing his ideas in rhymed verse.

There are painters who are poets, and there are poets who are musicians. Scriabin belongs to the second category. He made music out of words. Whole passages in the text of the *Acte préalable* are built on artful assonances and alliterations. "This is the way I orchestrate," he used to say. The variety of prosody is extraordinary; the metrical lines are precisely articulated. Intricate rhythmic designs in an unstable equilibrium, characteristic of Scriabin's musical scores, are absent from the text of the *Acte préalable*.

At twilight, to the sound of a tremolo chord, pianissimo (Scriabin played this chord for us but never wrote it down), a voice proclaims in a solemn, slow tempo:

> Once again the Deathless One bestows
> A blessed gift of Love on you;
> Once more the Infinite One shows
> In the Finite his image true.

The world is born. Space and time are created. The chorus sings:

> Eternity in a moment's ardor dwells,
> Illuminating the depths of space;
> Infinity's breath gives life its grace,
> And silence is alive with sounds of bells.

To Death is wed Eternal Father
Our flaming hearts to gather.

The Father dies in the throes of creation. His voice
is heard:

Children begotten by me,
Offspring of love's turmoil!
On me an assault I foresee;
Your victory I shall not foil.

I myself tore myself in twain
When I spawned you from my hidden recesses,
When I writhed in torment and pain
Craving for creative caresses.

You are destined to vanquish me now,
It is my law and your fate;
No retreat will I ever allow
To those who come here too late.

The people respond:

We are children begotten by you.
Obedient to paternal command,
We sadly depart to pursue
Our course toward a distant land.

We shall gather magical flowers
That bloom in the fields of our dreams.
Heirs to your inexhaustible powers,
We are floating in life-giving streams.

We are carried swiftly away,
Yet remaining under your sway,
    Rushing from eternity,

From saintly paternity,
In purposeful motion
Toward the human ocean,
Downward from light
Into tenebrous night
To imprint in fiery incarnation
Your image of divine adoration,
Of you alone
On the dark stone.

Cosmic evolution unfolds. Antinomies sharpen, only to meet in ever-closer reconciliation. Creative dreams are incarnated. The spirit is invested with flesh. The world blossoms forth. A dialogue between the masculine and feminine principles is heard:

FEMININE VOICE:

To you that come with morning light
In love's impetuous flight
Goes my responsive cry,
My ardor and my sigh.

MASCULINE VOICE:

What is this voice I hear
In sacred silence born,
So distant, yet so clear,
So lonely and forlorn?

There follows the song of the waves, a call of as yet unorganized matter:

We are the waves of Life!
Waves!
First
Waves,
Timid
Waves,
First
Murmurs,
Timid
Whispers,
First
Tremors,
Timid
Throbs,
Waves
Tender,
Waves
Rising,
Tender
Changes,
Swelling
Crests,
Tender
Wings,
Upwelling
Springs!

The choir of awakening senses is heard:

Tender joys
Of first caresses,
Secret sweetness
Of misty kisses!
Tender moans

Of first yieldings,
Secret bells,
Calls of desire,
Tender caresses
Of first approaches,
Secret tales
Of loving lights . . .

A soul is born from the union of the Ray of Light
and one of the waves. A wave speaks:

You sparkled, and the sweetness of delight
Burst forth within my misty flesh.
Fainting dreamily
I rise toward you.
Born of a dark consistence,
With waves a wave is fused.
In the embrace of my dreams
I was from my sisters torn away.

The sensuous world blooms:

What was it that by its auroral sparkle,
By a play of enchantment,
Hurled us down
Into the mist of our prisons?
It is a ray of light, a white ray
Which burst into song in us.
Its tenderness
Is filled with caresses;
It breaks apart
In lights and sounds of bells.
With joyous moans
The abyss resounds.

Rainbows are playing on us,
Dreams are in bloom
With its bright colors.
Sensuous spring tempts us.
Glinting lights surround us,
There are marvels around;
Secret calls are heard,
Voices from afar.
Dark waters are lit
By colors of the rainbow.
They shine with the treacherous
Eyes of the serpents,
They sparkle with the ambers
Of the depths of darksome swamps,
With the rainbow dazzle
Of spiderwebs . . .

The world is a caress, an enchantment; life is a yielding tenderness. Death itself is luminous and joyous. Toward it, toward its white sun, life rushes from its first moment of being; it thirsts for death, and in its flight toward death, life dooms itself to ecstasy:

Swarms of visions, choirs of dreams,
Legions of sparkling worlds.

The *Acte préalable* is a hymn to life, to abundant and radiant life; and it is also a hymn to death, in which life, sacrificing and surrendering itself, reaches its supreme efflorescence and fulfillment. In the hearts of the children who have forgotten their father, who dwell in the thrall of corruption, there sparkles a yearning for liberation.

The temples of past marvels
Encase us in their stifling prisons,
Only the pale light of dawn
Brightens them from the skies.
We are weary of parting,
We are pained by our chains . . .

A response is heard:

The same path that in its downward course
Brought you here into captivity
Will lead you to freedom
When your time is lived out,
When eternal motion
Which gave birth to this world
Will break down the walls,
And the Finite will joyously melt into the ether.

Bring forth the precious stones
From fragrant depths.
The sacred moment has arrived
To put together the broken dreams.

Man awakens:

The joyous hour has struck
And you awakened in us;
We are borne aloft
Toward a flaming dawn.
We behold a vision: The temple is in motion,
The sacrificial Victim and the Priest
Are at one in the Father, the Creator.

The Act concludes with a dance:

The dance is the prime cause,
Rendering righteous judgment;
It will fulfill your destiny
By its imperious splendor.
Our Father comes down to us
In the quickening heartbeats
Of our living dance.
Death comes down to us,
Sweetly dissolving the firmament
Of our living dance.
We are all embraced by love,
We are all a single current
Rushing to Eternity,
Toward saintly Paternity,
In purposeful motion
Away from the human ocean,
Upward toward light
From tenebrous night.
We imprinted in fiery incarnation
Your image of divine adoration,
Of you alone,
On the dark stone.
Flame up, sacred Temple
From the fire of our hearts!
Flame up in a sacred conflagration!
Melt blissfully in us, O sweet Father!
Melt with Death in ardent dance!

In his ecstatic exultation, Scriabin envisioned but a single aspect of being. But what place is the category of physical and moral evil to be assigned in Scriabin's vision? This evil is a necessary stage in cosmic evolution, an essential step that must be made before starting on the final ascent. Children must rise against the Father and forget him. Suffering, spiritual and bodily torment, will cease, and humanity will effloresce in the Grand Temple when the miracle of reunion is fulfilled. But why did the Eternal One allow his beloved children to suffer this great fall? Scriabin apostrophized thus:

> Why, oh why, did blessed Providence
> Sever the portal's guiding thread?
> It was to lure those possessed by torrid passion
> To empty the effervescent potion of lust,
> To suffer the horrors of ultimate doom
> And retrieve from the vial's bottom a sparkling
>   crystal,
> And from this multicolored crystal
> To erect a new temple of imperishable beauty.

So strong, so deep was Scriabin's consciousness of the cognitive value and mystical nature of necessary evil that when he revealed in the *Acte préalable* the image of the Teacher and Redeemer, he let him pass through the burning pit of sin. The Redeemer becomes a great sinner who had gone through the horror of outer darkness, who knew unimaginable sorrows and bore the plagues of the world, but was reborn and sanctified. He meets Death:

> "Are you the one that with avid stings
> Pierced the victims of Life's prisons?"
> "To you my caresses seemed like poniards;
> Your fear of me distorted my visage."
> "Why did you visit me in the form
> Of a blind monster with a cadaver's mouth?"
> "My child, the majesty of Death eluded you;
> You saw evil with fear in your eyes.
> I am the sweet concord in the temple of your soul,

A winged dream of your yearning for bliss—
I am dulcet oneness, a songful caress
In the blessed harmony of voices."

      The Eternal One returns to the multitudes, bring-
ing the blessed message of a joyous death. But his creatures
rise against him and destroy him.

      Disincarnated, he beheld
      The sprouting seeds of his instruction.

      This episode, in which Scriabin limns the image of
the hero, savior, and teacher, leaves an ambiguous impression, as if Scriabin himself did not fully comprehend his
own vision. It is also the weakest part of the entire poem.
Here Scriabin becomes a narrator, an instructor, a lecturer
expounding his ideas in verse. Who is that great sinner
who achieves sainthood, learns of the world's torment
through his own sufferings, and submits to tortures at the
hands of men but forgives them? Is he Christ? Definitely
not Christ the Redeemer. He is a wise teacher in the full-
ness of love, the beloved son of his Father, the first among
men to become awakened. He is far from the Superman
hero of the libretto of Scriabin's opera. The hero may be
the carrier of truth, but the teacher is its creator. The hero
learns that his life's aim is ecstasy; the teacher recreates
this aim. The hero calls for suffering and surrender in order to partake of a light of unknown delights; the teacher
promises absolute freedom. The hero of the opera ad-
dresses his adversaries in these words:

The sweet deception of religion
Does not enthrall me anymore;
My mind no longer is obscured
By its soft and tender mist.

Scriabin uses the same words in the text of the *Acte préalable,* but—what is highly significant—he inserts them in the speeches of the teacher's enemies. And yet these two images—that of a Superman and that of a wise teacher overflowing with love—are somehow related in their essential aspects. Both are animated by the expectation of ecstasy; both are suffused with the dream of blissful and liberating death.

Scriabin's ethical code was at first predominantly naturalistic in character. In his view, physical and moral evils lowered the vital tonus, weakened life's rhythm, and retarded its efflorescence. In the *Acte préalable,* we find a new ethical concept that is religious and mystical. Here evil is symbolized by the immersion of spirit into matter, a falling away from God. But there is also the vision of salvation through God:

Be bold, drink from these cups, O Mortals!
And enter your Father's portals!
Then let the rainbow crystals of your souls
Reflect the secrets of the distant goals!

The Destiny of Scriabin's Music

Reflecting on the exceptional position occupied by Scriabin in Russian music during the time immediately preceding World War I, we are struck by the strangeness and confusion that followed the destiny of his music. It gives us a measure of the capricious shifts in our tastes, of the precarious nature of our aesthetic judgments, proving that the survival of artistic works does not depend entirely on their intrinsic qualities, on their value, but on the circumstances, favorable or unfavorable, under which they are cast adrift, abandoned to themselves after the artist's death.

Although his country was at war, Scriabin's sudden death in April 1915 (caused by an abscess, as would later be the case with Alban Berg) had a great impact even beyond artistic circles. His disappearance was universally felt as an irreparable loss for Russian music. Scriabin personified the art of the avant-garde; he was recognized as the representative of innovative and revolutionary tendencies, a leader of the so-called modernists. And if this reputation exposed Scriabin to the attacks of conservative and academic musicians (who, however, recognized his talent while regretting his extreme uses of it), it also won him the fervent, almost fanatic admiration of ever-increasing numbers of music lovers—dominated naturally by the youth— whom Scriabin had succeeded in captivating after years of struggle.

Scriabin's last recitals, given in Petrograd a few weeks before he died, were enthusiastically received. The first performance of *Prométhée,* two years earlier, had assumed the proportions of a great event and precipitated passionate debates, which were not limited to music alone. It was known already that this work, scored for piano, orchestra, organ, and chorus, and including a special instrument, *clavier à lumières*—designed to produce a scale of colored lights in direct relation with the modulations and variations of tone colors—was to be followed by a greatly more ambitious and complex work, the *Acte préalable.* It was to accomplish, in a completely original form, a synthesis of all the arts, which Wagnerian music drama had only approximated.

In the meantime, a new star rose over the Russian horizon. It was Sergei Prokofiev. He had just graduated brilliantly from the Petrograd Conservatory as a pianist and composer. Prokofiev had not deliberately opposed himself to Scriabin, and yet they engaged manifestly upon widely divergent paths. The Russian public was also discovering the modern French school of composition through symphony concerts of Debussy and Ravel, conducted by Alexander Siloti and the Society of Contemporary Music in Petrograd. Although successful, these concerts had not attracted a large audience. The name of Schoenberg began to be known, too, but Russian musicians were puzzled by his music. The struggles and triumphs of Stravinsky in Paris aroused great interest, but his *Sacre du printemps* produced a disconcerting impression on musicians and critics of all categories.

After the Russian Revolution, the new regime, preoccupied with more urgent matters, let artists—painters, musicians, and poets—enjoy complete liberty of expression, a dispensation of which they took immediate advantage. At that time everything seemed possible. A political and economic revolution as radical as that of the Soviets should have logically brought about an aesthetic revolution, or so it was presumed. But with the disruption of all contact with the West, Soviet art remained bottled up. The music of Scriabin (and, to a lesser degree, that of Prokofiev) benefited the most from this isolation. Occasional concerts were dedicated to Scriabin's works, and his last piano sonatas were often heard at recitals. Young Russian composers adopted Scriabin's exalted modalities, his chromaticism, and inevitably exaggerated these traits. While old values were absorbed in the gigantic cauldron of demolition and reconstruction that Russia became, new generations faced the problem of physical survival in intolerably difficult conditions. They failed to find in the music of Scriabin a sympathetic voice; it did not respond to their emotions and aspirations. It was to them the echo of a dead and increasingly incomprehensible world. Later, when the Soviet government issued definite musical directives urging Soviet composers to abandon the so-called cosmopolitan trends and seek inspiration in national folklore, the works of Scriabin, surely "cosmopolitan" on all counts, were not banned from Soviet concert life, unlike Schoenberg's and most of Stravinsky's. But Scriabin's music nevertheless suffered neglect. After the death of Stalin, during the period of official benevolence, relative as it was, Scriabin's music, particularly his piano compositions, regained its rightful place.

Outside the Soviet domain, Scriabin's music is frequently heard in England, Germany, and the United States. But in France, where Scriabin is still regarded as one of the many epigones of Chopin, he is known to the general public and even to musicians only as the composer of a few piano preludes and the Etude in D-sharp Minor op. 8, which is often performed by French pianists. After the Second World War, in Paris in particular, Scriabin's music encountered a hostile milieu. There were many musical tendencies—although Stravinsky's influence was dominant—but all of these, while accepting Prokofiev's music, decisively opposed both the spirit and the idiom of Scriabin. Yet it was in Paris that Nikisch had conducted *Le Poème divin* with great success in 1904 and Koussevitzky had conducted *Prométhée* in 1921. Walter Gieseking had played Scriabin's Ninth Piano Sonata there in 1922. In later years foreign conductors presented *Le Poème de l'extase.* But these performances had but a reserved reception, not so much from the audience as from musicians and critics. If Scriabin's interpreters had persevered, his music might have gained recognition in Paris, but France was then at the height of an antiromantic reaction.

Scriabin was a romantic. This said, we must specify in what sense we employ the term. It designates, broadly speaking, a period of music history extending through more than a century, from Beethoven to, let us say, Alban Berg. Scriabin definitely belongs in this romantic lineage. Indeed, his first three sonatas and numerous piano pieces derive directly from Chopin in terms of pianistic writing, melodic, harmonic, and rhythmic turns, as well as in what is known as inspiration. Beginning with the Fourth Piano Sonata op. 30, we find influences of Liszt, particularly in the *Poème satanique.* But these influences are sporadic and disappear entirely in later works, along with those of Chopin. Scriabin's sonatas and short piano pieces, from op. 40 to op. 74, are written in a distinctly personal style. As for his three symphonies, and to some extent *Le Poème de l'extase,* they take their inspiration from Wagner.

The term *romantic* can, in a much broader sense, designate a constant of creative activity and not merely a historic phenomenon. In this interpretation, romanticism, which dominated the music of the nineteenth century, becomes an art for all ages. It is more or less explicitly manifest not only in the works of Bach and his sons Carl Philipp Emanuel and Wilhelm Friedemann, but even in the music of such preeminently classical composers as Haydn and Mozart. In this broader sense, romanticism reveals itself as singularly protean and is not easily circumscribed. Some say that it lacks a sense of proportion; it is unstable; the substance or content obscures the works' formal design; it is marked by repetitiousness, exaggeration, extreme expressivity, maudlin exacerbation, melancholy, vague reverie, self-abandonment to the power of imagination, exhibitionism, subjectivism . . . this list could be expanded indefinitely.

These elements of romanticism are not always concordant among themselves, but they seem to possess a trait in common. They appear to be diverse manifestations, perhaps self-contradictory, of the same tendency, of a power that impels an artist to overstep certain limits. Yet every creator must nourish this power, for without it his works would lack the requisite energy and intensity. A classicist manages to dominate this power while extracting from it what he needs, while a romantic risks succumbing to temptations that he can master only at the price of a struggle threatening to bring disorder and disequilibrium into his work. What identifies the romantic is not the subject matter, but the manner of its presentation.

But what is the boundary that the romantic, moved by an obscure need, unconsciously but persistently tries to overstep? It is the limit set by his art. Generally speaking, for a classicist, art is only an interlude, a celebration of some sort; it interrupts the course of time and serves as a break in the routine of life. It is an intermission, after which life resumes its course and returns to "serious business" as if nothing had changed. The goal of a romantic, on the other hand, is to erase such a distinction. A romantic definitely desires that everything be changed, with art not merely an entr'acte, but a celebration that goes on, that overflows into everyday existence and integrates with it in order to illuminate and, in effect, transform it. For a romantic, the main purpose is to convert a work of art into a means of action, not only on the aesthetic plane, but also on the plane of reality. The two worlds coalesce in this conception; the intention is to impart to artificial products of the creative imagination the status of real events (or likewise, to impart to real events the status of the imaginary). This is the clue to the importance of *Parsifal*.

When a romantic like Alban Berg attempts to give a sonorous representation to affective life in its most miniscule manifestations, its slightest nuances, we are not confronted with a "realist" solicitous of revealing psychological truth. Indeed, that truth is replaced by an altogether different truth— one brought to the extreme point of exasperation, rendered infinitely more potent by the subterfuges of an art at once violent and refined, it is imposed on us as eminently real and psychologically true. But this operation does not always succeed. And when it fails, a lack of proportion, extreme exaggeration, affectation, maudlin melodrama, and sentimental effusiveness are the price romanticism pays as a ransom for its ambitions.

With the exception of Scriabin, Russian music escaped the romantic possession. True, Chopin, Schumann, Liszt, and particularly Berlioz firmly established themselves in Russia; their works, widely performed, became popular and impressed themselves on the tastes of the Russian public and musicians. And yet their influence became pronounced only in techniques of composition for piano and orchestra (it is well known that

Rimsky-Korsakov's orchestrations owed a great deal to Berlioz). But it is through these composers' indirect influence that romanticism proved fertile in Russia. The novel romantic forms of composition, such as the symphonic poem, helped the Russian composers find themselves and formulate their aims, and render adequate judgment of their own potentialities and problems. But the spirit of romanticism, in the sense that has been detailed above, remained alien to Russian music. Although Wagnerian music drama had succeeded in captivating the cultured circles of the Russian public, composers in Russia seemed reluctant to adopt if not some individual Wagnerian procedures, such as the leitmotiv, then at any rate the dramatic system of Wagner, which Dargomyzhsky, Moussorgsky, Borodin, Rimsky-Korsakov, and Tchaikovsky explicitly rejected.

It must be noted, however, that Tchaikovsky is commonly regarded as a romantic, perhaps not in Russia itself but abroad, particularly in France. Yet Tchaikovsky owed infinitely more to Italian music than to German romanticism. The sentimentality, the pathos that permeate his music are but the excesses of his Italianism. He abandons himself all too willingly to his emotions, and he is complacent in his emotional flights. But he does not deliberately cultivate this emotionalism, and in this respect he differs from the expressionists, who actually create it. Indeed, Tchaikovsky's intentions and his tastes indicate classical affinities, as demonstrated by his veneration of Mozart.

Scriabin is the only true romantic musician produced by Russia. Nothing connects him with Russian composers who preceded him, nor had he any ties with his contemporaries. Whatever imitators he had were not disciples; no composer followed in the path opened by Scriabin. One might say that he was one of those artists who never carried a passport, to borrow an expression from Stravinsky, despite the fact that he had a quality that was typically Russian—namely, a pronounced national maximalism, a tendency to pursue his path to the end of his resources, to draw from his ideas and convictions all consequences, not only theoretical but practical as well, no matter how extravagant they might appear.

In the realm of Russian music, Scriabin is an absolutely unique phenomenon, an almost inconceivable exception. But when his art is viewed in the context of the literature of his time, he no longer appears as an isolated figure, the only one of his species. Scriabin's aesthetic code is remarkably similar to that of the vast intellectual and artistic movement that animated Russian philosophy and art early in the century as a reaction against the realism and positivism of the nineteenth century. The religious philosophy of Vladimir Soloviev, the French poets—particularly Baudelaire and Mallarmé—and German poets of the first romantic generation were the principal sources of this type of spiritual and idealistic renaissance that assumed the multiple aspects of an art commonly described as symbolist, even though this term very approximately defines most of its representatives. Some Russian symbolists, Valery Briussov in particular, confined themselves to a rather snobbish aestheticism and adopted a Parnassian attitude; others, like Viacheslav Ivanov (and to some extent Alexander Blok), regarded art as a superior mode of knowledge, an intuition analogous to that of the mystics, bearing the promise to reveal true reality and provide a passage to a transcendental world, to divinity.

Not realizing the importance of these trends, Scriabin began to be interested in modern poets only at a later stage of his career; consequently, he owed them nothing. And they, too, remained indifferent to Scriabin's ideas for a long time. And yet—and this is significant, because here we find a testimony to the grandeur and depth of Scriabin's thought, to his spontaneous and natural temperament—Scriabin's artistic activity, developed independently of these poets', moved nevertheless in the same direction. The religious, mystical spirit that inspired Scriabin's works was close to that which animated the poets. This is why both suffered the same fate after the revolution.

These poets and Scriabin were carried forward by the same demon of maximalism. There was nevertheless a difference between them. For Scriabin it was not enough to gain access to a transcendental reality, to know it and to take part in it: he wanted to take possession of this reality, to transform it according to his wishes, for art was to him a demiurgic act.

Scriabin therefore passed up the romantic composers and Wagner, and entered, unbeknownst to himself, the world of Novalis. He did not know his writings, but he retrieved the "magical idealism" of Novalis and appropriated the formula, "the world must be what I want it to be." The element of personal will characteristic of Novalis, his dream "permeated by a singular eroticism mixed with spiritual visions" (as Albert Béguin phrases it in his book *L'âme romantique et le rêve* [Paris, 1939]), lived again a century later in the soul of the Russian musician.

No wonder that Scriabin's music, imbued so deeply with literature, metaphysics, mysticism—an "impure" music if there ever was one—the essence of which Scriabin himself never tried to conceal, was irremediably tainted in France. During this time between the two wars, antiromanticism reigned supreme, and musicians, painters, and poets supported by the critical opinion of the elite, ensconced within the borders of their respective activities, devoutly preached a jealous cult of "purity" in theory, if not in practice.

But if we pay attention, as we should, not to the goals pursued by Scriabin, but to his accomplishments in pursuing these goals; if we consider not the titles of his works, but the works themselves; if we ignore what he said and wrote about them; if we disregard his own evaluation of their significance but turn to the works and listen to what they have to say to us; if we absorb the meaning that they possess in themselves—then a true image of Scriabin's art reveals itself, and all suspicions are dispelled. One could certainly remain aloof from this art or criticize it, but one must recognize that we are here confronted with an oeuvre which must be heard, understood, and judged on the same terms as any other production of "pure" music, whether it be Bach, Chopin, or Debussy.

Scriabin had a turn of mind usually called philosophical. He was singularly gifted for speculative thinking; he engaged passionately in the interplay of ideas, demonstrating considerable adroitness in handling them. When he discovered Oriental metaphysics in 1905—unfortunately by way of theosophy—he decided that he had finally found his true vision of the world, which allowed him to justify his deepest aspirations and formulate a complete exegesis of his music. This point was the most important for Scriabin; it was absolutely necessary for him to establish a concordance between his philosophy and his activity as a composer. Theories that he constructed had no other aim but to coordinate and formulate in rational terms his own musical experience. When Scriabin set to work, he was concerned not with the solution of metaphysical problems, but technical problems; not with modeling the world according to his fancy, but manipulating musical sounds. He did what all composers must do; he created sonorous forms that he could later attribute extramusical significance to and interpret in the light of his ideology. To judge by the titles of Scriabin's Third Symphony (*Le Poème divin*), *Le Poème de l'extase,* and *Prométhée* (*Le Poème du feu*), they are works of program music. But these titles were almost always added after composition.

It is perhaps dangerous to subdivide works of an artist into rigidly defined periods, to regard them as different phases of a composer's evolution, when in reality they overlapped. It is, however, difficult to avoid this artificial division. Although it simplifies a continuous organic development, disregarding digressions and returns, it allows us to draw a general outline and set down climactic points.

In Scriabin's works it is possible to establish two principal periods, with the line of demarcation coinciding approximately with the composition of the Fourth Piano Sonata op. 30, written in 1902–1903, even though some works written at a later date belong stylistically to the first period. The initial period would then comprise the first three sonatas and a number of smaller piano pieces, as well as the first and the second symphonies. All these works properly belong to the nineteenth century and are part of the romantic tradition. They are placed at the extreme end of an aesthetic movement that already betrayed signs of exhaustion. Apart from the unavoidable hesitations of the early years, Scriabin's art—his melodic invention, harmonic richness, and predilection for a concise well-balanced form—bears testimony to a close affinity with Chopin, although not in terms of imitation, but rather continuation. Scriabin succeeds in making the Chopinesque idiom more supple, more fluid, enhancing its modal ambiguities and multiplying its chromatic turns, which, however, are always inscribed within the framework of a strongly marked tonality. The aristocratic elegance, somewhat precious in its echoes of the fin de siècle, the dreamy and nostalgic mood of Scriabin's pieces of the first period, and even their titles—prelude, mazurka, étude—naturally evoke the spirit of Chopin; but other compositions of the same period are quite different.

A work of great importance in Scriabin's first period is the Third Piano Sonata op. 23, written in 1897. Its form is traditional, consisting of four movements—two Allegros frame an Allegretto and an Andante. The pianistic idiom is still Chopinesque, but we find here a power possessing savage energy.

There are rhythmic figures, ponderous or bounding by turns, and abrupt, assertive themes. This music is essentially that of action and not passion (if we take the word *passion* in its etymological sense of suffering), an action that breaks down all obstacles and, after the lyrical and playful interlude of the middle movements, is unleashed through the storm of the final *prestissimo con fuoco.* It is interesting to note that the Third Piano Sonata was written when Scriabin began to discover Nietzsche. It does not, however, represent an isolated or exceptional moment in the composer's production; quite the opposite. This sonata discloses to us the psychological and spiritual structure of all the sonatas that Scriabin was to compose, and also of *Le Poème divin,* which is basically a drama, an action, culminating after various peripeties in the affirmation of free will. What was to change was Scriabin's melodic and harmonic language, which is the character of this action.

The first two symphonies, op. 26 and op. 29, followed the same course of action. The first concludes with a chorus to the glory of music (a sort of counterpart to the "Ode to Joy" of Beethoven's Ninth Symphony). In the Second Symphony the finale proclaims in a major key, in march rhythms, the somber theme that introduced, in a minor key, the initial Allegro.

The Fourth Piano Sonata op. 30 inaugurates the second period of Scriabin's creative catalogue, which constitutes the principal part of his oeuvre. In it we can already discover certain essential traits of this period. It consists of two closely connected parts; the first, an Andante, opens with a long, lyrical phrase of nine measures. It blossoms against a background of trills, arpeggios, and light chords, and then hesitates and dissolves. This is followed by the thunderous start of a *prestissimo volando* based on a single theme derived from the introduction. Here, for the first time, Scriabin renounces the classical formula, which demands an exposition of two more or less contrasting themes, a development, and a recapitulation. (Unfortunately Scriabin was to return numerous times to it in his later works.) The tension subsides momentarily, the movement slows down, and the atmosphere grows somber; but the continuous musical line is preserved and finally leads back to the lyrical theme of the introduction. It broadens and, supported by chordal accompaniment, explodes in a gesture of defiance.

From a strictly constructive viewpoint, the Fourth Piano Sonata is, in its perfect cohesion, perhaps Scriabin's finest accomplishment. In later sonatas, *Le Poème divin*, *Le Poème de l'extase*, and *Prométhée*, Scriabin relinquishes the monothematism of the Fourth Piano Sonata and seeks to maintain unity by certain devices already employed, namely, the contraction and integration of movements into a unified whole unfolding without interruption; and a return in the end to an initial theme, which, amplified, enriched, and set in accelerated motion, acquires a new meaning. Finally, chords built on fourths that appear timidly, as a sort of presentiment, in the Fourth Piano Sonata, become integral parts in Scriabin's harmony beginning with the Fifth Piano Sonata and are rapidly implanted in *Prométhée*, which inaugurates a new harmonic system.

The Third Symphony (*Le Poème divin*) op. 43 dates from the same period as the Fourth Piano Sonata op. 30. And yet stylistically it corresponds principally to a stage that the Fourth Piano Sonata had already passed. Indeed the idiom of this sonata reflects the pianistic writing of Chopin but sporadically. The orchestration of *Le Poème divin*, while marking a great advance over the dense and heavy instrumentation of the Second Symphony, still betrays the influence of Wagner. The harmony of *Le Poème divin* is also somewhat Wagnerian, and its Lento in particular bears the imprint of *Tristan und Isolde*.

Le Poème divin appears to us, from a psychological as well as strictly musical standpoint, as an early version, so to speak, of *Le Poème de l'extase*, which marks Scriabin's definite departure from his past and a renewal of his musical language. The opulent orchestration of this work, while still proceeding from that of Wagner, is distinguished by an original use of woodwind instruments, individualization of different instrumental groups, and frequent emphasis on the highest register of the brass, particularly the trumpets, which imparts a brilliance in instrumental power, a transparency and sonorous cajolery that Scriabin had never before attained. The harmonic structure of *Le Poème divin* is still clearly tonal, and there are no aggregations of fourths. Quartal harmonies reappear in *Le Poème de l'extase*, which, in conjunction with the chromaticism and modal equivocation, contribute to a harmonic structure that, while not yet atonal, is already unstable and ambiguous.

In *Le Poème de l'extase* Scriabin finally breaks with the symphonic form in three movements. He still adheres to the traditional sonata-allegro form, but the symmetry it imposes interrupts the free flow of sonorities. To a lesser degree, this inconsistency in formal design is still discernible in *Prométhée*. The scholastic formula disappears in the last six sonatas, which no longer employ a key signature and whose structure is based on the interplay of two contrasting sonorous ideas and images, one violent and volitional, and the other tender, caressing, and sensual.

The evolution of Scriabin's musical idiom, beginning with the Fourth Piano Sonata and clearly articulated in *Le Poème de l'extase* and particularly the Fifth Piano Sonata, received its fullest expression in *Prométhée*. This evolution unfolded in parallel lines with the inner progress of Scriabin's thought; each reacted to and conditioned the other. This dual process was effected independently of all outside influences. Indeed, Scriabin took little interest in the music of the past or present. Having gone through his Chopinesque and Wagnerian periods, he lost all contact with works by other composers; they no longer impressed him, even though he conscientiously went to hear them performed. He shared with Debussy a taste for voluptuous sonorities but could not tolerate what he called Debussy's "passivity" and "essentially receptive sensuality." He looked over the piano score of *Pelléas et Mélisande* but soon put it aside and never referred to it again. But what truly made him suffer was the "brutality" of *Le Sacre du printemps;* he described it as "primal" music and said that Stravinsky's obstinate rhythms were "mechanized." If I am not mistaken, he knew nothing of Béla Bartók. As for Prokofiev, Scriabin heard much talk about him, but he had no interest in hearing any of his works. Schoenberg's symphonic poem *Pelleas und Melisande* bored him profoundly, but some of Schoenberg's piano pieces, which one of Scriabin's pupils played for him, aroused his curiosity.

It is all the more significant that Scriabin, ensconced as he was in his private universe, tried to solve the same problem that Debussy, Stravinsky, Schoenberg, and Bartók each independently addressed: the crisis, latent since Wagner, of classical tonality. But unlike Schoenberg, Scriabin did not consciously formulate his novel harmonic concepts, and he applied them methodically only during the composition of *Prométhée;* up to that point he took into consideration only the exigencies of his own sensitivity and put full trust in his intuition.

The initial chord in *Prométhée* can be reduced to a scale or mode of six notes—C, D, E, F-sharp, A, and B-flat—which, in various transpositions, constitutes the foundation of the entire melodic and harmonic structure of the score. This musical system, as pointed out with complete justification by Ivan Vishnegradsky, is based on a hexatonal irregular scale differing fundamentally from the classical diatonic scale both structurally and in the manner of employment. None of its six component tones assumes the function of the tonic; there is no hierarchy

or attractive force among them. This peculiarity is closely related to the manner in which Scriabin treats this scale; he uses
all its components simultaneously, often in superposed fourths.
Thus the concept of the scale is fused with that of the chord,
and this chord, embracing the entire scale, appears perfectly
stable, reposing upon itself without requiring resolution. It syn-
thesizes and summarizes the scale. From this standpoint any
transposition of the chord is equivalent to a freely effected mod-
ulation. The music moves as a concatenation of chords, disregarding any preconceived rules (within the limits of the mode)
and ignoring what is described as tonal logic.

Scriabin's hexatonal modes do not include a perfect
fifth, for its inclusion would entail a return to tonality; Scriabin
avoids this interval in his Sixth Piano Sonata op. 62, composed
shortly after *Prométhée* and introducing a seventh degree to his
scale.

It is clear that melodic and harmonic structures also
are fused, so that the melody simply unfolds in a certain order
and rhythm the sounds contained in the synthetic chord. But
although in theory this chord can be explained in terms of the
mode, in fact the mode is dictated by the chord; the point
of departure was a sonorous block that Scriabin heard and conceived as both a chord and a timbre. What brought the composer to an idiom as original as that of *Prométhée* and the piano
compositions from opus 61 to opus 74 was a search for harmonic complexes that would reflect unheard sonorities—in the
literal sense of the word—but that he heard and felt in the
sounds of bells and gongs. It was these sonorous images that
inspired Scriabin to construct the chord of *Prométhée* and the
last sonatas.

Scriabin's music assumes from this point on a very peculiar character, somewhat liturgical in expression, connected
with his psychological and spiritual evolution and his funda-

mental change in attitude toward the world. He ceases to oppose himself to the real world, seeking instead to identify himself with it.

Listening to *Prométhée* and particularly to the Sixth, Seventh, and Tenth Piano Sonatas, one is struck by the extent to which this music, while remaining essentially dynamic, ceases to be imperative or combative. For him, art is still an act that performs his desires; but the magus has now become a priest officiating at a religious ceremony in which the entire universe takes part and which culminates each time in an ecstatic dance.

Scriabin's death at the age of forty-three came only some five years after he had attained artistic maturity. If he had lived and settled in the West (he obviously could not have continued his work in postrevolutionary Russia), the fate of his art would undoubtedly have been quite different. But in what direction would he have proceeded? What influence would he have exercised on contemporary music, which today pretends to ignore him? These questions can never be answered.

Translated from the French by
Nicolas Slonimsky

The Musical Language of Scriabin

One may wonder why the name Scriabin should figure in an encyclopedia of religious music. He composed only instrumental works, for piano or orchestra. His music is undiluted in its purity; there is no resort to words or to dance. Only in the finale of his First Symphony did Scriabin employ a chorus, which sings a brief hymn to the glory of music. As for the voices at the very end of *Prométhée,* the performers are instructed to sing with their mouths closed. If we consider as religious only music containing texts from the scriptures, inspired by the scriptures, or expressing emotions of a religious character, then we must conclude that Scriabin wrote no religious music. But we will arrive at a different conclusion if we enlarge the conventional notion of religious music. Unless we do that, we will never understand the meaning of the legacy left to us by Scriabin, which is definitely religious in its nature.

The case of Scriabin is at once one of the simplest and most complex among composers. We can perhaps liken his oeuvre to that of Wagner, but apart from that, Scriabin is unique in the history of music. He was first and foremost a musician, the creator of forms of sonority; but he was also a poet. He left us two literary texts in verse: *Le Poème de l'extase* and *L'Acte préalable*. The former was published by the author himself in Geneva in 1906 and was written at about the same time as the score that bears the same title. Although the score does not follow the exposition of the text, there is a certain parallelism between them: the same emotions, the same spiritual impetus animate both.

The poetic text of *L'Acte préalable* was published in 1919 in Berlin, in the Russian magazine *Les Propylées*. The same magazine also contains random thoughts and sketches, sometimes separated by long intervals of time, which Scriabin was in the habit of jotting down. According to the author's intention, *L'Acte préalable,* of which only the text is extant, was to be a liturgical drama that would effect a synthesis of all arts in order to prepare the way for the consummation of the *Mysterium.* The magnetic idea of this work circumscribed almost the entire creative activity of Scriabin, imparting to it a perfect unity and providing the key to his thought.

Scriabin, musician and poet, was also a philosopher (we are taking this description *cum grano salis*). The artist Scriabin was extremely lucid in his utterances; he never ceased to reflect upon his actions and works, systematizing and rationalizing them. A subtle dialectician, he was nonetheless deficient in philosophical culture. He followed his own course and never tried to fully comprehend another's philosophical ideas; later he took possession of them, deformed them in order to adapt them for his own needs and incorporate them into his own ideology. So he proceeded with theosophy, which exerted a much less important influence on him than is usually claimed. Books on theosophy provided only a framework and a terminology that he used to establish ties with the esoteric tradition of a remote past, of which he regarded himself a natural heir. Toward the end of his life he lost all interest in theosophy and tried to immerse himself in Indian philosophic ambiance. In 1914 he even intended to take a trip to India, but the war supervened.

Scriabin's activity evolved on three planes at once: music, poetry, and philosophical discourse. The center of these three manifestations was obviously on the musical plane; the other modes of expression were but poetic and philosophic transcriptions of it. What is the message of Scriabin's music? Like any creation of man, it has a certain relation with the outside world; in this case, via a personal "mystique." Scriabin was never a contemplative artist; he was essentially an active spirit, maintaining a dynamic relationship with the world. There was in him, as it were, a sort of osmosis between the microcosm and macrocosm, but the latter he projected as the expansion of his inner self. Here we find a perfect convergence between the evolution of Scriabin's musical language and his spiritual evolution (as seen in his poetic writings and his reflections). They are two facets of the same process that led Scriabin from an exacerbated, proud, and solipsistic individualism to a pantheistic, pan-monistic *Weltanschauung* somewhat related to the doctrine of Plotinus.

The musical evolution of Scriabin is traditionally, and not unreasonably, divided into three periods. The first comprises the early opus numbers (beginning in 1885, when he was only thirteen years old), published in 1893, up to the Fourth Piano Sonata, op. 30 (written in 1904); the second comprises *Le Poème de l'extase,* op. 54 (1908) and the Fifth Piano Sonata, op. 53 (composed in 1907 and published in 1911); the third goes from *Prométhée,* op. 60 (1910), to the last opus numbers, concluding with op. 74 (1914). One important circumstance must be mentioned at the outset: Although Scriabin was a student at the Moscow Conservatory from 1882 to 1892 and a professor of the same conservatory from 1898 to 1903, he owed nothing to his predecessors nor to his Russian contemporaries, who in varying degrees followed the tradition of Glinka. Scriabin had no roots in his native country; he was to have epigones in Russia, but he had no ancestors there. His art evolved entirely in the romantic Western tradition, of which he was the sole Russian representative.

Russian poetry from the beginning of the nineteenth century was strongly influenced by English and German romanticism, particularly that of Byron and Schiller. But if musicians borrowed from the romantic poets certain poetic procedures, the very spirit of romanticism remained alien to them. Wagnerian music drama made no impression on Russian operas; Russian orchestration owes more to Berlioz than to Wagner.

In music history romanticism encompasses a period of about a century, but it can be taken in a much wider sense to designate a certain constant of creative activity, not merely a historical phenomenon. In this perspective a romantic artist can be described as one who strives to transcend the boundaries of his art by making it part of his life, which he thus illumines and transforms. Wagner's music dramas fit this description, for he was a romantic par excellence, particularly in *Parsifal*. Artistic activity for such a romantic is no longer, as it was for a classical musician, an interlude in the routine of everyday life. In this respect—but only in this respect—Scriabin is the sole heir of Wagner.

Scriabin's mentor in the first period was Chopin. Scriabin often used forms that the genius of the Polish composer had distinguished: valse, mazurka, polonaise, nocturne, impromptu. It is an intimate art, refined, hypersensitive, sometimes emotional, sometimes dreamy, caressing, aristocratically elegant. But very soon Scriabin's personality began to reveal itself, as evidenced in Impromptu, op. 10 (1895); Preludes nos. 14, 15, and 18 of op. 11 (1897); Preludes 1 and 4 of op. 15

(1897); and the frenetic violence of the Etude in D-sharp minor of op. 8 (1894). This newly won independence is most striking in Scriabin's rhythmic freedom, which continued to grow through the years. Scriabin rarely resorts to changes of meter, but upon this underlying framework he embroiders subtle, capricious rhythmic figures, which he, as one of the greatest pianists of his time, knew how to project to perfection in his own playing. One work dominates this second period: the Third Piano Sonata, op. 23 (1898). Its opening subject, of a violently affirmative, even aggressive nature, and the principal theme of the finale already presage *Le Poème divin,* op. 43 (1903). It must be observed that Scriabin's symphonies lagged behind his pianistic production. The First Symphony, op. 26 (1901) is in six movements, none of which is fully developed, and is essentially an orchestral transcription of an original work for piano. The Second Symphony, op. 29 (1903), surprises by its academism in comparison with the Third Piano Sonata, op. 23, which preceded it by five years.

The Fourth Piano Sonata, op. 30 (1903), marks a turning point in Scriabin's evolution. Here he breaks off from Chopin. He abandons the form of a sonata in several movements and never returns to it. The Fourth Piano Sonata progresses in a continuous flow; from the introductory Lento, of a serene nature, it is gradually enriched by transparent counterpoints and delicate ornaments. The tempo accelerates until it reaches a *prestissimo volando,* which concludes with a triumphant peroration through a reprise of the broadened first theme. The Fourth Piano Sonata unveils for the first time the true nature of Scriabin's art, essentially playful and sunny. Its rays throw a retrospective light onto the works of the first period, whose language is at times dolorous and full of pathos. It now appears that Scriabin ignored, or rather unconsciously wished to ignore, the human condition, its misery, its tragedy. Can one therefore say that this music has something "inhuman" in it? In contra-distinction to those of most romantics, the mystical experiences of Scriabin belong not to the night but to the light of day. The works that follow the Fourth Piano Sonata confirm this impression.

Around the time Scriabin wrote his Fourth Piano Sonata and was working on *Le Poème divin,* he conceived the project of an opera, which, however, he soon abandoned. The hero of this opera, an artist, obviously represents Scriabin himself, an image magnified by his ego, a Superman (Scriabin was then reading Nietzsche's *Also sprach Zarathustra*). We find the following lines in Scriabin's journal: "I am nothing. I am only what I create. All that exists comes from my consciousness, is the product of my action, which in turn is identical with what it produces. . . . The world is my creative act, and my creative act comprises the world. They are reciprocal. Nothing exists except the playful spirit, but this spirit is the loftiest and the most real of all possible realities. . . . Oh, if only I could give to the world a particle of my joy. . . . I want to seduce the world by my creative power, by its divine beauty. . . . I want to engulf all in myself. . . . I want to take the world as one takes a woman. . . . You do not exist, you are but a sport of my free fantasy. . . . I am God." The ultimate aim of the hero is ecstasy in dissolution and death. This ecstasy is but an individual state; those who witness the hero's transfiguration see nothing but a dead body.

With the project of his opera relinquished for the time being (but its idea was to be resumed later on), Scriabin completed in 1905 his Third Symphony, *Le Poème divin,* op. 43; it provides further evidence that, although a master of pianistic writing, Scriabin was not as yet completely at ease in orchestration. After a proclamatory phrase in the brass, which is either an appeal or a gesture of defiance, follows *Luttes.* But the battle implied in the title is launched by Scriabin himself, so that he might surmount it and, in the process, deploy his power; a similar projection is found in the episodes of temptation in the second movement, *Voluptés*. The real sense of *Le Poème divin* is unequivocally conveyed in the third movement, *Jeu divin*.

According to Scriabin, his First Symphony was lyrical, his Second, a dramatic work; and his Third, epical; but in reality, all three are lyrical and subjective expressions. Scriabin does not abandon subjectivity until the composition of *Prométhée*.

The text that Scriabin wrote for *Le Poème de l'extase* and the score itself relate to the period of transition. On the musical plane, the form is still sonata-allegro, even if the tonality of certain episodes remains ambiguous. But the central tone, C, is clearly affirmed in the ending, which recapitulates, in a somewhat modified form, the initial motif. Reading the text and listening to the music, one is struck by a curious ambiguity of the work: Is this overflowing joy that animates it, generating an ecstatic interplay of emotions, sensations, images, impetuous desires, and caresses, but an egocentric exhibition? Is it the hero of Scriabin's opera who affirms his divinity in *Le Poème de l'extase* and proclaims "I am"? Does this triumphant "I" reflect Scriabin's own personality? Some fragments of the opera libretto and *Le Poème de l'extase* follow a metaphysical code of aesthetics that posits the effective reaction of art upon the spiritual and material world. Art possesses a demiurgic power—the myths of Orpheus and Amphion are ever-present in Scriabin's thought. Unbeknownst to himself, he also espouses here the "magic idealism" of Novalis: reality is what the poet wills it to be. But what is the origin of the ambiguous impression that *Le Poème de l'extase* conveys? It is found in the disequilibrium between his musical language (which, though innovative, continues in the romantic tradition) and what he wants it to evoke. The composer can no longer be content with a personal transfiguration; he yearns to achieve a cosmic ecstasy, consciously transcending all boundaries of terrestrial existence. This is the central thought of his *Mysterium*.

Scriabin's Fifth Piano Sonata, op. 53, composed in 1907 and published in 1911, is also a work of transition, but it breaks more decisively with the past and turns toward the future. Here Scriabin takes the road of atonality: he abandons key signature and makes systematic use of accumulations of perfect fourths (which are already in evidence in the Fourth Piano Sonata); its general structure presages the "dialectical" construction of Scriabin's last sonatas.

With the composition of *Prométhée*, Scriabin's musical language undergoes a profound mutation, the true meaning of which can be understood only in the context of Scriabin's spiritual life, preserved by the entries in his journal. The harmonic foundation of *Prométhée* is based on a mode of six tones: C, F-sharp, B-flat, E, A, and D. This mode represents a transposition, necessarily approximative, of the upper partials of the natural harmonic series. It is simultaneously a chord and a tone color, a timbre. In his last sonatas, Scriabin adds to this chord-timbre a seventh tone, G, which provides the twelfth harmonic partial. From the very first measures, in the main subject, a new universe of sound opens before us. The theme is taken up again in the ending of *Prométhée* by a chorus singing with mouths closed, which imparts an even more mysterious sonority. Doubtless Scriabin was inspired here by the sound of bells and gongs, with which he was preoccupied at that time. They were to play a dominant role in *L'Acte préalable* and are discernible already in the Seventh Piano Sonata. Scriabin abandons the motives of strong volition, violence, and aggression; if there is still a lyric element, it is somewhat depersonalized; the chants resounded here no longer reflect an individual ego, but rather the macrocosm. Yet the spirit of a play is ever-present, grave and solemn in *Prométhée*, free and dancing in the piano sonatas in which contrasting elements are constantly in collision—the one, tender, caressing, erotic; the other, turbulent, winged, luminous. The emblem of Scriabin's creative imagination at this period is the dancing Shiva of the Hindu statuary, which creates and destroys worlds without end or beginning.

What was Scriabin to himself? How did he see himself? How did he conceive himself? He wrote in his journal: "The microcosm is a drop of water that reflects the sky. An individual is the cup from which the Unique imbibes limitation, suffering and death. An individual is the seal of the Unique imprinted on matter." Final ecstasy is no longer the goal that Scriabin freely set for himself; it is no longer his caprice. This goal is imposed upon him: it becomes his mission. Scriabin is now, in his own eyes, the prophet of the Unique, of the Father. He confided his thoughts to me in Brussels in 1908: "If I believed that there is another who could accomplish this mission, I would move aside, I would yield my place to him. But then I would no longer live." It was indeed impossible for him to renounce his dream. This dream was surely a delusion, but it gave a meaning to his entire creative activity; it was his sun. In this he was not unlike Mallarmé, who dreamed of writing a book that would put an end to all books.

After *Prométhée* and the last sonatas, nos. 6–10, Scriabin said that he would compose no other major works, so that he could devote himself exclusively to the *Mysterium,* for which he began to write the text during the summer of 1913. Yet he had to admit that he was spiritually unprepared for the *Mysterium.* As a result, he decided to embark on a preliminary work, which he called *L'Acte préalable.* It was a reduced version of the *Mysterium,* a compromise. The subject of the *Acte préalable,* as that of the *Mysterium,* was to be the history of humanity outlined in symbols and images, tracing its evolution from the Unique, its descent into the realm of matter, and its involution and reascent toward the Unique. But whereas the *Mysterium* was to consummate this return to the Father, the *Acte préalable* would only represent it. Like a liturgical Mass, it could be repeated in performance. Scriabin intended to restore in this work the unity of all arts, which he believed had been lost in the previous ages. The *Acte préalable* was not to be music plus words plus dance, reunited in a close parallelism. Scriabin had already experimented with such parallelism in *Prométhée,* whose score contains a color keyboard; but this experiment was a failure. This time, sound, light, words, and physical movements were to form a close-knit contrapuntal fabric. But even if we had at our disposal all these elements, we would not be able to produce the *Acte préalable.* Only Scriabin's own realization, his own mise-en-scène, could impart to it a vital spark. Moreover—and this is of the essence—the *Acte préalable* was to be perfected by communal effort—ordained by an individual, but performed by all those present, with participants contributing to the whole in various degrees.

The *Acte préalable* opens with a chorus proclaiming: "Once more you are summoned by the Eternal to bring a gift of love. Once more the Eternal wants to recognize in you the multiplicity and the diversity of existence." The principal figure, he whose mission is to restore the children to their Father and who is thus their representative, is precisely the one who had foundered most deeply in the element of matter, in the abyss of evil. And it is from the depth of this abyss that he ascends toward the source of light. It is because he had taken upon himself the horror of evil and assumed the gravity of sin that he, and with him all of mankind, is to attain ecstatic death in the Unique. "Christ, the Son," Scriabin wrote, "is the symbol of humanity that died and was resurrected in Him." Scriabin echoes here the celebrated formulation of Meister Eckhart: "The mouth of the river is larger than its source."

Scriabin completed the text of the *Acte préalable* during the winter of 1914–1915. He died before he could complete his revisions. Nothing is extant from its music, but it is possible that 5 Preludes, op. 74, contains a distant echo of the work.

Translated from the French by
Nicolas Slonimsky

Designer: Yvette Rutledge
Compositor: Graphic Composition, Inc.
Text: 13/14 Perpetua
Display: Perpetua
Printer: Edwards Bros., Inc.
Binder: Edwards Bros., Inc.